River's End

Nora Roberts

Series

Nora Roberts & *J. D. Robb*

REMEMBER WHEN

J. D. Robb

Anthologies

FROM THE HEART

A LITTLE MAGIC

A LITTLE FATE

MOON SHADOWS

(with Jill Gregory, Ruth Ryan Langan, and Marianne Willman)

The Once Upon Series

(with Jill Gregory, Ruth Ryan Langan, and Marianne Willman)

ONCE UPON A CASTLE

ONCE UPON A STAR

ONCE UPON A DREAM

ONCE UPON A ROSE

ONCE UPON A KISS

ONCE UPON A MIDNIGHT

***

SILENT NIGHT

(with Susan Plunkett, Dee Holmes, and Claire Cross)

OUT OF THIS WORLD

(with Laurell K. Hamilton, Susan Krinard, and Maggie Shayne)

BUMP IN THE NIGHT

(with Mary Blayney, Ruth Ryan Langan, and Mary Kay McComas)

DEAD OF NIGHT

(with Mary Blayney, Ruth Ryan Langan, and Mary Kay McComas)

THREE IN DEATH

SUITE 606

(with Mary Blayney, Ruth Ryan Langan, and Mary Kay McComas)

IN DEATH

THE LOST

(with Patricia Gaffney, Mary Blayney, and Ruth Ryan Langan)

THE OTHER SIDE

(with Mary Blayney, Patricia Gaffney, Ruth Ryan Langan, and Mary Kay McComas)

Also available . . .

THE OFFICIAL NORA ROBERTS COMPANION

(edited by Denise Little and Laura Hayden)

NORA ROBERTS

River's End

BERKLEY BOOKS, NEW YORK

THE BERKLEY PUBLISHING GROUP
Published by the Penguin Group
Penguin Group (USA) Inc.
375 Hudson Street, New York, New York 10014, USA
Penguin Group (Canada), 90 Eglinton Avenue East, Suite 700, Toronto, Ontario M4P 2Y3, Canada
(a division of Pearson Penguin Canada Inc.)
Penguin Books Ltd., 80 Strand, London WC2R 0RL, England
Penguin Group Ireland, 25 St. Stephen's Green, Dublin 2, Ireland (a division of Penguin Books Ltd.)
Penguin Group (Australia), 250 Camberwell Road, Camberwell, Victoria 3124, Australia
(a division of Pearson Australia Group Pty. Ltd.)
Penguin Books India Pvt. Ltd., 11 Community Centre, Panchsheel Park, New Delhi—110 017, India
Penguin Group (NZ), 67 Apollo Drive, Rosedale, Auckland 0632, New Zealand
(a division of Pearson New Zealand Ltd.)
Penguin Books (South Africa) (Pty.) Ltd., 24 Sturdee Avenue, Rosebank, Johannesburg 2196,
South Africa

Penguin Books Ltd., Registered Offices: 80 Strand, London WC2R 0RL, England

PRINTING HISTORY
G. P. Putnam's Sons hardcover edition / March 1999
Jove mass-market edition / May 2000
Berkley French flap edition / September 2011

Berkley French flap paperback ISBN: 978-0-425-24294-0

The Library of Congress has catalogued the G. P. Putnam's Sons hardcover edition of this book as follows:

Roberts, Nora.
  River's end / Nora Roberts.
      p.   cm.
  ISBN 0-399-14470-6 (acid-free paper)
  I. Title.
  PS3568.O243R58   1999   98-36160   CIP
  813'.54—dc21

PRINTED IN THE UNITED STATES OF AMERICA

10 9 8 7 6 5 4 3 2

To Mom and Pop
Thanks for being mine.

The woods are lovely, dark and deep
But I have promises to keep,
And miles to go before I sleep,
And miles to go before I sleep.

—ROBERT FROST

THE monster was back. The smell of him was blood. The sound of him was terror.

She had no choice but to run, and this time to run toward him.

The lush wonder of forest that had once been her haven, that had always been her sanctuary, spun into a nightmare. The towering majesty of the trees was no longer a grand testament to nature's vigor, but a living cage that could trap her, conceal him. The luminous carpet of moss was a bubbling bog that sucked at her boots. She ripped through ferns, rending their sodden fans to slimy tatters, skidded over a rotted log and destroyed the burgeoning life it nursed.

Green shadows slipped in front of her, beside her, behind her, seemed to whisper her name.

Livvy, my love. Let me tell you a story.

Breath sobbed out of her lungs, set to grieving by fear and loss. The blood that still stained her fingertips had gone ice-cold.

Rain fell, a steady drumming against the windswept canopy, a sly trickle over lichen-draped bark. It soaked into the greedy ground until the whole world was wet and ripe and somehow hungry.

She forgot whether she was hunter or hunted, only knew through some deep primal instinct that movement was survival.

She would find him, or he would find her. And somehow it would be finished. She would not end as a coward. And if there was any light in the world, she would find the man she loved. Alive.

She curled the blood she knew was his into the palm of her hand and held it like hope.

Fog snaked around her boots, broke apart at her long, reckless strides. Her heartbeat battered her ribs, her temples, her fingertips in a feral, pulsing rhythm.

She heard the crack overhead, the thunder snap of it, and leaped aside as a branch, weighed down by water and wind and time, crashed to the forest floor.

A little death that meant fresh life.

She closed her hand over the only weapon she had and knew she would kill to live.

And through the deep green light haunted by darker shadows, she saw the monster as she remembered him in her nightmares.

Covered with blood, and watching her.

Olivia

A simple child that lightly draws its breath,
And feels its life in every limb,
What should it know of death?

—WILLIAM WORDSWORTH

ONE

Beverly Hills, 1979

OLIVIA was four when the monster came. It shambled into dreams that were *not* dreams and ripped away with bloody hands the innocence monsters covet most.

On a night in high summer, when the moon was bright and full as a child's heart and the breeze was softly perfumed with roses and jasmine, it stalked into the house to hunt, to slaughter, to leave behind the indifferent dark and the stink of blood.

Nothing was the same after the monster came. The lovely house with its many generous rooms and acres of glossy floors would forever carry the smear of his ghost and the silver-edged echo of Olivia's lost innocence.

Her mother had told her there weren't any monsters. They were only pretend, and her bad dreams only dreams. But the night she saw the monster, heard it, smelled it, her mother couldn't tell her it wasn't real.

And there was no one left to sit on the bed, to stroke her hair and tell her pretty stories until she slipped back into sleep.

Her daddy told the best stories, wonderfully silly ones with pink giraffes and two-headed cows. But he'd gotten sick, and the sickness had made him do bad things and say bad words in a loud, fast voice that wasn't like Daddy's at all. He'd had to go away. Her mother had told her he'd had to go away until he wasn't sick anymore. That's why he could only come to see her sometimes, and Mama or Aunt Jamie or Uncle David had to stay right in the room the whole time.

Once, she'd been allowed to go to Daddy's new house on the beach. Aunt Jamie and Uncle David had taken her, and she'd been fascinated and delighted to watch through the wide glass wall as the waves lifted and fell, to see the water stretch and stretch into forever where it bumped right into the sky.

Then Daddy wanted to take her out on the beach to play, to build sand castles, just the two of them. But her aunt had said no. It wasn't allowed. They'd argued, at first in those low, hissing voices adults never think children can hear. But Olivia had heard and, hearing, had sat by that big window to stare harder and harder at the water. And as the voices got louder, she made herself *not* hear because they hurt her stomach and made her throat burn.

And she would *not* hear Daddy call Aunt Jamie bad names, or Uncle David say in a rough voice, *Watch your step, Sam. Just watch your step. This isn't going to help you.*

Finally, Aunt Jamie had said they had to go and had carried her out to the car. She'd waved over her aunt's shoulder, but Daddy hadn't waved back. He'd just stared, and his hands had stayed in fists at his sides.

She hadn't been allowed to go back to the beach house and watch the waves again.

But it had started before that. Weeks before the beach house, more weeks before the monster came.

It had all happened after the night Daddy had come into her room and awakened her. He'd paced her room, whispering to himself. It was a hard sound, but when she'd stirred in the big bed with its white lace canopy she hadn't been afraid. Because it was Daddy. Even when the moonlight spilled through the windows onto his face, and his face looked mean and his eyes too shiny, he was still her daddy.

Love and excitement had bounced in her heart.

He'd wound up the music box on her dresser, the one with the Blue Fairy from *Pinocchio* that played "When You Wish upon a Star."

She sat up in bed and smiled sleepily. "Hi, Daddy. Tell me a story."

"I'll tell you a story." He'd turned his head and stared at his daughter, the small bundle of tousled blond hair and big brown eyes. But he'd only seen his own fury. "I'll tell you a goddamn story, Livvy my love. About a beautiful whore who learns how to lie and cheat."

"Where did the horse live, Daddy?"

"What horse?"

"The beautiful one."

He'd turned around then, and his lips had peeled back in a snarl. "You don't listen! You don't listen any more than she does. I said *whore,* goddamn it!"

Olivia's stomach jumped at his shout, and there was a funny metal sting in her mouth she didn't recognize as fear. It was her first real taste of it. "What's a whore?"

"Your mother. Your fucking mother's a whore." He swept his arm over the dresser, sending the music box and a dozen little treasures crashing to the floor.

In bed, Olivia curled up and began to cry.

He was shouting at her, saying he was sorry. *Stop that crying right now!* He'd buy her a new music box. When he'd come over to pick her up, he'd smelled funny, like a room did after a grown-up party and before Rosa cleaned.

Then Mama came rushing in. Her hair was long and loose, her nightgown glowing white in the moonlight.

"Sam, for God's sake, what are you doing? There, Livvy, there, baby, don't cry. Daddy's sorry."

The vicious resentment all but smothered him as he looked at the two golden heads close together. The shock of realizing his fists were clenched, that they wanted, *yearned* to pound, nearly snapped him back. "I told her I was sorry."

But when he started forward, intending to apologize yet again, his wife's head snapped up. In the dark, her eyes gleamed with a fierceness that bordered on hate. "Stay away from her." And the vicious threat in her mother's voice had Olivia wailing.

"Don't you tell me to stay away from my own daughter. I'm sick and tired, sick and damn tired of orders from you, Julie."

"You're stoned again. I won't have you near her when you've been using."

Then all Olivia could hear were the terrible shouts, more crashing, the sound of her mother crying out in pain. To escape she crawled out of bed and into her closet to bury herself among her mountain of stuffed toys.

Later, she learned that her mother had managed to lock him out of the room, to call the police on her Mickey Mouse phone. But that night, all she knew was that Mama had crawled into the closet with her, held her close and promised everything would be all right.

That's when Daddy had gone away.

Memories of that night could sneak into her dreams. When they did, and she woke, Olivia would creep out of bed and into her mother's room down the hall. Just to make sure she was there. Just to see if maybe Daddy had come home because he was all better again.

Sometimes they were in a hotel instead, or another house. Her mother's work meant she had to travel. After her father got sick, Olivia always, always went with her. People said her mother was a star, and it made Olivia giggle. She knew stars were the little lights up in heaven, and her mother was right here.

Her mother made movies, and lots and lots of people came to see her pretend to be somebody else. Daddy made movies, too, and she knew the story about how they'd met when they were both pretending to be other people. They'd fallen in love and gotten married, and they'd had a baby girl.

When Olivia missed her father, she could look in the big leather book at all the pictures of the wedding when her mother had been a princess in a long white dress that sparkled and her father had been the prince in his black suit.

There was a big silver-and-white cake, and Aunt Jamie had worn a blue dress that made her look almost as pretty as Mama. Olivia imagined herself into the pictures. She would wear a pink dress and flowers in her hair, and she would hold her parents' hands and smile. In the pictures, everyone smiled and was happy.

Over that spring and summer, Olivia often looked at the big leather book.

The night the monster came, Olivia heard the shouting in her sleep. It made her whimper and twist. Don't hurt her, she thought. Don't hurt my mama. Please, please, please, Daddy.

She woke with a scream in her head, with the echo of it on the air. And wanted her mother.

She climbed out of bed, her little feet silent on the carpet. Rubbing her eyes, she wandered down the hallway where the light burned low.

But the room with its big blue bed and pretty white flowers was empty. Her mother's scent was there, a comfort. All the magic bottles and pots stood on the vanity. Olivia amused herself for a little while by playing with them and pretending she was putting on the colors and smells the way her mother did.

One day she'd be beautiful, too. Like Mama. Everyone said so. She sang to herself while she preened and posed in the tall mirror, giggling as she imagined herself wearing a long white dress, like a princess.

She tired of that and, feeling sleepy again, shuffled out to find her mother.

As she approached the stairs, she saw the lights were on downstairs. The front door was open, and the late-summer breeze fluttered her nightgown.

She thought there might be company, and maybe there would be cake. Quiet as a mouse, she crept down the stairs, holding her fingers to her lips to stop a giggle.

And heard the soaring music of her mother's favorite, *Sleeping Beauty*.

The living room spilled from the central hall, flowing out with high arched ceilings, oceans of glass that opened the room to the gardens her mother loved. There was a big fireplace of deep blue lapis and floors of sheer white marble. Flowers speared and spilled from crystal vases, and silver urns and lamps had shades the colors of precious jewels.

But tonight, the vases were broken, shattered on the tiles with their elegant and exotic flowers trampled and dying. The glossy ivory walls were splattered with red, and tables the cheerful maid Rosa kept polished to a gleam were overturned.

There was a terrible smell, one that seemed to paint the inside of Olivia's throat with something vile and had her stomach rippling.

The music crescendoed, a climactic sweep of sobbing strings.

She saw glass winking on the floor like scattered diamonds and streaks of red smearing the white floor. Whimpering for her mother, she stepped in. And she saw.

Behind the corner of the big sofa, her mother lay sprawled on her side, one hand flung out, fingers spread wide. Her warm blond hair was wet with blood. So much blood. The white robe she'd worn was red with it, and ripped to ribbons.

She couldn't scream, couldn't scream. Her eyes rounded and bulged in her head, her heart bumped painfully against her ribs, and a trickle of urine slipped down her legs. But she couldn't scream.

Then the monster that crouched over her mother, the monster with hands red to the wrists, with wet red streaks over his face, over his clothes, looked up. His eyes were wild, shiny as the glass that sparkled on the floor.

"Livvy," her father said. "God, Livvy."

And as he stumbled to his feet, she saw the silver-and-red gleam of bloody scissors in his hand.

Still she didn't scream. But now she ran. The monster was real, the monster was coming, and she had to hide. She heard a long, wailing call, like the howl of a dying animal in the woods.

She went straight to her closet, burrowed among the stuffed toys. There her mind hid as well. She stared blindly at the door, sucked quietly on her thumb and barely heard the monster as he howled and called and searched for her.

Doors slammed like gunshots. The monster sobbed and screamed, crashing through the house as it called her name. A wild bull with blood on his horns.

Olivia, a doll among dolls, curled up tight and waited for her mother to come and wake her from a bad dream.

• • •

THAT'S WHERE FRANK BRADY FOUND HER. HE MIGHT HAVE
overlooked her huddled in with all the bears and dogs and pretty dolls.
She didn't move, didn't make a sound. Her hair was a golden blond, shiny
as rain to her shoulders; her face a colorless oval, dominated by huge amber
eyes under brows as dark as mink pelt.

Her mother's eyes, he thought with grim pity. Eyes he'd looked into
dozens of times on the movie screen. Eyes he'd studied less than an hour
ago and found filmed and lifeless.

The eyes of the child looked at him, looked through him. Recogniz-
ing shock, he crouched down, resting his hands on his knees rather than
reaching for her.

"I'm Frank." He spoke quietly, kept his eyes on hers. "I'm not going
to hurt you." Part of him wanted to call out for his partner, or one of the
crime scene team, but he thought a shout might spook her. "I'm a policeman." Very slowly, he lifted a hand to tap the badge that hung from his
breast pocket. "Do you know what a policeman does, honey?"

She continued to stare, but he thought he caught a flicker in her eyes.
Awareness, he told himself. She hears me. "We help people. I'm here to
take care of you. Are these all your dolls?" He smiled at her and picked up
a squashy Kermit the Frog. "I know this guy. He's on *Sesame Street*. Do you
watch that on TV? My boss is just like Oscar the Grouch. But don't tell
him I said so."

When she didn't respond, he pulled out every Sesame Street character he could remember, making comments, letting Kermit hop on his
knee. The way she watched him, eyes wide and terrifyingly blank, ripped
at his heart.

"You want to come out now? You and Kermit?" He held out a hand,
waited.

Hers lifted, like a puppet's on a string. Then, when the contact was
made, she tumbled into his arms, shivering now with her face buried
against his shoulder.

He'd been a cop for ten years, and still his heart ripped.

"There now, baby. You're okay. You'll be all right." He stroked a hand down her hair, rocking for a moment.

"The monster's here." She whispered it.

Frank checked his motion then, cradling her, got to his feet. "He's gone now."

"Did you chase him away?"

"He's gone." He glanced around the room, found a blanket and tucked it around her.

"I had to hide. He was looking for me. He had Mama's scissors. I want Mama."

God. Dear God, was all he could think.

At the sound of feet coming down the hall, Olivia let out a low keening sound and tightened her grip around Frank's neck. He murmured to her, patting her back as he moved toward the door.

"Frank, there's—you found her." Detective Tracy Harmon studied the little girl wrapped around his partner and raked a hand through his hair. "The neighbor said there's a sister. Jamie Melbourne. Husband's David Melbourne, some kind of music agent. They only live about a mile from here."

"Better notify them. Honey, you want to go see your aunt Jamie?"

"Is my mama there?"

"No. But I think she'd want you to go."

"I'm sleepy."

"You go on to sleep, baby. Just close your eyes."

"She see anything?" Tracy murmured.

"Yeah." Frank stroked her hair as her eyelids drooped. "Yeah, I think she saw too damn much. We can thank Christ the bastard was too blitzed to find her. Call the sister. Let's get the kid over there before the press gets wind of this."

HE CAME BACK. THE MONSTER CAME BACK. SHE COULD SEE him creeping through the house with her father's face and her mother's scissors. Blood slid down the snapping blades like thin, glossy ribbons. In her father's voice he whispered her name, over and over again.

Livvy, Livvy love. Come out. Come out and I'll tell you a story.

And the long sharp blades in his hands hissed open and closed as he shambled toward the closet.

"No, Daddy! No, no, no!"

"Livvy. Oh honey, it's all right. I'm here. Aunt Jamie's right here."

"Don't let him come. Don't let him find me." Wailing, Livvy burrowed into Jamie's arms.

"I won't. I won't. I promise." Devastated, Jamie pressed her face into the fragile curve of her niece's neck. She rocked both of them in the delicate half-light of the bedside lamp until Olivia's shivers stopped. "I'll keep you safe."

She rested her cheek on the top of Olivia's head and let the tears come. She didn't allow herself to sob, though hot, bitter sobs welled and pressed into her throat. The tears were silent, sliding down her cheeks to dampen the child's hair.

Julie. Oh God, oh God, Julie.

She wanted to scream out her sister's name. To rave it. But there was the child, now going limp with sleep in her arms, to consider.

Julie would have wanted her daughter protected. God knew, she had tried to protect her baby.

And now Julie was dead.

Jamie continued to rock, to soothe herself now as Olivia slept in her arms. That beautiful, bright woman with the wickedly husky laugh, the giving heart and boundless talent, dead at the age of thirty-two. Killed, the two grim-faced detectives had told her, by the man who had professed to love her to the point of madness.

Well, Sam Tanner was mad, Jamie thought as her hands curled into brutal fists. Mad with jealousy, with drugs, with desperation. Now he'd destroyed the object of his obsession.

But he would never, never touch the child.

Gently, Jamie laid Olivia back in bed, smoothed the blankets over her, let her fingertips rest for a moment on the blond hair. She remembered the night Olivia had been born, the way Julie had laughed between contractions.

Only Julie MacBride, Jamie thought, could make a joke out of labor. The way Sam had looked, impossibly handsome and nervous, his blue eyes brilliant with excitement and fear, his black hair tousled so that she'd smoothed it with her own fingers to soothe him.

Then he'd brought that beautiful little girl up to the viewing glass, and there'd been tears of love and wonder in his eyes.

Yes, she remembered that, and remembered thinking as she smiled at him through that glass that they were perfect. The three of them, perfect together. Perfect for one another.

It had seemed so.

She walked to the window, stared out at nothing. Julie's star had been on the rise, and Sam's already riding high. They'd met on the set of a movie, fell wildly in love and were married within four months while the press raved and simpered over them.

She'd worried, Jamie admitted. It was all so fast, so Hollywood. But Julie had always known exactly what she wanted, and she'd wanted Sam Tanner. For a while, it had seemed as happy-ever-after as the stories Julie told her daughter at bedtime.

But this fairy tale had ended in a nightmare—blocks away, only blocks away while she'd slept, Jamie thought, squeezing her eyes shut as a sob clawed at her throat.

The sudden flash of lights had her jumping back, her heart pumping fast. David, she realized, and turned quickly to the bed to be certain Olivia slept peacefully. Leaving the light on low, she hurried out. She was coming down the stairs as the door opened and her husband walked in.

He stood there for a long moment, a tall man with broad shoulders. His hair of deep brown was mussed, his eyes, a quiet mix of gray and green, full of fatigue and horror. Strength was what she'd always found in him. Strength and stability. Now he looked sick and shaken, his usual dusky complexion pasty, a muscle jumping in his firm, square jaw.

"God, Jamie. Oh, sweet God." His voice broke, and somehow that made it worse. "I need a drink." He turned away, walked unsteadily into the front salon.

She had to grip the railing for balance before she could order her legs to move, to follow him. "David?"

"I need a minute." His hands shook visibly as he took a decanter of whisky from the breakfront, poured it into a short glass. He braced one hand on the wood, lifted the glass with the other and drank it down like medicine. "Jesus, God, what he did to her."

"Oh, David." She broke. The control she'd managed to cling to since the police had come to the door shattered. She simply sank to the floor in a spasm of sobs and shudders.

"I'm sorry, I'm sorry." He rushed to her and gathered her against him. "Oh, Jamie, I'm so sorry."

They stayed there, on the floor in the lovely room, as the light turned pearly with dawn. She wept in harsh, racking gasps until he wondered that her bones didn't shatter from the power of it.

The gasps turned to moans that were her sister's name, then the moans to silence.

"I'll take you upstairs. You need to lie down."

"No, no, no." The tears had helped. Jamie told herself they'd helped though they left her feeling hollowed-out and achy. "Livvy might wake up. She'll need me. I'll be all right. I have to be all right."

She sat back, scrubbing her hands over her face to dry it. Her head throbbed like an open wound, her stomach was a mass of cramps. But she got to her feet. "I need you to tell me. I need you to tell me everything." When he shook his head, her chin came up. "I have to know, David."

He hesitated. She looked so tired, so pale and so fragile. Where Julie had been long and willowy, Jamie was small and fine-boned. Both had carried a look of delicacy that he knew was deceptive. He'd often joked that the MacBride sisters were tough broads, bred to climb mountains and tramp through woods.

"Let's get some coffee. I'll tell you everything I know."

Like her sister, Jamie had refused live-in staff. It was her house, by God, and she wouldn't sacrifice her privacy. The day maid wouldn't be in for another two hours, so she brewed the coffee herself while David sat at the counter and stared out the window.

They didn't speak. In her head she ran over the tasks she would have to face that day. The call to her parents would be the worst, and she was already bracing for it. Funeral arrangements would have to be made—carefully, to ensure as much dignity and privacy as possible. The press would be salivating. She would make sure the television remained off as long as Olivia was in the house.

She set two cups of coffee on the counter, sat. "Tell me."

"There isn't much more than Detective Brady already told us," David began. "There wasn't any forced entry. She let him in. She was, ah, dressed for bed, but hadn't been to bed. It looked as though she'd been in the living room working on clippings. You know how she liked to send your folks clippings."

He rubbed both hands over his face, then picked up his coffee. "They must have argued. There were signs of a fight. He used the scissors on her." Horror bloomed in his eyes. "Jamie, he must have lost his mind."

His gaze came to hers, held. When he reached for her hand, she curled her fingers around his tightly. "Did he—was it quick?"

"I don't—I've never seen—he went wild." He closed his eyes a moment. She would hear, in any case. There would be leaks, there would be media full of truth and lies. "Jamie, she was . . . he stabbed her repeatedly, and slashed her throat."

The color drained from her face, but her hand stayed firm in his. "She fought back. She must have fought him. Hurt him."

"I don't know. They have to do an autopsy. We'll know more after that. They think Olivia saw some of it, saw something, then hid from him." He drank coffee in the faint hope it would settle his jittery stomach. "They want to talk to her."

"She can't be put through that." This time she jerked back, yanking her hand free. "She's a baby, David. I won't have them put her through that. They know he did it," she said with a fierce and vicious bitterness. "I won't have my sister's child questioned by the police."

David let out a long breath. "He's claiming he found Julie that way. That he came in and found her already dead."

"Liar." Her eyes fired, and color flooded back into her face, harsh and passionate. "Murdering bastard. I want him dead. I want to kill him myself. He made her life a misery this past year, and now he's killed her. Burning in hell isn't enough."

She whirled away, wanting to pound something, tear something to pieces. Then stopped short when she saw Olivia staring at her from the doorway with wide eyes.

"Livvy."

"Where's Mama?" Her bottom lip trembled. "I want my mama."

"Livvy." As temper drained into grief, and grief into helplessness, Jamie bent down and picked her up.

"The monster came and hurt Mama. Is she all right now?"

Over the child's head, Jamie's desperate eyes met her husband's. He held out a hand, and she walked over so the three of them stood wrapped together.

"Your mother had to go away, Livvy." Jamie closed her eyes as she pressed a kiss to Olivia's head. "She didn't want to, but she had to."

"Is she coming back soon?"

There was a ripple in Jamie's chest, like a wave breaking on rock. "No, honey. She's not coming back."

"She always comes back."

"This time she can't. She had to go to heaven and be an angel."

Olivia knuckled her eyes. "Like a movie?"

As her legs began to tremble, Jamie sat, cradling her sister's child. "No, baby, not like a movie this time."

"The monster hurt her and I ran away. So she won't come back. She's mad at me."

"No, no, Livvy." Praying for wisdom, Jamie eased back, cupped Olivia's face in her hands. "She wanted you to run away. She wanted you to be a smart girl, and run away and hide. To be safe. That was what she wanted most of all. If you hadn't, she'd have been very sad."

"Then she'll come back tomorrow." Tomorrow was a concept she knew only as later, another time, soon.

"Livvy." With a nod to his wife, David slid the child onto his lap, relieved when she laid her head against his chest and sighed. "She can't come back, but she'll be watching you from up in heaven."

"I don't want her to be in heaven." She began to cry now, soft, sniffling sobs. "I want to go home and see Mama."

When Jamie reached for her, David shook his head. "Let her cry it out," he murmured.

Jamie pressed her lips together, nodded. Then she rose to go up to her bedroom and call her parents.

TWO

THE press stalked, a pack of rabid wolves scenting heart blood. At least that was how Jamie thought of them as she barricaded her family behind closed doors. To be fair, a great many of the reporters were shocked and grieving and broadcast the story with as much delicacy as the circumstances allowed.

Julie MacBride had been well loved—desired, admired and envied—but loved all the same.

But Jamie wasn't feeling particularly fair. Not when Olivia sat like a doll in the guest room or wandered downstairs as thin and pale as a ghost. Wasn't it enough that the child had lost her mother in the most horrible of ways? Wasn't it enough that she, herself, had lost her sister, her twin, her closest friend?

But she had lived in the glittery world of Hollywood with its seductive shadows for eight years now. And she knew it was never enough.

Julie MacBride had been a public figure, a symbol of beauty, talent, sex with the girl-next-door spin, a country girl turned glamorous movie princess who'd married the reigning prince and lived with him in their polished castle in Beverly Hills.

Those who paid their money at the box office, who devoured glossy articles in *People* or absurdities in the tabloids, considered her theirs. Julie MacBride of the quick and brilliant smile and smoky voice.

But they didn't know her. Oh, they thought they did, with their exposés, their interviews and glossy articles. Julie had certainly been open and honest in most of them. That was her way, and she'd never taken her success for granted. It had always thrilled and delighted her. But no matter how much print and tape and film they'd run on the actress, they'd never really understood the woman herself: her sense of fun and foolishness, her love of the forest and mountains of Washington State where she'd grown up, her absolute loyalty to family, her unshakable love and devotion to her daughter.

And her tragic and undying love for the man who'd killed her.

That was what Jamie found hardest to accept. She'd let him in, was all she could think. In the end, she'd gone with her heart and had opened the door to the man she loved, even knowing he'd stopped being that man.

Would she have done the same? They'd shared a great deal, more than sisters, more than friends. Part of it came from being twins, certainly, but added to that was their shared childhood in the deep woods. The hours, the days, the evenings they'd spent exploring together. Learning, loving the scents and sounds and secrets of the forest. Following tracks, sleeping under the stars. Sharing their dreams as naturally as they had once shared the womb.

Now it was as if something in Jamie had died as well. The kindest part, she thought. The freshest and most vulnerable part. She doubted she would ever be whole again. Knew she would never be the same again.

Strong, she could be strong. Would have to be. Olivia depended on her; David would need her. She knew he'd loved Julie, too, had thought of her as his own sister. And her parents as his own.

She stopped pacing to glance up the stairs. They were here now, up with Olivia in her room. They would need her, too. However sturdy they were, they would need their remaining child to help them get through the next weeks.

When the doorbell rang, she jumped, then closed her eyes. She who had once considered herself fearless was shaking at shadows and whispers. She drew a breath in, let it out slowly.

David had arranged for guards, and the reporters were ordered not to come onto the property. But over that long, terrible day one slipped through now and then. She wanted to ignore the bell. To let it ring and ring and ring. But that would disturb Olivia, upset her parents.

She marched toward the door intending to rip off the reporter's skin, then through the etched-glass panels beside the wood she recognized the detectives who had come in the dark of the morning to tell her Julie was dead.

"Mrs. Melbourne. I'm sorry to disturb you."

It was Frank Brady who spoke, and he whom Jamie focused on. "Detective Brady, isn't it?"

"Yes, may we come in?"

"Of course." She stepped back. Frank noted that she had enough control to keep behind the door, not to give the camera crews a shot at her. It had been her control he'd noted, and admired, the night before.

She'd rushed out of the house, he recalled, even before they'd fully braked at the entrance. But the minute she'd seen the girl in his arms, she'd seemed to snap back, to steady. She'd taken charge of her niece, bundling her close, carrying her upstairs.

He studied her again as she led them into the salon.

He knew now that she and Julie MacBride had been twins, with Jamie the elder by seven minutes. Yet there wasn't as much resemblance as he might have expected. Julie MacBride had owned a blazing beauty— despite delicate features and that golden coloring, it had flamed out and all but burned the onlooker.

The sister had quieter looks, hair more brown than blond that was cut in a chin-length swing and worn sleek, eyes more chocolate than gold and lacking that sensuous heavy-lidded shape. She was about five-three, Frank calculated, probably about a hundred and ten pounds on slender bones where her sister had been a long-stemmed five-ten.

He wondered if she'd been envious of her sister, of that perfection of looks and the excess of fame.

"Can I get you anything? Coffee?"

It was Tracy who answered, judging that she needed to do something normal before getting down to business. "I wouldn't mind some coffee, Mrs. Melbourne. If it's not too much trouble."

"No . . . we seem to have pots going day and night. I'll see to it. Please sit down."

"She's holding up," Tracy commented when he was alone with his partner.

"She's got a way to go." Frank flicked open the curtains a slit to study the mob of press at the edge of the property. "This one's going to be a zoo, a long-running one. It's not every day America's princess gets cut to ribbons inside her own castle."

"By the prince," Tracy added. He tapped his pocket where he kept his cigarettes—then thought better of it. "We'll get maybe one more shot at him before he pulls it together and calls for a lawyer."

"Then we'd better make it a bull's-eye." Frank let the curtain close and turned as Jamie came back into the room with a tray of coffee.

He sat when she did. He didn't smile. Her eyes told him she didn't require or want pleasantries and masks. "We appreciate this, Mrs. Melbourne. We know this is a bad time for you."

"Right now it seems it'll never be anything else." She waited while Tracy added two heaping spoonsful of sugar to his mug. "You want to talk to me about Julie."

"Yes, ma'am. Were you aware that your sister placed a nine-one-one call due to a domestic disturbance three months ago?"

"Yes." Her hands were steady as she lifted her own mug. "Sam came home in an abusive state of mind. Physically abusive this time."

"This time?"

"He'd been verbally, emotionally abusive before." Her voice was brisk and clear. She refused to let it quaver. "Over the last year and a half that I know of."

"Is it your opinion Mr. Tanner has a problem with drugs?"

"You know very well Sam has a habit." Her eyes stayed level on Frank's. "If you haven't figured that out, you're in the wrong business."

"Sorry, Mrs. Melbourne. Detective Brady and I are just trying to touch all the bases. We have to figure you'd know your sister's husband, his routines. Maybe she talked to you about their personal problems."

"She did, of course. Julie and I were very close. We could talk about anything." For a moment, Jamie looked away, struggling to keep it all steady. Voice, hands, eyes. "I think it started a couple of years ago, social cocaine." She smiled, but it was thin and hard. "Julie hated it. They argued about it. They began to argue over a great many things. His last two movies didn't do as well as expected, critically or financially. Actors can be a tender species. Julie was worried because Sam became edgy, argumentative. But as much as she tried to smooth things over, her own career was soaring. He resented that, began to resent her."

"He was jealous of her," Frank prompted.

"Yes, when he should have been proud. They began to go out more, parties, clubs. He felt he needed to be seen. Julie supported him in that, but she was a homebody. I know it's difficult to equate the image, the beauty, glamour, with a woman who was happiest at home, in her garden, with her daughter, but that was Julie."

Her voice cracked. She cleared it, sipped more coffee and continued. "She was working on the feature with Lucas Manning, *Smoke and Shadows*. It was a demanding, difficult role. Very physical. Julie couldn't afford to work twelve or fourteen hours, come home, then polish herself up for night after night on the town. She wanted time to relax, time with Olivia. So Sam started going out on his own."

"There were some rumors about your sister and Manning."

Jamie shifted her gaze to Tracy, nodded. "Yes, there usually are when two very attractive people fire up the screen. People romanticize, and they enjoy gossip. Sam hounded her about other men, and Lucas in particular most recently. The rumors were groundless. Julie considered Lucas a friend and a marvelous leading man."

"How did Sam take it?" Frank asked her.

She sighed now and set down her mug, but didn't rub at the ache behind her eyes. "If it had been three or four years ago, he'd have laughed it off, teased her about it. Instead he hounded her, sniped at her. He accused her of trying to run his life, of encouraging other men, then of being with other men. Lucas was his prime target. It hurt Julie very much."

"Some women would turn to a friend, to another man under that kind of pressure." Frank watched her steadily as her eyes flared, her mouth tightened.

"Julie took her marriage seriously. She loved her husband. Enough, as it turned out, to stick by him until he killed her. And if you want to turn this around and make her seem cheap and ordinary—"

"Mrs. Melbourne." Frank lifted a hand. "If we want to close this case, to get justice for your sister, we need to ask. We need all the pieces."

She ordered herself to breathe, slowly in, slowly out, and poured more coffee she didn't want. "The pieces are simple. Her career was moving up, and his was shaky. The shakier it got, the more he did drugs and the more he turned the blame on her. She called the police that night last spring because he attacked her in their daughter's room and she was afraid for Livvy. She was afraid for all of them."

"She filed for divorce."

"That was a difficult decision for her. She wanted Sam to get help, to go into counseling, and she used the separation as a hammer. Most of all, she wanted to protect her daughter. Sam had become unstable. She wouldn't risk her child."

"Yet it appears she opened the door to him on the night of her death."

"Yes." Jamie's hand shook now. Once. She set the coffee down and folded both hands in her lap. "She loved him. Despite everything, she loved him and believed if he could beat the drugs they'd get back together. She wanted more children. She wanted her husband back. She was careful to keep the separation out of the press. Beyond the family, the only people who knew of it were the lawyers. She'd hoped to keep it that way as long as possible."

"Would she have opened the door to him when he was under the influence of drugs?"

"That's what happened, isn't it?"

"I'm just trying to get a picture," Frank told her.

"She must have. She wanted to help him, and she believed she could handle him. If it hadn't been for Livvy, I don't think she'd have filed papers."

But her daughter had been in the house that night, Frank thought. In the house, and at risk. "You knew them both very well."

"Yes."

"In your opinion, is Sam Tanner capable of killing your sister?"

"The Sam Tanner Julie married would have thrown himself in front of a train to protect her." Jamie picked up her coffee again, but it didn't wash away the bitterness that coated her throat. "The one you have in custody is capable of anything. He killed my sister. He mutilated her, ripping her apart like an animal. I want him to die for it."

She spoke coolly, but her eyes were ripe and hot with hate. Frank met that violent gaze, nodded. "I understand your feelings, Mrs. Melbourne."

"No, no, detective. You couldn't possibly."

Frank let it go as Tracy shifted in his chair. "Mrs. Melbourne," Frank began. "It would be very helpful if we were able to speak with Olivia."

"She's four years old."

"I realize that. But the fact is, she's a witness. We need to know what she saw, what she heard." Reading both denial and hesitation on her face, he pressed. "Mrs. Melbourne, I don't want to cause you or your family any more pain, and I don't want to upset the child. But she's part of this. A key part."

"How can you ask me to put her through that, to make her talk about it?"

"It's in her head. Whatever she saw or heard is already there. We need to ask her what that was. She knows me from that night. She felt safe with me. I'll be careful with her."

"God." Jamie lifted her hands, pressed her fingers to her eyes and tried to think clearly. "I have to be there. I have to stay with her, and you'll stop if I say she's had enough."

"That's fine. She'll be more comfortable with you there. You have my word, I'll make it as easy as I can. I have a kid of my own."

"I doubt he's ever witnessed a murder."

"No, ma'am, but his father's a cop." Frank sighed a little as he rose. "They know more than you want them to."

"Maybe they do." She wouldn't know, she thought as she led them out and up the stairs. David hadn't wanted children, and since she hadn't been sure she did either, she'd been content to play doting aunt to her sister's daughter.

Now she would have to learn. They would all have to learn.

At the door to the bedroom, she motioned the two detectives back. She opened it a crack, saw that her parents were sitting on the floor with Olivia, putting a child's puzzle together.

"Mom. Could you come here a minute?"

The woman who stepped out had Jamie's small build, but seemed tougher, more athletic. The tan and the sun-bleached tips of her brown hair told Frank she liked the outdoors. He gauged her at early fifties and imagined she passed for younger when her face wasn't drawn and etched with grief. Her soft blue eyes, bloodshot and bruised-looking, skimmed over Frank's face, then his partner's.

"This is my mother, Valerie MacBride. Mom, these are the detectives who . . . They're in charge," Jamie finished. "They need to talk to Livvy."

"No." Val's body went on alert as she pulled the door closed behind her. "That's impossible. She's just a baby. I won't have it. I won't have anyone reminding her of what happened."

"Mrs. MacBride——" But even as Frank spoke, she was turning on him.

"Why didn't you protect her? Why didn't you keep that murdering bastard away from her? My baby's dead." She covered her face with her hands and wept silently.

"Please wait here," Jamie murmured and put her arms around her mother. "Come lie down, Mom. Come on now."

When Jamie came back, her face was pale and showed signs of weeping. But her eyes were dry now. "Let's get this over with." She squared her shoulders, opened the door.

The man who looked up had folded his long legs Indian style. His hair was a beautiful mix of gold and silver around a narrow face that was tanned and handsome. The eyes of deep amber he'd passed to his younger daughter, and to her daughter, were fanned with lines and widely set under dark brows.

His hand, long and wide-palmed, reached out to lie on Olivia's shoulder in an instinctive gesture of protection as he studied the men behind Jamie.

"Dad." Jamie forced her lips into a smile. "This is Detective Brady and Detective Harmon. My father, Rob MacBride."

Rob rose, and though he offered his hand to each detective in turn, he kept himself between them and his granddaughter. "What's this about, Jamie?"

"They need to talk to Livvy." She pitched her voice low and gripped his hand before he could protest. "They need to," she repeated, squeezing. "Please, Dad, Mom's upset. She's lying down in your room. I'm going to stay here. I'll be right here with Livvy the whole time. Go talk to Mom. Please . . ." Because her voice threatened to break, she took a moment. "Please, we have to get through this. For Julie."

He bent, rested his brow against hers. Just stood that way for a moment, his body bowed, his hand in hers. "I'll talk to your mother."

"Where are you going, Grandpop? We haven't finished the puzzle."

He glanced back, fighting the tears that wanted to swim into his eyes. "I'll be back, Livvy love. Don't grow up while I'm gone."

She giggled at that, but her thumb had found its way into her mouth as she stared up at Frank.

She knew who he was—the policeman with long arms and green eyes. His face looked tired and sad. But she remembered he had a nice voice and gentle hands.

"Hi, Livvy." Frank crouched down. "Do you remember me?"

She nodded and spoke around her thumb. "You're Frank the policeman. You chased the monster away. Is it coming back?"

"No."

"Can you find my mama? She had to go to heaven and she must be lost. Can you go find her?"

"I wish I could." Frank sat on the floor, folded his legs as her grandfather had.

Tears welled into her eyes, trembled on her lashes and cut at Frank's heart like tiny blades. "Is it because she's a star? Stars have to be in heaven."

He heard Jamie's low sound of despair behind him, quickly controlled as she stepped forward. But he needed the child's trust now, so he laid a hand on her cheek and went with instinct. "Sometimes, when we're really lucky, very special stars get to stay with us for a while. When they have to go back, it makes us sad. It's all right to be sad. Did you know the stars are there, even in the daytime?"

"You can't see them."

"No, but they're there, and they can see us. Your mother's always going to be there, looking out for you."

"I want her to come home. We're going to have a party in the garden with my dolls."

"Do your dolls like parties?"

"Everybody likes parties." She picked up the Kermit she'd brought with her from home. "He eats bugs."

"That's a frog for you. Does he like them plain or with chocolate syrup?"

Her eyes brightened at that. "I like *everything* with chocolate syrup. Do you have a little girl?"

"No, but I have a little boy, and he used to eat bugs."

Now she laughed and her thumb popped back out of her mouth. "He did not."

"Oh yes. I was afraid he'd turn green and start hopping." Idly, Frank picked up a puzzle piece, fit it into place. "I like puzzles. That's why I became a policeman. We work on puzzles all the time."

"This is Cinderella at the ball. She has a bea-u-tiful dress and a pumpkin."

"Sometimes I work on puzzles in my head, but I need help with the pieces to make the picture in there. Do you think you can help me, Livvy, by telling me about the night I met you?"

"You came to my closet. I thought you were the monster, but you weren't."

"That's right. Can you tell me what happened before I came and found you?"

"I hid there for a long, long time, and he didn't know where I was."

"It's a good hiding place. Did you play with Kermit that day, or with puzzles?"

"I played with lots of things. Mama didn't have to work and we went swimming in the pool. I can hold my breath under the water for an ever, because I'm like a fish."

He tugged her hair, peeked at her neck. "Yep, there are the gills."

Her eyes went huge. "Mama says she can see them, too! But I can't."

"You like to swim?"

"It's the most fun of anything. I have to stay in the little end, and I can't go in the water unless Mama or Rosa or a big person's there. But one day I can."

"Did you have friends over that day, to play?"

"Not that day. Sometimes I do." She pursed her lips and industriously fit another piece of her puzzle into place. "Sometimes Billy or Cherry or Tiffy come, but that day Mama and me played, and we took a nap and we had some cookies Rosa made. And Mama read her script and she laughed and she talked on the phone: 'Lou, I love it!'" Livvy recited in such a smooth and adult tone, Frank blinked at her. "'I *am* Carly. It's about damn time I got my teeth into a romantic comedy with wit. Make the deal.'"

"Ah . . ." Frank struggled between surprise and admiration while Livvy tried to set another piece of her puzzle in place. "That's really good. You have a good memory."

"Daddy says I'd be a parrot if I had wings. I 'member lots of things."

"I bet you do. Do you know what time you went to bed?"

"I'm 'posed to go to bed at eight o'clock. Chickens go broody at eight. Mama told me the story about the lady with long, long hair who lived in the tower."

"Later you woke up. Were you thirsty?"

"No." She lifted her thumb to her mouth again. "I had a bad dream."

"My Noah has bad dreams, too. When he tells me about them, he feels better."

"Is Noah your little boy? How old is he?"

"He's ten now. Do you want to see his picture?"

"Uh-huh." She scooted closer as Frank took out his wallet and flipped through. Cocking her head, she studied the school photo of a boy with untidy brown hair and a wide grin. "He's pretty. Maybe he can come over to play."

"Maybe. Sometimes he has bad dreams about space aliens."

Forgive me, Noah, Frank thought with some amusement as he replaced his wallet, for sharing your darkest secret. "When he tells me about them, he feels better. You want to tell me about your bad dream?"

"People are yelling. I don't like when Mama and Daddy fight. He's sick and he has to get well, and we have to keep wishing really, really hard for him to get all better so he can come home."

"In your dream you heard your mother and father yelling?"

"People are yelling, but I can't hear what they say. I don't want to. I want them to stop. I want my mama to come. Somebody screams, like in the movies that Rosa watches. They scream and scream, and I wake up. I don't hear anything, 'cause it was just a dream. I want Mama."

"Did you go to find her?"

"She wasn't in bed. I wanted to get in bed with her. She doesn't mind. Then I . . ."

She broke off and gave a great deal of attention to her puzzle.

"It's all right, Livvy. You can tell me what happened next."

"I'm not supposed to touch the magic bottles. I didn't break any."

"Where are the magic bottles?"

"On Mama's little table with the mirror. I can have some when I get bigger, but they're toys for big girls. I just played with them for a minute."

She sent Frank such an earnest look, he had to smile. "That's all right then. What did you do next?"

"I went downstairs. The lights were on, and the door was open. It was warm outside. Maybe somebody came to see us, maybe we can have cake." Tears began to stream down her cheeks. "I don't want to say now."

"It's okay, Livvy. You can tell me. It's okay to tell me."

And it was. She could look into his green eyes and it was all right to say. "It smells bad, and things are broken, and they're red and wet and nasty. The flowers are on the floor and there's glass. You don't walk near glass in your bare feet 'cause it hurts. I don't want to step in it. I see Mama, and she's lying down on the floor, and the red and the wet is all over her. The monster's with her. He has her scissors in his hand."

She held up her own, fingers curled tight and a glazed look in her eye. "'Livvy. God, Livvy,'" she said in a horrible mimic of her father's voice. "I ran away, and he kept calling. He was breaking things and looking for me and crying. I hid in the closet." Another tear trembled and fell. "I wet my pants."

"That's all right, honey. That doesn't matter."

"Big girls don't."

"You're a very big girl. And very brave and smart." When she gave him a watery smile, he prayed he wouldn't have to put her through that night again.

He drew her attention back to her puzzle, made some foolish comment about talking pumpkins that had her giggling. He didn't want her parting thought of him to be of fear and blood and madness.

Still, when he turned at the door to glance back, Olivia's eyes were on him, quietly pleading, and holding that terrifyingly adult expression only the very young can manage.

As he started downstairs, he found his thoughts running with Jamie Melbourne's. He wanted Sam Tanner's blood.

"You were very good with her." Jamie's control had almost reached the end of its strength. She wanted to curl up and weep as her mother was. To mire herself in chores and duties as her husband was. Anything, anything but reliving this over again as she had through Olivia's words.

"She's a remarkable girl."

"Takes after her mother."

He stopped then, turned and looked at Jamie squarely. "I'd say she's got some of her aunt in her."

There was a flicker of surprise over her face, then a sigh. "She had nightmares last night, and I'll catch her just staring off into space with that—that vacant look in her eyes. Sucking her thumb. She stopped sucking her thumb before she was a year old."

"Whatever comforts. Mrs. Melbourne, you've got a lot on your mind, and a lot more to deal with. You're going to want to think about counsel-ing, not just for Olivia, but for all of you."

"Yes, I'll think about it. Right now, I just have to get through the moment. I want to see Sam."

"That's not a good idea."

"I want to see the man who murdered my sister. I want to look him in the eye. That's my therapy, Detective Brady."

"I'll see what I can do. I appreciate your time and cooperation. And again, we're sorry for your loss."

"See that he pays." She opened the door, braced herself against the calls and shouts of the press, of the curious, crowded in the street.

"We'll be in touch" was all Frank said.

Jamie closed the door, leaned heavily against it. She lost track of how long she stood there, eyes closed, head bent, but she jerked straight when a hand fell on her shoulder.

"Jamie, you need some rest." David turned her into his arms. "I want you to take a pill and lie down."

"No, no pills. I'm not having my mind or my feelings clouded." But she laid her head on his shoulder and some of the pressure eased out of her chest. "The two detectives were just here."

"You should have called me."

"They wanted to talk to me, and to Livvy."

"Livvy?" He pulled her back to stare at her. "For God's sake, Jamie, you didn't let them interrogate that child?"

"It wasn't like that, David." Resentment wanted to surface, but she was too tired for it. "Detective Brady was very gentle with her, and I stayed the whole time. They needed to know what she'd seen. She's the only witness."

"The hell with that. They have him cold. He was there, he had the weapon. He was fucking stoned as he's been half the time the last year."

At Jamie's quick warning look toward the stairs, he sucked in a breath, let it out slowly. Calm, he reminded himself. They all had to stay calm to get through this. "They have all the evidence they need to put him away for the rest of his miserable life," he finished.

"Now they have Livvy's statement that she saw him, she heard him." She lifted a hand to her head. "I don't know how it works, I don't know what happens next. I can't think about it."

"I'm sorry." He gathered her close again. "I just don't want you or Livvy, or any of us, to suffer more than we have to. I want you to call me before you let them talk to her again. I think we need to consult a child psychologist to make sure it isn't damaging to her."

"Maybe you're right. She likes Detective Brady, though. You can tell she feels safe with him. I upset my mother." For a moment, she burrowed against David's throat. "I need to go up to her."

"All right, Jamie." He slid his hands down her arms, linked fingers with her. "They're going to release Julie's body day after tomorrow. We can hold the memorial service the following day, if you're ready for it. I've started making the arrangements."

"Oh, David." Pathetically grateful, she shuddered back a sob. "You didn't have to do that. I was going to make calls later today."

"I know what you want for her. Let me take care of this for all of us, Jamie. I loved her, too." He brought her hands to his lips, pressed a kiss to her fingers.

"I know."

"I have to do something. Details are what I do best. I, ah, I've been working on a press release. There has to be one." He ran his hands up her arms again, back down in a gesture of comfort. "It's more your area than mine, but I figured simple was best. I'll run it by you before it's confirmed. But as for the rest . . . just let me take care of it."

"I don't know what I'd do without you, David. I don't know what I'd do."

"You'll never have to find out." He kissed her, softly. "Go up to your mother, and promise me you'll try to get some rest."

"Yes, I will."

He waited until she walked upstairs, then went to the door, stared out the glass panels at the figures sweltering outside in the high summer heat.

And thought of vultures over fresh kill.

THREE

S HE didn't want to take a nap. She wasn't sleepy. But Olivia tried, because Aunt Jamie had asked her to, and lay in the bed that wasn't hers.

It was a pretty room with little violets climbing up the walls and white curtains with tiny white dots on them that made everything soft and filmy when you looked through them. She always slept in this room when she came to visit.

But it wasn't home.

She'd told Grandma she wanted to go home, that she could come, too. They could have a tea party in the garden until Mama got home.

But Grandma's eyes had gotten bright and wet, and she'd hugged Olivia so hard it almost hurt.

So she hadn't said anything more about going home.

When she heard the murmur of voices down the hall, behind the door of the room where her grandparents were staying, Olivia climbed out of bed and tiptoed from the room. Aunt Jamie had said, when Olivia asked, that Grandma and Grandpop were taking naps, too. But if they were awake, maybe they could go out and play. Grandma and Grandpop liked to be outside best of all. They could play ball or go swimming or climb a tree.

Grandpop said there were trees that reached right up and brushed the sky in Washington. Olivia had been there to visit when she was a tiny baby and again when she'd been two, so she couldn't remember very well. She thought Grandpop could find a sky-brushing tree for her so she could climb all the way up and call her mother. Mama would hear if she could just get closer to heaven.

When she opened the door, she saw her grandmother crying, her aunt sitting beside her holding her hands. It made her stomach hurt to see Grandma cry, and it made her afraid when she saw her grandpop's face. It was so tight and his eyes were too dark and mean. His voice, when he spoke, was quiet but hard, as if he were trying to break the words instead of say them. It made Olivia cringe back to make herself small.

"It doesn't matter why he did it. He's crazy, crazy with jealousy and drugs. What matters is he killed her, he took her away from us. He'll pay for it, every day of his miserable life, he'll pay. It'll never be enough."

"We should've made her come home." Tears continued to slide down Grandma's cheeks. "When she told us she and Sam were having trouble, we should have told her to bring Livvy and come home for a while. To get her bearings."

"We didn't know he'd gotten violent, didn't know he'd hurt her." Grandpa's fists balled at his sides. "If I'd known, I'd have come down here and dealt with the son of a bitch myself."

"We can't go back, Dad." Jamie spoke wearily, for some of that responsibility was hers. She had known and said nothing. Julie had asked her to say nothing. "If we could, I know I'd be able to see a hundred different things I could do to change it, to stop it. But I can't, and we have to face the now. The press—"

"Fuck the press."

From her peep through the doorway, Olivia widened her eyes. Grandpop never said the bad word. She could only goggle as her aunt nodded calmly.

"Well, Dad, before much longer they might look to fuck us. That's the way of it. They'll canonize Julie, or make her a whore. Or they'll do both. We have to, for Livvy's sake, take as much control as we can. There'll be speculation and stories about her marriage and relationship with Sam—speculation about other men. Particularly Lucas Manning."

"Julie was not a cheat." Grandma's voice rose, snapped.

"I know that, Mom. But that's the kind of game that's played."

"She's dead," Grandpop said flatly. "Julie's dead. How much worse can it get?"

Slowly, Olivia backed up from the door. She knew what dead meant. Flowers got dead when they were all brown and stiff and you had to throw them away. Tiffy's old dog, Casey, had died and they'd dug a hole in the yard and put him inside, covered him up with dirt and grass.

Dead meant you couldn't come back.

She kept moving away from the door while the breath got hot and thick in her chest, while flashes of blood and broken glass, of monsters and snapping scissors raced through her head.

Then that breath burst out, burning over her heart as she started to run. And she started to scream.

"Mama's not dead. Mama's not dead and in a hole in the yard. She's coming back. She's coming back soon."

She kept running, away from the shouts of her name, down the steps, down the hall. At the front door, she fought with the knob while tears flooded her cheeks. She had to get outside. She had to find a tree, a sky-brushing tree, so she could climb up and call Mama home.

She fought it open and raced out. There were crowds of people, and she didn't know where to go. Everyone was shouting, at once, like a big wave of sound crashing over her head, hurting her ears. She pressed her hands to them, crying, calling for her mother.

A dozen cameras greedily captured the shot. Ate the moment and her grief and her fear.

Someone shouted for them to leave her alone, she's just a baby. But the reporters surged forward, caught in the frenzy. Sun shot off lenses, blinded her. She saw shadows and shapes, a blur of strange faces. Voices boomed out questions, commands.

Look this way, Olivia! Over here.

Did your father try to hurt you?

Did you hear them fighting?

Look at me, Olivia. Look at the camera.

She froze like a fawn in the crosshairs, eyes dazed and wild. Then she was being scooped up from behind, her face pressed into the scent and shape of her aunt.

"I want Mama, I want Mama." She could only whisper it while Aunt Jamie held her tight.

"She's just a child." Unable to stop herself, Jamie lifted her voice to a shout. "Damn you, God damn every one of you, she's only a child."

She turned back toward the house and shook her head fiercely before her husband and her parents could step out. "No, stay inside. Don't give them any more. Don't give them another thing."

"I'll take her upstairs." Grandma's eyes were dry now. Dry and cold and calm. "You're right, Jamie. We deal with them now." She pressed her lips to Olivia's hair as she started upstairs. For her, Olivia was the now.

THIS TIME OLIVIA SLEPT, DEEP IN THE EXHAUSTION OF TER-
ror and misery, while her grandmother watched over her. That, Val decided, was her job now.

In less soothing surroundings, Frank Brady thought of the child he'd seen that morning. He kept the image of her, those wide brown eyes holding trustingly to his, while he did his job.

Sam Tanner was the now for Frank.

Despite the hours in prison and the fact that his system was jumping for a hit, Sam's looks had suffered little. It appeared as though he'd been prepped for the role of the afflicted lover, shocked and innocent and suffering, but still handsome enough to make the female portion of the audience long to save him.

His hair was dark, thick and untidy. His eyes, a brilliant Viking blue, were shadowed. His love affair with cocaine had cost him some weight, but that only added a romantic, hollowed-out look to his face.

His lips tended to tremble. His hands were never still.

They'd taken away his bloody clothes and given him a washed-out gray shirt and slacks that bagged on him. They'd kept his belt and his shoelaces. He was on suicide watch, but had only begun to notice the lack of privacy. The full scope of his situation was still buried under the fog of shock and withdrawal from his drug of choice.

The interrogation room had plain beige walls and the wide expanse of two-way glass. There was a single table, three chairs. His tended to wobble if he tried to lean back. A water fountain in the corner dispensed stingy triangular cups of lukewarm water, and the air was stuffy.

Frank sat across from him, saying nothing. Tracy leaned against the wall and examined his own fingernails. The silence and overheated room had sweat sliding greasily down Sam's back.

"I don't remember any more than I told you before." Unable to stand the quiet, Sam let the words tumble out. He'd been so sure when they'd finished talking to him the first time, they'd let him go. Let him go so he could find out what they'd done with Julie, with Olivia.

Oh God, Julie. Every time he thought of her, he saw blood, oceans of blood.

Frank only nodded, his eyes patient. "Why don't you tell me what you told me before? From the beginning."

"I *keep* telling you. I went home—"

"You weren't living there anymore, were you, Mr. Tanner?" This from Tracy, and just a little aggressive.

"It's still my home. The separation was just temporary, just until we worked some problems out."

"Right." Tracy kept studying his fingernails. "That's why your wife filed papers, got sole custody of the kid, why you had limited visitation and bought that palace on the beach."

"It was just formality." Color washed in and out of Sam's face. He was desperate for a hit, just one quick hit to clear his head, sharpen his focus. Why didn't people understand how hard it was to *think*, for Christ's sake. "And I bought the Malibu house as an investment."

When Tracy snorted, Frank lifted a hand. They'd been partners for six years and had their rhythm down as intimately as lovers. "Give the guy a chance to tell it, Tracy. You keep interrupting, you'll throw him off. We're just trying to get all the details, Mr. Tanner."

"Okay, okay. I went home." He rubbed his hands on his thighs, hating the rough feel of the bagging trousers. He was used to good material, expertly cut. By God, he thought as he continued to pick and pluck at his pant legs, he'd earned the best.

"Why did you go home?"

"What?" He blinked, shook his head. "Why? I wanted to talk to Julie. I needed to see her. We just needed to straighten things out."

"Were you high, Mr. Tanner?" Frank asked it gently, almost friend to friend. "It'd be better if you were up-front about that kind of thing. Recreational use . . ." He let his shoulders lift and fall. "We're not going to push you on that, we just need to know your state of mind."

He'd denied it before, denied it right along. It was the kind of thing that could ruin you with the public. People in the business, well, they understood how things were. But cocaine didn't play well at the box office.

But a little coke between friends? Hell, that wasn't a big deal. Not a big fucking deal, as he was forever telling Julie when she nagged him. If she'd just . . .

Julie, he thought again, and pressed his fingers to his eyes. Was she really dead?

"Mr. Tanner?"

"What?" The eyes that had women all over the world sighing blinked. They were bloodshot, bruised and blank.

"Were you using when you went to see your wife?" Before he could deny it again, Frank leaned forward. "Before you answer, I'm going to tell you that we searched your car and found your stash. Now we're not going to give you grief about possession. As long as you're up-front."

"I don't know what you're talking about." He scrubbed the back of his hand over his mouth. "Anybody could have put that there. You could've planted it, for all I know."

"You saying we planted evidence?" Tracy moved fast, a lightning strike of movement. He had Sam by the collar and half out of the chair. "Is that what you're saying?"

"Easy, take it easy. Come on now." Frank lifted both hands. "Mr. Tanner's just confused. He's upset. You didn't mean to say we'd planted drugs in your car, did you?"

"No, I—"

"Because that's serious business, Mr. Tanner. A very serious accusation. It won't look good for you, especially since we have a number of people who'll testify you like a little nose candy now and then. Just a social thing," Frank continued as Tracy let out a snort of disgust and went back to leaning on the wall. "We don't have to make a big deal out of that. Unless you do. Unless you try saying we planted that coke when we know it was yours. When I can look at you right now and see you could use a little just to smooth the edges a bit."

Face earnest, Frank leaned forward. "You're in a hell of a fix here, Sam. A hell of a fix. I admire your work, I'm a big fan. I'd like to cut you a break, but you're not helping me or yourself by lying about the drugs. Just makes it worse."

Sam worried his wedding ring, turning it around and around on his finger. "Look, maybe I had a couple of hits, but I was in control. I was in control." He was desperate to believe it. "I'm not an addict or anything, I just took a couple of hits to clear my head before I went home."

"To talk to your wife," Frank prompted. "To straighten things out."

"Yeah, that's right. I needed to make her understand we should get back together, get rid of the lawyers and fix things. I missed her and Livvy. I wanted our life back. Goddamn it, I just wanted our life back."

"I don't blame you for that. Beautiful wife and daughter. A man would be crazy to give it all up easy. You wanted to straighten out your troubles, so you went over there, and talked to her."

"That's right, I—no, I went over and I found her. I found her. Oh, Jesus Christ." He closed his eyes then, covered his face. "Oh God, Julie. There was blood, blood everywhere, broken glass, the lamp I bought her for her birthday. She was lying there in the blood and the glass. I tried to pick her up. The scissors were in her back. I pulled them out."

Hadn't he? He thought he'd pulled them out, but couldn't quite remember. They'd been in his hand, hot and slick with blood.

"I saw Livvy, standing there. She started running away."

"You went after her," Frank said quietly.

"I think—I must have. I think I went a little crazy. Trying to find her, trying to find who'd done that to Julie. I don't remember. I called the police." He looked back at Frank. "I called the police as soon as I could."

"How long?" Tracy pushed away from the wall, stuck his face close to Sam's. "How long did you go through the house looking for that little girl, with scissors in your hand, before you broke down and called the cops?"

"I don't know. I'm not sure. A few minutes, maybe. Ten, fifteen."

"Lying bastard!"

"Tracy—"

"He's a fucking lying bastard, Frank. He'd've found that kid, she'd be in the morgue next to her mother."

"No. No." Horror spiked in his voice. "I'd never hurt Livvy."

"That's not what your wife thought, is it, Tanner?" Tracy jabbed a finger into Sam's chest. "She put it in writing that she was afraid for you to be alone with the kid. You're a cokehead, and a sorry son of a bitch, and I'll tell you just how it went down. You thought about her in that big house, locking you out, keeping you away from her and your kid because she couldn't stand the sight of you. Maybe you figure she's spreading her legs for another man. Woman who looks like that, there's going to be other men. And you got yourself all coked up and drove over there to show her who was boss."

"No, I was just going to talk to her."

"But she didn't want to talk to you, did she, Tanner? She told you to get out, didn't she? Told you to go to hell. Maybe you knocked her around a little first, like you did the other time."

"It was an accident. I never meant to hurt her. We were arguing."

"So you picked up the scissors."

"No." He tried to draw back, tried to clear the images blurring in his head. "We were in Livvy's room. Julie wouldn't have scissors in Livvy's room."

"You were downstairs and you saw them on the table, sitting there, shiny, sharp. You grabbed them and you cut her to pieces because she was done with you. If you couldn't have her, no one was going to have her. That's what you thought, isn't it, Tanner? The bitch deserved to die."

"No, no, no, I couldn't have done that. I couldn't have." But he remembered the feel of the scissors in his hands, the way his fingers had wrapped around them, the way blood had dripped down the blade. "I loved her. I loved her."

"You didn't mean to do it, did you, Sam?" Frank picked up the ball, sliding back into the seat, his voice gentle, his eyes level. "I know how it is. Sometimes you love a woman so much it makes you crazy. When they don't listen, don't hear what you're saying, don't understand what you need, you have to find a way to make them. That's all it was, wasn't it? You were trying to find a way to make her listen, and she wouldn't. You lost your temper. The drugs, they played a part in that. You just didn't have control of yourself. You argued, and the scissors were just there. Maybe she came at you. Then it just happened, before you could stop it. Like the other time when you didn't mean to hurt her. It was a kind of accident."

"I don't know." Tears were starting to swim in his eyes. "I had the scissors, but it was after. It had to be after. I pulled them out of her."

"Livvy saw you."

Sam's face went blank as he stared at Frank. "What?"

"She saw you. She heard you, Sam. That's why she came downstairs. Your four-year-old daughter's a witness. The murder weapon has your prints all over it. Your bloody footprints are all over the house. In the living room, the hall, going up the stairs. There are bloody fingerprints on the doorjamb of your little girl's bedroom. They're yours. There was no one else there, Sam, no burglar like you tried to tell us yesterday. No intruder. There was no sign of a break-in, nothing was stolen, your wife wasn't raped. There were three people in the house that night. Julie, Livvy and you."

"There had to be someone else."

"No, Sam. No one else."

"My God, my God, my God." Shaking, he laid his head on the table and sobbed like a child.

When he had finished sobbing, he confessed.

FRANK READ THE SIGNED STATEMENT FOR THE THIRD TIME, got up, walked around the tiny coffee room and settled for the nasty dregs in the pot. With the cup half full of what even the desperate would call sludge, he sat at the table and read the confession again.

When his partner came in, Frank spoke without looking up. "This thing's got holes, Tracy. It's got holes you could drive that old Caddy you love so much through without scraping the paint."

"I know it." Disgusted, Tracy set a fresh pot on to brew, then went to the scarred refrigerator to steal someone's nicely ripened Bartlett pear. He bit in, grunted with satisfaction, then sat. "But the guy's whacked, Frank. Jonesing, jittery. And he was flying that night. He's never going to remember it step-by-step."

He swiped at pear juice dribbling down his chin. "We know he did it. We got the physical evidence, motive, opportunity. We place him at the scene. Hell, we got a witness. Now we got a confession. We did our job, Frank."

"Yeah, but it doesn't sit right in the gut. Not all the way right. See here where he says he broke the music box, the kid's Disney music box. There was no music box. He's getting the two nights confused, blending them into one."

"He's a fucking cokehead," Tracy said impatiently. "His story about coming in after a break-in doesn't wash. She let him in—her sister confirmed it was something she'd do. This guy ain't no Richard Kimble, pal. No one-armed man, no TV show. He picked up the scissors, jammed them into her back while she was turned. She goes down—no defensive wounds—then he just keeps hacking at her while she's trying to crawl away. We got the blood trail, the ME's report. We know how it went down. Makes me sick."

He pitched the pear core into the trash, then scraped his chair back to get fresh coffee.

"I've been working bodies for seven years now," Frank murmured. "It's one of the worst I've seen. A man does that to a woman, he's got powerful feelings for her." He sighed himself, rubbed his tired eyes. "I'd like a cleaner statement, that's all. Some high-dollar lawyer's going to dance through those holes before this is done."

With a shake of his head, he rose. "I'm going home, see if I remember what my wife and kid look like."

"Lawyer or no lawyer," Tracy said as Frank started out, "Sam Tanner's going down for this, and he'll spend the rest of his worthless life in a cage."

"Yeah, he will. And that little girl's going to have to live with that. That's what makes me sick, Tracy. That's what eats through my gut."

He thought about it on the drive home, through the impossible traffic on the freeway, down the quiet street where the houses, all tiny and tidy like his own, were jammed close together with patches of lawn gasping from the lack of rain.

Olivia's face was lodged in his mind, the rounded cheeks of childhood, the wounded, too-adult eyes under striking dark brows. And the whisper of the first words she'd spoken to him:

The monster's here.

Then he pulled into the short driveway beside his little stucco house, and it was all so blessedly normal. Noah had left his bike crashed on its side in the yard, and his wife's impatiens were wilting because she'd forgotten to water them, again. God knew why she planted the things. She killed them with the regularity of a garden psychopath. Her ancient VW Bug was already parked, emblazoned with the bumper stickers and decals of her various causes. Celia Brady collected causes the way some women collected recipes.

He noted that the VW was leaking oil again, swore without any real heat and climbed out of his car.

The front door burst open, then slammed like a single gunshot. His son raced out, a compact bullet with shaggy brown hair, bruised knees and holey sneakers.

"Hey, Dad! We just got back from protesting whale hunting. Mom's got these records with whales singing on them. Sounds like alien invaders."

Frank winced, knowing he'd be listening to whale song for the next several days. "I don't suppose we've got dinner?"

"We picked up the Colonel on the way home. I talked her into it. Man, all that health food lately, a guy could starve."

Frank stopped, laid a hand on his son's shoulder. "You're telling me we have fried chicken in the house? Don't toy with me, Noah."

Noah laughed, his dark green eyes dancing. "A whole bucket. Minus the piece I swiped on the way home. Mom said we'd go for it because you'd need some comfort food."

"Yeah." It was good to have a woman who loved you enough to know you. Frank sat down on the front stoop, loosened his tie and draped an arm around Noah's shoulders when the boy sat beside him. "I guess I do."

"The TV's had bulletins and stuff all the time about that movie star. Julie MacBride. We saw you and Tracy going into that big house, and they showed pictures of the other house, the bigger one where she got killed. And just now, right before you got home? There was this little girl, the daughter. She came running out of the house. She looked really scared."

Noah hadn't been able to tear his eyes from the image, even when those huge terrified eyes seemed to stare right into his and plead with him for help.

"Gee, Dad, they got right up in her face, and she was crying and screaming and holding her hands over her ears, until somebody came and took her back inside."

"Oh, Christ." Frank braced his elbows on his knees, put his face into his hands. "Poor kid."

"What are they going to do with her, if her mother's dead and her father's going to jail and all?"

Frank blew out a breath. Noah always wanted to know the whats and the whys. They didn't censor him—that had been Celia's stand, and Frank had come around to believing her right. Their boy was bright, curious, and knew right from wrong. He was a cop's son, Frank thought, and he had to learn that there were bad guys, and they didn't always pay.

"I don't know for sure. She has family who love her. They'll do the best they can."

"On the TV, they said she was in the house when it happened. Was she?"

"Yes."

"Wow." Noah scratched at a scab on his knee, frowned. "She looked really scared," he murmured. Noah did understand bad guys existed, that they didn't always pay. And that being a child didn't mean you were safe from them. But he couldn't understand what it would be like to be afraid of your own father.

"She'll be all right."

"Why did he do it, Dad?" Noah looked up into his father's face. He almost always found the answers there.

"We may never know for certain. Some will say he loved her too much, others will say he was crazy. That it was drugs or jealousy or rage. The only one who'll ever really know is Sam Tanner. I'm not sure he understands why himself."

Frank gave Noah's shoulders a quick squeeze. "Let's go listen to whales sing and eat chicken."

"And mashed potatoes."

"Son, you might just see a grown man cry."

Noah laughed again and trooped inside with his father. But he, too, loved enough to understand. And he was sure he would hear his father pacing the floor that night, as he did when his job troubled him most.

FOUR

C ONFESSION may be good for the soul, but in Sam Tanner's case it was also good for snapping reality into sharp focus. Less than an hour after he wrote his tearful statement admitting the brutal and drug-hazed murder of his wife, he exercised his civil rights.

He called the lawyer he'd claimed had only complicated his marital problems and demanded representation. He was panicked and ill and had by this point forgotten half of what he'd confessed.

So it was a lawyer who specialized in domestic law who first claimed the confession had been given under duress, ordered his client to stick to his right to remain silent and called out the troops.

Charles Brighton Smith would head the defense team. He was a sixty-one-year-old fox with a dramatic mane of silver hair, canny blue eyes and a mind like a laser. He embraced high-profile cases with gusto and loved nothing better than a tumultuous court battle with a media circus playing in the center ring.

Before he flew into L.A., he'd already begun assembling his team of researchers, clerks, litigators, experts, psychologists and jury profilers. He'd leaked his flight number and arrival time and was prepared—and elegantly groomed—for the onslaught of press when he stepped off the plane.

His voice was rich and fruity, drawing up through the diaphragm like an opera singer's. His face was stern and carefully composed to show concern, wisdom and compassion as he made his sweeping opening statement.

"Sam Tanner is an innocent man, a victim of this tragedy. He's lost the woman he loved in the most brutal of fashions, and now that horror has been compounded by the police in their rush to close the case. We hope to correct this injustice swiftly so that Sam can deal with his grief and go home to his daughter."

He took no questions, made no other comments. He let his bodyguards plow through the crowd and lead him to the waiting limo. When he settled inside, he imagined the media would be rife with sound bites from his entrance.

And he was right.

After seeing the last news flash of Smith's Los Angeles arrival, Val MacBride shut off the television with a snap. It was all a game to them, she thought. To the press, the lawyers, the police, the public. Just another show to bump ratings, to sell newspapers and magazines, to get their picture on the covers or on the news.

They were using her baby, her poor murdered baby.

Yet it couldn't be stopped. Julie had chosen to live in the public eye, and had died in it.

Now they would use that, the lawyers. That public perception would be twisted and exploited to make a victim out of the man who'd killed her. He would be a martyr. And Olivia was just one more tool.

That, Val told herself, she could stop.

She went quietly from the room, stopping only to peek in on Olivia. She saw Rob, sprawled on the floor with their grandchild, his head close to her as they colored together.

It made her want to smile and weep at the same time. The man was solid as a rock, she thought with great gratitude. No matter how hard you leaned on him, he stayed straight.

She left them to each other and went to find Jamie.

The house was built on the straight, clean lines of a T. In the left notch Jamie had her office. When she'd come to Los Angeles eight years before to act as her sister's personal assistant, she'd lived and worked out of the spare room in Julie's dollhouse bungalow in the hills.

Val remembered worrying a bit about both of them then, but their calls and letters and visits home had been so full of fun and excitement she'd tried not to smother the light with nagging and warnings. They'd lived in that house together for two years, until Julie had met and married Sam. And less than six months afterward, Jamie had been engaged to David. A man who managed rock and roll bands, of all things, she'd thought at the time. But he'd turned out to be as steady as her own Rob.

She'd considered her girls safe then, safe and happy and settled with good men. How could she have been so wrong?

She pushed that thought away as useless and knocked lightly on Jamie's office door before opening it.

The room had Jamie's sense of style and organization. Ordinarily the sleek vertical blinds would have been open to the sunlight and the view of the pool and flowers. But the paparazzi and their telescopic lenses had the house under siege. The blinds were shut tight, the lamps on though it was mid-afternoon.

We're like hostages, Val thought as her daughter sent her a harried smile and continued to talk on her desk phone.

Val sat in the simple button-backed chair across from the desk and waited.

Jamie looked tired, she noticed, and nearly sighed when she realized how little attention she'd paid over the last few days to the child she had left.

As her heart stuttered, Val closed her eyes, took several quiet breaths. She needed to focus on the matter at hand and not get mired in her grief.

"I'm sorry, Mom." Jamie hung up the phone, pushed both hands through her hair. "There's so much to do."

"I haven't been much help."

"Oh, yes, you have. I don't know how we'd manage without you and Dad. Livvy—I can't handle this and give her the attention she needs right now. David's shouldered a lot of the load."

She rose and went to the small refrigerator for a bottle of water. Her system had begun to revolt at the gallons of coffee she'd gulped down. In the center of her forehead was a constant, dull headache no medication seemed to touch.

"But he has his own work," she continued as she poured two glasses. "I've had people offer to field some of the calls and cables and notes, but . . ."

"This is for family," Val finished.

"Yes." Jamie handed her mother a glass, eased her hip on the desk. "People are leaving flowers at the gate of Julie's house. I needed to make arrangements for them to be taken to hospitals. Lucas Manning, bless him, is helping me with that. The letters are just starting to come in, and though Lou, Julie's agent, is going to help handle them, I think we're going to be snowed under in another week or two."

"Jamie—"

"We already have a mountain of condolences from people in the business, people she knew or worked with. And the phone calls—"

"Jamie," Val said more firmly. "We have to talk about what happens next."

"This is what happens next for me."

"Sit down." When the phone rang, Val shook her head. "Let it go, Jamie, and sit down."

"All right. All right." Giving in, Jamie sat, let her head fall back.

"There's going to be a trial," Val began, and this had Jamie sitting up again.

"There's no point in thinking about that now."

"It has to be thought of. Sam's fancy new lawyer's already on TV, prancing and posing. Some people are hot to say he couldn't have done it. He's a hero, a victim, a figure of tragedy. More will say it before it's over."

"You shouldn't listen."

"No, and I don't intend to anymore." Val's voice went fierce. "I don't intend to take any chances that Livvy will hear any of it, will be exposed to any of it or be used as she was the other day when she got outside. I want to take her home, Jamie. I want to take her back to Washington as soon as possible."

"Take her home?" For a moment, Jamie's mind went completely blank. "But this is her home."

"I know you love her. We all do." Val set her glass aside to take her daughter's hand. "Listen to me, Jamie. That little girl can't stay here, closed up in this house like a prisoner. She can't even go outside. We can't risk her going to her window without knowing some photographer will zoom in and snap her picture. She can't live like that. None of us can."

"It'll pass."

"When? How? Maybe, maybe it would have eased up a little, but not now that there's going to be a trial. She won't be able to start preschool in the fall, or play with her friends without bodyguards, without having people look at her, stare, point, whisper. And some won't bother to whisper. I don't want her to face that. I don't think you do either."

"Oh God, Mom." Torn to bits again, Jamie rose. "I want to raise her. David and I talked about it."

"How can you do that here, honey? With all the memories, all the publicity, all the risks. She needs to be protected from that but not locked in a house, however lovely, in the center of it all. Are you and David willing to give up your home, your work, your lifestyle, to take her away, to devote your time to her? Your father and I can give her a safe place. We can cut her off from the press." She took a deep breath. "And I intend to see a lawyer myself, right away, to start custody proceedings. I won't have that man getting near her, ever again. It's what's right for her, Jamie. It's what Julie would want for her."

What about me? Jamie wanted to scream it. What about what I need, what I want? She was the one who soothed Livvy's nightmares, who comforted and rocked and sat with her in the long dark hours. "Have you talked to Dad about this?" Her voice was dull now, her face turned away.

"We discussed it this morning. He agrees with me. Jamie, it's what's best. You and David could come, spend as much time as you like. She'll always be yours, too, but not here, Jamie. Not here."

• • •

FRANK PUSHED AWAY FROM HIS DESK, SURPRISED WHEN HE saw Jamie Melbourne. She took off her dark glasses as she crossed the squad room, then passed them restlessly from hand to hand.

"Detective Brady, I'd like to speak with you if you have a moment."

"Of course. We'll go in the coffee room." He tried a smile. "But I'm not recommending the coffee."

"No, I'm trying to stay away from it just now."

"Do you want to speak with Detective Harmon?"

"It's not necessary to pull both of you away from your work." She moved into the cramped little room. "I came on impulse. Not an easy feat," she added as she walked to the stingy window. At least it was a window, she thought. At least she could look outside. "There are still reporters. Not as many, but a number of them camped out. I think I ran over that snippy one from Channel Four."

"Never liked him anyway."

She leaned her hands on the windowsill and laughed. Then couldn't stop. The bubble of sound had burst a hole in her dam of control. Her shoulders shook and the laugh turned to sobs. She held on to the sill, rocking back and forth until Frank drew her gently into a chair, gave her a box of tissues and held her hand.

He said nothing, just waited for her to empty out.

"I'm sorry, I'm sorry." Frantically she pulled tissue after tissue out of the box. "This isn't what I came here to do."

"If you don't mind my saying so, Mrs. Melbourne, it's about time you let that go. The longer you hold it in, the bigger it gets."

"Julie was the emotional one. She felt everything in big soaring waves." Jamie blew her nose. "And she was one of those women who looked gorgeous when she cried." She mopped her raw and swollen eyes. "You could have hated her for that." She sat back. "I buried my sister yesterday. I keep trying to take a step back from that now that it's done, but it won't stop coming into my head."

She let out a long breath. "My parents want to take Olivia back to Wash-

ington. They want to apply for full custody and take her away." She pulled
out another tissue, then began to fold it neatly, precisely, into squares. "Why
am I telling you? I was going to tell David, cry on his shoulder, then I found
myself going into the garage, getting into the car. I guess I needed to tell
someone who wasn't so involved, yet wasn't really separate. You won."

"Mrs. Melbourne—"

"Why don't you call me Jamie now that I've cried all over you? I'd
certainly be more comfortable calling you Frank."

"Okay, Jamie. You're facing the worst anybody faces, and things are
coming at you from all directions at once. It's hard to see."

"You think my mother's right, about Livvy."

"I can't speak for your family." He got up, poured some water. "As a
parent," he continued, offering the paper cup, "I think I'd want my kid
as far away from this mess as possible, at least temporarily."

"Yes, my head knows that." But her heart, her heart didn't know how
much more it could take. "Yesterday morning, before the service, I took
Livvy out in the backyard. It's screened by trees, it seemed safe enough.
I wanted to try to talk to her, to try to help her understand. This morning there was a picture of the two of us out there in the paper. I never
even saw the photographer. I don't want that for her."

She drew in a deep breath. "I want to see Sam."

Frank sat again. "Don't do that to yourself."

"I'll have to see him in court. I'll have to look him in the face, day
after day during the trial. I need to see him now, before it begins. I need
to do that before I let Livvy go."

"I don't know if he'll agree to it. His lawyers are keeping him on a
short leash."

"He'll see me." She got to her feet. "He won't be able to stop himself.
His ego won't let him."

HE TOOK HER BECAUSE HE DECIDED SHE'D FIND A WAY TO
do what she felt she had to do with or without his help.

She said nothing as they dealt with security and protocol. Nothing when they entered the visitors' area with its long counters and glass partitions. Frank showed her to a stool. "I have to back off here. I can't have any contact with him without his lawyer at this point. I'll be right outside."

"I'll be fine. Thank you."

She'd braced herself so she didn't jolt at the harsh sound of the buzzer. A door opened, and Sam was led in.

She'd wanted him to be pale, to look ill and gray and battered. How could he, she thought as her hands fisted in her lap, how could he look so perfect, so carelessly handsome? The hard lights didn't detract from his appearance, nor the faded, ill-fitting prison clothes. If anything, they added to the appeal.

When he sat, offered her a long, pain-filled stare out of those deep blue eyes, she all but expected to hear a director call out *Cut! Print!*

She kept her gaze level and reached for the phone. He mirrored the move on the other side of the glass. She heard him clear his throat.

"Jamie, I'm so glad you came. I've been going out of my mind. Julie." He closed his eyes. "Oh God, Julie."

"You killed her."

His eyes flew open. She read the shock in them, and the hurt. Oh, she thought, oh yes, he was good.

"You can't believe that. Sweet Jesus, Jamie, you of all people know how much we loved each other. I'd never hurt her. Never."

"You've done nothing but hurt her for more than a year now, with your jealousy, your accusations, your drugs."

"I'm going into rehab. I know I've got a problem, and if I'd listened to her, if I'd only listened, I'd have been there that night and she'd still be alive."

"You were there that night, and that's why she's dead."

"No. No." He pressed a hand to the glass as if he could pass through it and reach her. "I found her. You have to listen to me, Jamie—"

"No, I don't." She felt the calm slide over her, into her. "No, Sam, I don't. But you have to listen to me. I pray every day, every hour, every minute of every day that you'll suffer, that you'll pay for what you've done. It'll never be enough, no matter what they do to you, it'll never be enough, but I'll dream of you, Sam, in a cage for the rest of your life. That'll help me get through."

"They'll let me out." Panic and nausea spewed into his throat, burned there. "The cops don't have dick, all they want is headlines. And when I get out, I'm taking Livvy and I'm starting over."

"Livvy's as dead to you as Julie. You'll never see her again."

"You can't keep my own daughter away from me." Rage leaped into his eyes, with glimmers of hate at the edges. "I'll get out, and I'll take back what's mine. You were always jealous of Julie. Always knew you were second best. You wanted what she had, but you won't get it."

She said nothing, let him rave. His voice was an ugly buzz in her ear. She never took her eyes off his face, never flinched at the violence she saw there, or the vileness of the names he called her.

And when he'd run out, when his breath was heaving and his fists clenched, she spoke calmly. "This is your life now, Sam. Look around you. Walls and bars. If they ever let you out, if they ever unlock the cage, you'll walk out an old man. Old and broken and ruined. Nothing but a blip on a film clip running on late-night television. They won't even remember your name. They won't even know who you are."

She smiled then, for the first time, and it was fierce and bright. "And neither will Olivia."

She hung up the phone, ignoring him when he beat on the glass, watching coolly as the guard came over to restrain him. He was shouting, she could see his mouth moving, see the angry color flood his face as the guard muscled him toward the door.

When they closed the door behind him, when she knew the lock had snicked into place, she let out a long breath. And felt the beginnings of peace.

THE MINUTE SHE ARRIVED HOME, DAVID RUSHED INTO THE foyer. His arms came around her, clutched her tight. "My God, Jamie, where were you? I was frantic."

"I'm sorry. There was something I needed to do." She drew back, touched his cheek. "I'm fine."

He studied her for a minute, then his eyes cleared. "Yes, I can see that. What happened?"

"I got something out of my system." She kissed him, then drew away. Eventually she'd tell him what she'd done, Jamie thought. But not now. "I need to talk to Livvy."

"She's upstairs. Jamie, your father and I talked. I know they want to take her north, away from this."

She pressed her lips together. "You agree with them."

"I'm sorry, honey, but yes, I do. It's going to be ugly here, for God knows how long. I think you should go, too."

"You know I can't. I'll be needed at the trial, and even if they didn't need me," she continued before he could speak, "I'd have to see it through. I'd have to, David, for myself as much as for Julie." She gave his arm an absent squeeze. "Let me talk to Livvy."

She climbed the steps slowly. It hurt, she thought. Every step was painful. It was amazing, really, just how much pain the human heart could take. She opened the door to the pretty room she'd decorated specifically for her niece's visits.

And saw the curtains drawn, the lights blazing in the middle of the day. Just another kind of prison, she thought as she stepped inside.

Her mother sat on the floor with Livvy, playing with an elaborate plastic castle and dozens of little people. Val glanced up, kept her eyes on Jamie's, her hand on Livvy's shoulder.

The gesture told Jamie just how torn her mother was, so she managed to fix on a smile as she moved forward.

"Well, what's all this?"

"Uncle David bought me a castle." Sheer delight bubbled in Olivia's voice. "There's a king and a queen and a princess and a dragon and *everything*."

"It's beautiful." God bless you, David, Jamie thought and settled onto the floor. "Is this the queen?"

"Uh-huh. Her name's Magnificent. Right, Grandma?"

"That's right, baby. And here're King Wise and Princess Delightful."

While Olivia played, Jamie laid a hand over her mother's. "I wonder if you could go down and see if there's fresh coffee."

"Of course." Understanding, Val turned her hand up so their palms met.

When they were alone, Jamie sat quietly, watching.

"Livvy, do you remember the forest? Grandma's house up in the woods, all the big trees and the streams and the flowers?"

"I went there when I was a baby, but I don't remember. Mama said we'd go back sometime and she'd show me her best places."

"Would you like to go there, to Grandma's house?"

"To visit?"

"To live. I bet you could have the same room your mother had when she was a little girl. It's a big old house, right in the forest. Everywhere you look there are trees, and when the wind blows, they sigh and shiver and moan."

"Is it magic?"

"Yes, a kind of magic. The sky's very blue, and inside the forest, the light is green and the ground's soft."

"Will Mama come?"

Yes, Jamie thought, it was amazing how much pain the heart could take and go on beating. "Part of her never left, part of her's always there. You'll see the places we played when we were girls. Grandma and Grandpop will take very good care of you."

"Is it far, far away?"

"Not so very far. I'll come visit you." She drew Olivia onto her lap. "As often as I can. We'll walk in the woods and wade in the streams until Grandma calls us home for cookies and hot chocolate."

Olivia turned her face into Jamie's shoulder. "Will the monster find me there?"

"No." Jamie's arms tightened. "You'll always be safe there. I promise."

But not all promises can be kept.

FIVE

Olympic Rain Forest, 1987

I N the summer of Olivia's twelfth year, she was a tall, gangly girl with a wild mane of hair the color of bottled honey. Eyes nearly the same shade were long lidded under dark, slashing brows. She'd given up her dreams of being a princess in a castle for other ambitions. They'd run from explorer to veterinarian to forest ranger, which was her current goal.

The forest, with its green shadows and damp smells, was her world, one she rarely left. She was most often alone there, but never lonely. Her grandfather taught her how to track, how to stalk deer and elk with a camera. How to sit quietly as minutes became hours to watch the majestic journey of a buck or the grace of a doe and fawn.

She'd learned to identify the trees, the flowers, the moss and the mushrooms, though she'd never developed a proficient hand at drawing them as her grandmother had hoped.

She spent quiet days fishing with her grandmother, and there had learned patience. She'd taken on a share of the chores of the lodge and campground the MacBrides had run in Olympic for two generations, and there had learned responsibility.

She was allowed to roam the woods, to wade in the streams, to climb the hills. But never, never to go beyond their borders alone.

And from this, she learned freedom had limits.

She'd left Los Angeles eight years before and had never been back. Her memories of the house in Beverly Hills were vague flickers of high ceilings and shining wood, pretty colors and a pool with bright blue water surrounded by flowers.

During the first months she'd lived in the big house in the forest, she'd asked when they would go back to where she lived or when her mother would come for her, where her father was. But whenever she asked questions, her grandmother's mouth would clamp tight and her eyes would go shiny and dark.

From that, Olivia learned to wait.

Then she learned to forget.

She grew tall, and she grew tough. The fragile little girl who hid in closets became little more than a memory, and one that ghosted into dreams. Living in the present was another lesson she learned, and learned well.

With her chores at the campground over for the day, Olivia wandered down the path toward home. The afternoon was hers now, as much a reward as the salary her grandmother banked for her twice monthly in town. She thought about fishing, or hiking up to high ground to dream over the lake, but felt too restless for such sedentary activities. She'd have enjoyed a swim even this early in the season, but it was one of her grandmother's hard-and-fast rules not to swim alone.

Olivia broke it from time to time and was always careful to dry her hair completely before coming home.

Grandma worried, she thought now. Too much, too often and about nearly everything. If Olivia sneezed, she'd race to the phone to call the doctor unless Grandpop stopped her. If Olivia was ten minutes late coming home, her grandmother was out on the porch calling.

Once she'd nearly called Search and Rescue because Olivia had stayed

at the campground playing with other children and forgotten to come
home until dark.

It made Olivia roll her eyes to think of it. She'd never get lost in the
forest. It was home, and she knew every twist and turn as well as she knew
the rooms in her own house. She knew Grandpop had said as much because
she'd heard them arguing about it more than once. Whenever they did,
Grandma would be better for a few days, but then it would start again.

She moved through the gentle green light and soft shadows of the forest and into the clearing where the MacBride house had stood for generations.

The mica in the old stone glinted in the quiet sunlight. When it rained,
the hidden colors in the rock, the browns and reds and greens, would
come out and gleam. The windows sparkled, always there to let in the
light or the comforting gloom. It was three levels, each stacked atop the
other at a different angle with decks jutting out everywhere to stitch it
all together. Flowers and ferns and wild rhododendrons hugged the foundation, then sprawled out in a hodgepodge garden her grandfather babied
like a beloved child.

Huge pansies with purple and white faces spilled out of stone pots,
and an enormous bed of impatiens, sassy and pink, danced along the edge
of the lower deck.

She'd spent many satisfying hours with her grandfather and his flowers. Her hands in the dirt and her head in the clouds.

She started down the stone walkway, varying giant and baby steps to
avoid all the cracks. She skipped up the steps, spun into a quick circle,
then pulled open the front door.

She had only to step inside to realize the house was empty. She called
out anyway, from habit, as she walked through the living room with its
big, ragged sofas and warm yellow walls.

She sniffed, pleased to catch the scent of fresh cookies. Only sighed
a little when she reached the kitchen and discovered they were oatmeal.

"Why can't they be chocolate-chip," she muttered, already digging
into the big glass jar that held them. "I could eat a million chocolate-chip
cookies."

She settled for the oatmeal, eating fast and greedily as she read the note on the refrigerator.

Livvy. I had to run into town, to go to the market. Your aunt Jamie and uncle David are coming to visit. They'll be here tonight.

"Yes!" Olivia let out a whoop and scattered crumbs. "Presents!"

To celebrate, she reached for a third cookie, then muttered a quiet "damn" under her breath at the rest of the message.

Stay at home, honey, so you can help me with the groceries when I get back. You can tidy up your room—if you can find it. Stop eating all the cookies. Love, Grandma

"Sheesh." With true regret, Olivia put the top back on the jar.

Now she was stuck in the house. Grandma might be *hours* shopping. What was she supposed to do all day? Feeling put upon, she clumped up the back stairs. Her room wasn't that bad. It just had her stuff, that was all. Why did it matter so much if it was put away when she'd only want to get it out again?

Her various projects and interests were scattered around. Her rock collection, her drawings of wildlife and plants with the scientific names painstakingly lettered beneath. The chemistry set she'd been desperate for the previous Christmas was shoved on a shelf and ignored, except for the microscope which held a prominent position on her desk.

There was a shoe box crammed with what she considered specimens— twigs, dead bugs, bits of ferns, hair, scrapings of tobacco and scraps of bark.

The clothes she'd worn yesterday were in a heap on the floor. Precisely where she'd stepped out of them. Her bed was unmade and in a tangle of blankets and sheets—exactly the way it had been when she'd leaped out of it at dawn.

It all looked perfectly fine to Olivia. But she marched over to the bed, dragged the covers up, slapped the pillows a couple of times. She kicked discarded shoes under the bed, tossed clothes in the direction of the hamper or the closet. She blew away dust and eraser bits from the surface of her desk, stuffed pencil stubs in the glass jar, pushed papers in the drawer and considered it a job well done.

She thought about curling up on her window seat to dream and sulk

for a while. The trees were stirring, the tops of the soaring Douglas firs
and western hemlocks sighing and shifting in the incoming breeze. The
western sky had taken on the bruised and fragile look of an incoming
storm. She could sit and watch it roll in, see if she could spot the line of
rain before it fell.

Better, much better, would be to go outside, to smell it, to lift her
face up and draw in the scent of rain and pine. An alone smell, she always
thought. The better to be absorbed in solitude.

She nearly did just that, was already turning toward the tall glass
doors that led to the deck off her room. But all the boxes and games and
puzzles jammed on her shelves pricked her conscience. Her grandmother
had been asking her to sort through and straighten out the mess for weeks.
Now, with Aunt Jamie coming—and surely bringing presents with her—
there was bound to be a lecture on the care and appreciation of your
possessions.

Heaving a long-suffering sigh, Olivia snatched down old, neglected board
games and jigsaw puzzles and made a teetering stack. She'd take them up
to the attic, she decided, then her room would be practically perfect.

Carefully she went up the stairs and opened the door. When the light
flashed on, she glanced around, looking for the best place to store her
castoffs in the huge cedar-scented space. Old lamps, not quite ready to
be shipped off to Goodwill, stood bare of bulbs and shades in a corner
where the roofline dipped low. A child-size rocking chair and baby furniture that looked ancient to Olivia were neatly stacked against one wall
along with storage boxes and chests. Pictures that had once graced the
walls of the house or the lodge were ghosted in dust covers. A creaky
wooden shelf her grandfather had made in his wood shop held a family
of dolls and stuffed animals.

Val MacBride, Olivia knew, didn't like to throw things away either.
Possessions ended up being transferred to the attic or to the lodge or
simply recycled within the house.

Olivia carried her boxes to the toy shelf and stacked them on the floor
beside it. More out of boredom than interest, she poked into some of the
drawers, pondered baby clothes carefully wrapped in tissue and scattered

with cedar chips to keep them sweet. In another was a blanket, all pink and white with soft satin edgings. She fingered it as it stirred some vague memory. But her stomach got all hot and crampy, so she closed the drawer again.

Technically she wasn't supposed to come to the attic without permission, and she was never allowed to open drawers or chests or boxes. Her grandmother said that memories were precious, and when she was older she could take them out. It was always when she was older, Olivia thought. It was never, never now.

She didn't see why it was such a big deal. It was just a bunch of old junk, and she wasn't a kid anymore. It wasn't as if she'd break something or lose it.

Anyway, she didn't really care.

The rain started to patter on the roof, like fingers lightly drumming on a table. She glanced toward the little window that faced the front of the clearing. And saw the chest.

It was a cherry wood chest with a domed lid and polished-brass fittings. It was always kept deep under the overhang, and always locked. She noticed such things. Her grandfather said she had eyes like a cat, which had made her giggle when she'd been younger. Now it was something she took pride in.

Today, the chest wasn't shoved back under the roofline, and neither was it locked. Grandma must have put something away, Olivia thought and strolled casually over as if she weren't particularly interested.

She knew the story about Pandora's box and how the curious woman had opened it and set free all the ills upon the world. But this wasn't the same thing, she told herself as she knelt in front of it. And since it wasn't locked, what was the harm in opening it up and taking a peek inside?

It was probably just full of sentimental junk or musty old clothes or pictures turning yellow.

But her fingers tingled—in warning or anticipation—as she lifted the heavy lid.

The scent struck her first and made her breath come fast and hard.

Cedar, from the lining. Lavender. Her grandfather had a sweep of it planted on the side of the house. But under those, something else. Something both foreign and familiar. Though she couldn't identify it, the waft of it had her heart beating fast, like a quick, impatient knocking in her chest.

The tingling in her fingers became intense, making them shake as she reached inside. There were videos, labeled only with dates and stored in plain black dust covers. Three thick photo albums, boxes of varying sizes. She opened one very like the box her grandparents used to store their old-fashioned Christmas balls.

There, resting in foam for protection, were half a dozen decorative bottles.

"The magic bottles," she whispered. It seemed the attic was suddenly filled with low and beautiful laughter, flickering images, exotic scents.

On your sixteenth birthday, you can choose the one you like best. But you mustn't play with them, Livvy. They might break. You could cut your hand or step on glass.

Mama leaned over, her soft hair falling over the side of her face. Laughing, her eyes full of fun, she sprayed a small cloud of perfume on Olivia's throat.

The scent. Mama's perfume. Scrambling up to her knees again, Olivia leaned into the chest, breathed long and deep. And smelled her mother.

Setting the box aside, she reached in for the first photo album. It was heavy and awkward, so she laid it across her lap. There were no pictures of her mother in the house. Olivia remembered there had been, but they'd disappeared a long time before. The album was full of them, pictures of her mother when she'd been a young girl, pictures of her with Jamie, and with her parents. Smiling, laughing, making faces at the camera.

Pictures in front of the house and in the house, at the campground and at the lake. Pictures with Grandpop when his hair had been more gold than silver, and with Grandma in a fancy dress.

There was one of her mother holding a baby. "That's me," Olivia whispered. "Mama and me." She turned the next page and the next, all but devouring each photo, until they abruptly stopped. She could see the marks on the page where they'd been removed.

Impatient now, she set it aside and reached for the next.

Not family photos this time but newspaper clippings, magazine articles. Her mother on the cover of *People* and *Newsweek* and *Glamour*. Olivia studied these first, looking deep, absorbing every feature. She had her mother's eyes. She'd known that, remembered that, but to see it so clearly, to look with her own into them, the color, the shape, the slash of dark eyebrows.

Excitement, grief, pleasure swirled through her in a tangled mass as she stroked a finger over each glossy image. She'd been so beautiful, so perfect.

Then her heart leaped again as she paged through and found a series of pictures of her mother with a dark-haired man. He was handsome, like a poet, she thought as her adolescent heart sighed. There were pictures of them in a garden, and in a big room with dozens of glittering lights, on a sofa with her mother snuggled into his lap with their faces close and their smiles for each other.

Sam Tanner. It said his name was Sam Tanner. Reading it, she began to shiver. Her stomach cramped, a dozen tight fists that twisted.

Daddy. It was Daddy. How could she have forgotten? It was Daddy, holding hands with Mama, or with his arm around her shoulders.

Holding scissors bright with blood.

No, no, that couldn't be. It was a dream, a nightmare. Imagination, that was all.

She began to rock, pressing her hands to her mouth as the images began to creep in. Panic, burning fingers of it, had her by the throat, squeezing until her breath came in strangled gasps.

Broken glass sparkling on the floor in the lights. Dying flowers. The warm breeze through the open door.

It wasn't real. She wouldn't let it be real.

Olivia pushed the book aside and lifted out the last with hands that trembled. There'd be other pictures, she told herself. More pictures of her parents smiling and laughing and holding each other.

But it was newspapers again, with big headlines that seemed to scream at her.

JULIE MACBRIDE MURDERED
SAM TANNER ARRESTED
FAIRY TALE ENDS IN TRAGEDY

There were pictures of her father, looking dazed and unkempt. More of her aunt, her grandparents, her uncle. And of her, she saw with a jolt. Of her years before with her eyes wild and blank and her hands pressed to her ears.

JULIE'S CHILD, ONLY WITNESS TO MOTHER'S SLAYING

She shook her head in denial, ripping quickly through the pages now. There, another face that awakened memories. His name was Frank, she thought. He chased the monster away. He had a little boy and he'd liked puzzles.

A policeman. Soft, hunted sounds trembled in her throat. He'd carried her out of the house, the house where the monster had come. Where all the blood was.

Because her mother was dead. Her mother was dead. She knew that, of course she knew that. But we don't talk about it, she reminded herself, we never talk about it because it makes Grandma cry.

She ordered herself to close the book, to put it all away again, back in the chest, back in the dark. But she was already turning the pages, searching the words and pictures.

Drugs. Jealousy. Obsession.

Tanner Confesses!

Tanner Retracts Confession. Proclaims His Innocence.

Four-Year-Old Daughter Chief Witness.

The Tanner trial took one more dramatic turn today as the videotaped testimony of Tanner's daughter, four-year-old Olivia, was introduced. The child was questioned in the home of her maternal aunt, Jamie Melbourne, and videotaped with permission of her grandparents, acting as guardians. Previously Judge Sato ruled that the taped statement could be introduced as evidence, sparing the minor the trauma of a court appearance.

She remembered, she remembered it all now. They'd sat in Aunt Jamie's living room. Her grandparents had been there, too. A woman with red hair and a soft voice had asked her questions about the night the monster had come. Grandma had promised it would be the last time she would have to talk about it, the very last time.

And it was.

The woman had listened and asked more questions. Then a man had talked to her, a man with a careful smile and careful eyes. She'd thought since it was the last time, she'd be able to go back home. That it would all go away.

But she'd come to Washington instead, to the big house in the forest. Now, she knew why.

Olivia turned more pages, narrowed her eyes against tears until they were stinging dry. And with her jaw tight and her eyes clear, read another flurry of headlines.

SAM TANNER CONVICTED
GUILTY! JURY CONVICTS TANNER
TANNER SENTENCED TO LIFE

"You killed my mother, you bastard." She said it with all the hate a young girl could muster. "I hope you're dead, too. I hope you died screaming."

With steady hands, she closed the book, carefully replaced it along with the others in the chest. She shut the lid, then rose to go turn off the lights. She walked down the stairs, through the empty house to the back porch.

Sitting there, she stared out into the rain.

She didn't understand how she could have buried everything that had happened, how she could have locked it up the way her grandmother locked the boxes and books in the chest.

But she knew she wouldn't do so again. She would remember, always. And she would find out more, find out everything she could about the night her mother died, about the trial, about her father.

She understood she couldn't ask her family. They thought she was still a child, one who needed to be protected. But they were wrong. She'd never be a child again.

She heard the sound of the Jeep rumbling up the lane through the rain. Olivia closed her eyes and concentrated. A part of her hardened, then wondered if she'd inherited acting skills from either of her parents. She tucked the hate, the grief and the anger into a corner of her heart. Sealed it inside.

Then she stood up, a smile ready for her grandmother when the Jeep braked at the end of the drive.

"Just who I wanted to see." Val tossed up the hood of her jacket as she stepped out of the Jeep. "We're loaded here, Livvy. Get a jacket and give me a hand, will you?"

"I don't need a jacket. I won't melt." She stepped out into the rain. The steady drum of it was a comfort. "Are we having spaghetti and meatballs for dinner?"

"For Jamie's first night home?" Val laughed and passed Olivia a grocery bag. "What else?"

"I'd like to make it." Olivia shifted the bag, then reached in for another.

"You—really?"

Olivia jerked a shoulder and headed into the house. The door slapped shut behind her, then opened again as Val pushed in with more bags. "What brought this on? You always say cooking is boring."

That had been when she'd been a kid, Olivia thought. Now was different. "I have to learn sometime. I'll get the rest, Grandma." She started out, then turned back. The anger was inside her, didn't want to stay locked up. It wanted to leap out, she realized, and slice at her grandmother. And that was wrong. Deliberately, she walked over and gave Val a fierce hug. "I want to learn to cook like you."

While Val blinked in stunned pleasure, Olivia hurried outside for the rest of the bags. What had gotten into the girl? Val wondered as she unpacked fresh tomatoes and lettuce and peppers. Just that morning she'd whined about fixing a couple of pieces of toast, all but danced with impatience to get outside. Now she wanted to spend her free afternoon cooking.

When Olivia came back in, Val lifted her eyebrows. "Livvy, did you get in trouble at the campground?"

"No."

"Are you after something? That fancy new backpack you've had your eye on?"

Olivia sighed, shoved the damp hair out of her eyes. "Gran, I want to learn how to cook spaghetti. It's not a big deal."

"I just wondered about the sudden interest."

"If I don't know how to cook, I can't be independent. And if I'm going to learn, I'd might as well learn right."

"Well." Pleased, Val nodded. "My girl's growing up on me." She reached over, brushed Olivia's cheek with her fingertips. "My pretty little Livvy."

"I don't want to be pretty." Some of the fire of that buried anger smoked into her eyes. "I want to be smart."

"You can be both."

"I'd rather work on smart."

Changes, Val thought. You couldn't stop them, could never hold a moment. "All right. Let's get this stuff put away and get started."

With patience Val explained what ingredients they'd use and why, which of the herbs they'd add from the kitchen garden and how their flavors would blend. If she noticed that Olivia paid almost fierce attention to every detail, she was more amused than concerned.

If she could have heard her granddaughter's thoughts, she might have wept.

Did you teach my mother how to make the sauce? Olivia wondered. Did she stand here with you when she was my age at this same stove and learn how to brown garlic in olive oil? Did she smell the same smells and hear the rain beating on the roof?

Why won't you tell me about her? How will I know who she was if you don't? How will I know who I am?

Then Val laid a hand on her shoulder. "That's good, honey. That's fine. You've got a real knack."

Olivia stirred the herbs into the slow simmer of the sauce. And for now, let the rest go.

SIX

B ECAUSE the first night Jamie and David came to visit was always treated as a special occasion, the family ate in the dining room with its long oak table set with white candles in silver holders, fresh flowers in crystal vases and Great-Grandma Capelli's good china.

Food was abundant, as was conversation. As always, the meal spun out for two hours while the candles burned down and the sun that had peeked out of the clouds began to slide behind the trees.

"Livvy, that was just wonderful." Jamie groaned and leaned back to pat her stomach. "So wonderful, I haven't left room for any tiramisù."

"I have." Rob twinkled, giving Olivia's hair a tug. "I'll just shake the spaghetti into my hollow leg. She's got your hand with the sauce, Val."

"My mother's, more like. I swear it was better than mine. I was beginning to wonder if our girl would ever do more than fry fish over a campfire."

"Blood runs true," Rob commented and winked at his granddaughter. "That Italian was bound to pop out sooner or later. The MacBride side was never known for its skill in the kitchen."

"What are they known for, Dad?"

He laughed, wiggled his brows at Jamie. "We're lovers, darling."

Val snorted, slapped his arm, then rose. "I'll clear," Jamie said, starting to get up.

"No." Val pointed a finger at her daughter. "You don't catch KP on your first night. Livvy's relieved, too. Rob and I will clean this up, then maybe we'll all have room for coffee and dessert."

"Hear that, Livvy?" David leaned over to murmur in her ear. "You cook, you don't scrub pots. Pretty good deal."

"I'm going to start cooking regularly." She grinned at him. "It's a lot more fun than doing dishes. Do you want to take a hike tomorrow, Uncle David? We can use my new backpack."

Olivia slanted her grandmother a look, struggling not to smirk.

"You spoil her, David," Val stated as she stacked dishes. "She wasn't going to get that backpack until her birthday this fall."

"Spoil her?" His face bland, David poked a finger into Olivia's ribs and made her giggle. "Nah, she's not even ripe yet. Plenty of time yet before she spoils. Do you mind if I switch on the TV in the other room? I've got a client doing a concert on cable. I promised I'd catch it."

"You go right on," Val told him. "Put your feet up and get comfortable. I'll bring coffee in shortly."

"Want to come up and talk to me while I unpack?" Jamie asked her niece.

"Could we take a walk?" Olivia had been waiting for the right moment. It seemed everyone had conspired to make it now. "Before it gets dark?"

"Sure." Jamie stood, stretched. "Let me get a jacket. It'll do me good to work off some of that pasta. Then I won't feel guilty if I don't make it over to the health club at the lodge tomorrow."

"I'll tell Grandma. Meet you out back."

Even in summer, the nights were cool. The air smelled of rain and wet roses. The long days of July held the light even while a ghost moon rose in the eastern sky. Still, Olivia fingered the flashlight in her pocket. They would need it in the forest. It was the forest she wanted. She would feel safe there, safe enough to say what she needed to say and ask what she needed to ask.

"It's always good to be home." Jamie took a deep breath and smiled at her father's garden.

"Why don't you live here?"

"My work's in L.A. So's David's. But we both count on coming up here a couple of times a year. When I was a girl, your age, I suppose, I thought this was the whole world."

"But it's not."

"No." Jamie angled her head as she looked over at Olivia. "But it's one of the best parts. I hear you're a big help at the campground and the lodge. Grandpop says he couldn't do without you."

"I like working there. It's not like work." Olivia scuffed a boot in the dirt and angled away from the house toward the trees. "Lots of people come. Some of them don't know *anything*. They don't even know the difference between a Douglas fir and a hemlock, or they wear expensive designer boots and get blisters. They think the more you pay for something the better it is, and that's just stupid." She slanted Jamie a look. "A lot of them come from Los Angeles."

"Ouch." Amused, Jamie rubbed her heart. "Direct hit."

"There're too many people down there, and cars and smog."

"That's true enough." All that felt very far away, Jamie realized, when you stepped into the deep woods, smelled the pine, the soft scent of rot, felt the carpet of cones and needles under your feet. "But it can be exciting, too. Beautiful homes, wonderful palm trees, shops, restaurants, galleries."

"Is that why my mother went there? So she could shop and go to restaurants and have a beautiful home?"

Jamie stopped short. The question had snapped out at her, an unexpected backhanded slap that left her dazed. "I—she . . . Julie wanted to be an actress. It was natural for her to go there."

"She wouldn't have died if she'd stayed home."

"Oh, Livvy." Jamie started to reach out, but Olivia stepped back.

"You have to promise not to say anything to anyone. Not to Grandma or Grandpop or Uncle David. Not to anyone."

"But, Livvy—"

"You *have* to promise." Panic snuck into her voice, tears into her eyes. "If you promise you won't say anything, then you won't."

"All right, baby."

"I'm not a baby." But this time Olivia let herself be held. "Nobody ever talks about her, and all her pictures got put away. I can't remember unless I try really hard. Then it gets all mixed up."

"We just didn't want you to hurt. You were so little when she died."

"When he killed her." Olivia drew back. Her eyes were dry now and glinting in the dim light. "When my father killed her. You have to say it out loud."

"When Sam Tanner killed her."

The pain reared up, hideously fresh. Giving in to it, Jamie sat beside a nurse log, breathed out slowly. The ground was damp, but it didn't seem to matter.

"Not talking about it doesn't mean we don't love her, Livvy. Maybe it means we loved her too much. I don't know."

"Do you think about her?"

"Yes." Jamie reached out a hand, clasping Olivia's firmly. "Yes, I do. We were very close. I miss her every day."

With a nod, Olivia sat beside her, idly played her light on the ground. "Do you think about him?"

Jamie shut her eyes. Oh God, what should she do, how should she handle this? "I try not to."

"But do you?"

"Yes."

"Is he dead, too?"

"No." Nerves jittering, Jamie rubbed a hand over her mouth. "He's in prison."

"Why did he kill her?"

"I don't know. I just don't know. It doesn't do any good to wonder, Livvy, because it'll never make sense. It'll never be right."

"He used to tell me stories. He used to carry me on his back. I remember. I'd forgotten, but I remember now."

She continued to play the light, dancing it over the rotting log that nurtured seedlings she recognized as hemlock and spruce, the rosettes of tree moss that tumbled over it, the bushy tufts of globe lichen that tangled with it. It kept her calm, seeing what she knew, putting a name to it.

"Then he got sick and went away. That's what Mama told me, but it wasn't really true. It was drugs."

"Where are you hearing these things?"

"Are they true?" She looked away from the log, the flourishing life. "Aunt Jamie, I want to know what's true."

"Yes, they're true. I'm sorry they happened to you, to Julie, to me, to all of us. We can't change it, Livvy. We just have to go on and do the best we can."

"Is what happened why I can never come visit you? Why Grandma teaches me instead of my going to school with other kids? Why my name's MacBride instead of Tanner?"

Jamie sighed. She heard an owl hoot and a rustle in the brush. Hunters and hunted, she thought. Only looking to survive the night. "We decided it was best for you not to be exposed to the publicity, to the gossip, the speculations. Your mother was famous. People were interested in her life, in what happened. In you. We wanted to get you away from all that. To give you a chance, the chance Julie would have wanted for you to have a safe, happy childhood."

"Grandma locked it all away."

"Mom—Grandma . . . It was so hard on her, Livvy. She lost her daughter." The one she couldn't help but love best. "You helped get her through it. Can you understand that?" She gripped Olivia's hand again. "She needed you as much as you needed her. She's centered her life on you these last years. Protecting you was so important—and maybe by doing that she protected herself, too. You can't blame her for it."

"I don't want to. But it's not fair to ask me to forget everything. I can't talk to her or Grandpop." The tears wanted to come again. Her eyes stung horribly as she forced them back. "I need to remember my mother."

"You're right. You're right." Jamie draped an arm around Olivia's shoulders and hugged. "You can talk to me. I won't tell anyone else. And we'll both remember."

Content with that, Olivia laid her head on Jamie's shoulder. "Aunt Jamie, do you have tapes of the movies my mother was in?"

"Yes."

"One day I want to see them. We'd better go back in." She rose, her eyes solemn as she looked at Jamie. "Thanks for telling me the truth."

What a shock it was, Jamie thought, to expect a child and see a woman. "I'll make you another promise right here, Livvy. This is a special place for me, a place where if you make a promise, you have to keep it. I'll always tell you the truth, no matter what."

"I promise, too." Olivia held out her hand. "No matter what."

They walked out, hands linked. At the edge of the clearing, Olivia looked up. The sky had gone a deep, soft blue. The moon, no longer a ghost, cut its white slice out of the night. "The first stars are out. They're there, even in the daytime, even when you can't see them. But I like to see them. That's Mama's star." She pointed up to the tiny glimmer near the tail of the crescent moon. "It comes out first."

Jamie's throat closed, burned. "She'd like that. She'd like that you thought of her, and weren't sad."

"Coffee's on!" Val called through the door. "I made you a latte, Livvy. Extra foam."

"We're coming. She's happy you're here, so I get latte." Olivia's smile was so sudden, so young, it nearly broke Jamie's heart. "Let's get our share of tiramisù before Grandpop hogs it all."

"Hey, for tiramisù, I'd take my own father down without a qualm."

"Race you." Olivia darted off like a bullet, blond hair flying.

IT WAS THAT IMAGE—THE LONG BLOND HAIR SWINGING, THE girlish dare, the swift race through the dark—that Jamie carried with her through the evening. She watched Olivia scoop up dessert, stage a mock battle with her grandfather over his serving, nag David for details about his meeting Madonna at a party. And she wondered if Olivia was mature enough, controlled enough, to tuck all her thoughts and emotions away or if she was simply young enough to cast them aside in favor of sweets and attention.

As much as she'd have preferred it to be the latter, she decided Olivia had inherited some of Julie's skills as an actress.

There was a weight on her heart as she prepared for bed in the room that had been hers as a girl. Her sister's child was looking to her now, as she had during those horrible days eight years before. Only this time, she wasn't such a little girl and wouldn't be satisfied with cuddles and stories.

She wanted the truth, and that meant Jamie would have to face parts of the truth she'd tried to forget.

She'd dealt with the unauthorized biographies, the documentaries, the television movie, the tabloid insanity and rumors dealing with her sister's life and her death. They still cropped up from time to time. The young, beautiful actress, cut down in her prime by the man she loved. In a town that fed itself on fantasy and gossip, grim fairy tales could often take on the sheen of legends.

She'd done her best to discourage it. She gave no interviews to the press, cut no deals, endorsed no projects. In this way she protected her parents, the child. And herself.

Still, every year, a new wave of Julie MacBride stories sprang up. Every year, she thought, leaning on the pedestal sink and staring at her own face in the mirror, on the anniversary of her death.

So she fled home every summer, escaped it for a few days, let herself be tucked away as she'd let Olivia be tucked away.

They were entitled to their privacy, weren't they? She sighed, rubbed her eyes. Just as Olivia was entitled to talk about the mother she'd lost. Somehow, she had to see to it that they managed to have both.

She straightened, pushed the hair back from her face. She'd let her hairdresser talk her into a perm and some subtle highlighting around her face. She had to admit, he'd been right. It gave her a softer, younger look. Youth wasn't just a matter of vanity, she thought. It was a matter of business.

She was beginning to see lines creeping around her eyes, those nasty little reminders of age and wear and tear. Sooner or later, she'd have to consider a tuck. She'd mentioned it to David, and he'd just laughed.

Lines? What lines? I don't see any lines.

Men, she thought now, but they'd both known his response had pleased her.

Still, it didn't mean she could afford to neglect her skin. She took the time to smooth on her night cream, using firm, upward strokes along her throat, dabbing on the eye cream with her pinkies. Then she added a trail of perfume between her breasts in case her husband was feeling romantic.

He often was.

Smiling to herself, she went back into the bedroom where she'd left the light burning for David. He hadn't come up yet, so she closed the door quietly, then moved to the chevel glass. She removed her robe and took inventory.

She worked out like a fiend three days a week with a personal trainer she secretly called the Marquessa de Sade. But it paid off. Perhaps her breasts would no longer qualify as perky, but the rest of her was nice and tight. As long as she could pump and sweat, there'd be no need for nips and tucks anywhere but her eyes.

She understood the value of keeping herself attractive—in her public relations work and in her marriage. The actors and entertainers she and David worked with seemed to get younger every time she blinked. Some of his clients were beautiful and desirable women, *young* women. Succumbing to temptation, Jamie knew, was more often the rule rather than the exception in the life she and David lived.

She also knew she was lucky. Nearly fourteen years, she mused. The length of their marriage was a not-so-minor miracle in Hollywood. They'd had bumps and dips, but they'd gotten through them.

She'd always been able to depend on him, and he on her. And the other not-so-minor miracle was that they loved each other.

She slipped back into her robe, belting it as she walked to the deck doors and threw them open to the night. She stepped out, to listen to the wind sigh through the trees. To look for Julie's star.

"How many times did we sit out on nights like this and dream? We'd whisper together when we were supposed to be in bed. And we'd plan. Such big, shiny plans. I've got so much I dreamed of, so much I wouldn't have had if you hadn't had the big dreams first. I might never have met David if not for you. Would never have had the courage to start my own company. So many things I wouldn't have done, wouldn't have seen if I hadn't followed after you."

She leaned on the rail, closing her eyes as the wind toyed with her hair, the hem of her robe, shivered along her bare skin. "I'll make sure Livvy dreams big, too. That nothing stops her from grabbing hold of what she needs most. And I'm sorry, Julie. I'm sorry I had a part in trying to make her forget you."

She stepped back, rubbing her arms as the air turned chilly. But she stayed outside, watching the stars until David found her.

"Jamie?" When she turned, his eyes warmed. "You look beautiful. I was afraid you'd gone to bed while I puffed cigars and told lies with your father."

"No, I wanted to wait for you." She stepped into his arms, nestled her head on his shoulder. "I waited just for this."

"Good. You've been quiet tonight. Are you all right?"

"Hmm. Just a little lost in thoughts." Too many she couldn't share with him. A promise had been given. "Tomorrow it'll be eight years. Sometimes it seems like a lifetime ago, and others like yesterday. It means so much to me, David, that you come with me every year. That you understand why I have to be here. I know how hard it is for you to juggle your schedule to carve out these few days."

"Jamie, she mattered to all of us. And you . . ." He drew her back to kiss her. "You matter most."

With a smile, she laid her hand on his cheek. "I must. I know how much you love tramping through the woods and spending an afternoon fishing."

He grimaced. "Your mother's taking me out on the river tomorrow."

"My hero."

"I think she knows I hate fishing and makes me go out every summer to pay her back for stealing her daughter."

"Well then, the least her daughter can do is make it worth your while."

"Oh yeah?" His hands were already sliding down to mold her bottom through the thin robe. "How?"

"Come with me. I'll show you."

OLIVIA DREAMED OF HER MOTHER AND WHIMPERED IN HER sleep. They huddled together in a closet filled with animals who stared with glassy eyes. She shivered in the dark, holding tight, so tight because the monster raged outside the door. He was calling her name, roaring it out while he stomped on the floor.

She buried her face against her mother's breast, pressed her hands over her ears as something crashed close, so close to where she tried to disappear.

Then the door burst open and the closet bloomed with light. In the light she saw the blood, all over her hands, all over her mother's hair. And Mama's eyes were like the eyes of the animals. Glassy and staring.

"I've been looking for you," Daddy said, and snapped the scissors that shined and dripped.

As she tossed in sleep, others dreamed of Julie.

Images of a lovely young girl laughing in the kitchen as she learned to make red sauce like her grandmother's. Of a much-loved companion who raced through the woods with her pale hair flying. Of a lover who sighed in the night. A woman of impossible beauty dancing in a white dress on her wedding day.

Of death, so terrible, so stark it couldn't be remembered in the light.

And those who dreamed of her wept.

Even her killer.

IT WAS STILL DARK WHEN VAL KNOCKED BRISKLY ON THE bedroom door. "Up and at 'em, David. Coffee's on and the fish are biting."

With a pitiful moan, David rolled over, buried his head under the pillow. "Oh, my God."

"Ten minutes. I'll pack your breakfast."

"The woman's not human. She can't be."

With a sleepy laugh, Jamie nudged him toward the edge of the bed. "Up and at 'em, fish boy."

"Tell her I died in my sleep. I'm begging you." He pushed the pillow off his head and managed to bring his wife's silhouette into focus. She smiled when his hand closed warmly over her breast. "Go catch fish, and if you're very good, I'll reward you tonight."

"Sex doesn't buy everything," he said with some dignity, then crawled out of bed. "But it buys me." He tripped over something in the dark, cursed, then limped to the bathroom while his wife snickered.

She was sound asleep when he came back, gave her an absent kiss and stumbled out.

Light was filtering through the windows when the shakes and whispers woke her. "Huh? What?"

"Aunt Jamie? Are you awake?"

"Not until I've had my coffee."

"I brought you some."

Jamie pried one eye open, focused blearily on her niece. She sniffed once, caught the scent and sighed. "You are my queen."

With a laugh, Olivia sat on the side of the bed as Jamie struggled up. "I made it fresh. Grandma and Uncle David are gone, and Grandpop left for the lodge. He said he had paperwork to do, but he just likes to go over there and talk to people."

"You got his number." Eyes closed, Jamie took the first sip. "So what are you up to?"

"Well . . . Grandpop said that I could have the day off if you wanted to go for a hike. I could take you on one of the easy trails. It's sort of practice for being a guide. I can't really be one until I'm sixteen, even though I know all the trails better than mostly anyone."

Jamie opened one eye again. Olivia had a bright smile on her face and a plea in her eye. "You've got my number, too, don't you?"

"I can use my new backpack. I'll make sandwiches and stuff while you're getting dressed."

"What kind of sandwiches?"

"Ham and Swiss."

"Sold. Give me twenty minutes."

"All right!" Olivia darted out of the room, leaving Jamie to take the first two of that twenty minutes to settle back and enjoy her coffee.

IT WAS WARM AND BRIGHT, WITH A WILD BLUE SKY OF HIGH summer. A perfect day, Jamie decided, to think of what is rather than what had been.

She flexed her feet in her ancient and reliable boots and studied her niece. Olivia had her hair tucked up in a fielder's cap with the RIVER'S END LODGE AND CAMPGROUND logo emblazoned on the crown. Her T-shirt was faded, the overshirt unbuttoned and frayed at the cuffs. Her boots looked worn and comfortable, the backpack brightly blue.

She had a compass and a knife sheath hooked to her belt.

She looked, Jamie realized, supremely competent.

"Okay, what's your spiel?"

"My spiel?"

"Yeah, I've hired you to guide me on the trail today, to show me the ropes, to make my hiking experience a memorable one. I know nothing. I'm an urban hiker."

"Urban hiker?"

"That's right. Rodeo Drive's my turf, and I've come here to taste nature. I want my money's worth."

"Okay." Olivia squared her shoulders, cleared her throat. "Today we're going to hike the John MacBride Trail. This trail is an easy two-point-three-mile hike that loops through the rain forest, then climbs for a half a mile to the lake area, which offers magnificent views. Um . . . More experienced hikers often choose to continue the hike from that point on one of the more difficult trails, but this choice gives the visitor . . . um, the chance to experience the rain forest as well as the lake vistas. How was that?"

"Not bad."

It was, Olivia thought, almost word for word from one of the books on sale at the lodge gift shop. All she'd done was to focus on bringing the page into her head and basically reading it off.

But she'd fix that. She'd learn to personalize her guides. She'd learn to be the best there was.

"Okay. As your guide, and the representative of River's End Lodge and Campground, I'll be providing your picnic lunch and explanations of the flora and fauna we see on our tour. I'll be happy to answer any questions."

"You're a natural. Ready when you are."

"Neat. The trailhead begins here, at the original site of the first Mac-Bride homestead. John and Nancy MacBride traveled west from Kansas in 1853 and settled here on the edges of the Quinault rain forest."

"I thought rain forests were in the tropics," Jamie said and fluttered her lashes at Olivia as they moved toward the trees.

"The Quinault Valley holds one of the few temperate rain forests in the world. We have mild temperatures and a lot of rainfall."

"The trees are so *tall!* What are they?"

"The overstory of trees is Sitka spruce; you can identify them by the flaky bark. And Douglas fir. They grow really tall and straight. When they get old, the bark's dark brown and has those deep grooves in it. Then there's western hemlock. It's not usually a canopy tree, and it's shade-tolerant so it's understory. It doesn't grow as fast as the Douglas fir. You see the cones, all over the place?" Olivia stooped to pick one up. "This one's a Doug-fir, see the three points? There'll be lots of them inside the forest, but you won't see saplings because they're not shade-tolerant. The animals like them, and bears like to eat their bark."

"Bears! *Eek!*"

"Oh, Aunt Jamie."

"Hey, I'm your city-slicker client, remember?"

"Right. You don't have to worry about bear if you take simple safety precautions," Olivia parroted. "The black bear lives in this area. The biggest problem with them is they like to steal food, so you've got to use proper storage for food and garbage. You never, never leave food or dirty dishes unattended in your campsite."

"But you have food in your backpack. What if the bears smell it and come after us?"

"I have the food wrapped in double plastic, so they won't. But if a bear comes around, you should make lots of noise. You need to be calm, give them room so they can go away."

They stepped out of the clearing and into the trees. Almost immediately the light turned soft and green with only a few stray shimmers of sun sneaking through the canopy of trees. Those thin fingers were pale, watery and lovely. The ground was littered with cones, thick with moss and ferns. The green covered the world in subtly different shapes, wildly different textures.

A thrush called out and darted by, barely ruffling the air.

"It looks prehistoric."

"I guess it is. I think it's the most beautiful place in the world."

Jamie laid her hand on Olivia's shoulder. "I know." And a safe place, Jamie thought. A wise place for a child to go. "Tell me what I'm seeing as we go, Livvy. Make it come alive for me."

They walked at an easy pace, with Olivia doing her best to use a tour guide's voice and rhythm. But the forest always captured her. She wondered why it had to be explained at all when you could just see.

The light was so soft it was as if she could feel it on her skin, the air so rich with scent it almost made her head reel. Pine and damp and the dying logs that were the life source for new trees. The deceptively fragile look of the moss that spilled and spread and climbed everywhere. The sounds—the crunch of boots over needles and cones, the stirring of small animals that darted here and there on the day's business, the call of birds, the sudden surprising gurgle of water in a little stream. They all came together for her in their own special kind of silence.

It was her cathedral, more magnificent and certainly more holy to her than any of the pictures she'd seen of the glorious buildings in Rome or Paris. This ground lived and died every day.

She pointed out a ring of mushrooms that added splashes of white and yellow, the lichens that upholstered the great trunks of trees, the papery seeds spilled by the grand Sitka spruce, the complicated tangle of vine maples that insisted on growing close to the trail.

They wound between nurse logs, shaggy with moss and sprouts, brushed through feathery crops of ferns and spotted, thanks to Olivia's sharp eye, an eagle lording it over the branches high overhead.

"Hardly anyone uses this trail," Olivia said, "because the first part of it's private. But the public trails start to loop there now, and you begin to see people."

"Don't you like to see people, Livvy?"

"Not so much in the forest." She offered a sheepish smile. "I like to think it's mine, and no one will ever change it. See? Listen." She held up a hand, closed her eyes.

Intrigued, Jamie did the same. She heard the faint tinkle of music, could just make out the slick twang of country and western.

"People take away the magic," Olivia said solemnly, then started up the upward slant of the trail.

As they climbed, Jamie began to pick up more sounds. A voice, a child's laugh. Where the trees thinned, sunlight sprinkled in until that soft green twilight was gone.

The lakes spread out in the distance, sparkling with sun, dotted with boats. And the great mountains speared up against the sky while the dips and valleys and gorges cut through with curves and slashes.

Warmer now, she sat and tugged off her overshirt to let the sun play on her arms. "There's all kinds of magic." She smiled when Olivia shrugged off her pack. "You don't have to be alone for it to work."

"I guess not." Carefully, Olivia unpacked the food, the thermos, then, sitting Indian style, offered Jamie her binoculars. "Maybe you can see Uncle David and Grandma."

"Maybe Uncle David dived overboard and swam home." With a laugh, Jamie lifted the field glasses. "Oh, there are swans. I love the way they look. Just gliding along. I should've brought my camera. I don't know why I never think of it."

She lowered the glasses to pick up one of the sandwiches Olivia had cut into meticulously even halves. "It's always beautiful here. Whatever the season, whatever the time of day."

She glanced down, noticed that Olivia was watching her steadily. It gave her a little chill to see that measuring look in a child's eyes. "What is it?"

"I have to ask you for a favor. You won't want to do it, but I thought about it a lot, and it's important. I need you to get me an address." Olivia pressed her lips together, then blew out a breath. "It's for the policeman, the one who took me to your house that night. His name is Frank. I remember him, but not very well. I want to write to him."

"Livvy, why? There's nothing he can tell you that I can't. It can't be good for you to worry so much about this."

"It has to be better to know things than to wonder. He was nice to me. Even if I can only write and tell him I remember he was nice to me, I'd feel better. And . . . he was there that night, Aunt Jamie. You weren't there. It was just me until he came and found me. I want to talk to him."

She turned her head to stare out at the lakes. "I'll tell him my grand-parents don't know I'm writing. I won't tell lies. But I need to try. I only remember his name was Frank."

Jamie closed her eyes, felt her heart sink a little. "Brady. His name is Frank Brady."

SEVEN

F RANK Brady turned the pale-blue envelope over in his hands. His name and the address of the precinct had been handwritten, neat and precise and unmistakably childlike, as had the return address in the corner.

Olivia MacBride.

Little Livvy Tanner, he mused, a young ghost out of the past.

Eight years. He'd never really put that night, those people, that case aside. He'd tried. He'd done his job, justice had followed through as best it could, and the little girl had been whisked away by family who loved her.

Closed, finished, over. Despite the stories on Julie MacBride that cropped up from time to time, the gossip, the rumors, the movies that ran on late-night television, it was done. Julie MacBride would be forever thirty-two and beautiful, and the man who'd killed her wouldn't see the outside of a cage for another decade or more.

Why the hell would the kid write to him after all this time? he wondered. And why the hell didn't he just open the letter and find out?

Still, he hesitated, frowning at the envelope while phones shrilled around him and cops moved in and out of the bull pen. He found himself wishing his own phone would ring so he could set the letter aside, pick up a new case. Then with a quiet oath, he tore the envelope open, spread out the single sheet of matching stationery and read:

Dear Detective Brady,

I hope you remember me. My mother was Julie MacBride, and when she was killed you took me to my aunt's house. You came to see me there, too. I didn't really understand then about murder or that you were investigating. You made me feel safe, and you told me how the stars were there even in the daytime. You helped me then. I hope you can help me now.

I've been living with my grandparents in Washington State. It's beautiful here and I love them very much. Aunt Jamie came to visit this week, and I asked her if she could give me your address so I could write to you. I didn't tell my grandparents because it makes them sad. We never talk about my mother, or what my father did.

I have questions that nobody can answer but you. It's awfully important to me to know the truth, but I don't want to hurt my grandmother. I'm twelve years old now, but she doesn't understand that when I think about that night and try to remember it gets mixed up and that makes it worse. Will you talk to me?

I thought maybe if you wanted to take a vacation you could even come here. I remember you had a son. You said he ate bugs and had bad dreams sometimes about alien invaders, but he's older now so I guess he doesn't anymore.

Christ, Frank thought with a stunned laugh. The kid had a memory like an elephant.

There's lots to do up here. Our lodge and campground are really nice, and I could even send you our brochures. You can go fishing or hiking or boating. The lodge has a swimming pool and nightly entertainment. We're also close to some of the most beautiful beaches in the Northwest.

Even as Frank felt his lips twitch at her sales pitch, he scanned the rest.

> *Please come. I have no one else to talk to.*
> *Yours truly,*
> *Olivia*

"Jesus." He folded the letter, slipped it back in its envelope and into his jacket pocket. But he wasn't able to tuck Olivia out of his mind so easily.

HE CARRIED BOTH THE LETTER AND THE MEMORY OF THE girl with him all day. He decided he'd write her a gentle response, keep it light—sympathetic but noncommittal. He could tell her how Noah was starting college in the fall, and how he'd been named Most Valuable Player in his basketball tournament. Chatty, easy. He'd use his work and his family commitments as an excuse not to go up to see her.

What good would it do to go to Washington and talk to her? It would only upset everyone involved. He couldn't possibly take on a responsibility like that. Her grandparents were good people.

He'd done a background check on them when they'd filed for custody. Just tying up loose ends, he told himself now as he'd told himself then. And maybe in the first couple of years he'd done a few more checks—just to make sure the kid was settling in all right.

Then he'd closed the book. He meant it to stay closed.

He was a cop, he reminded himself as he turned down the street toward home. He wasn't a psychologist, a social worker, and his only connection to Olivia was murder.

It couldn't possibly help her to talk to him.

He pulled into the drive behind a bright blue Honda Civic. It had replaced his wife's VW four years before. Both bumpers were crowded with stickers. His wife might have given up her beloved Bug, but she hadn't given up her causes.

Noah's bike had been upgraded to a secondhand Buick the boy pampered like a lover. He'd be loading it up and driving it off to college in a matter of weeks. The thought of that struck Frank as it always did—like an arrow to the heart.

The flowers that danced around the door thrived, due to Noah's attention. God knew where he'd gotten the green thumb, Frank thought as he climbed out of the car. Once the boy was away at school, both he and Celia would kill the blooms within a month.

He stepped in the front door to the sound of Fleetwood Mac. His heart sank. Celia liked to cook to Fleetwood Mac, and if she'd decided to cook it meant that Frank would be sneaking into the kitchen in the middle of the night, searching out his well-hidden stashes of junk food.

The living room was tidy—another bad sign. The fact that there were no newspapers or shoes scattered around meant Celia had gotten off early from her job at the women's shelter and was feeling domestic.

He and Noah suffered when Celia shifted into a domestic mode. There would be a home-cooked meal that had much more to do with nutrition than taste, a tidy house where he'd never be able to find anything and very likely freshly folded laundry. Which meant half his socks would be missing.

Things ran much more smoothly in the Brady household when Celia left the domestic chores to her men.

When Frank stepped into the kitchen, his worst fears were confirmed. Celia stood happily stirring something at the stove. There was a fresh loaf of some kind of tree-bark bread on the counter beside an enormous yellow squash.

But she looked so damn pretty, he thought, with her bright hair pulled back in a smooth ponytail, her narrow, teenage-boy hips bumping to the beat and her long, slim feet bare.

She carried a look of competent innocence that he'd always thought disguised a boundless determination. There was nothing Celia Brady wanted to accomplish that she didn't manage to do.

Just, he thought, as she'd managed him one way or another since she'd been a twenty-year-old coed and he the twenty-three-year-old rookie who'd arrested her during a protest against animal testing.

The first two weeks of their relationship they'd spent arguing. The second two weeks they'd spent in bed. She'd refused to marry him, so they'd fought about that. But he had his own share of determination. During the year they'd lived together, he'd worn her down.

Unexpectedly he came up behind her and hugged her tight. "I love you, Celia."

She turned in his arms and gave him a quick kiss. "You're still eating the black beans and squash. It's good for you."

He figured he'd live through it—and he had mini-pizzas buried in the depths of the freezer. "I'll eat it, and I'll still love you. I'm a tough guy. Where's Noah?"

"Out shooting hoops with Mike. He's got a date with Sarah later."

"Again?"

Celia had to smile. "She's a very nice girl, Frank. And with him going off to college in a few weeks, they want to spend as much time together as they can."

"I just wish he wasn't so hung up on this one girl. He's only eighteen."

"Frank, after a half term in college, Sarah won't be more than a vague memory. Now, what's really wrong?"

He didn't bother to sigh, but took the beer she held out to him. "Do you remember the MacBride case?"

"Julie MacBride?" Celia's eyebrows lifted. "Of course. It was the biggest high-profile case of your career, and you still get sad if one of her movies comes on TV. But what about the MacBride case? You closed it years ago. Sam Tanner's in prison."

"The little girl."

"Yes, I remember. She broke your heart." Celia rubbed his arm. "Softie."

"Her grandparents got custody, took her up to Washington State. They own a place up there, lodge, campground on the Olympic Peninsula. Attached to the national forest."

"The Olympic National Forest?" Celia's eyes went bright. "Oh, that's beautiful country. I hiked up that way the summer I graduated from high school. They've really kept the greedy bloodsuckers at bay."

To Celia greedy bloodsuckers were anyone who wanted to chop down a tree, demolish an old building, hunt rabbits or pour concrete over farmland.

"Tree hugger."

"Ha ha. If you had any idea how much damage can be done by loggers who don't have the foresight to—"

"Don't start, Cee, I'm already eating beans and squash."

She pouted a moment, then shrugged a shoulder and started to rise. Since putting her back up hadn't been part of his strategy, he reached in his pocket for the letter. "Just read this, and tell me what you think."

"So now you're interested in what I think." But after reading the first couple lines, she sat again, and the light of battle in her eyes melted into compassion. "Poor little thing," she murmured. "She's so sad. And so brave."

She smoothed her fingers over the letter, then handed it back to Frank before she went back to stir her pot. "You know, Frank, a family vacation before Noah heads off to college would be good for all of us. And we haven't been camping since he was three and you took an oath never to spend another night sleeping on the ground."

Half the weight the letter had put on his shoulders slid off. "I really do love you, Celia."

OLIVIA DID HER BEST TO BEHAVE NORMALLY, TO TUCK THE nerves and excitement away so her grandparents wouldn't notice. Inside, she was breathless and jittery, and her head ached a little, but she did her morning chores and managed to eat a little lunch so no one would comment on her lack of appetite.

The Bradys would be there soon.

She'd been relieved when her grandfather had been called to the campground right after lunch to handle some little snag. It hadn't been hard to make excuses to stay behind instead of going with him, though she'd felt guilty about being less than honest.

The guilt had her working twice as hard as she might have on cleaning the terrace outside the lodge dining room and weeding the gardens that bordered it.

It was also the perfect spot from which to watch arrivals and departures.

Olivia weeded the nasturtiums that tumbled over the low stone wall in cheery yellows and oranges, deadheaded the bright white Shasta daisies behind them and kept one eye on the turn toward Reception.

Her hands sweated inside her garden gloves, which she'd worn only because she wanted to be adult and shake hands with the Brady family without having grime on her fingers and under her fingernails. She wanted Frank to see that she was grown-up enough to understand about her mother, about her father.

She didn't want him to see a scared little girl who needed to be protected from monsters.

She was going to learn to chase the monsters away herself, Olivia thought. Then, despite her plans, she absently swiped a hand over her cheek and smeared it with soil.

She'd brushed her hair and smoothed it into a neat ponytail that she'd slipped through the opening in the back of her red cap. She wore jeans and a River's End T-shirt. Both had been clean that morning, and though she'd tried to keep them that way, the knees of her jeans were soiled now.

That would only prove that she'd been working, she told herself. That she was responsible.

They should be here by now, she thought. They had to be here soon, they just had to. Otherwise her grandfather might come back. He might recognize Frank Brady. He probably would. Grandfather remembered everyone and everything. Then he'd find ways to keep her from talking to Frank, to keep her from asking questions. All the planning, the care, the hopes she had would be for nothing if they didn't get there soon.

A couple strolled out onto the terrace, sat at one of the little iron tables. One of the staff would come out to serve them drinks or snacks, Olivia knew. Then she'd lose the solitude.

Olivia worked her way along the border, half listening as the woman read about the trails in her guidebook. Planning tomorrow's hike, debating whether to take one of the long ones and order one of the picnic lunches the lodge provided.

Ordinarily Olivia might have stopped working long enough to recommend just that plan, to give her own description of the trail the woman seemed to favor. The guests enjoyed the personal touch, and her grandparents encouraged her to share her knowledge of the area with them. But she had too much on her mind for chitchat and continued to work steadily down the edge of the terrace until she was nearly out of sight.

She saw the big old car bumping up the drive, but noted immediately that the man driving it was too young to be Frank Brady. He had a pretty face—what she could see of it, as he wore a cap and sunglasses. His hair spilled out of the cap, wavy and sun-streaked brown.

The woman in the passenger seat was pretty, too. His mother, Olivia guessed, though she didn't look very old either. Maybe she was his aunt, or his big sister.

She ran through the reservations in her head, trying to remember if they had a couple coming in that day, then she spotted another figure sprawled in the backseat.

Her heart began to thud in her chest, the answering echo a dull beat in her head. Slowly she got to her feet as the car coasted around the last turn and parked.

She knew him right away. Olivia didn't consider it at all strange that her bleary memory of his face shot into sharp focus the minute Frank stepped out of the car. She remembered perfectly now, the color of his eyes, the sound of his voice, the way his hand had felt, big and gentle on her cheek.

Her aching head spun, once, sickly, as he turned his head and saw her. She felt her knees tremble, but she pulled off her gloves and stuck them in her back pocket. Her mouth was dust dry, but she forced a polite smile on her face and started forward.

So did he.

For Olivia, at that moment, the woman and the young man who got out of the car faded into the background. As did the wall of great trees, the searing blue sky above them, the flutter of butterflies, the chatter of birds.

She saw only him, as she'd seen only him the night he'd opened the closet door.

"I'm Olivia," she said in a voice that sounded very far away to her own ears. "Thank you for coming, Detective Brady." She held out her hand.

How many times, Frank wondered, would this one little girl break his heart? She stood so poised, her eyes so solemn, her smile so polite. And her voice shook.

"It's nice to see you again, Olivia." He took her hand in his, held it. "Livvy. Don't they call you Livvy anymore?"

"Yes." Her smile warmed, just a little. "Did you have a nice trip?"

"Very nice. We decided to drive, so we needed my son's car. It's the only one big enough to be comfortable for that long. Celia?"

He reached out, then slipped his arm around his wife's shoulders. It was a gesture Olivia noticed. She liked to study the way people were together. The woman fit easily against him, and her smile was friendly. Her eyes sympathetic.

"This is Celia, my wife."

"Hello, Livvy. What a beautiful place. You know I camped in your campgrounds once, when I was Noah's age. I've never forgotten this area. Noah, this is Livvy MacBride, her family owns the lodge."

He glanced over, nodded—polite but distant. "Hey" was all he said as he tucked his hands in his back pockets. Behind the dark glasses, he took in every feature of her face.

She was taller than he expected. Gangly. He reminded himself his image of her was stuck on the little girl with her hands clamped over her ears and her face wild with fear and grief.

He'd never forgotten how she'd looked. He'd never forgotten her.

"Noah's a man of few words these days," Celia said soberly, but the way her eyes laughed had Olivia smiling again.

"You can leave your car here if you want while you check in. All the lake-view units were booked, but you have a really nice view of the forest. It's one of the family units on the ground floor and has its own patio."

"It sounds wonderful. I remember taking pictures of the lodge all those years ago." To put Olivia at ease, Celia laid a hand on her shoulder and turned to study the building. "It looks as if it grew here, like the trees."

It was grand and old and dignified. Three stories, with the main section under a steeply pitched roof. Windows were generous, to offer the guests stunning views. The wood had weathered to a soft brown and, with the deep green trim, seemed as much a part of the forest as the giant trees that towered over it.

Pathways were fashioned of stone with small evergreens and clumps of ferns and wildflowers scattered throughout. Rather than manicured, the grounds looked appealingly wild and untouched.

"It's not intrusive at all. Whoever built it understood the importance of working with nature instead of beating it back."

"My great-grandfather. He did the original building, then he and his brother and my grandfather added on to it. He named it, too." Olivia resisted the urge to rub her damp palms on her jeans. "There's no river that ends here or anything. It's a metaphor."

"For finding rest and shelter at the end of a journey," Celia suggested and made Olivia smile.

"Yeah, exactly. That's what he wanted to do. It was really just an inn at first, and now it's a resort. But we want that same restful atmosphere and are dedicated to preserving the area and seeing to it that the lodge adds to rather than detracts from the purity of the forest and lakes."

"You're talking her language." Frank winked. "Celia's a staunch conservationist."

"So is anyone with brains," Olivia said automatically and had Celia nodding in approval.

"We're going to get along just fine. Why don't you show me around the lodge while these big strong men deal with the luggage?"

Olivia glanced back at Frank as Celia led her off. Impatience all but shimmered around her, but she did as she was asked and opened one half of the great double doors.

"I never made it inside during my other trip," Celia was saying. "I was on a pretty tight budget, and I was busy turning my nose up at any established creature comforts. I was one of the first hippies."

Olivia stopped, blinked. "Really? You don't look like a hippy."

"I only wear my love beads on special occasions now—like the anniversary of Woodstock."

"Was Frank a hippy, too?"

"Frank?" Celia threw back her head and laughed in sheer delight. "Oh no, not Mister Conservative. That man was born a cop—and a Republican. Well," she said with a sigh, "what can you do? Oh, but this is lovely."

She turned a half circle in the main lobby, admiring the floors and walls of natural pine and fir, the great stone fireplace filled in the warmth of August with fresh flowers rather than flames. Chairs and sofas in soft earth tones were arranged in cozy groups.

Several guests were enjoying coffee or wine while they sat and contemplated the views or studied their guidebooks.

There was Native American art in paintings and wall hangings and rugs, and copper pails that held generous bouquets of fresh flowers or greenery.

It seemed more like a sprawling living room than a lobby, which, Celia imagined, had been just the intention.

The front desk was a polished wood counter manned by two clerks in crisp white shirts and hunter green vests. Daily activities were handwritten on an old slate board, and a stoneware bowl of pastel-colored mints sat on the counter.

"Welcome to River's End." The female clerk had a quick grin for Olivia before she turned a welcoming smile on Celia. "Will you be staying with us?"

"Yes, Celia Brady and family. My husband and son are getting our luggage."

"Yes, Mrs. Brady, we're happy to have you." While she spoke, the clerk tapped her fingers over the keyboard below the counter. "I hope you had a pleasant trip."

"Very." Celia noted the name tag pinned to the vest. "Thank you, Sharon."

"And you'll be staying with us for five nights. You have our family package, which includes breakfast for three every morning, any one of our guided tours . . ."

Olivia tuned out Sharon's welcome address and explanation and looked toward the door. Her stomach began to flutter again as Frank came in with Noah behind him. They were loaded down with luggage and backpacks.

"I can help you with that. Sharon, I can show the Bradys to their rooms and tell them where everything is."

"Thanks, Livvy. You can't do better than with a MacBride as your guide, Mrs. Brady. Enjoy your stay."

"It's this way." Struggling not to hurry, Olivia led the way down a hallway off the lobby, turned right. "The health club is to the left and complimentary to guests. You can reach the pool through there or by going out the south entrance."

She rattled off information, meal service times, room service availability, lounge hours, rental information for canoes, fishing gear, bikes.

At the door to their rooms, she stood back, and despite nerves found herself pleased when Celia let out a little gasp of pleasure.

"It's great! Just great! Oh, Frank, look at that view. It's like being in the middle of the forest." She moved immediately to the patio doors and flung them open. "Why do we live in the city?"

"It has something to do with employment," Frank said dryly.

"The master bedroom is in here, and the second bedroom there."

"I'll go dump my stuff." Noah headed off to the other end of the sitting room.

"You'll want to unpack, get settled in." Olivia linked her hands together, pulled them apart. "Is there anything I can get you, or any questions . . . I—there are some short, easy trails if you want to do any exploring this afternoon."

"Frank, why don't you play scout?" Celia smiled, unable to resist the plea in Olivia's eyes. "Noah and I will probably laze by the pool for a bit. Livvy can show you around now and you can stretch your legs."

"Good idea. Do you mind, Livvy?"

"No. No, I don't mind. We can go right out this way." She gestured to the patio doors. "There's an easy half-mile loop; you don't even need any gear."

"Sounds perfect." He kissed Celia, ran a hand down her arm. "See you in a bit."

"Take your time." She walked to the door after them, watched the girl lead the man toward the trees.

"Mom?"

She didn't turn, kept watching until the two figures slipped into the shadows of the forest. "Hmmm?"

"Why didn't you tell me?"

"Tell you what, Noah?"

"That's Julie MacBride's kid, isn't it?"

Celia turned now to where Noah stood in the doorway of his room, his shoulder nonchalantly propped against the frame, his eyes alert and just a bit annoyed.

"Yes. Why?"

"We didn't come up here to play in the woods and go fishing. Dad hates fishing, and his idea of a vacation is lying in the hammock in the backyard."

She nearly laughed. It was exactly true. "What's your point?"

"He came up to see the kid. Does that mean something new's come up on the Julie MacBride murder?"

"No. It's nothing like that. I didn't know you had any interest in that business, Noah."

"Why wouldn't I?" He pushed away from the doorway and picked up one of the bright red apples in a blue bowl on the table. "It was Dad's case, and a big one. People still talk about it. And he thinks about it." Noah jerked his chin in the direction his father had taken. "Even if he doesn't talk about it. What's the deal, Mom?"

Celia lifted her shoulders, let them fall. "The girl—Olivia—wrote to him. She has some questions. I don't think her grandparents have told her very much, and I don't think they know she wrote your father. So, let's give the two of them a little room."

"Sure." Noah bit into the apple, and his gaze drifted toward the window where the tall young girl had led the man toward the trees. "I was just wondering."

EIGHT

THE trees closed them in, like giant bars in an ancient prison. Frank had expected a kind of openness and charm, and instead found himself uneasily walking through a strange world where the light glowed eerily green and nature came in odd, primitive shapes.

Even the sounds and smells were foreign, potent and ripe. Dampness clung to the air. He'd have been more comfortable in a dark alley in East L.A.

He caught himself glancing over his shoulder and wishing for the comforting weight of his weapon.

"You ever get lost in here?" he asked Olivia.

"No, but people do sometimes. You should always carry a compass, and stay on the marked trails if you're a novice." She tipped up her face to study his. "I guess you're an urban hiker."

He grinned at the term. "You got that right."

She smiled, and the humor made her eyes glow. "Aunt Jamie said that's what she is now. But you can get lost in the city, too, can't you?"

"Yeah. Yeah, you can."

She looked away now, slowing her pace. "It was nice of you to come. I didn't think you would. I wasn't sure you'd even remember me."

"I remember you, Livvy." He touched her arm lightly, felt the stiffness and control a twelve-year-old shouldn't have. "I've thought about you, wondered how you were."

"My grandparents are great. I love living here. I can't imagine living anywhere else. People come here for vacation, but I get to live here all the time." She said it all very fast, as if she needed to get out everything good before she turned a corner.

"You have a nice family," she began.

"Thanks. I think I'll probably keep them."

Her smile came and went quickly. "I have a nice family, too. But I . . . That's a nurse log," she pointed out as nerves crept back into her voice. "When a tree falls, or branches do, the forest makes use of them. Nothing's wasted here. That's a Douglas fir, and you can see the sprouts of western hemlock growing out of it, and the spread of moss, the ferns and mushrooms. When something dies here, it gives other things a chance to live."

She looked up at him again, her eyes a shimmering amber behind a sheen of tears. "Why did my mother die?"

"I can't answer that, Livvy. I can never really answer the why, and it's the hardest part of my job."

"It was a waste, wasn't it? A waste of something good and beautiful. She was good and beautiful, wasn't she?"

"Yes, yes she was."

With a nod, she began to walk again and didn't speak until she was certain she'd fought back the tears. "But my father wasn't. He couldn't have been good and beautiful, not really. But she fell in love with him, and she married him."

"Your father had problems."

"Drugs," she said flatly. "I read about it in newspapers my grandmother has put away in our attic. He took drugs and he killed her. He couldn't have loved her. He couldn't have loved either of us."

"Livvy, life isn't always that simple, that black-and-white."

"If you love something, you take care of it. You protect it. If you love enough, you'd die to protect it." She spoke softly, but her voice was fierce. "He says he didn't do it. But he did. I saw him. I can still see him if I let myself." She pressed her lips together. "He would have killed me, too, if I hadn't gotten away."

"I don't know." How did he answer this child, with her quiet voice and old eyes. "It's possible."

"You talked to him. After."

"Yes. That's part of my job."

"Is he crazy?"

Frank opened his mouth, closed it again. There were no pat answers here. "The court didn't think so."

"But did you?"

Frank let out a sigh. He could see how they'd circled around now, see parts of the roofline, the glint of the windows of the inn. "Livvy, I think he was weak, and the drugs played into that weakness. They made him believe things that weren't true and do things that weren't right. Your mother separated from him to protect you as much, probably more, than herself. And, I think, hoping it would push him into getting help."

But it didn't, Olivia thought. It didn't make him get help, it didn't protect anyone.

"If he wasn't living there anymore, why was he in the house that night?"

"The evidence indicated she let him in."

"Because she still loved him." She shook her head before Frank could answer. "It's all right. I understand. Will they keep him in jail forever?"

There are so few forevers, Frank thought. "He was given a sentence of twenty years to life, the first fifteen without possibility of parole."

Her eyes narrowed in a frown of concentration. Fifteen years was longer than she'd been alive, but it wasn't enough. "Does that mean he can just get out in seven more years? Just like that, after what he did?"

"No, not necessarily. The system . . ." How could he possibly explain the twists and turns of it to a child? "He'll go before a panel, like a test."

"But the people on the panel don't know. They weren't there. It won't matter to them."

"Yes, it will matter. I can go." And he would, Frank decided, and speak for the child. "I'm allowed to go and address the panel because I was there."

"Thank you." The tears wanted to come back, so she held out a hand to shake his. "Thank you for talking to me."

"Livvy." He took her hand, then touched his free one to her cheek. "You can call or write me anytime you want."

"Really?"

"I'd like it if you did."

The tears stopped burning, her nerves smoothed out. "Then I will. I'm really glad you came. I hope you and your family have a good time. If you want, I can sign you up for one of the guided hikes while you're here, or I can show you which trails you can take on your own."

Going with instinct, Frank smiled at her. "We'd like that, but only if we can hire you as guide. We want the best."

She studied him with calm and sober eyes. "Skyline Trail's only thirty-one miles." When his mouth fell open, she smiled a little. "Just kidding. I know a nice day hike if you like to take pictures."

"What's your definition of a nice day hike?"

Her grin flashed, quick and surprising. "Just a couple of miles. You'll see beaver and osprey. The lodge can make up a boxed lunch if you want a picnic."

"Sold. How about tomorrow?"

"I'll check with my grandfather, but it should be all right. I'll come by about eleven-thirty." She glanced down at his scuffed high-tops. "You'd be better off with boots, but those are okay if you don't have them. I'll see you tomorrow."

"Livvy?" he called when she turned back toward the trees. "Should I buy a compass?"

She tossed a quick smile over her shoulder. "I won't let you get lost."

She walked into the trees, going fast now until she was sure no one could see. Then she stopped, hugging herself hard, rocking, letting the tears spill out.

They were hot and stinging; her chest ached with them as it hitched.

But after they'd fallen, after she was able to breathe again, to scrub her face dry with her hands, she felt better.

And at age twelve, Olivia decided what she would do with and how she would live her life. She would learn all there was to learn about the forest, the lakes, the mountains that were her home. She would live and she would work in the place she loved, the place where her mother had grown up.

She would, over time, find out more about her mother. And about the man who killed her. She would love the first with all her heart. Just as she would hate the second.

And she would never, never fall in love the way her mother had.

She would become her own woman. Starting now.

She stopped to wash her face in the stream, then sat quietly until she was sure all traces of tears and tattered emotions were gone. Her grand-parents were to be protected—that was another promise she made her-self. She would see to it that nothing she did ever caused them pain.

So when she walked into the clearing and saw her grandfather weed-ing his flowers, she crossed to him, knelt beside him with a smile. "I just did this over at the lodge. The gardens look really nice there."

"You got my green thumb, kiddo." He winked at her. "We won't talk about the color of your grandmother's."

"She does okay with houseplants. A family just checked into the lodge. A couple and their son." Casually, Olivia uprooted a weed. She didn't want to lie to him, but she thought it wisest to skirt around the bare truth. "The mother said she'd hiked around here when she was a teenager, but I don't think the other two know a bush from a porcupine. Anyway, they'd like me to go out with them tomorrow, just a short hike. I thought I'd take them to Irely Lake, along the river so they could take pictures."

He sat back on his heels, the line of worry already creasing his fore-head. "I don't know, Livvy."

"I'd like to do it. I know the way, and I want to start learning even more about running the lodge and campground, more about the trails and even the backcountry areas. I've gone along on guided hikes before, and I want to see if I can do one by myself. It's just down to Irely. If I do a good job, I could start training to guide other hikes during the summer and maybe give talks and stuff for kids. When I'm older, I could even do overnights, and be a naturalist like they have in the park. Only I'd be better, because I grew up here. Because it's home."

He reached out to skim his knuckles over her cheek. He could see Julie in her eyes, Julie, when she'd been a young girl and telling him of her dreams to be a great actress. Her dream had taken her away from him. Olivia's would keep her close.

"You're still young enough to change your mind a dozen times."

"I won't. But anyway, I won't know if I'm good or if it's really what I want until I try. I want to try, just a little bit, tomorrow."

"Just down to Irely?"

"I showed the father the loop trail from the inn before I left. He kept talking about getting lost." She shared an easy chuckle with Rob. "I think Irely's about all he can handle."

Knowing she'd won, she got up, brushed off her jeans. "I'm going to go see if Grandma needs any help with dinner." Then she stopped, leaned down to wrap her arms around Rob's neck. "I'm going to make you proud of me."

"I am proud of you, baby."

She hugged tighter. "Just wait," she whispered, then darted inside.

OLIVIA WAS EXACTLY ON TIME. SHE'D DECIDED THAT WOULD be important to how she lived her life from now on. She would always be prompt; she would always be prepared.

She arrived early at the lodge to collect the boxed lunch for the hike. It would be her job to carry the supplies. She was young and strong, she thought as she stowed them in her backpack. She would get older, and she would get stronger.

She shouldered the pack, adjusted the straps.

She had her compass, her knife, bottled water, spare plastic bags to seal up any trash or garbage, her camera, a notepad and pencils, a first-aid kit.

She'd spent three hours the night before reading, studying, absorbing information and history. She was going to see to it that the Bradys had an entertaining, and an educational, afternoon.

When she walked around to the patio entrance of the unit, she saw Noah sitting in one of the wooden chairs. He was wearing headphones and tapping his fingers restlessly on the arm of the chair. His legs were long, clad in ripped jeans and stretched out to cross at the ankles of high-top Nikes.

He wore sunglasses with very dark lenses. It occurred to her she'd yet to see him without them. His hair was damp as if he'd recently come from the shower or the pool. It was casually slicked back and drying in the sun.

She thought he looked like a rock star.

Shyness wanted to swallow her, but she straightened her shoulders. If she was going to be a guide, she had to learn to get over being shy around boys and everyone else. "Hi."

His head moved a little, his fingers stopped tapping. She realized he'd probably had his eyes closed behind those black lenses and hadn't even seen her.

"Yeah, hi." He reached down to turn off the cassette that was singing in his ears. "I'll get the troops."

When he stood up, she had to tip back her head to keep her eyes on his face. "Did you try the pool?"

"Yeah." He gave her a grin and had the woman's heart still sleeping in the child's breast stirring. "Water's cold." He opened the patio door. "Hey, the trailblazer's here." There was a muffled response from behind the bedroom door before he turned back to Olivia. "You might as well sit down. Mom's never ready on time."

"There's no hurry."

"Good thing."

Deciding it was more polite to sit since he'd asked her to, she lowered herself to the stone patio. She fell into a silence that was part shyness and part simple inexperience.

Noah studied her profile. She interested him because of her connection to his father and to Julie MacBride and, he admitted, because of her connection to murder. Murder fascinated him.

He would have asked her about it if he hadn't been certain both his parents would have skinned him for it. He might have risked that, but he remembered the image of the small child with her hands over her ears and tears flooding her cheeks.

"So . . . what do you do around here?"

Her gaze danced in his direction, then away. "Stuff." She felt the heat climb into her cheeks at the foolishness of the answer.

"Oh yeah, stuff. We never do that in California."

"Well, I do chores, help out at the campground and here at the lodge. I hike and fish. I'm learning about the history of the area, the flora and fauna, that sort of thing."

"Where do you go to school?"

"My grandmother teaches me at home."

"At home?" He tipped down his sunglasses so she got a glimpse of deep green eyes. "Some deal."

"She's pretty strict," Olivia mumbled, then leaped to her feet in relief when Frank stepped out.

"Celia's coming. I figured I should go get our lunch."

"I have it." Olivia shifted her pack. "Cold fried chicken, potato salad, fruit and pound cake. Sal, that's the chef, he makes the best."

"You shouldn't carry all that," Frank began, but she stepped back.

"It's part of my job." Then she looked past him, saw Celia and felt shy again. "Good morning, Mrs. Brady."

"Good morning. I saw a deer out my window this morning. She stepped through the fog like something out of a fairy tale. By the time I snapped out of it and dug out my camera, she was gone."

"You'll probably see more. The blacktail is common in the forest. You might catch sight of a Roosevelt elk, too."

Celia tapped the camera hanging from a strap around her neck as she stepped out. "This time, I'm prepared."

"If you're ready, we'll get started." Olivia had already, subtly she hoped, checked out their shoes and clothes and gear. It would do well enough for the short, easy hike. "You can stop me anytime you want to take pictures or rest or ask questions. I don't know how much you know about Olympic, or the rainforest," she began as she started the walk.

She'd practiced her presentation that morning as she'd dressed and led into it very much as she had when her aunt had played tourist for her.

When she mentioned bear, Celia didn't squeal as Jamie had, but sighed. "Oh, I'd love to see one."

"Jeez, Mom, you would."

Celia laughed and hooked an arm around Noah's neck. "Hopeless city boys, Livvy. Both of them. You've got your work cut out for you with these two."

"That's okay, it's good practice."

She identified trees for them, but got the feeling only Celia was particularly interested. Though Noah did seem to perk up when she spotted an eagle for him high in the moss- and lichen-draped trees. But when she cut over to the river and the world opened up a bit, all three of her charges seemed to get into the spirit.

"This is the Quinault," Olivia told them. "It runs to the coast. The Olympic Range rings the interior."

"God, it's beautiful. It takes your breath away." Celia had her camera up, busily framing and snapping. "Look at the way the mountains stand against the sky, Frank. White and green and gray against that blue. It's like taking a picture of a painting."

Olivia scrambled around in her head for what she knew about the mountains. "Ah, Mount Olympus is actually less than eight thousand feet at its peak, but it rises from the rain forest at almost sea level, so it looks bigger. It has, I think it's six, glaciers. We're on the western slopes of the range."

She led them along the river, pointing out the clever dams the beavers built, the stringlike petals of wild goldthread, the delicate white of marsh marigold. They passed other hikers on the trail, singles and groups.

Celia stopped often for pictures, and her men posed with patience if not enthusiasm. When Olivia managed to catch a red-legged frog, Celia took pictures of that as well, laughing in delight when it let out its long feeble croak.

Then she surprised Olivia by stroking a long finger over the frog's back. Hardly any of the women Olivia knew wanted to pet frogs. When she released it, she and Celia smiled at each other in perfect unity.

"Your mother's found a soul sister," Frank muttered to Noah.

Olivia was about to point out an osprey nest when a toddler raced down the trail, evading the young parents who called and rushed after him.

He tripped and came to a skidding halt on knees and elbows almost at Olivia's feet. And wailed like a thousand bagpipes.

She started to bend down, but Noah was faster and had the boy scooped up, jiggling him cheerfully. "Uh-oh. Wipeout."

"Scotty! Oh, honey, I told you not to run!" The frantic mother grabbed for him, then looked back at her out-of-breath husband. "He's bleeding. He's scraped his knees."

"Damn it. How bad? Let's see, buddy."

As the boy screamed and sobbed, Olivia slipped off her pack. "You'll need to wash his cuts. I have some bottled water and a first-aid kit."

She went to work so efficiently, Frank signaled Celia back.

"You'll have to hold him still," Olivia said. "I can't clean it if he's kicking."

"I know it hurts, honey, I know. We're going to make it all better." The mother kissed Scotty's cheeks. "Here, let me clean off the cuts. Thanks so much." She took the cloth Olivia had dampened and struggled with her husband to keep the child still long enough to see the damage.

"Just scrapes. Knocked the bark off, buddy." The father kept his voice light, but his face was very pale as his wife cleaned the blood away.

Olivia handed over antiseptic, and one glance at the little bottle had Scotty switching from wails to ear-piercing screams.

"Hey, you know what you need." Noah pulled a candy bar out of his back pocket, waved it in front of Scotty's face. "You need to spoil your lunch."

Scotty eyed the chocolate bar through fat tears. His lips trembled, but instead of a screech he let out a pitiful whimper. "Candy."

"You bet. You like candy? This is pretty special candy. It's only for brave boys. I bet you're brave."

Scotty sniffled, reached out, too intent on the bar to notice his mother quickly bandaging his knees. "'Kay."

"Here you go, then." Noah held it out, then tugged it just out of reach with a grin. "I forgot. I can only give this candy to somebody named Scotty."

"I'm Scotty."

"No kidding? Then this must be yours."

"Thanks. Thanks so much." The mother shifted the now-delighted child to her hip and shoved back her hair with her free hand. "You're lifesavers."

Olivia glanced up from where she was repacking her first-aid kit. "You should make sure you pick up one of these if you're going to do much hiking. The River's End Lodge gift shop carries them, or you can get them in town."

"First on my list. Along with emergency chocolate. Thanks again." She looked over to Frank and Celia. "You've got great kids."

Olivia started to speak, then ducked her head and said nothing. But not so quickly that Celia hadn't seen the look of unhappiness. "You two make a good team," she said cheerfully. "And that little adventure worked up my appetite. When's lunch, Liv?"

Olivia looked up, blinked. Liv, she thought. It sounded strong and sure and smart. "There's a nice area just a little farther down. We might get lucky and see a couple of beavers instead of just their dams."

She picked her spot, a shady area just off the trail where they could sit and watch the water, or gaze off toward the mountains. The air was warm, the sky clear in one of those perfect summer days the peninsula could offer.

Olivia nibbled at her chicken and held herself back just a little. She wanted to watch the Bradys together. They seemed so easy, so meshed. Later, when she was older and looked back on that comfortable hour, she would call it a rhythm. They had a rhythm of movement, of speech, of silences. Little bits of humor that were intimately their own, tossed-off comments, teasing, body language.

And she would realize, remembering, that however much she and her grandparents loved one another, they didn't have quite that same connection.

A generation stood between them. Her mother's life, and her death.

But just then all she knew was that she felt a tug of longing, an ache of envy. It made her ashamed. "I'm going to walk down a little more." She got up, ordering herself to do so casually. "I'll see if I can spot some beavers. If I do, I'll come back and get you."

"Poor little thing," Celia murmured when Olivia walked down the trail. "She's lonely. I don't even think she knows how lonely she is."

"Her grandparents are good people, Celia."

"I'm sure they are. But where are the other kids? The ones her age she should be playing with on a beautiful day like this?"

"She doesn't even go to school," Noah put in. "She told me her grandmother teaches her at home."

"They've put her in a bubble. A spectacular one," Celia added as she looked around, "but it's still closed."

"They're afraid. They have reason to be."

"I know, but what will they do when she starts to beat her wings against the bubble? And what will she do if she doesn't?"

Noah got to his feet. "I think I'll walk down, too. Never seen a beaver."

"He has a kind heart," Celia commented, smiling after him.

"Yeah, and he also has a curious mind. I hope he doesn't try to pump her."

"Give him some credit, Frank."

"If I didn't, I'd be going to look for beavers, too, instead of taking a nap." With that, he stretched out and laid his head in his wife's lap.

NOAH FOUND HER SITTING ON THE BANK OF THE RIVER, VERY quiet and very still. It made a picture in his mind—very much like, yet so very different from, the one he had of her as a small child running from grief.

Here she simply sat, her cap over her butterscotch hair, her back straight as a die, staring out over water that ran fast and bright and clear.

She wasn't running from grief this time, he thought. She was learning to live with it.

It was sort of her personal river's end, he supposed.

Her head turned quickly at his approach. She kept her gaze steady on his face, those rich eyes of hers solemn, as he moved to her and sat down.

"They come to play here," she told him in a low voice. "They don't mind people too much. They get used to them. But you have more luck if you don't make a lot of noise and movement."

"I guess you spend a lot of time just hanging around."

"There's always something to see or do." She kept scanning the river. He made her feel odd in a way she couldn't decide was pleasant or not. She only knew it was different from anything she'd felt before. A kind of drumming just under her heart. "I guess it's nothing like Los Angeles."

"Nothing at all." At that point in his life, L.A. *was* the world. "It's okay, though. Mom's big on nature and shit. You know, save the whales, save the spotted owl, save the whatever. She gets into it."

"If more people did, we wouldn't need to save them in the first place."

She spoke with just enough heat to make him smile. "Yeah, that's what she says. I got no problem with it. Mostly I like my nature in the city park, with a basketball hoop."

"I bet you've never even been fishing."

"Why should I?" He sent her a quick flash of a grin that had the drumming inside her picking up its beat. "I can walk right into McDonald's and buy a fish sandwich."

"Yuck."

"Hey, you want yuck? Sticking a defenseless worm on some hook and drowning it so you can pull up some flopping, slimy fish." The fact that she smiled a little, that her eyes shimmered with a mild and adult kind of humor, pleased him. "That's disgusting."

"That's skill," she corrected, almost primly, but she was looking at him now, instead of at the river. "Isn't it crowded in the city, and full of noise and traffic and smog and stuff?"

"Sure." He leaned back comfortably on his elbows. "That's why I love it. Something's always happening."

"Something's always happening here, too. Look." Forgetting her shyness, she laid a hand on his leg.

A pair of beavers swam cheerfully upriver, their slick heads skimming the surface, ripples shimmying over the water in widening pools around them. Then, like a dream, a heron rose up over the opposite bank and glided with a majestic flap of wings across the river, so close its shadow flowed over them.

"Bet you never saw that in the city."

"Guess not."

He amused himself with the beavers. They were really pretty cute, he decided, circling, splashing, flipping over to swim on their backs.

"You know about my mother."

Noah looked over sharply. She was facing the water again, her face set, her jaw tight. There were a dozen questions he'd wanted to ask if he found the opportunity, but now that she'd opened the door he found he couldn't.

She was just a kid.

"Yeah. It's rough."

"Have you ever seen any of her movies?"

"Sure. Lots of them."

Olivia pressed her lips together. She had to know. Someone had to tell her. He would. She hoped he'd treat her like a grown-up instead of someone who needed constant protecting. "Was she wonderful in them?"

"Haven't you ever seen one?" When she shook her head, he shifted, not sure how to answer. The best answer, his mother often said, was the simple truth. "She was really good. I mostly like action flicks, you know, but I've watched hers on TV. Man, she was beautiful."

"I don't mean how she looked." Her voice snapped out, surprising him into staring. "I mean how she *was*. Was she a good actress?"

"Sure. Really good. She made you believe. I guess that's what it's all about."

Olivia's shoulders relaxed. "Yes." She nodded. "She left here because she wanted to act. I just wanted to know if she was good. 'She made you believe.'" Olivia murmured it, then tucked that single statement into her heart. "Your father . . . he came here because I asked him to. He's a great man. You should know that. You have parents who care about things, about people. You should never forget that."

She got to her feet. "I'll go get them so they can see the beavers before we head back."

Noah sat where he was. He hadn't asked her the questions in his head, but she'd answered one of them. How did it feel to be the daughter of someone famous who'd died in a violent way.

It felt lousy. Just lousy.

Noah

It takes two to speak the truth—
one to speak, and another to hear.

—HENRY DAVID THOREAU

NINE

Washington State University, 1993

THERE was nothing to be nervous about. Noah reminded himself of that as he checked the address of the trim two-story house. He'd been planning this trip, this connection for a long time. And that, he supposed as he parked his rental car at the curb in the quiet tree-lined neighborhood, was exactly why he was nervous.

Maybe he sensed his life could change today, that seeing Olivia Mac-Bride again could alter the course he was on. He was willing to take that new direction. There was no gain without risk, after all. That's where the damp palms and jumpy belly came from.

It was nothing personal.

He combed back his hair by using the fingers of his hands in two quick rakes. He'd thought about getting a trim before coming here, but hell, he was on vacation.

More or less.

Two weeks away from the newspaper, where his struggle to make a name for himself as a crime reporter wasn't as satisfying as he'd thought it would be. Politics, print space, editors and advertising concerns got in the way of stories he wanted to tell.

And he wanted to tell them his way.

That was why he was here. To write the one story he'd never been able to forget, and to tell it his way.

Julie MacBride's murder.

One of the keys to it lived on the second floor of this pretty house that had been converted into four apartments. They and others like it had been designed to accommodate the overflow from the college campus. For those who could afford separate housing, he thought. Who could pay the price for privacy. And who wanted it badly enough—who didn't look for the pace and companionship, the bursts of energy in college life.

Personally, he'd loved his years on campus at UCLA. Maybe the first semester had been mostly a blur of parties, girls and drunken late-night philosophical discussions only the young could understand. But he'd buckled down after that.

He'd wanted his degree in journalism. And his parents would have killed him if he'd washed out.

Those two incentives had worked for him in equal measure.

And what, he wondered, was Olivia's incentive?

If after nearly three years on the job he'd learned he wasn't a reporter at heart, he was still a good one. He'd done his research. He knew Olivia MacBride was majoring in natural resource science, that her grades were a straight four point oh. He knew she'd spent one year, her freshman year, on campus in a dorm. And that she'd moved out and into her own apartment the following fall.

He knew she belonged to no clubs or sororities and was monitoring two extra classes while shouldering an eighteen-credit load during her spring semester.

That told him she was focused, dedicated and probably a little more than obsessive about her studies.

But there were things he couldn't research through computers, through transcripts. It didn't tell him what she wanted, what she hoped for.

What she felt about her parents.

To know all that, he needed to know her. To write the book that fermented in the back of his heart and his mind, he had to get inside her head.

The two images of her that burned brightest in his mind were of the child's tear-stained face and the young girl's solemn eyes. As he walked into the house, noted the hallway cutting the space precisely in two, he wondered what he would see now.

He climbed the steps, noted the small plaque that identified apartment 2-B. No name, he thought. Just the number. The MacBrides still guarded their privacy like the last gold coin in an empty sack.

"Here goes nothing," he muttered, and pressed the buzzer.

He had a couple of basic plans of approach in mind, believing it best to be flexible until he gauged his ground. Then she opened the door and every plan, every practical thought ran out of his mind like water from a tipped bowl. Slow and steady and completely.

She wasn't beautiful, certainly not if you measured her by her mother's staggering image. It was almost impossible to do otherwise when you saw the eyes, rich golden brown under slashing dark brows.

She was tall and slim, but with an efficient toughness to her build he found surprisingly, almost ridiculously sexy. Her hair had darkened since he'd seen her last, but was shades lighter than her eyes and drawn back in a smooth ponytail that left her face unframed.

The child's face had refined, sharpened and taken on the edge of young womanhood Noah always thought of as faintly feline.

She wore jeans, a WSU sweatshirt, no shoes and a vaguely annoyed expression.

He found himself standing, staring foolishly, unable to do anything but grin at her.

She cocked one of those killer eyebrows, and a surprising kick of lust joined his sheer pleasure at seeing her again. "If you're looking for Linda, she's across the hall. Two-A."

She said it as though she said it often and in a voice that was throatier than he remembered.

"I'm not looking for Linda. I'm looking for you." And the thought crossed his mind that he always had been. That was so absurd, he dismissed it immediately. "And you just put a huge hole in my ego by not remember-ing me."

"Why should I remember . . . ?" She trailed off, focusing those fasci-nating eyes on him as she hadn't when she'd thought he was just another of the nuisance men who flocked around her across-the-hall neighbor. And as she did, her lips parted, those eyes warmed. "You're Noah. Noah Brady. Frank's son." Her gaze shifted from his, over his shoulder. "Is he—"

"No, it's just me. Got a minute?"

"Yes. Yes, of course. Come in." Flustered, she stepped back. She'd been deep into the writing of a paper on the root symbiosis of fungus. Now she went from being buried in science to flying back over time, into memories.

And into the lovely little crush she'd had on him when she'd been twelve.

"I can make some coffee, or I probably have something cold."

"Either's fine." He took the first-time visitor's circling scan of the tidy room, the organized desk with its humming computer, the soft cream walls, the deep blue sofa. The space was compact, creatively arranged and comfortably simple. "Nice place."

"Yes, I like it." Relished, hoarded the blissful thrill of living alone for the first time in her life.

She didn't fuss, fluttering around as some women were prone to, apologizing for the mess even when there wasn't one. She simply stood there, looking at him as if she didn't know quite where to begin.

He looked back and wondered the same thing himself.

"Ah . . . I'll just be a minute."

"No rush."

He followed her into the kitchen, flustering her again. It was hardly more than a passageway, with stove, refrigerator and sink lining one side and stingy counter space between.

Despite the limited space, he managed to wander around. When he stood at the window, they were close enough to bump shoulders. She rarely let a man get close. "Coke or coffee?" she asked when she'd pulled open the fridge and taken a quick survey.

"Coke's fine. Thanks."

He would have taken the can from her, but she was already reaching for a glass.

For God's sake, Olivia, she scolded herself, open your mouth and speak. "What are you doing in Washington?"

"I'm on vacation." He smiled at her, and the drumming that had been under her heart six years before started up as if it had never stopped. "I work for the *L.A. Times.*" She smelled of soap and shampoo, and something else, something subtle. Vanilla, he realized, like the candles his mother liked.

"You're a reporter."

"I always wanted to write." He took the glass from her. "I didn't realize it until I was in college, but that's what I wanted." And because he felt her wariness slide between them like a band of smoke, he smiled again and decided there was no hurry about telling her what he'd come for. "I had a couple of weeks coming, and the friend I was going to flake out at the beach with for a few days couldn't get away after all. So I decided to head north."

"You're not up here on assignment, then."

"No." That was the truth, absolutely true, he told himself. "I'm on my own. I decided to look you up, since you're the only person I know in the entire state of Washington. How do you like college?"

"Oh, very much." Making a deliberate effort to relax, she led him back into the living room. "I miss home off and on, but classes keep me busy."

She sat on the couch, assuming he'd take the chair, but he sat beside her and companionably stretched out his legs. "What are you working on?" He nodded toward the computer.

"Fungus." She laughed, took a nervous sip of her drink. He was wonderful to look at, the untidy sun-streaked brown of his hair, the deep green eyes that reminded her of home, the easy sensuality of his smile.

She remembered she'd once thought he looked like a rock star. He still did.

"I'm a natural resource science major."

He started to tell her he knew, stopped himself. Too many explanations, he thought, and ignored the little whisper of guilt in his ear. "It fits."

"Like a glove," she agreed. "How are your parents?"

"They're great. You told me once I should appreciate them. I do." He shifted, his eyes meeting hers, holding hers, until the blood that had always remained calm and cool around men heated. "More, I guess, since I moved out, got my own place. That distance of the adult child, you know?"

"Yes, I do."

"Do you still work at the lodge?"

"Summers, over breaks." Do other men look at me this way? she wondered. Wouldn't she have noticed if one had ever looked at her as if her face were all that mattered? "I—did you ever learn to fish?"

"No." He grinned again and his fingers trailed lightly over the back of her hand.

"So it's still fish sandwiches at McDonald's?"

"They never miss. But I can occasionally do better. How about dinner?"

"Dinner?"

"As in eating, the evening meal. Even a natural resource science major must have heard of the ritual evening meal. Why don't you have yours with me tonight?"

Her ritual evening meal usually consisted of whatever she had time to toss together in her miniature kitchen or, failing that, what she picked up on the way home from a late class.

Besides, she had a paper to finish, a test to study for, a lab project to prepare for. And he had the most beautiful green eyes. "That would be nice."

"Good. I'll pick you up at seven. Got a favorite place?"

"Place? Oh, no, no, not really."

"Then I'll surprise you." He got up, giving her hand an absentminded squeeze as she rose to lead him to the door. "Don't fill up on fungus," he told her, and grinned one last time before he left.

Olivia quietly closed the door, quietly turned to lean back against it. She let out a long breath, told herself she was being ridiculous, that she was too old to indulge in silly crushes. Then for the first time in longer than she could remember, she had a purely frivolous thought:

What in God's name was she going to wear?

. . .

HE'D BRING UP THE SUBJECT OF HER FATHER, OF THE BOOK, during dinner. Gently, Noah told himself. He wanted her to have time to consider it, to understand what he hoped to do and the vital part she'd play in it.

It couldn't be done without her cooperation. Without her family's. Without, he thought, as he stuck his hands in his pockets and climbed the steps to her apartment again, Sam Tanner.

She wasn't a kid anymore. She'd be sensible. And when she understood his motivations, the results he wanted to accomplish, how could she refuse? The book he wanted to craft wouldn't just be about murder, about blood and death, but about people. The human factor. The motivations, the mistakes, the steps. The heart, he thought.

This kind of story began and ended with the heart. That's what he had to make her understand.

He was connected to it, and had been if not from the minute his father had answered the call to go to the house in Beverly Hills, then from the instant he himself had seen the image of the child on his living-room television screen.

He didn't just want to write about it. He had to.

He'd be straight with her about that.

Before he could push the buzzer of 2-B, the door of 2-A opened.

"Well, hello."

And this, he thought, must be Linda. The smile was a knee-jerk reaction to the smoldering brunette with laser blue eyes. His blood ran just a few beats faster, as the little red dress painted over female curves meant it to.

He knew her type and appreciated it. Just as he appreciated the way she moved, the metronome sway of hips, as she stepped out into the hall, crossing to him on ice-pick heels the same hot sex color as the dress.

"Can you give me a hand with this? I'm just . . . all thumbs tonight."

She dangled a thin gold bracelet from her fingertips, breathed in and out slow and deep, just in case he hadn't noticed the really lovely breasts straining against the slick red.

"Sure." There was nothing more flattering to the male ego than an obvious woman. He took the bracelet, circled it around her wrist and enjoyed the way she shifted her body closer, angled in to tip her face back and look into his.

"If Liv's had you tucked away, it's no wonder she never goes out."

He fastened the bracelet and wallowed in the come-and-get-me fragrance pumping off Linda's skin. "Doesn't she?"

"All work and all work, that's our Liv." She laughed and gave a skilled shake of her head that tossed her luxurious dark curls. "Me, I like to play."

"I bet you do." He still had Linda's wrist in his hand, and the friendly grin on his face, when the door behind him opened.

He forgot Linda had ever been born. He forgot the book. He very nearly forgot his name.

Olivia was anything but obvious. She stood in the doorway, wearing a dress of quiet blue that covered a lot more area than Linda's red. And made him wonder just what was under all that soft material. She'd left her hair loose so that it fell straight as rain and gave him a glimpse of glints of gold at her ears.

He already knew he'd have to get close, very close, to catch her scent. Her lips were unpainted, her eyes cool.

No, she was definitely not a kid anymore, he thought, thankfully.

"You look great."

She only lifted her eyebrows, skimmed her gaze over Linda. "I'll just get a jacket."

She pivoted, walked back into her apartment on long, wonderful hiker's legs.

There was no reason to be angry, she told herself as she snatched up her jacket and bag. No reason for this grinding sense of disappointment. She wouldn't have known he was flirting with Linda if she hadn't been watching for his car like a love-struck teenager. If she hadn't scurried over to the door to look out the Judas hole and watch him come toward the door.

There was no point in feeling let down because she had agonized for two hours over the right dress, the right hairstyle. It was her own problem. Her own responsibility.

She turned back toward the door and bumped right into him.

"Sorry. Let me help you with that." He was close now, and drew in her scent as he took the jacket from her. It was perfect for her. Just perfect.

"I didn't mean to interrupt."

"Interrupt what?" He slipped the jacket on for her and indulged himself in a sniff at her hair.

"You and Linda?"

"Who? Oh." He laughed, taking Olivia's hand and walking to the door. "Not exactly shy, is she?"

"No."

"Did you finish your paper?"

"Yes, barely."

"Good. You can tell me all about fungus."

It made her laugh. He held her hand all the way down to the car, then he skimmed his fingers over her hair, brushing it back just as she started to climb in.

Her heart stumbled, and fell right at his feet.

HE'D FOUND AN ITALIAN PLACE JUST CASUAL ENOUGH NOT to intimidate. Tiny white candles flickered on soft, salmon-colored cloths. Conversation was muted and punctuated with laughter. The air was ripe with good, rich scents.

He was easy to talk to. He was the first man, outside of family, she'd ever had dinner with who seemed actually interested in her studies and her plans to use them. Then she remembered his mother.

"Is your mother still involved with causes?"

"She and her congressmen are on a first-name basis. She never lets up. I think the current focus is the plight of the mustang. Are you going to let me taste that?"

"What?" She'd just lifted a forkful of portobello mushroom. "Oh. Sure."

When she would have put the bite on his plate, he simply took her wrist, guided her hand toward his mouth. Heat washed into her belly as his eyes watched hers over the fork.

"It's terrific."

"Ah, there is a wide variety of edible mushrooms in the rain forest."

"Yeah. Maybe I'll make it back up there one of these days and you can show me."

"I'm—we're hoping to add a naturalist center to the lodge. There'd be lectures and talks on how to identify the edibles."

"Edible fungus—it never sounds as appetizing as it is."

"Actually, the mushroom isn't the fungus. It's a fruiting body of the fungus organism. Like an apple from the apple tree."

"No kidding?"

"When you see a fairy ring, it's the fruit of the continuous body of the fungus that grows in the soil, expanding year after year and—" She caught herself. "And you can't possibly care."

"Hey, I like to know what I'm eating. Why do they call them fairy rings?"

She blinked at him. "I suppose because that's what they look like."

"Are there fairies in your forest, Liv?"

"I used to think so. When I was little, I'd sit there, in the green light, and think if I was very quiet, I'd see them come out and play."

"And you never did?"

"No." So she'd given up fairy tales. Science was reliable. "But I saw deer and elk and marten and bear. They're magical enough for me."

"And beaver."

She smiled, relaxing back as the waiter cleared, then served the main course. "Yes. There's still a dam where I took your family that day."

She sampled her angel-hair pasta with its generous chunks of tomato and shrimp. "They always give you more than you could possibly eat."

"Says who?" He dug into his manicotti, with shells bursting with cheese and spices.

It amazed her that he managed not only to do justice to his meal but also to put away a good portion of hers. Then still had room to order dessert and cappuccino.

"How can you eat like that and not weigh three hundred pounds?" she wanted to know.

"Metabolism." He grinned as he scooped up a spoonful of the whipped-cream-and-chocolate concoction on his plate. "Same with my dad. Drives my mother crazy. Here, try this. It's amazing."

"No, I can't—" But he already had the spoon to her lips, and she opened them automatically. The rich glory of it melted on her tongue. *"Hmm,* well. Yes."

He had to pull himself back a little. Her response, the half-closed eyes, the just-parted lips made him think of sex. Made him realize he wanted his mouth on hers, so all those tastes would mingle.

"Let's take a walk." He scribbled a tip and his signature on the bill, pocketed his credit card. Air, he told himself; he needed a little air to clear her and his fantasies out of his head.

But they were still there when he drove her home, when he walked her to her door, when she turned and smiled at him.

She saw it now, clear and dark in his eyes. Desire for her, the anticipation of that first kiss. A tremble shivered up the center of her body.

"This was nice." Could you possibly be more inane, Liv? she asked herself. "Thanks."

"What are you doing tomorrow?"

"Tomorrow?" Her mind went as blank as glass. "I have classes."

"No, tomorrow night."

"There's . . ." Studying, another paper, extra lab work. "Nothing."

"Good. Seven, then."

Now, she thought, he would kiss her now. And she'd probably implode. "All right."

"'Night, Liv." He only ran his hand down her arm, over the back of hers, then walked away.

TEN

H E took her to McDonald's, and she laughed until her sides burned. She fell in love with him over fish sandwiches and fries, under glaringly bright lights and through the noisy chatter of children.

She forgot the vow she'd made as a child that she would never, never love anyone so much she'd be vulnerable to him. That she would never hook her heart to a man and give him the power to break it, and her.

She simply rode that wonderful, that wild and windy crest of first love.

She told him what she hoped to do, describing the naturalist center she'd already designed in her mind and had shared with no one but family.

The biggest dream in her life was easy to share with him. He listened, he watched her face. What she wanted seemed to matter to him.

Because she fascinated him, he put aside all the work he'd done that day—the sketchy outline for the book, the notes, the more detailed plans for interviews—and just enjoyed her.

He told himself there was plenty of time. He had the best part of two weeks, after all. What was wrong with taking the first few days with her?

He wondered if the center she spoke of with such passion was her way of opening the bubble his mother had described or just another way to expand its boundaries and stay inside.

"It'll be a lot of work."

"It's not work when you're doing what you love."

That he understood. His assignments at the paper had become a grind, but every time he opened himself up to the book, dived into the research, pored over his notes and files, it was a thrill. "Then you can't let anything stop you."

"No." Her eyes were alive with the energy of it. "Just a few more years, and I'm going to make it happen."

"Then I'll come see it." His hand closed over hers on the white plastic table. And you, he thought.

"I hope so." And because she did, because she found she could, she turned her hand over and linked her fingers with his.

They talked about music, about books, about everything couples talk about when they're desperate to find every shared interest and explore it.

When he discovered she had not only never been to a basketball game, but had never watched one on television, he looked totally, sincerely shocked.

"You've got a huge hole in your education here, Liv." He had her hand again as they walked to his car. "I'm sending you copies of my tapes of the Lakers."

"They would be a basketball team."

"They, Olivia, would be gods. Okay." He settled behind the wheel. "We've managed to introduce you to the cultural delights of fast food; we have the only true sport heading your way. What's next?"

"I don't know how to thank you for helping me this way."

"It's the least I can do."

He already knew what was next, as he'd spent part of his day scoping out the area around the college. He had a pretty good idea it wasn't only fish sandwiches and sports Olivia had missed.

He took her dancing.

The club was loud, crowded and perfect. He'd already decided if he was alone with her he wouldn't be able to stop himself from moving too fast.

He was an observer, a measurer of people. It had taken only one evening with her for him to realize she was every bit as lonely as the young girl he remembered on the banks of the river. And that she was completely untouched.

There were rules. He believed strongly in rules, in rights and wrongs and in consequences. She wasn't ready for the needs she stirred up inside him.

He wasn't sure he was ready for them himself.

He saw her dazzled and wary look when they shoved their way through the crowd. Amused by it, delighted by her, he leaned close to her ear.

"Mass humanity at ritual. You could do a paper."

"I'm a naturalist."

"Baby, this is nature." He found them a table, jammed in with other tables, leaned forward to shout over the driving scream of music. "Male, female, basic courtship rituals."

She glanced toward the tiny dance floor where dozens of couples managed to squeeze in together and writhe. "I don't think that qualifies as courtship."

But it was interesting enough to watch. She'd always avoided places like this. Too many people in too small a space. It tended to create pressure in her chest, to release little flutters of panic in her throat. But she didn't feel uneasy tonight, bumped up against Noah, his hand lightly covering hers on the table.

He ordered a beer, and she opted for sparkling water. By the time the waitress had managed to swerve, shuffle and elbow her way through with their order, Olivia was relaxed.

The music was loud, and not particularly good, but it meshed nicely with that drumming under her heart. A kind of primitive backbeat to her own longings.

Since she couldn't hear her own thoughts, she forgot them and just watched.

Courtship. She supposed Noah was right, after all. The plumage—in this case leather and denim, bold colors or basic black. The repeated movements that signaled a demand to be noticed by the opposite sex, a sexual invitation, a willingness to mate. Eye contact, the flirtation glance toward, then away, then back again.

She found herself smiling. Hadn't she seen the ritual, in various forms, in countless species?

She said essentially this to Noah, speaking almost against his ear to be heard, and felt his rumble of laughter before he turned his face and she saw his smile.

Just as she realized how incredibly stupid she must have sounded, he tugged her to her feet.

"Are we leaving?"

"No, we're joining."

Now the panic came, fast and hard to fill her chest. "No, I can't." She tried to pull her hand free as he headed for the dance floor. "I don't dance."

"Everyone dances."

"No, really." Her skin went hot all over, burning from the inside out. "I don't know how."

They were on the edge of the dance floor, surrounded, closed in, and his hands were on her hips. His face was close. "Just move." His body did just that against hers, and turned the panic into a different, deeper, far more intimate fear. "It doesn't matter how."

He guided her hips, side to side, shifted so that they moved in a small circle. The music was fast, driven by a frenzied riff on an electric guitar and the vocalist's roar. Beside them someone let out a wild laugh. Someone bumped her hard from behind and brought her up against Noah, curves to angles, heat to heat.

Her hands gripped his shoulders now. Her face was flushed, her eyes, dark and wide, on his, her lips parted as the breath rushed in and out.

Through all the scents—the clash of perfume, sweat, spilled beer—he smelled only her. Fresh and quiet, like a meadow.

"Olivia." She couldn't hear his voice, but watched in dazed amazement as her name formed on his lips. It seemed that the only thing inside her now was the warm, sweet longing.

"The hell with it." He had to have her, if only one taste. His arms wrapped tight around her waist, urging her up to her toes. He felt the quick intake of her breath, and the tremble that followed it. And hesitated, hesitated, drawing out the moment, the now, the ache and the anticipation until they were both reeling from it.

Then he brushed his mouth over hers, soft, smooth. Nibbled her in, patient pleasure. Slid into her silkily, as if he'd always belonged there.

He heard her moan, low and long, over the thunder in his own blood. Slow, easy, he ordered himself. Sweet God. He wanted to dive, to devour, to demand more and still more as the surprisingly sharp, stunningly sexy taste of her flooded through him.

Her body was pressed against his, slender and strong. Her arms had locked around his neck, holding on. Holding him. Her mouth was full, and just shy enough to speak of innocence.

Just a little more, he thought and changed the angle of the kiss to take it.

The music crashed around them, building to a frenzy of guitars, a feral pounding of drums, a shouting stream of voices.

And she floated, drifted, glided. She imagined herself a single white feather, weightless, spinning slowly, endlessly, through the soft green light of the forest. Her heart swelled and its beat quieted to a thick, dull thud. The muscles in her stomach loosened and dipped. As she skimmed her fingers into his hair, tipped her head back in surrender, she could have wept from the discovery.

This, she thought, is life. Is beginnings. Is everything.

"Olivia." He said her name again, ended the kiss while he still had the power to do so, then just nudged her head to the curve of his shoulder.

The band ripped into another number, pumping the crowd to a fever pitch.

While they swayed together in the melee, Noah wondered what the hell he was going to do now.

He kissed her again at her door, and this time she felt little licks of heat from him, quick riffs of frustration that were oddly thrilling. Then he was closing the door between them and leaving her staring blankly at the solid panel of wood.

She pressed a hand to her heart. It was beating fast, and wasn't that wonderful? This was what it was like to be in love, to be wanted. She held the feeling close, closing her eyes, savoring it. Then her lids flew open again.

She should have asked him in. What was wrong with her? Why was she such an idiot around men? He'd wanted her, she was sure of it. She wanted him. Finally there was someone who made her feel.

She flung open her door, raced down the steps, and burst outside just as his car pulled away from the curb. She watched the red taillights wink away and wondered why she could never quite match her pace to anyone else's.

HE WORKED THROUGH THE MORNING. AND THOUGHT ABOUT calling her a dozen times. Then he shut down his laptop and changed into sweat shorts. The punishing workout he subjected himself to in the hotel's gym helped purge some of the guilt and frustration.

He needed to change directions, he decided as he did a third set of curls with free weights. He should never have gone this far down this road with Olivia.

He puffed out short breaths, added another rep while sweat ran satisfactorily down his back.

He'd have bet a year's pay that she was a virgin. He had no right to touch her. However horrible an experience she'd been through, she'd lived the first eighteen years of her life completely sheltered. Like some princess in an enchanted forest in a fairy tale. He was years older—not the six that separated them chronologically, but in experience. He had no right to take advantage of that.

As he switched to flies, the practical side of his mind reminded him she was also smart, strong and capable. She was ambitious and her eyes were as ancient as a goddess's. Those were traits she owned that appealed to him every bit as much as the shyness she tried to hide.

He hadn't taken advantage of her. She'd responded, she'd all but melted against him, goddamn it. She had to feel something of what he felt. That bond, that connection, the absolute rightness of it.

Then he circled back around and berated himself for thinking with his glands.

That had to stop. He'd call her, ask her if they could meet for coffee later. Something simple. Then he'd tell her about the book he was preparing to write. He'd explain things carefully, how he was going to contact everyone involved in the case. That he'd started with her because she'd been the reason the idea had formed in his mind in the first place.

He wondered if the seed had been planted the first time he'd seen her.

He set the weights aside, mopped his face with a towel. He'd call her as soon as he'd gone up to his room and showered. And he'd do what he now realized he should have done as soon as she'd opened her apartment door to him.

Feeling better, looser, he bypassed the elevator and took the stairs to the ninth floor.

And jolted to a halt when he saw her standing in front of his door, digging through an oversized purse.

"Liv?"

"God!" She nearly stumbled back, then stared at him. "You startled me." She kept her hands buried in her bag until she was sure they wouldn't shake. "I was just about to write you a note and slip it under your door."

She sent him a smile and stood there looking neat and fresh in jeans and a boxy jacket. When he didn't respond, she shifted uneasily. "I hope you don't mind that I came by."

"No, sorry." He couldn't afford to let her dazzle him again. "I just wasn't expecting you. I was down in the gym."

"Really? I would never have guessed."

His quick grin had the worst of the tension smoothing out of her stomach. He dug his keycard out of his pocket, slid it into the door. "Come on in. And you can tell me instead of writing a note."

"I had some time between classes." That was a lie. She was, for the first time in her college career, skipping class. How could she be expected to concentrate on wildlife ecology when she was planning to ask him to take her to bed?

Oh God, how could she possibly tell him why she'd come? How would she begin?

"Time enough for coffee?"

"I . . . yes. I was going to invite you to dinner—a home-cooked meal."

"Oh yeah? Much better than coffee." He tried to think. He could talk to her more privately at her apartment. She'd be more comfortable there. She was obviously nervous now, standing in his cramped hotel room, with her hands locked together while she flicked uneasy glances toward the bed.

So they'd get out. All he had to do was keep his hands off her in the meantime.

"I need to clean up a little," he told her.

"Ah . . ." He looked wonderful, damp from his workout, the muscles in his arms toned and tough. She remembered how strong they'd been when they'd banded around her. "I just have to pick up a few things at the market."

"Tell you what. Give me a chance to take a shower, and we'll both go to the market. Then I can watch you cook."

"All right."

He grabbed jeans from the back of a chair, hunted up a shirt. "There's a very miserly honor bar under the TV. Help yourself. We've got cable," he added as he dug socks and underwear out of a drawer. "Just have a seat. Give me ten minutes."

"Take your time." The minute he closed the door to the bathroom, she lowered herself to the edge of the bed. Her knees were shaking.

Good Lord, how was she going to manage this and not make a complete fool of herself? Marketing, they were going marketing. She wanted to giggle wildly. She'd just come from the drugstore where she'd had to gather every fiber of her courage to walk to the counter and buy condoms.

Now they lay in her purse, weighing like lead. Not because of the heft of the decision she'd made, but because of the fear that she'd misread what she'd seen in his eyes the night before. What she'd tasted when he'd kissed her.

She had intended to ask him to dinner, but that would have been after. After she'd knocked on his door, after he'd opened it and she'd smiled and stepped to him, slipped her arms around him, kissed him.

She'd imagined it so perfectly that when she'd knocked and he hadn't answered, she'd been completely baffled, and now nothing was going as she'd scripted it in her head.

She'd come here to offer herself, to tell him she wanted him to be the one. She'd imagined more—the way his eyes would focus on her face, so deep, so intense, until her vision blurred and his mouth would cover hers.

The way he'd pick her up—even the quick rushing feel in her stomach the sweep of that would cause. How he'd carry her to the bed.

She let out a breath and got up to pace. Of course she'd built up the room differently in her mind. It had been larger, with prettier colors, a soft spread over the bed, a mountain of pillows.

She'd added candlelight.

This room was small, with colors of gray and faded rose. Bland, she thought, as so many hotel rooms were. But it didn't matter. She closed her eyes and listened to the water drumming in the shower.

What would he do if she went in, if she quietly stripped, stepped into the steam and spray with him? Would their bodies come together then? Wet and hot and ready.

She didn't have the courage for it. Sighing, she walked to the honor bar, perused the selections without interest, wandered to the desk where he'd set up his computer and piles of disorganized notes and files.

She'd wait until he came out. She was better at dealing with matters, both small and vital, in a clear, face-to-face fashion. She wasn't the sultry seductress and never would be.

Would that disappoint him?

Annoyed with herself, she shook her head. She had to stop second-guessing him, criticizing herself. When he came back out again, she would simply let him know she wanted him, and see what happened next.

Idly, she tidied his notes, tapping edges together. She liked the fact that he'd brought work with him. She respected the ambition, the dedication, the energy. It was important to respect someone you loved.

He hadn't talked very much about his work, she thought now, then rolled her eyes. Because she'd been too busy babbling about herself. She'd ask him about it, she decided. About what he liked best in his work, how it felt to see his words in print and know that people read them.

She thought it must be a wonderful, satisfying feeling, and smiled over it as she stacked his notes.

The name MacBride, scrawled in black ink on a yellow legal pad caught her eye, had her frowning, lifting the sheet of paper.

Within seconds, her blood had gone cold and she was riffling through his work without a thought for his privacy.

NOAH RUBBED A TOWEL OVER HIS HAIR AND WORKED OUT exactly what he would say to Olivia. Once they'd come to an agreement on professional terms, they'd work on the personal ones. He could go to River's End and spend some time with her that summer. To do the interviews, certainly. But to be with her. He'd never known a woman he was so compelled to be with.

He'd have to arrange for more time off from the newspaper. Or just fucking quit, he thought, staring at his own face in the steamy mirror. Of course he'd have to figure out how the hell he was going to live until the book was written and sold. But he'd work that out.

He never doubted it would sell. He was meant to write books, and he was damn sure he was meant to write this one.

And he was beginning to think, not entirely easily, that he was meant to be with Olivia.

None of that would happen until he took the first step.

He took one, into the bedroom, and heard the world crash around his ears. She was standing by his desk, his papers in her hands, and a look of iced fury in those amber eyes.

"You son of a bitch." She said it quietly, but the words ripped the air like a scream. "You scheming, calculating bastard."

"Just a minute."

"Don't touch me." She slapped him back with the words even as he started toward her. "Don't think about touching me. You're here on your own, not as a reporter. Fucking liar, it was all for a story."

"No." He stepped to the side to block her before she could stride to the door. "Just wait. I'm not here for the paper."

She still held his notes and, looking him dead in the eye, crumpled them in her hand and tossed them in his face.

"Just how big a fool do you think I am?"

"I don't." He grabbed her arms. He expected her to struggle, to claw and spit and scratch. Instead she went rigid. She turned off. He could see in her eyes the way she simply shut off. A little desperate, he gave her a quick, light shake.

"Listen, goddamn it. It's not for the paper. I want to write a book. I should have told you, I meant to tell you. Then . . . Jesus, Liv, you know what happened. The minute I looked at you everything got confused. I wanted to spend some time with you. I needed to. That's a first for me. Every time I looked at you . . . I just went under."

"You used me." She'd be cold, she'd stay cold. Nothing he could say, nothing he could do could penetrate the wall of ice. She wouldn't permit it. She wouldn't let herself fall into that trap again.

"If I did, I'm sorry. I let what I felt for you get in the way of what was right. Last night, walking away from you was the hardest thing I've ever done. I wanted you so much it ached right down to the bone."

"You'd have slept with me to get information for your book." Stay cold, she ordered herself. Pain couldn't cut through ice.

"No." It ripped at his guts that she would think it, that she would believe it. "You have to know better than that. What happened between us had nothing to do with the book. It was about you and me. I wanted you, Liv, from the minute you opened your door, but I couldn't touch you until I'd explained everything. I was going to talk to you about it tonight."

"Were you?" There was a snap of amusement in her voice—frigid amusement that cut like frosted razors. "That's very convenient, Noah. Take your hands off me."

"You have to listen to me."

"No, I don't. I don't have to listen to you. I don't have to look at you. I don't have to think about you ever again once I'm out of this room. So I'll finish this, here and now. Pay attention."

She pushed his hands away, and her eyes were level, a burning gold. "This is my life, not yours. My business, no one else's. I won't cooperate with your goddamn book, and neither will my family. I'll see to it. And if I find out you've tried to contact anyone I care about, anyone who matters to me, I'll do everything I can to make you suffer."

She shoved him back. "Stay away from me and mine, Brady. If you call me again, if you contact me again, I'll ask my aunt to use every bit of her influence to see you're fired from the *Times*. And if you've done your research, you know just how much influence she has."

The threat taunted his own temper, had him yanking it back. "I've hurt you. I'm sorry. I didn't realize what I'd feel for you, how huge it could be. I didn't plan what happened here, between us."

"As far as I'm concerned, nothing happened between us. I despise you and everyone like you. Keep away from me." She snatched up her bag, shoved by him to the door. "I once told you that your father was a great man. He is. Beside him, Noah, you're very small."

She didn't even bother to slam the door. He watched it close with a quiet click.

She didn't run, but she wanted to. Her chest was full and heavy, her eyes stinging with tears she refused to shed. He'd used her; he'd betrayed her. She'd let herself love, she'd let herself trust, and what she'd gotten had been lies.

He'd never wanted her. He'd wanted her mother, her father. He'd wanted the blood and the grief. She would never, never give them to him.

She would never give her trust to anyone again.

She wondered if her mother had felt anything like this when she'd known the man she'd loved was a lie. If she'd felt this emptiness, this sick sadness, this burning betrayal.

Olivia let rage coat over misery and promised herself she'd never think of Noah Brady again.

ELEVEN

Venice, California, 1999

NOAH Brady figured his life was just about perfect. Thanks to the critical and popular success of his first book, he had his trim little bungalow on the beach and the financial resources to live pretty much as he liked.

He loved his work—the intensity and punch of writing true crime with the bent of sliding into the mind and heart of those who chose murder as a solution, or as recreation. It was much more satisfying than the four years he'd worked as a reporter, forced to accept assignments and to gear his style to fit the newspaper.

God knew it paid better, he thought, as he jogged the last of his daily three-mile run along the beach.

Not that he was in it for the money, but the money sure as hell didn't hurt.

Now with his second book just hitting the bookstores, the reviews and sales solid, he figured it didn't get much better.

He was young, healthy, successful and blissfully unattached—since he'd recently untangled himself from a relationship that had started off intriguing, sexy and fun and had degenerated into mildly annoying.

Who'd have thought that Caryn, self-described party girl and wanna-be actress, would have morphed into a clinging, suffocating female who whined and sulked every time he wanted an evening on his own?

He knew he'd been in trouble when more and more of her things started taking up permanent residence in his closet and drawers. When her makeup began making itself at home on his bathroom counter. He'd come dangerously close to living with her mostly by default. No, not default, *his* fault, Noah corrected, because he'd been so preoccupied with the research and writing on his next book he'd barely noticed.

Which, of course, is what pissed her off enough to send her into a raging, tearful snit when she'd tossed accusations of selfishness and neglect at him while she'd tossed her things into a tote bag the size of Kansas. She'd broken two lamps—one nearly over his head, but he'd been quicker—had upended his prized gloxinia into a mess of soil, broken leaves and shattered pottery. Then she'd walked out on him, flipping back her long, straight California blond hair.

As he'd stood, just a little dazed in the middle of the debris, she'd shot him a killing look out of brimming blue eyes and had told him he could reach her at Marva's when he was man enough to apologize.

Noah decided he was man enough to be relieved when the door slammed behind her.

That hadn't stopped her from leaving messages on his machine that ranged from snotty to weepy to raging. He didn't know what was wrong with her. She was a stunningly beautiful woman in a town that worshiped beautiful women. She was hardly going to spend time alone if she wanted a man to play with.

It never occurred to him that she might have been in love with him. Or at least believed herself to be.

His mother would have said that was typical of him. He was able to see inside strangers, victims, witnesses, the guilty and the innocent with uncanny insight and interest. But when it came to personal relationships, he barely skimmed the surface.

He'd wanted to once, and the results had been disastrous. For Olivia, and for him.

It had taken him months to get over those three days he'd spent with her. To get over her. In time he'd managed to convince himself it had been the book after all, the thirst to write it, that had tilted his feelings for her into something he'd nearly thought was love.

She'd simply interested him, and attracted him, and because of that— and inexperience—he'd handled the entire situation badly. He'd found ways to put that aside, just as he'd put the idea of that particular book aside. He'd found other women, and other murders.

When he thought of Olivia, it was with regret, guilt and a wondering about what might have been.

So he tried not to think of it.

He jogged toward the tidy, two-story bungalow the color of butter-milk. The sun splattered over the red-tile roof, shot out from the windows. It might have been late March, but southern California was experiencing a sultry heat wave that delighted him.

Out of habit, he went around to the front of the house to get his mail. The floods of color in his flower beds were the envy of his neighbors.

He went inside, moving straight through the living area he'd furnished sparsely, and dumped the mail on the kitchen counter, then pulled a large bottle of spring water from the fridge.

He glanced at his answering machine, saw he'd already accumulated four messages since he'd gone out for his run. Fearing at least one would be from the now-dreaded Caryn, he decided to make coffee and toast a couple of bagels before he played them back.

A guy needed fuel for certain tasks.

He tossed his sunglasses on top of his pile of mail and got down to the first order of business. While the coffee brewed, he switched on the portable TV, flipping through the morning talk shows to see if there was a topic of interest to him.

His bedroom VCR would have taped the *Today* show while he'd been out. He'd catch up with that later, see what was up in the world, skim through it for the news headlines. He'd brought the morning papers in before his run, and he'd get to them as well, spending at least an hour, if not two, absorbing the top stories, the metro reports, the crime.

You just never knew where the next book would come from.

He glanced again at the light blinking on his answering machine but decided his mail was a higher priority than his phone messages. Not that he was procrastinating, he thought as he sat at the counter with his single-man's breakfast and listened with half an ear to *Jerry Springer*.

He scooped back his hair, thought vaguely about a haircut and worked his way through the usual complement of bills and junk mail. There was a nice little packet of reader mail forwarded by his publisher that he decided to read and savor later, his monthly issue of *Prison Life* and a postcard from a friend vacationing in Maui.

Then he picked up a plain white envelope with his name and address carefully handwritten on it. The return address was San Quentin.

He received mail from prisoners routinely, but not, Noah thought with a frown, at his home address. Sometimes they wanted to kick his ass on general principles, but for the most part they were certain he'd want to write their story.

He hesitated over the letter, not sure if he should be annoyed or concerned that someone in one of those cages had his home address. But when he had opened it and skimmed the first lines, his heart gave a quick jerk that was both shock and fascination.

Dear Noah Brady,

My name is Sam Tanner. I think you'll know who I am. We are, in a way, connected. Your father was the primary investigating officer in my wife's murder, and the man who arrested me.

You may or may not be aware that he has attended all of my parole hearings since I began serving my sentence. You could say Frank and I have kept in touch.

I read with interest your book Hunt by Night. *Your clear-sighted and somewhat dispassionate look into the mind and methods of James Trolly made his systematic selection and mutilation of male prostitutes in West*

*Hollywood more chilling and real than any of the stories in the media
during his spree five years ago.*

As an actor I have a great appreciation for a strong, clearheaded writer.

*It has been some years since I've bothered to speak to reporters, to the
freelance journalists and writers who initially clamored to tell my story. I
made mistakes in whom I trusted, and was paid back by having my words
twisted to suit the public's thirst for scandal and gossip.*

*In reading your work, I've come to believe that you're interested in the
truth, in the real people and events that took place. I find this interesting,
given my connection to your father. Almost as if it's been fated. I've come
to believe in fate over these last years.*

*I would like to tell you my story. I'd like you to write it. If you're
interested, I think you know where to find me.*

I'm not going anywhere for a few more months.

Sincerely,
Sam Tanner

"Well, well." Noah scratched his chin and read over the high points
of the letter again. When his phone rang, he ignored it. When Caryn's
angry voice shot out accusing him of being an insensitive pig, cursing
him and swearing revenge, he barely heard.

"Oh, I'm interested all right, Sam. I've been interested in you for
twenty years."

He had files stuffed full on Sam Tanner, Julie MacBride and the Beverly
Hills murder his father had investigated. He'd kept them and had continued to accumulate data even after his painful visit to Olivia at college.

He'd put the book aside, but not his interest in the case. And not his
determination to one day write the book that would tell the story from
all angles.

But he'd put it aside for six years, he thought now, because every time
he started to work on it again, he saw the way Olivia had looked at him
when she'd stood by the desk in that little hotel room, with his papers
gripped in her hands.

This time when that image tried to form, he blocked it out. He couldn't, and wouldn't, channel his work because of a blighted love affair.

An exclusive series of interviews with Sam Tanner. They'd have to be exclusive, Noah thought as he got to his feet to pace. He was going to make that a condition from the get-go.

He'd need a list of everyone involved, even peripherally. Family, friends, employees, associates. Excitement pumped through his blood as he began to outline his research strategy. Court transcripts. Maybe he could track down some of the members of the jury. Police reports.

The thought of that brought him up short. His father. He wasn't at all sure his father was going to be happy with the idea.

He headed to the shower to clean up. And to give himself time to think.

THE BRADY HOUSE HADN'T CHANGED A GREAT DEAL OVER the years. It was still the same pale rose stucco, the lawn nicely mowed and the flowers on the edge of death. Since his father had retired from the force the year before, he'd piddled with a variety of hobbies including golf, photography, woodworking and cooking. He'd decided he hated golf after the first nine holes. He'd also decided that he had no eye for photography, no affinity for wood and no skill in the kitchen.

Six months after his retirement, Celia sat him down, told him she loved him more than she had the day they'd married. And if he didn't find something to do and get out of her house she was going to kill him in his sleep.

The local youth center saved his life and his marriage. Most afternoons he could be found there, coaching the kids on the basketball court as he'd once coached his son, listening to their complaints and triumphs and breaking up the inevitable fights and squabbles.

Mornings, after Celia had gone off to work, he spent puttering, doing crosswords or sitting in the backyard reading one of the paperback mystery novels he'd become addicted to since murder was no longer a part of his daily routine.

That's where Noah found him, his long legs stretched out in front of him as he relaxed in a lawn chair under a stingy patch of shade.

He wore jeans, ancient sneakers and a comfortably wrinkled cotton shirt. His hair had gone a shimmering pewter gray but remained full and thick.

"Do you know how hard it is to kill geraniums?" Noah glanced at the withered pink blooms struggling along the back deck. "It almost has to be premeditated."

"You'll never convict me." Pleased to see his son, Frank set aside the latest John Sandford novel.

Merely shaking his head, Noah unwound the hose, switched it on and gave the desperate flowers another shot at life.

"Didn't expect to see you until Sunday."

"Sunday?"

"Your mother's birthday." Frank narrowed his eyes. "You didn't forget?"

"No. I've already got her present. It's a wolf." He turned his head to grin. "Don't panic, she doesn't get to keep it here. She gets to adopt one in the wild, and they keep tabs on it for her. I figured she'd go for that— and the earrings I picked up."

"Show-off," Frank grumbled and crossed his feet at the ankles. "You're still going out to dinner with us Sunday, though?"

"Wouldn't miss it."

"You can bring that girl if you want, the one you've been seeing."

"That would be Caryn, who just left me a message on my machine calling me a pig. I'm steering clear of her."

"Good. Your mother didn't like her."

"She only met her once."

"Didn't like her. 'Shallow,' 'snooty,' 'stupid' I believe were the three words she used."

"It's annoying how she's always right." Satisfied the geraniums would live another day, Noah turned off the hose and began to wind it back on its wheel.

Frank said nothing for a moment, just watched while his son carefully aligned the hose. Carefully enough to make Frank's lips twitch. "You know, I was a pretty good detective. I don't think you came here to water my flowers."

When he couldn't use the hose to stall any longer, Noah slid his hands in the back pockets of his jeans. "I got a letter this morning. Guy in San Quentin wants me to tell his story."

"And?" Frank raised his eyebrows. "You get fairly regular correspondence from criminals these days, don't you?"

"Yeah, most of it's useless. But I'm interested in this case. Been interested in it for a while." He took off his sunglasses, met his father's eyes levelly. "About twenty years now. It's Sam Tanner, Dad."

There was a little hitch in Frank's heart rate. Beat, hesitation, beat. He didn't jolt. He'd been a cop too long to jump at shadows and ghosts, but he braced. "I see. No, I don't see," he said immediately and pushed out of his chair. "I put that son of a bitch away and now he writes to you? He wants to talk to the son of the man who helped send him over, who's made goddamn sure he stayed over for twenty years? That's bullshit, Noah. Dangerous bullshit."

"He mentioned the connection." Noah kept his tone mild. He didn't want to argue, hated knowing he was going to upset his father, but his decision was already made. "Why did you go to all his parole hearings?"

"Some things you don't forget. And because you don't, because you can't, you make sure the job stays done." And he'd made a promise to a young girl with haunted eyes as they'd stood in the deep shadows of the forest. "He hasn't forgotten either. What better way to pay me back than to use you?"

"He can't hurt me, Dad."

"I imagine that's just what Julie MacBride thought the night she opened the door to him. Stay away from him, Noah. Put this one aside."

"You haven't." He held up a hand before Frank could speak. "Just listen a minute. You did your job. It cost you. I remember how it was. You'd pace the floor at night, or come out here to sit in the dark. I know there were others that followed you home, but nothing ever like this one.

So I never forgot it either. I guess you could say it's followed me, too. This one's part of us. All of us. I've wanted to write this book for years. I have to talk to Sam Tanner."

"If you do that, Noah, and go on to write this book, drag out all that ugliness again, do you realize what it might do to Tanner's other victims? The parents, the sister. Her child?"

Olivia. No, Noah told himself, he was not going to cloud the issue with Olivia. Not now. "I thought about what it might do to you. That's why I'm here. I wanted you to know what I'm going to do."

"It's a mistake."

"Maybe, but it's my life now, and my job."

"You think he'd have contacted you if you weren't mine?" Fear and fury sprang out in equal measures, turning Frank's eyes hard, snapping into his voice like the crack of a bullet. "The son of a bitch refuses to talk to anyone for years—and they've tried to get to him. Brokaw, Walters, Oprah. No comment, no interviews, no nothing. Now, just months before he's likely to get out, he contacts you, offers you the story on a plate. Damn it, Noah, it doesn't have to do with your work. It has to do with mine."

"Maybe." Noah's tone chilled as he slipped his sunglasses back on. "And maybe it has to do with both. Whether or not you respect my work, it's what I do. And what I'm going to keep doing."

"I never said I didn't respect your work."

"No, but you never said otherwise either." It was a bruise Noah just realized he'd been nursing. "I'll take my breaks where I find them and make them work for me. I learned that from you. I'll see you Sunday."

Frank stepped forward, started to speak. But Noah was already striding away. So he sat, feeling his age, and stared down at his own hands.

NOAH'S FOUL MOOD DROVE HOME WITH HIM, LIKE A SEPArate energy, an irritable passenger in the stone-gray BMW. He kept the top down, the radio up, trying to blow away the anger, drown out his thoughts.

He hated the sudden discovery that he was hurt because his father had never done a tap dance of joy over the success of his books.

It was stupid, he thought. He was old enough not to need the whistles and claps of parental approval. He wasn't eighteen and scoring the winning basket at the tail of the fourth quarter any longer. He was a grown man both happy and successful in his profession. He was well paid, and his ego got all the boosts it required from reviews and royalty checks, thank you very much.

But he knew, had known all along, that his father disapproved of the path he'd taken with his writing. Because neither had wanted to confront the other, little had been said.

Until today, Noah thought.

Sam Tanner had done more than offer a story to be told. He'd put the first visible crack in a relationship Noah had counted on all his life. It had been there before, hidden, from the first moment he'd decided to write about all the ripples on the river of murder.

Fiction would have been fine, Noah knew. Entertaining. But digging and exposing the realities, stripping down killers, victims, survivals for public consumption. That's what his father disliked—and couldn't understand.

And just now, because he didn't know how to explain it, Noah's mood teetered on the edge of vile.

Spotting Caryn's car parked in front of his house tripped it over the rest of the way.

He found her sitting on his back deck, her long, smooth legs clad in tiny pink shorts, a wide-brimmed straw hat protecting her face from the sun. When he opened the glass door, she looked up, her eyes brimming behind the amber lenses of her designer sunglasses. Her lips trembled.

"Oh, Noah. I'm so sorry. I don't know what came over me."

He cocked his head. It would've been fascinating if it hadn't been so tedious. It was a pattern he recognized from their weeks together. Fight, curse, accuse, throw things, slam out. Then come back with tearful eyes and apologize.

Now, unless she'd decided to deviate from form, she would slither around him and offer sex.

When she rose, smiling tremulously as she crossed to him and slid her arms around him, he decided she just didn't have the imagination to improvise.

"I've been so unhappy without you these last few days." She lifted her mouth to his. "Let's go inside so I can show you how much I've missed you."

It worried him a little that he wasn't tempted, not in the least.

"Caryn. It's not going to work. Why don't we just say it was fun while it lasted?"

"You don't mean it."

"Yes." He had to nudge her back so she'd stop rubbing against him. "I do."

"There's someone else, isn't there? All the time we were living together, you were cheating on me."

"No, there's no one else. And we weren't living together. You just started staying here."

"You bastard. You've already had another woman in our bed." She rushed past him, into the house.

"It's not *our* bed. It's my bed. Goddamn it." He was more weary than angry, until he walked into the bedroom and saw she was already ripping at his sheets. "Hey! Cut it out."

He made a grab for her, but she rolled onto the bed, leaped off the other side. Before he could stop her, she'd grabbed the bedside lamp and heaved it at him. The best he could do was block it so the base didn't rap him between the eyes.

The sound of the glass crashing on the floor snapped the already unsteady hold on his temper.

"Okay, that's it. Get out. Get the hell out of my house and stay away from me."

"You never cared. You never thought about my feelings."

"You're right, absolutely." He went for her as she made a beeline for his prized basketball trophy. "I didn't give a damn about you." He panted it out as he struggled to get her out without losing any of his own skin to her long, lethal nails. "I'm a pig, a creep, a son of a bitch."

"I hate you!" She shrieked it, slapping and kicking as he dragged her to the front door. "I wish you were dead!"

"Just pretend I am. And I'll do the same for you." He shoved her outside, shut the door, then leaned back against it.

He let out a long breath, rolled his shoulders. Then because he hadn't heard her car start, glanced out the window. Just in time to see her rake her keys over the glossy finish of his BMW.

He roared like a wounded lion. By the time he had flung open the door and burst out, she was leaping into her own car, squealing away.

Hands clenched, he looked at the damage. Deep, nasty scratches formed letters on the hood. PI. At least she hadn't had the satisfaction of finishing the thought, he decided.

Okay, fine. He'd have the car repaired while he was out of town. It seemed like a very good time to head north to San Quentin.

TWELVE

N OAH'S first distant glimpse of San Quentin made him think of an
old fortress now serving as some sort of thematic resort complex.
Disneyland for cons.

The building was the color of sand and stretched out over San
Francisco Bay with its multilevels and towers and turrets with a faintly
exotic air.

It didn't smack of prison unless you thought of the armed guards in
those towers, the spread of security lights that would turn the air around
it orange and eerie at night. And all the steel cages it held inside.

He'd opted to take the ferry from San Francisco to Marin County
and now stood at the rail while it glided over water made choppy by the
wind. He found the architecture of the prison odd and somehow very
Californian, but doubted the inmates had much appreciation for the structure's aesthetics.

It had taken him only hours to clear through channels for permission
to visit. It made Noah wonder if Tanner had connections on the inside
that had helped smooth the way.

Didn't matter, Noah decided while the wind cut through his hair like jagged shards of glass. The results were what counted.

He'd taken a day to read through his files on the MacBride murder, to study, refresh his memory, to consider. He knew the man he would meet as well as anyone from the outside was able to, he imagined.

At least he knew the man Tanner had been.

A hardworking, talented actor with an impressive string of successful movies under his belt by the time he'd met Julie MacBride, his co-star in *Summer Thunder*. He'd also, by all accounts, had an impressive string of females associated with his name before he'd married. It had been a first marriage for both of them, though he'd been seriously involved with Lydia Loring, a very hot property during the seventies. The gossip columns had had a field day with their stormy and very public breakup once he'd set his sights on Julie.

He'd enjoyed his fame, his money and his women. And had continued to enjoy the first two after his marriage. There'd been no other women after Julie. Or, Noah mused, he'd been very, very discreet.

Insiders called him difficult, temperamental, then had begun to use terms like "explosive temper," "unreasonable demands" when his two films after *Summer Thunder* had tanked at the box office.

He'd begun to show up late and unprepared for shooting, had fired his personal assistant, then his agent.

It became one of Hollywood's worst-kept secrets that he was using, and using heavily.

So he'd become obsessive about his wife, delusional about the people around him, focused on Lucas Manning as his nemesis and, in the end, violent.

In 1975, he'd been the top box-office actor in the country. By 1980, he'd become an inmate in San Quentin. It was a long way to fall in a short amount of time.

The careless spread of staggering wealth and fame, the easy access to the most beautiful women in the world, the scrambling of maître d's to provide the best tables, the A-list for parties, the cheers of fans. How would it feel to have that sliding through your fingers? Noah wondered. Add arrogance, ego, mix it with cocaine, a little freebasing, jealousy over an up-and-coming box-office rival and a shattered marriage, and you had a perfect formula for disaster.

It would be interesting to see what the last twenty years had added, or taken away, from Sam Tanner.

He was back in his rental car when the ferry docked, and anxious to get on with it. Though he hoped to be done with the initial interview in time to get back to the airport and catch the evening flight home, he'd tossed a few things in a bag just in case he decided to stay over.

He hadn't mentioned the trip to anyone.

As he waited his turn, he drummed his fingers on the wheel to the Spice Girls and inexplicably thought of Olivia MacBride.

Oddly, the image that came to his mind was of a tall, gangly girl with pale hair and tanned arms. Of sad eyes as they'd sat on a riverbank watching beavers splash. He had done his research, but had found nothing public on her since her childhood. A few speculations now and then in the press, a recap story, the reprint of that stunning photo of her grief when she'd been four—that was all the mass media could manage.

Her family had pulled the walls up, he thought, and she'd stayed behind them. Just as her father had stayed behind the thick sand-colored walls of his prison. It was an angle he intended to pursue.

When the time came, he'd do whatever it took to convince her to speak with him again, to cooperate with the book. He could only hope that after six years her bitterness toward him would have lost its edge. That the sensible—and wonderfully sweet—science student he'd spent such a lovely few days with would see the value and the purpose of what he meant to do.

Beyond that, he couldn't think of what it would be like to see her again. So he tucked her away in his mind and concentrated on today.

He drove his rental car down the road toward the prison, passed an old pier and a pumping station. He caught a glimpse of a paved trail which he assumed led down to the water, and what might have been a little park, though he wondered why anyone would want to loiter or picnic in the shadow of those forbidding walls.

The visitors' parking lot skirted a small, attractive beach, with the waters a dull iron gray beyond. He'd considered a tape recorder, or at least a notebook, but had decided to go in cold. Just impressions, this time. He didn't want to give Tanner the idea he was making a commitment.

The visitors' entrance was a long hall with a side door halfway down. The single window was covered with notices, preventing views from either side. There was a sign on the door that had a chill sliding down his spine even as his lips quirked in wry amusement:

PLEASE DO NOT KNOCK. WE KNOW YOU ARE OUT THERE. WE WILL GET TO YOU AS SOON AS POSSIBLE.

So he stood, alone in the empty hallway with the wind whistling stridently, waiting for those who knew he was there to get to him.

When they did, he relayed his business, gave his ID, filled out the required forms. There was no small talk, no polite smiles.

He'd been the route before—in New York, in Florida. He'd been on death row and felt the ice slick through his gut at the sound of doors sliding shut and footsteps echoing. He'd spoken to lifers, the condemned and already damned.

He'd smelled the hate, the fear and the calculation, as much a stink in the air as sweat and piss and hand-rolled cigarettes.

He was taken down a hallway, bypassing the main visitors' area, and shown into a small, cheerless room with a table and two chairs. The door was thick with a single window of reinforced glass.

And there, Noah had his first look at what had become of Sam Tanner.

Gone was the pampered screen idol with the million-dollar smile. This was a hard man, body and face. Noah wondered how much his mind had toughened as well. He sat, one hand chained, the bright orange prison jumpsuit baggy and stark. His hair was cut brutally short and had gone a nearly uniform ash gray.

The lines dug deep into his face gave him the look of a man well beyond his age of fifty-eight. And Noah remembered another inmate once telling him prison years were long dog years. Every one behind bars was the equal of seven out in the world.

The eyes were a sharp and cold blue that took their time studying

Noah, barely flicked toward the guard when they were told they had thirty minutes.

"Glad you could make it, Mr. Brady."

That hadn't changed, Noah realized. The voice was as smooth and rich and potent as it had been in his last movie. Noah sat as the door closed and the locked snicked into place at his back.

"How did you get my home address, Mr. Tanner?"

A ghost of a smile played around his mouth. "I still have some connections. How's your father?"

Noah kept his eyes level and ignored the jolt in his gut. "My father's fine. I can't say he sends his best."

Sam's teeth bared in a fleeting grin. "A straight-up cop, Frank Brady. I see him and Jamie . . . now and again. She's still a pretty woman, my former sister-in-law. I wonder just how close her and your old man are."

"Did you get me all the way up here to annoy me, Tanner, with speculations on my father's personal life?"

The smile came back, small and sly. "I haven't had much interesting conversation lately. Got any reals?"

Noah lifted a brow. He knew most of the basic prison terms. "No, sorry. I don't smoke."

"Fucking California." With his free hand, Sam reached inside his jumpsuit, carefully removed the tape that affixed a single hand-rolled cigarette and wooden match to his chest. "Making prisons nonsmoking facilities. Where do they come up with this shit?"

He lighted the match with his thumbnail, then puffed the cigarette to life. "Used to be I had the resources for a full brick a day. A couple packs of reals is decent currency inside. Now I'm lucky to get a carton a month."

"It's lousy the way they treat murderers these days."

Those hard blue eyes only glimmered—amusement or disdain, Noah couldn't be sure. "Are you interested in crime and punishment, Brady, or are you interested in the story?"

"One goes with the other."

"Does it?" Sam blew out a stream of ugly-smelling smoke. "I've had a long time to think about that. You know, I can't remember the taste of good scotch, or the smell of a beautiful woman. You can deal with the sex. There are plenty inside who'll bend over for you if that's what you want. Otherwise you've always got your hand. But sometimes you wake up in the middle of the night just aching for the smell of a woman."

He jerked a shoulder. "There ain't no substitute. Me, I read a lot to get through those times. I used to stick to novels, pick a part in one and imagine playing it when I got out. I loved acting." He said it with the same cold look in his eyes. "I loved everything about it. It took me a long time to accept that part of my life was over, too."

Noah angled his head. "Is it? What role are you playing here, Tanner?"

Abruptly, Sam leaned forward, and for the first time life sprang into his eyes, hot and real. "This is all I've got. You think because you come in here and talk to cons you understand what it's like? You can get up and walk out anytime. You'll never understand."

"There's not much stopping me from getting up and walking out now," Noah said evenly. "What do you want?"

"I want you to tell it, to put it all down. To say how it was then, how it is now. To say why things happened and why they didn't. Why two people who had everything lost it all."

"And you're going to tell me all that?"

"Yeah, I'm going to tell you all of it." Sam leaned back, drawing out the last stingy sliver of his smoke. "And you're going to find out the rest."

"Why? Why me, why now?"

"Why you?" Sam dropped the smoldering bit of paper and tobacco on the floor, absently crushed it out. "I liked your book," he said simply. "And I couldn't resist the irony of the connection. Seemed almost like a sign. I'm not one of the pitiful who found God in here. God has nothing to do with places like this, and He doesn't come here. But there's fate, and there's timing."

"You want to consider me fate, okay. What's the timing?"

"I'm dying."

Noah skimmed his gaze coolly over Sam's face. "You look healthy enough to me."

"Brain tumor." Sam tapped a finger on his head. "Inoperable. The doctors say maybe a year, if I'm lucky—and if I'm lucky, I'll die in the world and not inside. We're working on that. It looks like the system's going to be satisfied with my twenty now that I'm dead anyway."

He seemed to find that amusing and chuckled over it. It wasn't a sound that encouraged the listener to join in. "You could say I've got a new sentence, short stretch with no possibility of parole. So, if you're interested, you'll have to work fast."

"You've got something new to add to everything that's been said, printed, filmed over the last couple of decades?"

"Do you want to find out?"

Noah tapped a finger on the table. "I'll think about it." He rose. "I'll get back to you."

"Brady," Sam said as Noah moved to the door. "You didn't ask if I killed my wife."

Noah glanced back, met his eyes dead on. "Why would I?" he said and signaled for the guard.

Sam smiled a little. He thought the first meeting had gone well and never doubted Frank Brady's son would come back.

NOAH SAT IN PRISON SUPERVISOR DITERMAN'S OFFICE, SUR-prised and a little flattered that his request for a meeting had been so quickly granted. Hollywood would never have cast George Diterman in the role of head of one of the country's most active prisons. With his thinning patch of hair, small build and round black-framed glasses, he looked like a man very low on the feeding chain of a midlevel accounting firm.

He greeted Noah with a brisk handshake and a surprisingly charming smile. "I enjoyed your first book," he began as he took his place behind his desk. "And I'm already enjoying the second."

"Thank you."

"And should I assume you're here gathering information to write another?"

"I've just spoken with Sam Tanner."

"Yes, I'm aware of that." Diterman folded his small, neat hands on the edge of his desk. "I cleared the request."

"Because you admire my work or because of Tanner?"

"A little of both. I've been in this position in this facility for five years. During that period Tanner has been what you'd call a model prisoner. He stays out of trouble, he does his work in the prison library well. He follows the rules."

"Rehabilitated?" Noah asked with just enough cynicism in his tone to make Diterman smile again.

"That depends on which definition you choose. Society's, the law's, this house's. But I can say that at some point, he decided to do his time clean."

Diterman unlaced his fingers, pressed them together, laced them tidily again. "Tanner's authorized me to give you access to his records and to speak to you frankly about him."

He works fast, Noah mused. Fine. He'd been waiting a long time to begin this book, and he intended to work fast himself. "Then why don't you, Supervisor, speak frankly to me about Inmate Tanner."

"According to reports, he had a difficult time adjusting when he first came here. There were a number of incidents—altercations between him and the guards, between him and other prisoners. Inmate Tanner spent a large portion of 1980 in the infirmary being treated for a number of injuries."

"He got into fights."

"Consistently. He was violent and invited violence. He was transfered to solitary several times during his first five years. He also had an addiction to cocaine and found sources within the prison to feed that addiction. During the fall of 1982 he was treated for an overdose."

"Deliberate or accidental?"

"That remains unclear, though the therapist leaned toward accidental. He's an actor, a good one." Diterman's eyes remained bland, but Noah read sharp intelligence in them. "My predecessor noted several times that Tanner was a difficult man to read. He played whatever role suited him."

"Past tense."

"I can only tell you that for the past several years he's settled in. His work in the library appears to satisfy him. He keeps to himself as much as it's possible to do so. He avoids confrontations."

"He told me he has an inoperable brain tumor. Terminal."

"Around the first of the year he complained of severe, recurring headaches, double vision. The tumor was discovered. Tests were run, and the consensus is he has perhaps a year. Most likely less than that."

"How'd he take it?"

"Better than I think I would. There are details of his file and his counseling and treatment I can't share with you, as I'll require not only his permission, but other clearance."

"If I decide to pursue this, to interview him, to listen, I'll need your cooperation as well as his. I'll need names, dates, events. Even opinions. Are you willing to give me those things?"

"I'll cooperate as much as I'm able. To be frank, Mr. Brady, I'd like to hear the entire story myself. I had a tremendous crush on Julie MacBride."

"Who didn't?" Noah murmured.

HE DECIDED TO STAY THE NIGHT IN SAN FRANCISCO, AND after settling into a room with a view overlooking the bay, he ordered up a meal and set up his laptop. Once he'd plugged into the Internet, he did a search on Sam Tanner.

For a man who'd spent two decades behind bars without granting a single interview, there was a wealth of hits. A number of them dealt with movies, his roles, summaries and critiques. Those could wait.

He found references to a number of books on the case, including unauthorized biographies of both Sam and Julie. Noah had a number of them in his library and made a note to himself to read through them again. There were articles on the trial, mostly rehashes.

He found nothing particularly fresh.

When his meal arrived, Noah ate his burger and typed one-handed, bookmarking any areas he might want to explore again.

He'd seen the photographs that popped before. The one of Sam, impossibly handsome, and a luminous Julie, both beaming beautifully into the camera. Another of Sam, shackled, being led out of the court-house during the trial and looking ill and dazed.

And both of those men, Noah thought, were inside the cool-eyed and calculating inmate. How many others would he find before his book was done?

That, Noah admitted, was the irresistible pull. Who lived behind those eyes? What was it that gripped a man and drove him to butcher the woman he claimed to love, the mother of his child? To destroy everything he swore mattered to him?

Drugs? Not enough, in Noah's opinion. And not in the court's opinion either, he recalled. The defense had fallen back on drugs during the sentencing phase, attempting to get the sentence reduced due to mitigating circumstances. It hadn't swayed the results.

The brutality of the crime had outweighed everything else. And, Noah thought now, the pathetic video testimony of the victim's four-year-old child. No jury could have turned their backs on that little girl, her tearful description of what she'd seen that night, and given Sam Tanner any pity.

Twenty to life, the first fifteen without possibility of parole.

Noah didn't intend to be judge or jury but to align facts. As far as he was concerned, drugs didn't matter. Drugs might blur the edges, remove inhibitions. They might bring out the beast, but the beast had to exist in order to act.

The hand that had plunged the scissors repeatedly into Julie MacBride had belonged to a monster. He didn't intend to forget that.

He could research the crime objectively, he could distance himself from the horror of it. That was his job. He could sit and listen to Sam Tanner, talk with him, become intimate with his mind and put it all down on paper. He could dissect the man, prowl around in his brain and note the changes that may or may not have taken place inside him over the last two decades.

But he wouldn't forget that one night in high summer, Sam Tanner hadn't been a man.

He started to begin a new search on Julie MacBride, then on impulse changed it to River's End Lodge and Campground. He sat back and sipped his coffee as their home page came up. Technology, he mused, was a wonderful thing.

There was an arty and appealing photo of the lodge, exactly as he remembered it. A couple of interior photos showed the lobby and one of the guest suites. There was a chatty little description, which touched on the history, the accommodations, the beauty of the national forest.

Another click took him to the recreational offerings—fishing, canoeing, hiking, a naturalist center . . .

He paused there and grinned. She'd done it, then. Built her center. Good for you, Liv.

They offered guided tours, a heated pool, health-club facilities.

He skimmed down, noting that weekend, full-week and special packages were offered. The proprietors were listed as Rob and Val MacBride.

Nowhere did he find Olivia's name.

"You still there, Liv?" he wondered. "Yeah, you're still there. With the forest and the rivers. Do you ever think of me?"

Annoyed he'd had the thought, the question, he pushed away from the desk and stalked to the window. He looked out at the city, at lights, at traffic.

And wondered what had become of his ancient backpack.

Turning away, he flicked on the television, just for the noise. There were times when he couldn't think in silence. Because he was a man, and there was a remote at hand, he couldn't resist surfing the channels. He let out a short laugh when Julie MacBride, young, gorgeous and alive, filled the screen. Those striking amber eyes were glowing with love, with pleasure, with the sheen of tears as she raced down a long sweep of white stairs and into the arms of Sam Tanner.

Summer Thunder, Noah mused. Last scene. No dialogue. The music swells . . . He watched, hearing the flood of violins as the couple embraced, as Julie's warm flow of laughter joined it. As Sam lifted her off her feet, circling, circling in celebration of love found.

Fade-out.

Fate? Noah thought. Well, sometimes there was just no arguing with it.

He picked up a notebook, plopped down on the bed with it and began to make a list of names and questions.

Jamie Melbourne
David Melbourne
Rob and Val MacBride
Frank Brady
Charles Brighton Smith
Prosecution team? Who's still alive?
Lucas Manning
Lydia Loring
Agents, managers, publicists?
Rosa Sanchez (housekeeper)
Other domestic staff?

At the bottom of the list, he wrote "Olivia MacBride."

He wanted more from her than memories of one violent night. He wanted what she remembered of her parents together, what she remembered of them individually. The tone of their household, the undercurrents of marital distress.

There were always other angles to pursue. Had Julie been involved with Lucas Manning—giving credence to her husband's jealousy?

Would she have told her sister? Would the child have sensed it? The servants?

And wasn't it interesting, Noah decided, that his daughter hadn't been among the things Sam Tanner claimed to miss?

Oh yes, Olivia was key, Noah thought, and circled her name. This time, he couldn't allow himself to be distracted by feelings, by basic attraction, by even the connection of friendship.

They were both older now, and that was behind them. This time when they met, it would be the book first.

He wondered if she still wore her hair pulled back in a ponytail, if she still had that brief hesitation before she smiled.

"Give it a rest, Brady," he muttered. "That's history."

He pushed himself up, then dug in his briefcase for the numbers he'd looked up and scribbled down before leaving L.A. Rain began to lash the windows as he made the call, and he adjusted his vague plans of going out and indulging in some San Francisco nightlife to a solo beer at the bar downstairs.

"Good afternoon, Constellations."

"Noah Brady calling for Jamie Melbourne."

"Ms. Melbourne is with a client. May I take a message?"

"Tell her I'm Frank Brady's son, and I'd like to speak with her. I'm out of town at the moment." He glanced at the phone, then reeled off the number. "I'll be in for another hour."

That was a test, he mused as he hung up. Just to see how quickly the Brady name got a call back.

He stretched back out on the bed and had surfed through the channels twice when his phone rang. "Brady."

"Yes, this is Jamie Melbourne."

"Thanks for getting back to me." Within six minutes, Noah thought with a glance at his watch.

"Is this about your father? I hope he's well."

"He's fine, thanks. This is about Sam Tanner." He paused, waited, but there was no response. "I'm in San Francisco. I spoke with him earlier today."

"I see. I was under the impression he spoke to no one, particularly reporters or writers. You're a writer, aren't you, Noah?"

The first name, putting him in his place, he decided. Maintaining control. A good and subtle move. "That's right. He spoke to me, and I'm hoping you will, too. I'd like to set up an appointment with you. I should be back in town by tomorrow evening. Do you have any time free Thursday or Friday?"

"Why?"

"Sam Tanner wants to tell his story. I'm going to write it, Ms. Melbourne, and I want to give you every opportunity to tell your part of it."

"The man killed my sister and broke the hearts of every member of my family. What else do you need to know?"

"Everything you can tell me—unless you want the information I gather coming only from his point of view. That's not what I'm after here."

"No, you're after another best-seller, aren't you? However you can get it."

"If that were true, I wouldn't have called you. Just talk to me—off the record if you want. Then make up your mind."

"Have you spoken with anyone else in my family?"

"No."

"Don't. Come to see me Thursday at four. At my home. I'll give you an hour, no more."

"I appreciate it. If I could have your address?"

"Get it from your father." She snapped that out, her controlled voice finally breaking. "He knows it."

Noah winced as she broke the connection, though the click was quiet, almost discreet. Definitely stepping onto shaky ground there, he decided. She was predisposed not to cooperate, not to be objective about what he intended to accomplish.

He flipped through channels without interest as he considered. Sam hadn't told him about his death sentence in confidence. Perhaps he'd pass that information to Jamie, see if it made any difference to her. He could also use her reluctance to cooperate in his strategy with Sam.

Playing one against the other would result in more information from both of them—if he did it well.

And he'd just keep his own long-term and personal fascination with the case his little secret for now.

He drifted off with the rain pattering on the windows and the television blaring, and dreamed a dream he wouldn't remember of giant trees and green light, and a tall woman with golden eyes.

THIRTEEN

THE same guard took Noah to the same room. This time he'd brought a notepad and a tape recorder. He set them both on the table. Sam glanced at them, said nothing, but Noah caught a quick glint in his eyes that might have been satisfaction. Or relief.

Noah took his seat, switched on the recorder. "Let's go back, Sam. Nineteen seventy-three."

"*Fever* was released in May, and was the biggest moneymaker of the summer. I got an Oscar nomination for it. I listened to 'Desperado' every time I turned on the radio. The sixties were pretty well dead," Sam said with what might have been amusement, "and disco hadn't quite reared its ugly head. I was unofficially living with Lydia and having great sex and monumental fights. Pot was out, snow was in. There was always a party going on. And I met Julie MacBride."

He paused, just a heartbeat of silence. "Everything that had happened to me before that moment took second place."

"You were married that same year."

"Neither one of us was the cautious type, or the patient type." His gaze drifted off, and Noah wondered what images he could see playing against the ugly bare walls. "It didn't take us long to figure out what we wanted. What we wanted was each other. For a while, that was enough for both of us."

"Tell me," Noah said simply, and waited while Sam took out his contraband cigarette, lighted it.

"She'd been in Ireland with her sister, taking a couple weeks between projects. We met in Hank Midler, the director's, office. She came in— wearing jeans and a dark blue sweater. Her hair was pulled back. She looked maybe sixteen. She was the most beautiful thing I'd ever seen in my life."

His gaze arrowed back, shot straight into Noah's eyes. "That's not an exaggeration. It's the truth. I was used to women—to having them, enjoying them. One look at her, and she might have been the first. I think I knew, right then, she'd be the last. You may not understand that."

"Yes, I do understand it." He'd experienced that rush, that connection, when this man's daughter had opened her apartment door and given him a faintly annoyed frown.

"Been in love, have you, Brady?"

"I've been in something."

Sam let out a short laugh, then looked past Noah again, seemed to dream. "My belly clutched up," he murmured. "And my heart . . . I could actually feel it shaking inside me. When I took her hand it was like . . . yes. You. Finally. Later, she told me it had been exactly the same for her, as if we'd been moving through our lives to get to that moment. We talked about the script, went about the business as if both of us weren't reeling. Afterward, I asked her to dinner, and we agreed to meet at seven. When I got home, I told Lydia it was over."

He paused, laughed a little, drew deep on the cigarette. "Just over. I wasn't kind about it, wasn't cruel. The fact was, she'd simply ceased to exist for me. All I could think of was that at seven I'd see Julie again."

"Was Julie involved with anyone at that time?"

"She'd been seeing Michael Ford. The press played it up, but it wasn't serious. Two weeks after we met, we moved in together. Quietly, or as quietly as we were able to."

"You met her family?"

"Yes, that was important to her. It was a lot of work for me to bring Jamie around. She was very protective of Julie. She didn't trust me, thought Julie was just another fling. Hard to blame her," he said with a jerk of his shoulders. "I'd had plenty."

"Did it bother you that Julie's name was linked to a number of men at that time? Ford was just the latest."

"I didn't think of it then." Sam pulled the stub of the cigarette out of his mouth, crushed it out with a restrained violence that had Noah's eyes narrowing. "It was only later, when things got out of control. Then I thought about it. Sometimes it was all I could think about. The men who'd had her, the men who wanted her. The men she wanted. She was pulling away from me, and I wanted to know who was going to take my place. Who the hell was she turning to when she was turning away from me? Lucas Manning."

Even after twenty years, saying the name scored his tongue. "I knew there was something between them."

"So you killed her to keep her."

The muscles in Sam's jaws quivered once, and his eyes went blank. "That's one theory."

Noah gave him a pleasant smile. "We'll talk about the rest of the theories some other time. What was it like working with her on the movie?"

"Julie?" Sam blinked, lifted a hand to rub it distractedly over his face.

"Yes." Noah continued in the same mild tone. He'd thrown Sam off rhythm, exactly as he'd intended. He wasn't about to settle for well-rehearsed lines and perfect phrasing. "You were getting to know each other on two levels during the shoot. As lovers, and as actors. Let's talk about what she was like as an actor."

"She was good. Solid." Sam dropped his hands into his lap, then lifted them onto the table as if he wasn't quite sure what to do with them. "A natural. The term's overused, but it applied to her. She didn't have to work as hard as I did. She just felt it."

"Did that bother you? That she was better than you?"

"I didn't say she was better." His hands stilled, and his gaze whipped up, two hot blue points. "We came at it from two different places, different schools. She had a phenomenal memory, and that helped her with lines. She never forgot a fucking line. But she tended to put herself into her director's hands, almost naively trusting him to make it all come together. She didn't know enough about the rest of the craft to risk input on angles, lighting, pacing."

"But you did," Noah interrupted before Sam could fall back into a rhythm.

"Yeah, I did. Midler and I went head-to-head plenty on that film, but we respected each other. I was sorry to hear he died a couple of years ago. He was a genius."

"And Julie trusted him."

"She practically worshiped him. The chance to work with him was the main reason she'd taken the part. And he knew how to showcase her, knew how to coax the best from her. She was like a sponge, soaking up the thoughts and feelings of her character, then pouring them out. I built the character, layer by layer. We made a good team."

"Julie won the New York Film Critics' Award for her portrayal of Sarah in *Summer Thunder.* You were nominated but didn't win. Did that cause any friction between you?"

"I was thrilled for her. She was upset that I hadn't won. She'd wanted it more than I had. We'd been married less than a year at that time. We were as close to royalty as you can get in that town. We were completely in love, completely happy, and riding the wave. She shared everything with me then, understood me as no one ever had."

"And the next year, when she was nominated for an Oscar for best actress for *Twilight's Edge,* and your movie got mixed reviews. How did that affect your relationship?"

A muscle twitched under Sam's left eye, but he continued to speak coolly. "She was pregnant. We concentrated on that. She wanted a healthy baby a lot more than she wanted a statue."

"And you? What did you want?"

Sam smiled thinly. "I wanted everything. And for a while, that's just what I had. What do you want, Brady?"

"The story. From all the angles." He leaned forward and switched off the tape recorder. "I'm heading back to L.A.," he continued as he began to pack his briefcase. "I'll be talking to Jamie Melbourne tomorrow."

He noted the way Sam's fingers jerked and curled on the table. "Is there anything you want me to pass along to her?"

"She won't take anything from me but my death. She'll be getting that soon enough. She was jealous of Julie," he said in a rush, and had Noah pausing. "Julie could never see it, or never wanted to admit it, but Jamie had plenty of built-up jealousy over Julie's looks, her success, her style. She played the devoted sister, but if she'd had the chance, if she'd had the talent, she'd have knocked Julie aside, stepped over her and taken her place."

"Her place with you?"

"She settled for Melbourne, music agent with no talent of his own. She played second lead to Julie all her life. When Julie was dead, Jamie finally got the spotlight."

"Is that another theory?"

"If she hadn't tagged on to Julie, she'd still be running that lodge up in Washington. You think she'd have a big house, her business, her pussy-whipped husband if Julie hadn't cleared the way?"

Oh, there was resentment here, bitterness that had brewed for more than two decades. "Why should that matter to you?"

"She's kept me in here, made damn sure I didn't get a decent shot at parole these last five years. Made it her goddamn mission to keep me inside. And all the while she's still sucking up what Julie left behind. You talk to her, Brady, you have a nice chat with her, and you ask her if she wasn't the one who talked Julie into filing for divorce. If she wasn't the one who pushed it all over the edge. And if she wasn't the one who built her whole fucking big-time business off her dead sister's back."

THE MINUTE HIS PLANE TOOK OFF, NOAH ORDERED A BEER and opened his laptop. He wanted to get his thoughts and impressions into words while they were still fresh, and he wanted to get home, spread his notes out around him, start making calls, setting up interviews.

The rush of anticipation racing through his blood was a familiar sensation and told him he was committed now. There was no going back. The endless stream of research, digging, backtracking and puzzling didn't intimidate him. It energized him.

From now until it was done, Sam Tanner would be the focus of his life.

He wants to run the show, Noah wrote. *So do I. It's going to be an interesting tug-of-war. He's smart. I think people have underestimated him, seeing him purely as a spoiled and selfish pretty boy with a filthy temper. He's learned control, but the temper's still under it. And if his reaction to Jamie Melbourne is any indication, his temper can still be mean.*

I wonder how much of what he tells me will be the truth, what he sees as the truth, or outright lies.

One thing I'm sure of is that he wants the spotlight again. He wants to be recognized. He wants the attention that's been denied him since he walked into San Quentin. And he wants it on his terms. I don't think he's looking for sympathy. I don't think he gives a good goddamn about understanding. But this is his story. He's chosen the time to tell it, and he's chosen me to tell it to.

It's a good twist—the son of the cop who took him down writing the book. The press will play on it, and he knows it.

His comments on Jamie Melbourne are interesting. Truth, perception or lie? It'll be even more interesting to find out.

Most intriguing of all is the fact that he's yet to ask about Olivia, or to mention her by name.

He wondered if Jamie would.

NOAH UNDERSTOOD THAT JAMIE MELBOURNE'S PUBLICITY firm, Constellations, was one of the most prestigious in the entertainment business. It had branches in Los Angeles and New York and represented top names.

He also understood that prior to her sister's death, Jamie had represented only Julie, and had worked primarily out of her own home.

It was an unarguable fact that Jamie's star had risen after her sister's murder.

What that meant, Noah mused as he drove through the gates to the elaborate home in Holmby Hills, was yet to be seen.

According to his research, the Melbournes had moved into the estate in 1986, selling their more modest home and relocating here where they were known for their lavish parties.

The main house was three stories in sheer wedding-cake white with a long, flowing front porch at the entrance flanked by columns. Rooms speared out from the central structure in two clean lines on opposite sides, with walls of glass winking out on richly blooming gardens and fussy ornamental trees.

Two gorgeous golden retrievers bounded across the lawn to greet him, tails slapping the air and each other in delight.

"Hey there." He opened the car door and fell instantly in love. He was bending over, happily scratching ears and murmuring nonsense when Jamie walked over carrying a ratty tennis ball.

"They're Goodness and Mercy," she said, but didn't smile as Noah looked up at her.

"Where's Shirley?"

A faint wisp of humor played around her mouth. "She has a good home." Jamie held up the ball. As one, both dogs quivered and sat, staring up with desperately eager eyes. Then she threw it, sending it sailing for the dogs to chase.

"Good arm," Noah murmured.

"I keep in shape. It's too nice an afternoon to sit inside." And she'd yet to decide if she wanted him in her home. "We'll walk."

She turned, heading away from where the dogs were wrestling deliriously over the ball.

Noah had to agree she kept in shape. She was fifty-two, and could have passed easily for forty—and was all the more attractive as she wasn't going for twenty.

There were a few lines, but they added strength to her face, and it was her eyes that drew the attention rather than the creases fanning out from them. They were dark, intelligent and unflinching. Her hair was a soft brown, cut in a just-above-chin-length wedge that set off the shape of her face and added to the image of a mature woman of style and no fuss.

She was small framed, slimly built and wore rust-colored slacks and a simple camp shirt with confidence and comfort. She walked like a woman who was used to being on her feet and knew how to get where she wanted to go.

"How is your father?" she asked at length.

"He's fine, thanks. I guess you know he retired last year."

She smiled now, briefly. "Yes. Does he miss his work?"

"I think he did, until he got involved with the neighborhood youth center. He loves working with kids."

"Yes, Frank's good with children. I admire him very much." She walked past a glossy bush that smelled delicately of jasmine. "If I didn't, you wouldn't be here now."

"I appreciate that, and your taking the time to see me, Ms. Melbourne."

She didn't sigh out loud, but he saw the rise and fall of her shoulders. "Jamie. He's spoken to me about you often enough that I think of you as Noah."

"Has he? I didn't realize the two of you had had that much contact."

"Frank was an integral part of the most difficult period of my life."

"Most people tend to separate themselves from people who remind them of difficult periods."

"I don't," she said briefly and walked toward a large fan-shaped swimming pool bordered in white stone and cool pink flowers. "Your father helped me through a tremendous loss, helped see that my family got justice. He's an exceptional man."

Your father's a great man, Olivia had told him once. And later, *Beside him, you're very small.*

Noah turned off the ache of that and nodded. "I think so."

"I'm glad to hear it."

As they skirted the pool, he could see the deep green of tennis courts in the distance. Tucked behind oleanders and roses was a scaled-down version of the main house.

"I don't like your work," she said abruptly.

"All right."

She stopped, turned to him. "I don't understand it. Or why you do it. Your father dedicated his life to putting people who take the lives of others in prison. And you're dedicating yours to putting their names in print, to glorifying what they've done."

"Have you read my work?"

"No."

"If you had, you'd know I don't glorify the people I write about or what they've done."

"Writing about them is glory enough."

"Writing about them lays it out," Noah corrected. "The people, the acts, the history, the motives. The whys. My father was interested in the whys, too. How and when aren't always enough. Don't you want to know why your sister died, Jamie?"

"I know why she died. She died because Sam Tanner killed her. Because he was jealous and sick and vicious enough not to want her to live without him."

"But they'd loved each other once, enough to marry and make a child. Enough, even when they were supposedly having serious marital difficulties, for her to open the door to him."

"And for that last act of love, he killed her." This time, Jamie's voice was hot and bitter. "He used her feelings, her loyalty, her need to keep her family together. He used them against her just as surely as he used the scissors."

"You could tell me about her the way no one else can. About what she thought, what she felt, about what happened to turn her life into a nightmare."

"What about her privacy?"

"She's never had that, has she?" He said it gently. "I can promise to give her the truth."

She looked away again, wearily. "There are a lot of degrees in the truth."

"Give me yours."

"Why is he letting you do this? Why is he talking to you, to anyone after all these years?"

"He's dying." He said it straight and watched her face.

Something flickered across it, glinted in her eyes, then was gone. "Good. How long is it going to take him?"

A hard woman, Noah thought, hard and honest. "He has brain cancer. They diagnosed it in January and gave him under a year."

"Well, justice wins. So he wants his brief time in the sun again before he goes to hell."

"That may be what he wants," Noah said evenly. "What he'll get is a book written my way. Not his."

"You'll write it with or without my cooperation."

"Yes, but I'll write a better book with it."

She believed he meant it. He had his father's clear, assessing eyes. "I don't want to hate you for it," she said almost to herself. "I've centered all my hate on one place all these years. I don't want to diffuse it at this point— especially now that his time is nearly up."

"But you have something to say, haven't you? Things you haven't said yet."

"Maybe I do. I spoke with my husband about this yesterday. He surprised me."

"How?"

"He thinks we should give you your interviews. To counterbalance what Sam tells you, David thinks, to make sure whatever ugliness he's formed in his mind doesn't stand on its own. We were there, part of their lives. We know what happened to it. So, yes, maybe I do have something to say."

She ripped at a hibiscus, tore the fragile pink blossom to shreds. "I'll talk to you, Noah, and so will David. Let's go inside so I can check my calendar."

"Got any time now?" He smiled, a quick and charming flash. "You said I could have an hour, and we've only used about half that."

"That part must come from your mother," Jamie mused. "The fast dazzle. Frank's more subtle."

"Whatever works."

"All right. Come inside."

"I need to get my things out of the car. Taping interviews protects both of us."

"Just ring. Rosa will let you in."

"Rosa? Would that be Rosa Sanchez?"

"Rosa Cruz now, and yes, the same Rosa who worked for Julie at one time. She's been with David and me for the past twenty years. Go get your tape recorder, Noah, you're still on the clock."

He made it fast, though the dogs conned him into throwing the ball for them and made him wonder why he didn't get himself a dog of his own.

When he rang the bell, he noted that the long glass panes on either side of the grand white door were etched with calla lilies, and the marble urns that flanked them were spilling over with fuchsia in tones of deep reds and purples that were obviously well loved and well tended.

The woman who answered the door was very short and very wide, so that he thought of a barrel in a smartly pressed gray uniform. Her hair was the same color as the cloth and wound tidily, almost ruthlessly back into a nape bun. Her face was round and deep gold, her eyes a nut brown that snapped with disapproval.

All in all, Noah thought, she made a better guard than Goodness and Mercy, who were at that moment happily peeing on the tires of his rental car.

"Mr. Brady." Her voice was richly Mexican and cold as February. "Ms. Melbourne will see you in the solarium."

"Thanks." He stepped into a foyer wide as a ballroom and had to muffle a whistle of interest at the flood of crystal in the chandelier and what seemed like acres of white marble on the floor.

Rosa's heels clicked over it busily, giving him little time to study the art and furnishings of the living room. But what he did see told him the dogs weren't allowed to do any romping in that area.

The solarium was a towering glass dome snugged onto the south side of the house, crowded with flowers and plants and their exotic mix of scents. Water glistened its way down a stone wall and into a little pool where white water lilies floated.

Seats and benches were tucked here and there, and a pretty conversation area was arranged beside the tall glass. Jamie was already waiting on a generously sized rattan chair with cushions striped in cheery green and white.

On the rippled glass of a round table was a clear pitcher filled with amber iced tea, two tall glasses and a plate of what Noah thought of as girl cookies—tiny, frosted and shaped like hearts.

"Thank you, Rosa."

"You have a cocktail party at seven." Rosa relayed this with her eyebrows beetled into one straight line.

"Yes, I know. It's all right."

She only sniffed, then muttered something in Spanish before she left them alone.

"She doesn't like me."

"Rosa's very protective." As he sat, Jamie leaned forward to pour the tea.

"It's a great house." He glanced over her shoulder, through the glass to the flood of flowers beyond. "Your dahlias are terrific, a nice match with the wild indigo and dusty miller."

Jamie's brows rose. "You surprise me, Noah. The horticultural limits of most young hunks stop at roses." The grimace he didn't quite hide made her laugh and relax. "And you can be embarrassed. Well, that's a relief. Was it the flower comment or the hunk reference?"

"Flowers are a hobby of mine."

"Ah, the hunk then. Well, you're tall, built and have a very handsome face. So there you are." She continued to smile, and indulged herself in a cookie. "Your parents keep hoping you'll find the right woman and settle down."

"What?"

Thoroughly amused now, she lifted the plate, offered it. "Haven't they mentioned that to you?"

"No. Jesus." He took a cookie, shaking his head as he set up his tape recorder. "Women aren't high on my list right now. I just had a narrow escape."

"Really?" Jamie tucked her legs up under her. "Want to talk about it?"

His gaze shifted, met hers. "Not while I'm on the clock. Tell me about growing up with Julie."

"Growing up?" He'd broken her rhythm. "Why? I thought you'd want to discuss that last year."

"Eventually." The cookies weren't half bad, so he had another. "But right now I'd like to know what it was like being her sister. More, her twin sister. Tell me about that, about when you were kids."

"It was a good childhood, for both of us. We were close, and we were happy. We had a great deal of freedom, I suppose, as children often do who grow up outside of the city. My parents believed in giving us responsibilities and freedom in equal measure. It's a good formula."

"You grew up in a fairly isolated area. Did you have any other friends?"

"Hmm, a few, certainly. But we were always each other's best friend. We enjoyed each other's company, and liked most of the same things."

"No squabbles, no sibling rivalry?"

"Nothing major. We had spats—I doubt anyone can fight like sisters or aim for the weak spots with more accuracy. Julie wasn't a pushover, and gave as good as she got."

"She get a lot?"

Jamie nibbled on her cookie, smiled. "Sure. I wasn't a pushover either. Noah, we were two strong-minded young girls growing up in each other's pockets. We had a lot of room, but we were . . . enclosed all the same. We sniped, we fought, we made up. We irritated each other, competed with each other. And we loved each other. Julie would take her licks, and she'd take her swipes. But she could never hold a grudge."

"Could you?"

"Oh yes." The smile again, slightly feline now. "That was one thing I was always better at. With Julie, she'd go her round, aim her punches, then she'd forget it. One minute she'd be furious, stomp off with her nose in the air. And the next, she'd be laughing and telling me to hurry up and look at something, or it would be, 'Oh come on, Jamie, get over it and let's go for a swim.' And if I didn't get over it quickly enough, she'd keep poking at me until I did. She was irresistible."

"You said holding grudges was the one thing you were better at. What was she better at?"

"Almost everything. She was prettier, sharper, quicker, stronger. Certainly more outgoing and ambitious."

"Didn't you resent that?"

"Maybe I did." She looked at him blandly. "Then I got over it. Julie was born to be spectacular. I wasn't. Do you think I blamed her for that?"

"Did you?"

"Let's put this on another level," Jamie said after a moment. "Using an interest we both apparently share. Do you blame one rose for being a deeper color, a bigger bloom than the other? One isn't less than another, but different. Julie and I were different."

"Then again, a lot of people overlook the smaller bloom and choose the more spectacular one."

"But there's something to be said for slow bloomers, isn't there? She's gone." Jamie picked up her glass and sipped, watching Noah over the rim. "I'm still here."

"And if she'd lived? What then?"

"She didn't." Her gaze shifted away now, toward something he couldn't see. "I'll never know what would have been in store for both of us if Sam Tanner hadn't come into our lives."

FOURTEEN

I was madly in love with Sam Tanner. And I spent many delightful hours devising ways in which he would die the most hideous and painful, and hopefully embarrassing, of deaths."

Lydia Loring sipped her mineral water and lime from a tall, slim glass of Baccarat crystal and chuckled. Her eyes, a summery baby blue, flirted expertly with Noah and had him grinning back at her.

"Care to describe one of the methods for the record?"

"Hmmm. Well, let's see . . ." She trailed off, recrossing her very impressive legs. "There was the one where he was found chained to the bed and wearing women's underwear. He'd starved to death. It took many horrible days."

"So I take it the two of you didn't end your relationship in an amicable fashion."

"Hell. We didn't do anything in an amicable fashion. We were animals from the first minute we laid hands on each other. I was crazy about him," she added, running her finger around the rim of her glass. "Literally. When they convicted him, I opened a bottle of Dom Perignon, seventy-five, and drank every single drop."

"That was several years after your relationship ended."

"Yes, and several years before my lovely vacation at Betty Ford's. I do, occasionally, still miss the marvelous zip of champagne." She lifted a shoulder. "I had problems, so did Sam. We drank hard, played hard, worked hard. We had outrageous sex, vicious fights. There was no moderation for either of us back then."

"Drugs."

"Rehabilitated," she said, holding up a hand and flashing a killer smile. "My body's a temple now, and a damn good one."

"No arguing there," Noah responded and made her purr. "But there were drugs."

"Honey, they were passed out like candy. Coke was our favorite party favor. Word was after Sam fell for Julie, she put a stop to that. But me, I just kept on flying. Wrecked my health, toppled my career, screwed up my personal life by marrying two money-grubbing creeps. When the eighties dawned, I was sick, broke, ruined. I got clean and clawed my way back. Sitcom guest shots, bit parts in bad movies. I took whatever I could get, and I was grateful. Then six years ago I got *Roxy*."

She smiled over the situation comedy that had boosted her back to the top. "A lot of people talk about reinventing themselves. I did it."

"Not everyone would be so up-front about the mistakes they made along the way. You've always been brutally honest about what you did, where you were."

"Part of my personal philosophy. I had fame once, and I handled it badly. I have it again, and I don't take any of it for granted."

She glanced around the spacious dressing room with its plump sofa, fresh flowers. "Some say *Roxy* saved my life, but they're wrong. *I* saved my life, and part of the process was putting my relationship with Sam Tanner in perspective. I loved him. He loved Julie. And look what that got her."

She plucked a glossy green grape from a bowl, popped it in her mouth. "Look what getting dumped by him got me."

"How did you feel about her?"

"I hated her." She said it cheerfully, without a hint of guilt. "Not only did she have what I wanted, but she came off looking like the wholesome girl next door while I was the used-up former lover. I was thrilled when their marriage hit the rocks, when Sam started showing up at clubs and parties again. The old Sam. Looking for action, asking for trouble."

"Did you give it to him? The action? The trouble?"

For the first time since the interview began, she hesitated. Stalling, she rose to refill her glass. "I was different back then. Selfish, single-minded. Destructive. He'd come into a party, make some comment about Julie being tired or tied up. But I knew him, knew that edge in his eyes. He was unhappy and angry and restless. I was between marriages to Asshole Number One and Asshole Number Two. And I was still in love with Sam. Pitifully in love with him."

She turned then, looking smart and sophisticated in the snazzy red suit she would wear to shoot the upcoming scene. "This is painful. I didn't realize it would be painful. Well . . ." She lifted her glass in salute and offered him her signature self-mocking smile. "Builds character. At one of those ubiquitous parties we indulged ourselves in during that regrettable era, Sam and I shared a couple of lines for old times' sake. I won't say who hosted the party, it doesn't really matter. It could have been anyone. We were in a bedroom, sitting at this ornate glass table. The mirror, the silver knife, the pretty little straws. I egged him on about Julie. I knew what buttons to push."

Her gaze turned inward, and this time he thought he saw regret in them. "He said he knew she was fucking Lucas—Lucas Manning. He was going to put a stop to that, by Christ, and she was going to pay for cheating on him. She was keeping his daughter away from him, turning the kid against him. He'd see them all in hell before she replaced him with that son of a bitch. They didn't know who they were dealing with, and he'd show them just who they were dealing with. He was ranting, and I pushed him along, telling him exactly what he wanted to hear. All I could think was, he'll leave her and come back to me. Where he belongs. Instead he turned on me, shoved me away. We ended up screaming at each other. Just before he slammed out he looked at me, sneered at me. He said I'd

never have any class, never be anything but a second-rate whore pretending to be a star. That I'd never be Julie.

"Two days later, she was dead. He made her pay," Lydia said with a
sigh. "If he'd killed her that night, the night he left me at that party, I don't
think I'd have survived it. For purely selfish reasons I'm grateful he waited
just long enough so I was sure he'd forgotten me again. You know, it took
me years to realize how lucky I was he never loved me."

"Did he ever hit you?"

"Sure." The humor came back into her eyes. "We hit each other. It
was part of our sexual dance. We were violent, arrogant people."

"But there weren't any reports of abuse or violence in his marriage
until the summer she died. What do you think about that?"

"I think she was able to change him, for a time. Or that he was able to
change himself, for a time. Love can do that, or very great need. Noah . . ."
She came back and sat. "I believe he really, really wanted to be the person
he was with her. And it was working. I don't know why it stopped working. But he was a weak man who wanted to be strong, a good actor who
wanted to be a great one. Maybe, because of that, he was always doomed
to fail."

There was a brisk knock at the door. "Ms. Loring? You're needed on
the set."

"Two minutes, honey." She set her glass aside, grinned at Noah.
"Work, work, work."

"I appreciate your squeezing some time into your schedule for me."

When he rose, she eyed him up and down, with a sly cat smile on her
face. "I imagine I could . . . squeeze more if you're interested . . ."

"I'm bound to have some follow-up questions along the way."

She stepped closer, tapped a finger to his cheek. "You look like such
a bright young man, Noah. I think you know I was talking about a more
personal session."

"Yeah. Ah, the thing is, Lydia, you scare me."

She threw back her head and laughed in delight. "Oh, what a lovely
thing to say. What if I promise to be gentle?"

"I'd say you're a liar." Relieved by her laugh, he grinned back at her.

"There, I said you were bright. Well . . ." She hooked her arm through his as they walked to the door. "You know how to get in touch now if you change your mind. Older women are very creative, Noah."

She turned, gave him a sharp, little nip on the bottom lip that had both heat and nerves swimming into his blood.

"Now you're really scaring me. One last thing?"

"*Mmmm.*" She turned again, leaned back against the door. "Yes?"

"Was Julie having an affair with Lucas Manning?"

"All business, aren't you? I find that very sexy. But since I don't have time to attempt a worthwhile seduction, I'll tell you that I don't know the answer. At the time, there were two camps on that subject. The one that believed it—delighted in believing it—and the one that didn't, and wouldn't have if Julie and Lucas had been caught in bed naked at the Beverly Hills Hotel."

"Which camp were you in?"

"Oh, the first, of course. I got off hearing anything negative or juicy about Julie in those days. But that was then, and this isn't. Later, years later, when Lucas and I had our obligatory affair—" She lifted her brows when his eyes narrowed. "Oh, didn't dig that up, I see. Yes, Lucas and I had a few memorable months together. But he never told me if he'd slept with her. So I can only tell you I don't know. But Sam believed it, so it hardly matters."

It mattered, Noah thought. Every piece mattered.

LIKE ANY SELF-RESPECTING RESIDENT OF LOS ANGELES, NOAH conducted a great deal of business on the freeway. As he wound through traffic toward home, he used his cell phone to try to contact Charles Brighton Smith.

Sam Tanner's renowned defense attorney was seventy-eight, still practicing law when the mood struck him, on his fifth wife—this one a gorgeous twenty-seven-year-old paralegal—and currently enjoying the sun and surf at his island retreat on St. Bart's.

With tenacity, Noah managed to get as far as an administrative assistant who informed him in snippy tones that Mr. Smith was incommunicado, but the message and request for an interview would be related at the earliest convenience.

Interpreting that to mean anytime from tomorrow to never, Noah went to work on accessing a copy of the trial transcript.

He toyed with swinging off the exit to his parents' house, then decided he would treat his father professionally, try to keep their personal relationship separate. Somehow.

It was time, he thought, to sit down at his machine and begin working out an outline for the book. He'd already decided on the form. It wouldn't begin with the murder, as he'd once planned, but with all that had led up to it.

A section on Sam Tanner's rise through Hollywood, paralleled by a section on Julie MacBride's. The meeting that had changed them, the fast-forward love affair sliding, from all reports, into a blissful marriage that had produced a much-loved child.

Then the disintegration of that marriage, of love turning to obsession and obsession to violence.

And a section on the child. One who had seen the horrors of that violence. A section on the woman she'd become and how she lived with it.

Murder didn't stop with death. That, Noah thought as he turned toward home, was something he'd learned from his father. And what, most of all, he tried to illustrate in his work.

It hurt that the man he admired and respected most didn't understand that.

He parked, jingling his keys in his hand as he walked toward his front door. It annoyed him that he couldn't seem to shake that need for his father's approval. If I'd been a cop, he thought, scowling, that would've been just dandy. Then we'd sit around over a beer and talk shop, crime and punishment, and he'd brag about his son, the detective, at his weekly pinochle game.

But I write about murders instead of investigating them, so it's like some slightly embarrassing secret.

"Get over it, Brady," he muttered, then started to jab the key in the lock.

He didn't need to. He didn't have to be a homicide detective to see the door was unlocked and not quite closed. The muscles of his stomach clutched into one tight, nasty ball as he gently nudged the door open.

He stood, staring in shock at the destruction of his house.

It looked as if a team of mad demons had danced over every surface, ripped and torn at every fabric, smashed every piece of glass.

He leaped inside, already swearing and felt only a quick flutter of relief when he saw his stereo equipment still in place.

Not a burglary then, he thought, hearing the buzz of blood in his head as he waded through the mess. Papers were strewn everywhere, glass and pottery crunched under his feet.

He found his bedroom in worse condition. The mattress had been shredded, the filling spilling out like guts from a belly wound. Drawers were upended and thrown against the wall to splinter the wood. When he found his favorite jeans sliced from the waist down to their frayed hems, the buzz turned to a roar.

"She's crazy. She's fucking insane."

Then anger turned to sheer horror. "No, no, no," he hissed under his breath as he raced from the bedroom into his office. "Oh God, oh shit."

His basketball trophy was now stuck dead center in his computer monitor. The keyboard, ripped away from the unit, was covered with potting soil from the ornamental lemon tree that had thrived in the corner. His files were scattered, torn, covered with dirt.

Before it had been destroyed, his computer had been used to generate the single clean sheet of paper and message that was taped to the base of the trophy:

I WON'T STOP UNTIL YOU DO.

Rage washed through him like a tidal wave, in one vicious, screaming flood. Before he could think, he dug for his phone, then only cursed bitterly when he found the receiver smashed.

"Okay, Caryn, you want war, you got war. Lunatic bitch."

He stormed back into the living room for the briefcase he'd dropped, tearing through it for his cell phone.

When he realized his hands were shaking, he walked outside, sucked in air, then just sat down and dropped his head into his hands.

He was sick, dizzy, with the fury still pumping through him in fast, hot beats. But under it was the baffled outrage of the victim. When he was able to use the phone, he didn't call Caryn, but his father.

"Dad. I've got a problem here. Can you come over?"

Twenty minutes later, Frank pulled up and Noah was sitting in exactly the same spot. He hadn't worked up the energy to go back inside but got to his feet now.

"Are you all right?" Moving fast, Frank came up the walk, took his son by the arm.

"Yeah, but . . . well, take a look for yourself." He gestured toward the door, then braced himself to step inside.

"God almighty, Noah." This time Frank laid a hand on Noah's shoulder in support, even as he scanned the room, picking up details in the chaos. "When did you find this?"

"About a half hour ago, I guess. I had an appointment in Burbank, just got back. I've been gone all day doing research."

"Did you call the cops?"

"No, not yet."

"That's the first step. I'll do it." He took Noah's phone and made the call. "The electronics are still here," he began when he disconnected. "You keep any cash in the house?"

"Yeah, some." He stepped through the debris and into the office, kicking papers out of the way. He found his desk drawer in the corner, with a fifty-dollar bill under it. "I probably had a couple of hundred," he said, holding up the bill. "I'd guess the rest is buried under here somewhere. Everything's still here, Dad. It's just trashed."

"Yeah, I think we can rule out burglary." He studied the monitor, felt a twinge of his own. He remembered when Noah had won that MVP trophy, the pride and excitement they'd shared. "Got a beer?"

"I did, before I left this morning."

"Let's see if you still do. And we'll go sit out on the deck."

"It'll take me weeks to replace some of this data," Noah said as he rose. "Some I'll never be able to replace. I can buy a goddamn new computer, but not what was in it."

"I know. I'm sorry, Noah. Let's go outside and sit down until the uniforms get here."

"Sure, what the hell." More sick than angry now, Noah found two beers in the refrigerator, popped tops on both and sat with Frank on the back deck.

"You got any idea who or why on this?"

Noah let out a short laugh, then tipped back the beer to drink deeply. "Just a little bunny boiler I know."

"Excuse me?"

"Caryn." Noah dragged a hand through his hair, then sprang up to pace. "A little clip from *Fatal Attraction*. She didn't take it well when I stopped seeing her. She's been calling, leaving crazy messages. And the other day she was out here when I got home, all dewy-eyed and apologetic. When I didn't bite, she got nasty. Keyed my car on the way out."

"You still have any of her messages on your machine?"

"No. My strategy was to ignore her so she'd go away." He looked in through the deck door and the light of battle came back into his eyes. "Didn't work. She's going to pay for this."

"You know what she drives?"

"Sure."

"We'll check with the neighbors, see if anyone saw her or her car in the area today. You give the cops her address and let them go have a talk with her."

"Talk's not what I have in mind."

"The best thing for you to do is stay clear. I know you're pissed, Noah," he continued when Noah whirled around. "And we can have her charged with breaking and entering, destruction of property, malicious mischief, and all manner of things if we can prove she did this."

"Prove it, my ass. Who else? I knew she did it the minute I walked in."

"Knowing and proving are different things. Could be she'll admit to it under a little pressure. But for now, you let the cops take the report, do their job, and you steer clear. Don't talk to her." Worry clouded Frank's eyes at the battle light gleaming in his son's. "Has she ever gotten physically violent with you?"

"Jesus, I outweigh her by sixty pounds." He sat again, then looked up quickly. "I never touched her that way. The last time she was here, she went at me and I hauled her out the door."

Frank worked up a smile. "You sure can pick 'em."

"I'm giving celibacy a try for a while." With a sigh, Noah picked up his beer again. "Women are too much trouble. A couple of hours ago I got hit on by a TV star old enough to be my mother, and for a minute, it didn't seem like such a bad idea."

"Your appointment in Burbank," Frank said, primarily to keep Noah's mind off his problem for a little while.

"Yeah, Lydia Loring, she looks damn good." He rubbed the bottle of beer between both hands. "I'm interviewing people connected to Sam Tanner and Julie MacBride. I've been to San Quentin. I've talked to Tanner twice."

Frank puffed out his cheeks. "What do you want me to say?"

"Nothing." Disappointment was just one more weight in his gut. "But I'm hoping you'll cooperate, talk to me about the case, your investigation. I can't write the whole story, do justice to it, without your end. Sam Tanner has brain cancer. He has less than a year to live."

Frank lowered his eyes to his beer. "Some things come around," he murmured. "They take their own sweet time, but they come around."

"Don't you want to know?" Noah waited until Frank looked up again. "You never forgot this case, never really let go of it, or the people in it. He confessed, he recanted, then he shut up for twenty years. Only three people know what happened that night, and only two of them are still alive. One's dying."

"And one was four years old, Noah. For pity's sake."

"Yeah, and her testimony damned him. Tanner will talk to me. I'll convince Olivia MacBride to talk to me. But you're the one who strings them together. Are you going to talk to me?"

"He's still looking for glory. At the end, he's still looking for glory, and he'll twist what he tells you so that he gets it. The MacBride family deserves better."

"I thought I deserved your respect. But I guess we don't always get what we deserve." He got to his feet. "The cops're here."

"Noah." Frank stood, touched a hand to his son's arm. "Let's table this until we get what's going on here with you straightened out. Then we'll talk again."

"Fine."

"Noah." Frank tightened his grip, accepted the look of anger in his son's eyes. "Let's get through one problem at a time." He nodded toward the living area. "This is a pretty big one."

"Sure." Noah resisted the nasty urge to shrug the hand away. "One problem at a time."

IT WAS ONE TEDIOUS ROUTINE FOLLOWED BY ANOTHER. TELL-ing his story to the police, answering their questions, watching them look over what was left of his things was only the first. He called his insurance company, reported the loss, dealt with the curiosity of the neighbors who wandered down.

Then he locked himself inside and wondered where to begin.

It seemed most practical to start in the bedroom, to see if he had any clothes worth salvaging or if he'd walk around naked until he could get more. He managed to pick through, find enough for one mixed load and dumped it all together in the washing machine.

He ordered a pizza, got out another beer and, sipping it, studied the living room. He wondered if it wouldn't be better all around to just hire a crew to come in with shovels and haul the entire mess away.

"Start from scratch, Brady," he muttered. "It could be liberating."

He was still scoping it out when someone knocked on his door. Since it was too soon for the pizza, he considered ignoring it. But decided even another nosy neighbor was better than stewing in his own helpless disgust.

"Hey, Noah, don't you ever return phone calls? I've been . . . Whoa, some party. Why wasn't I invited?"

Resigned, Noah closed the door behind his oldest friend. Mike Elmo had been part of his life since grade school. "It was a surprise party."

"I bet." Mike hooked his thumbs in the pockets of the Dockers he'd bought because the commercials had convinced him women couldn't resist a guy wearing them and blinked out of eyes red rimmed from the contacts he couldn't quite adjust to. "Man, this sucks."

"Want a beer?"

"You bet. You get ripped off?"

"Just ripped." Noah took the path he'd already kicked clear into the kitchen. "Caryn's a little irritated that I dumped her."

"Wow, she do this? Seriously twisted." He shook his head, his chestnut-brown eyes soft and sad. "I told you."

Noah snorted and offered the beer. "You told me she was your lifetime fantasy woman and tried to pump me for every sexual detail."

"So my fantasy woman's twisted. What're you going to do?"

"Drink this beer, eat some pizza and start cleaning it up."

"What kind of pizza?"

"Pepperoni and mushroom."

"Then I can give you a hand." Mike plopped his chunky butt on a torn cushion. "So do you think Caryn'd have sex with me now that you've split?"

"Jesus, Mike." Noah enjoyed his first laugh in hours. "Sure, I'll even put in a good word for you."

"Cool. Rebound sex is very intense." He stretched out his short legs, crossed his ankles. "Oh yeah, I get a lot of rebound sex. Guys like you shake a woman off, they're prime for me."

"I sure do appreciate your support and sympathy during this difficult time."

"You can count on me." He offered Noah his surprisingly sweet, puppy-dog smile out of his half-homely face. "Hey, it's only stuff, and not really good stuff anyway. You go back to Ikea, or hit Pier 1 or something, and dump it all back in. Take you a few hours."

Because he'd been thinking the same thing about the bulk of his furniture, Noah scowled. "She broke my basketball trophy."

Mike straightened, and a look of utter horror whitened his face. "Not the MVP—not from the championship game of eighty-six?"

"Yeah." And since that had gotten the kind of rise out of his friend that soothed the soul, he narrowed his eyes. "She broke it by shoving it into my computer monitor."

"That sick, evil bitch broke your computer? Christ, God." He was up now, stumbling through the wreckage to Noah's office.

Computers were Mike's first love. Women could come and go—and for him it was usually the latter—but a good motherboard was always there for you. He actually yelped when he saw the damage, then leaped toward the once-sleek trophy.

"Jesus, she killed it dead. She mutilated it. Butchered it. What kind of a mind does this?" He turned back to Noah, his eyes wide and bright and blinking as his contacts haloed his vision. "She should be hunted down like a dog."

"I called the cops."

"No, for this you need a vigilante like Dark Man, you need ruthlessness like the Terminator."

"I'll give them a call next. Think you can salvage anything off the hard drive? She trashed every stinking one of my disks."

"She's the Antichrist, Noah." He shook his head sadly. "I'll see what I can do, but don't hold out any hope. There's the pizza," he said when he heard the knock. "Let me fuel up, then I'll do what I can do. And you know what? I don't even want rebound sex with her now."

FIFTEEN

IT took Noah a week to get his house in order. The sorting, cleaning, dumping was purely a pain in the ass, but the demands of it kept him from feeling helpless.

A new computer was a priority, and with Mike egging him on, he bought a system that sent his friend into raptures of delight and envy.

He wouldn't have bought all the damn software games if Mike hadn't kept pushing them on him. And he sure as hell wouldn't have sat up half the night playing video pinball if he hadn't bought it in the first place.

But he told himself that was beside the point. He'd needed the distraction.

He outfitted his living room with cargo furniture, ordering straight out of an in-store catalog by pointing at a page and telling the salesman: "Give me that."

This delighted the salesman and saved Noah a headache.

Within two weeks, he could walk through his house without cursing and made serious inroads on reorganizing his office and regenerating lost data.

He had his car back, a new mattress, and a half-baked promise through

Smith's admin for a meeting when the lawyer returned to California the following month.

And he managed to track down Lucas Manning.

Manning wasn't quite as cheerfully forthcoming as Lydia Loring had been, but he agreed to talk about Julie. Noah met him at Manning's Century City suite of offices. It always surprised and slightly disillusioned Noah that actors had big, plush executive offices.

They might as well be CEOs, he thought as he was cleared through several levels of security.

Manning greeted Noah with a professional smile and assessed him with eyes of storm gray. The years had turned his once burnished-gold-coin hair into the brilliance of polished pewter and filed down his face to the sharp points and angles of a scholar. According to the polls, women continued to find him one of the most appealing leading men in the business.

"I appreciate your taking the time to talk to me."

"I might not have." Manning gestured to a chair. "But Lydia campaigned for you."

"She's quite a woman."

"Yes, she is. So was Julie, Mr. Brady, and even after all this time it's not easy for me to talk about what happened to her."

No need for small talk, Noah thought, and following Manning's lead, he took out his recorder and pad. "You worked together."

"One of the happiest experiences of my life. She was a brilliant natural talent, an admirable woman and a good friend."

"There are those who believed, and still believe, that you and Julie MacBride were more than friends."

"We could have been." Manning eased back, laid his hands on the ornately carved arms of his chair. "If she hadn't been in love with her husband, we would have been. We were attracted to each other. Part of that was the intimacy of the roles we played, and part was simply a connection."

"Sam Tanner believed you acted on that connection."

"Sam Tanner didn't value what he had." Manning's trained voice hardened at the edges and made Noah wonder if the delivery was emotion or simply skill. "He made her unhappy. He was jealous, possessive, abusive. In my opinion, his addiction to drugs and alcohol didn't spark this abuse, it simply uncovered it."

There was a bitterness still toward Tanner, Noah thought, every bit as ripe as Tanner's was toward him. "Did she confide in you?"

"To an extent." He lifted the fingers of one hand off the arm of the chair, then dropped them again, like a pianist hitting keys. "She wasn't a whiner. I admit, I pressed her to talk to me, and we'd grown close during the filming, remained friends afterward. I knew she was troubled. At first she made excuses for him, then she stopped. Ultimately, she told me, in confidence, that she'd filed for divorce to snap him out of it, to force him to get help."

"Did you and Tanner ever discuss it?"

Manning's lips twisted into a smile. Wry and experienced. "He had a reputation for having a violent temper, for causing scenes. My career had just taken off, and I intended to be in it for the long haul. I avoided him. I'm not of the school that believes any press is good press, and I didn't want to see headlines splashed around gloating that Tanner and Manning had brawled over MacBride."

"Instead they gloated that Manning and MacBride were an item."

"There was nothing I could do about that. One of the reasons I agreed to this interview was to set the record straight about my relationship with Julie."

"Then I have to ask, Why haven't you set the record straight before now? You've refused to discuss her in interviews since her death."

"I set the record straight." Manning angled his head slightly, lowered his chin. It was an aggressive stance with those storm-cloud eyes just narrowed. "In court," he continued. "Under oath. But the media, the masses were never really satisfied. For some the idea of scandal, of illicit sex, was as much of a fascination as murder. I refused to play into it, to demean Julie that way."

Maybe, Noah mused. Or maybe the mystery of it gave your rocketing career one more boost. "And now?"

"Now you're going to write the book. Rumors around this town are that it'll be the definitive work on the Julie MacBride murder." He smiled thinly. "I'm sure you know that."

"There are a lot of rumors around this town," Noah said equably. "I let my agent worry about that end of it. I just do the work."

"Lydia said you were sharp. You're going to write the book," he repeated. "I'm part of the story. So I'll answer the questions I've refused to answer for the last twenty years. Julie and I were never lovers. Tanner and I never fought over her. The fact is, I'd have been delighted if both of those misconceptions had been true. The morning I heard what had happened to her remains the worst day of my life."

"How did you hear?"

"David Melbourne called me. Julie's family wanted to block as much media as possible, and he knew the minute the press got wind of it, they'd start hammering me for comments, interviews, statements. Of course he was right," Manning murmured. "It was early. The call woke me. My private number. Julie had my private number."

He closed his eyes and pain flickered over his face. "He said, 'Lucas, I have terrible, terrible news.' I remember exactly how his voice broke, the grief in it. 'Julie's dead. Oh God, God, Julie's dead. Sam killed her.'"

He opened his eyes again, emotion rushing into them. "I didn't believe it. Wouldn't. It was like a bad dream, or worse, worse, some scene I'd be forced to play over and over again. I'd just seen her the day before. She'd been beautiful and alive, excited about a script she'd just read. Then David told me she was dead."

"Were you in love with her, Mr. Manning?"

"Completely."

Manning gave him two full hours. Noah had miles of tape, reams of notes. He believed part of Manning's interview had been calculated, rehearsed. Timing, phrasing, pause and impact. But in it there was truth.

And with truth there was progress.

He decided to celebrate by meeting Mike at an off-the-strip bar called Rumors for a couple of drinks.

"She's giving me the eye." Mike rolled his own watering eyes to the left and muttered into his pilsner.

"Which eye?"

"The *eye,* you know. The blonde in the short skirt."

Noah considered his order of nachos. The energy from a good day's work bubbled under the surface of his skin and conversely helped him relax. "There are one hundred and thirty-three blondes in short skirts in here. They all have eyes."

"The one two tables over to the left. Don't look."

Though he hadn't intended to, Noah shrugged. "Okay. I'm going up to San Francisco again in a couple of days."

"Why?"

"Work. The book. Remember?"

"Oh yeah, yeah. I'm telling you, she's definitely eyeing me. She just did the hair flip. Hair flipping's the second stage."

"Go make a move, then."

"I'm biding my time, scoping it out. What's it like inside San Quentin, anyway?" Mike tried a little eyebrow wiggle on the blonde to get her reaction.

"Depressing. You walk through a door, it locks behind you. Your hair stands on end when you hear that click."

"So does he still look like a movie star? You never said."

"No, he looks like a man who's spent twenty years in prison. Are you going to eat any of these?"

"After I talk to the blonde. I don't want nacho breath. Okay, that was five full seconds of eye contact. I'm going in."

"My money's on you, pal." Then Noah muttered as Mike swaggered away, "She'll eat him alive."

He amused himself watching the action. The dance floor was packed, bodies crammed against bodies in a shower of flashing colored lights and all bumping and twisting to the music.

It made him think of the night he'd taken Olivia dancing. And how he'd stopped hearing the music or anything but the beat of his own blood once his mouth tasted hers.

"Put it away, pal," he muttered, and, scowling, picked up his beer. "You blew that one."

He sipped his beer and watched the show. He'd always enjoyed an occasional night in a club, getting blasted with music and voices, being pressed in with people and movement. Now he was sitting alone, while his oldest friend worked the blonde, and wishing he'd stayed home.

He pushed aside the nachos without interest, lifted his beer again and spotted Caryn crossing the floor toward his table.

"Of all the gin joints in all the towns," he mumbled and took a longer, deeper drink.

"I thought you were playing hermit." She'd decked herself out in a leather dress of electric blue that coated her like a tattoo and screamed to an abrupt halt just past her crotch. Her hair was in a thousand wild fuck-me curls, and her mouth was painted a hot, wet red.

It occurred to him that it was just that look that had made him think with his glands when he'd first seen her. He said nothing, lifted his glass again and did his best to stare through her.

"You set the cops on me." She leaned down, planting her palms on the table and her impressive breasts directly at eye level. "You got some nerve, Noah, getting your father to call out his gestapo friends to give me grief."

He flicked his gaze up to hers, then over her shoulder where one of her friends was pulling desperately at her arm and muttering her name.

His lips curved in a viciously cold smile, and he pitched his voice just over the roar of music. "Why don't you do us all a favor and get her out of here?"

"I'm talking to you." Caryn jabbed a nail, painted the same wild blue as her dress, into his chest. "You pay attention to me when I'm talking to you, you bastard."

The control snapped in, even as he imagined squeezing his hands around her neck until her eyes popped. "Back off."

She jabbed him again, hard enough this time to break skin. Then let out a squeal of shock when he grabbed her wrist.

"Keep out of my way. You think you can trash my house, destroy my things and I'll do nothing? You keep the hell out of my way."

"Or what?" She tossed her hair back, and to his disgust he saw it wasn't fear in her eyes, but excitement, edged with a glint of lust. "Going to call

Daddy again?" She raised her voice now, to just under a scream. Even in the din, it cut and had heads turning. "I never touched your precious things. I wouldn't lower myself to go back in that house after the way you treated me, and you can't prove any different. If I'd been there I'd have burned it down—and I'd have made sure you were inside when I did."

"You're sick." He shoved her hand aside. "And you're pitiful." He was pushing his chair back when she slapped him. The ring on her finger nicked the corner of his mouth, and he tasted blood. His eyes went dark and flat as he got to his feet. "You keep crossing that line, Caryn, and you're going to get run over."

"We got a problem here?"

Noah merely glanced at security. The man's shoulders were wide as a canyon and his big, sharp smile didn't hold any humor. Before he could speak, Caryn had launched herself against the boulder of his chest, blinking until her eyes filled.

"He wouldn't leave me alone. He grabbed me."

"Oh, for Christ's sake."

"That's a damn lie." This from Mike, who'd hopped to Noah's side. "She started on him. She's a lunatic, wrecked his house last week."

"I don't know what they're talking about." Tears slid gracefully down her cheeks as she tipped her face back to the bouncer's. "He hurt me."

"I saw what happened." A brunette with amused eyes and a slight Southern drawl strolled up. "I was sitting right over there." She gestured behind her, kept her voice low. "This guy was having a beer at this table, minding his own business. She came up to him, got in his face, started poking at him and yelling abuse. Then she slugged him."

The outrage had Caryn shrieking. She took a swipe at the brunette, missing by a mile as the bouncer nipped her around the waist. Her exit, kicking and screaming, caused quite a stir.

"Thanks." Noah dabbed the back of his hand on his lip.

The brunette's smile was slow and friendly. "Any time."

"I'm going to get you a fresh beer. Sit, relax." Mike fussed around him like a mother. "Man, that woman is over the edge and then some. I'll get the beer and some ice."

"Your friend's very sweet." She offered Noah a hand. "I'm Dory."

"Noah."

"Yes, I got that from Mike already. He likes my friend." She fluttered a hand toward the table where the blonde sat looking wide-eyed and prettily distressed. "She likes him. Why don't you join us?"

She had a voice like cream, and skin to match, intelligent interest in her eyes and a sympathetic smile. And he was just too damn tired to start the dance. "I appreciate it, but I'm going to take off. Go home, soak my head. I'm considering entering a monastery."

She laughed, and because he looked as if he could use it, touched a light kiss to his cheek. "Don't do anything rash. Ten, twenty years from now, you'll look back and smile at this little incident."

"Yeah, that's about right. Thanks again, and tell Mike I'll catch him later."

"Sure." She watched him go with a little tug of regret.

HE WAS LOST IN THE FOREST, THE LOVELY, DEEP WOODS WITH the low glow of light edged with green. There was silence, such silence he could swear he heard the air breathing. He couldn't find his way over the slick carpet of moss, through the tangle of dripping vines, beyond the great columns of trees that rose like an ancient wall.

He was looking for something . . . someone. He had to hurry, but whichever direction he took, he remained cupped there, in the ripe and green darkness. He heard the faint murmur of water from a stream, the sigh of the air and the drumming inside his head that was the frantic beat of his own blood.

Then, under it, like a whisper, came his name. *Noah . . . Noah . . .*

"Noah."

He shot up in bed, fists raised, eyes still glazed and blinded by the dream, his heart cartwheeling madly in his chest.

"And you used to wake up with a smile on your face."

"What? What?" He blinked his vision clear as the sharpest edge of the dream dulled and faded. "Mom?" He stared at her, then flopped back, buried his face in his pillow. "Jeez. Why don't you just bash me over the head with a tire iron next time?"

"Let's just say I didn't expect to find you still in bed at eleven o'clock in the morning." She sat on the edge of the bed, then rattled the bakery box she carried. "I brought pastries."

His pulse had nearly leveled out, so he opened one eye—and it was full of suspicion. "Not that carob crap?"

She sighed heavily. "All my hard work for nothing. You still have your father's stomach. No, not carob. I brought my only son poisonous white sugar and fat."

The suspicion remained, but around it was greedy interest. "What do I have to do for them?"

She leaned over, kissed the top of his head. "Get out of bed."

"That's it?"

"Get out of bed," she said again. "I'll go make coffee."

The idea of coffee and food thrilled him so much he was out of bed and pulling on his jeans before it struck him how weird it was to have his mother drop by with pastries on a Sunday morning.

He started out, rolled his eyes and went back for a T-shirt. She'd never let him chow down bare-chested. Since he'd gone that far, he brushed his teeth and splashed some water on his face.

Coffee was just scenting the air when he walked out.

"You know, you're a very creative young man," Celia began. "It baffles me that you didn't take a little more time, a little more care in furnishing your home."

"I just live here." He slid onto a stool at the counter. "And this stuff suits the place."

"Actually, it does." She glanced back at the simple, straight lines and dark blue cushions. "There's just not much of Noah around here."

"I lost a lot of stuff." He lifted his shoulder. "I'll pick it up here and there, eventually."

"Hmm." She said nothing more, and turned away to get out mugs and plates until she could bank some of the fury. Every time she thought about what had been done to him, she wanted to march over to wherever that Caryn creature lived and wade in.

"So, what's Dad up to?"

"A basketball game, what else?" She poured the coffee, arranged the pastries on a plate. He'd already grabbed one when she turned and opened the fridge. "You know, you'd be so much better off using your juicer than buying this processed stuff."

His answer was muffled around Bavarian cream and only made her shake her head as she poured orange juice into a glass for him.

Leaning on the counter, she watched him eat. His eyes were heavy, she noted, his hair tousled and his T-shirt torn at the shoulder. Love, wonderfully warm, spurted through her.

He grinned a little, licking cream and chocolate off his thumb. She was so damn pretty, he thought, her hair bright as polished copper, her eyes an all-seeing blue. "What?"

"I was just thinking how good-looking you are."

The grin widened as he reached for another pastry. "I was thinking the same thing about you. I get my good looks from my mom. She's a beaut. And right now, she's got something on her mind."

"Yes, she does." Taking her time, Celia moved around the counter, took a stool. She propped her feet on the stool between them, lifted her coffee and sipped. "You know how I've made it a policy not to interfere in your life, Noah?"

His grin faded. "Ah . . . yeah. I always appreciated that."

"Good. Because with that foundation between us, I expect you to listen to what I have to say."

"Uh-oh."

She let that pass, tossed back the hair she still wore long enough to wrap into a fat braid. "Mike called me this morning. He told me what happened last night."

"Biggest mouth in the west," Noah muttered.

"He was worried about you."

"Nothing to worry about, and he shouldn't have bothered you with it."

"Like he shouldn't have bothered me when you were twelve and that pimply-faced bully decided you'd make a nice punching bag every day after school?" She cocked an eyebrow. "He was three years older and twice your size, but did you tell me he was pounding on you?"

Noah tried to sulk into his coffee, but his lips curved. "Dick Mertz. You drove over to his house and went head-to-head with his Neanderthal father, told him to send his little Nazi out and you'd go a couple of rounds with him."

"There are times," Celia said primly, "when it's difficult to remain a pacifist."

"It was a proud moment in my life," Noah told her, then sobered. "I'm not twelve anymore, Mom, and I can handle my own bullies."

"This Caryn isn't some playground misfit either, Noah. She's proven she's dangerous. She threatened you last night. For God's sake, she talked about burning your house down around you."

Mike, you moron. "It's just talk, Mom."

"Is it? Are you sure?" When he opened his mouth, she merely stared until he shut it again. "I want you to get a restraining order."

"Mom—"

"It's basically all the police can do at this point, and it might very well intimidate her enough to make her stop, go away."

"I'm not getting a restraining order."

"Why?" A trickle of the genuine fear she felt broke through in the single word. "Because it's not macho?"

He inclined his head. "Okay."

"Oh!" Frustrated, she slammed her coffee down and pushed off the stool. "That's unbelievably stupid and shortsighted. What is your penis, your shield?"

"It's about as effective a shield as a piece of paper would be," he pointed out as she stormed around the room. "She'll lose interest quicker if I lie back a bit, then she'll latch onto some other poor bastard. The fact is, I'm going to be doing a lot of traveling over the next several months. I'm heading up to San Francisco in a few days."

"Well, I hope you don't come back to a pile of ashes," Celia snapped, then blew out a breath. "I'm so *angry,* and I've got nowhere to put it."

He smiled, opened his arms. "Put it here, pal."

She sighed again, hugely, then walked over to wrap her arms around him. "I want to punch her, just once. Just one good shot."

He had to laugh, and tightened his grip into a fierce squeeze. "If you ever get the chance, I'll go your bail. Now stop worrying about me."

"It's my job. I take my work very seriously." She eased back, looked up. Despite the man's face, the man's stubble of beard, he was still her little boy. "Now, I guess we move on to phase two. I know you and your father are tiptoeing around each other."

"Let it go, Mom."

"Not when it involves the two most important people in my life. The two of you were like a couple of polite strangers at my birthday dinner."

"Would you rather we'd fought about it?"

"Maybe. Boy, I seem to have latent violent tendencies." She smiled a little, smoothed a hand over his hair, wished she could smooth out his troubles as easily. "I hate seeing both of you unhappy and distant."

"This is *my* job," he pointed out. "And I take it very seriously."

"I know you do."

"He doesn't."

"That's not true, Noah." Her brow furrowed because she heard the unhappiness under the anger. "He just doesn't completely understand what you do and why you do it. And this particular case was—is—very personal to him."

"It's personal to me, too. I don't know why," he said when she studied him. "It just is, always has been. I have to follow through."

"I know that, and I think you're right."

The tension and resentment eased off his shoulders. "Thanks."

"I only want you to try to understand your father's feelings on it, and actually, I think you'll come to as you go deeper into the people and the events. Noah, he ached for that little girl. I don't think he's ever stopped aching for her. There've been other cases, other horrors, but that child stayed with him."

She stayed with me, too, he thought. Right inside me. But he didn't say it. He hadn't wanted to think it. "I'll be going up to Washington, to see if she's still there."

Celia hesitated, suffered through the tug-of-war with loyalties. "She's still there. She and your father have kept in touch."

"Really?" Noah considered as he got up to pour more coffee. "Well then, that should make things easier."

"I'm not sure anything will make this easier."

AN HOUR LATER, WHEN HE WAS ALONE AND SLIGHTLY QUEASY from having inhaled four pastries, Noah decided it was as good a day as any to travel. This time he'd drive to San Francisco, he thought as he went to the bedroom to toss what few clothes he had in a bag. It would give him time to think, and he could make arrangements on the way for a few days at River's End.

It would give him time to prepare himself for seeing Olivia again.

SIXTEEN

S AM'S nerves slithered under his skin like restless snakes. To keep them at bay he recited poetry—Sandburg, Yeats, Frost. It was a trick he'd learned during his early stage work, when he'd suffered horribly, and he had refined it in prison, where so much of the life was waiting, nerves and despair.

At one time he'd tried to calm himself, control himself, by running lines in his head. Bits and pieces of his movies in which he would draw the character up from his gut, become someone else. But that had led to a serious bout of depression during the first nickel of his time inside. When the lines were done, he was still Sam Tanner, he was still in San Quentin and there was no hope that tomorrow would change that.

But the poetry was soothing, helped stroke back that part of himself that was screaming.

When he'd come up for parole the first time, he'd actually believed they would let him go. They, the tangled mass of faces and figures of the justice system, would look at him and see a man who'd paid with the most precious years of his life.

He'd been nervous then, with sweat pooling in his armpits and his gut muscles twisted like thin rope. But beneath the fear had been a simple and steady hope. His time in hell was done, and life could begin again.

Then he'd seen Jamie, and he'd seen Frank Brady, and he'd known they'd come to make certain the doors of hell stayed locked.

She'd spoken of Julie, of her beauty and talent, her devotion to family. Of how one man had destroyed all that, out of jealousy and spite. How he had endangered and threatened his own child.

She'd wept while she'd addressed the panel, Sam recalled, quiet tears that had trickled down her cheeks as she spoke.

He'd wanted to leap to his feet when she'd finished, shouting, Cut! One-take wonder! A brilliant performance!

But he'd recited poetry in his head and remained still, his face blank, his hands resting on his thighs.

Then Frank had had his turn, the dedicated cop focused on justice. He'd described the scene of the murder, the condition of the body in the pitiless, formal detail of police-speak. Only when he'd talked of Olivia, of how he'd found her, did emotion slip into his voice.

It had been all the more effective.

Olivia had been nineteen then, Sam thought now. He'd tried to imagine her as a young woman—tall and slim with Julie's eyes and that quick smile. But he'd only seen a little girl with hair as golden as dandelion who'd always wanted a story at bedtime.

He'd known as Frank had looked at him, as their eyes had met and held, that parole wouldn't be granted. He'd known that this same scene would be repeated year after year, like a film clip.

The rage he'd felt wanted to spew from his mouth like vomit. In his head he'd found Robert Frost and gripped the lines like a weapon.

I have promises to keep, and miles to go before I sleep.

For the last five years he'd formed and refined those promises. Now, the son of the man who'd murdered his hope was going to help him keep them.

That was justice.

Over a month had passed since Noah had first come to see him. Sam had begun to worry that he wouldn't come back, that the seeds he'd so carefully planted hadn't taken root after all. Those plans, those hopes, those promises that had kept him alive and sane would shatter, leaving him only the sharp edges of failure.

But he'd come back, was even now being led to this miserable little room. Interior scene, day, Sam thought as he heard the locks slide open. Action.

Noah walked to the table, set down his briefcase. Sam could smell his shower on him, the hotel soap. He was dressed in jeans, a soft cotton shirt, black Converse high-tops. There was a small healing cut at the corner of his mouth.

Sam wondered if he knew how young he was, how enviably young and fit and free.

Noah took his tape recorder, a notebook and a pencil out of the briefcase. And when the door was shut and locked at his back, tossed a pack of Marlboros and a book of matches in front of Sam.

"Didn't know your brand."

Sam tapped a fingertip on the pack, and his smile was sly and wry. "One's the same as the other in here. They'll all kill you, but nobody lives forever."

"Most of us don't know when or how it's going to end for us. How does it feel being someone who does?"

Sam continued to tap his finger on the pack. "It's a kind of power, or would be if I were in the world. In here, one day's the same as the next anyway."

"Regrets?"

"About being in here, or dying?"

"Either. Both."

With a short laugh, Sam opened the cigarettes. "Neither one of us has enough time for that list, Brady."

"Just hit the high points."

"I regret I won't have the same choices you do when this hour's up. I regret I can't decide: you know, I'd think I'd like a steak tonight, medium rare and a glass of good wine to go with it and strong black coffee after. Ever had prison coffee?"

"Yeah." It was a small thing to sympathize with. "It's worse than cop coffee. What else do you regret?"

"I regret that when I'm finally able to make that choice again, have that steak, I'm not going to have much time to enjoy it."

"That seems fairly simple."

"No, there are those who have choices and those who don't. It's never simple to the ones who don't. What choice have you made?" He slid a cigarette out of the pack, angled it toward the recorder. "With this. How far are you going to go with this?"

"All the way."

Sam looked down at the cigarette, effectively shuttering his eyes and whatever was in them. He opened the book of matches, tore one off, struck it to flame. Now, with his eyes closed he drew in that first deep gulp of Virginia tobacco.

"I need money." When Noah only lifted an eyebrow, Sam took a second drag. "I'm getting out when my twenty's up, my lawyer's done that dance. I'm going to live on the outside for maybe six months. I want to live decently, with some dignity, and what I've got isn't going to run to that steak."

He took another drag, a calming breath while Noah waited him out. "It took everything I had to pay for my defense, and what you make in here isn't what you'd call a living wage. They'll pay you for the book. You'll get an advance, and with your second best-seller out there, it won't be chump change."

"How much?"

The snakes began to stir under his skin again. He couldn't keep his promises without financial backing. "Twenty thousand—that's one large one for every year I've been in. That'll buy me a decent room, clothes, food. It won't set me up at the BHH, but it'll keep me off the streets."

It wasn't an unusual demand, nor did Noah consider it an unreasonable amount. "I'll have my agent draw up an agreement. That suit you?"

The snakes coiled up and slept. "Yeah, that suits me."

"Do you plan to stay in San Francisco when you're released?"

"I think I've been in San Francisco long enough." Sam's lips curved again. "I want the sun. I'll go south."

"L.A.?"

"Nothing much for me there. I don't think my old friends will be planning a welcome-home party. I want the sun," he said again. "And some privacy. Choices."

"I spoke with Jamie Melbourne."

Sam's hand jerked where it rested on the table. He lifted it, bringing the cigarette that smoldered between his fingers to his lips. "And?"

"I'll be talking to her again," Noah said. "I'll be contacting the rest of Julie's family as well. I haven't been able to hook up with C. B. Smith yet, but I will."

"I'm one of his few failures. We didn't part ways with great affection, but he had one of his young fresh faces spring the lock at twenty."

"Affection isn't what you're going to get from the people I interview."

"Have you talked to your father?"

"I'm doing background first." Eyes sharp, Noah inclined his head. "I won't agree to getting your approval on who I interview or what I use in the book. We go with this, you'll have to sign papers waiving those rights. Even if my publishers wouldn't insist on that, and they will, I would. Your story, Sam, but my book."

"You wouldn't have a book without me."

"Sure I would. It'd just be a different book." Noah leaned back, his pose relaxed, his eyes hard as iron. "You want choices? There's your first one. You sign the papers, you take the twenty thousand and I write the book my way. You don't sign, you don't get the money and I write it my way."

There was more of his father in him than Sam had realized before. A toughness the beach-boy looks and casual style skimmed over. Better that way, Sam decided. Better that way in the end.

"I'm not going to live to see the book in print anyway. I'll sign the papers, Brady." His eyes went cold, eyes that understood murder and had learned to live with it. "Just don't fuck me up."

Noah angled his head. "Fine. But remember, you don't want to fuck me up either."

He understood murder, too. He'd been studying it all his life.

. . .

NOAH ORDERED A STEAK, MEDIUM RARE, AND A BOTTLE OF Côte d'or. As he ate, he watched the lights that swept over the bay glint and glow against the dark and listened to the replay of his latest interview with Sam Tanner.

But most of all he tried to imagine what it would be like to be eating that meal, drinking that wine, for the first time in over twenty years.

Would you savor it, he wondered, or feed like a wolf after a long winter's famine?

Sam, he thought, would savor it, bite by bite, sip by sip, absorbing the flavors, the texture, the deep red color of the wine in the glass. And if his senses threatened to overload from the sudden flood of stimuli, he'd slow down even more.

He had that kind of control now.

How much of the reckless, greedy-for-pleasure, out-of-control man he had been still strained for release inside him?

It was smarter to think of Sam as two men, the one he'd been, the one he was now, Noah decided. Pieces of both had always been there, he imagined, but this was very much a story of what had been and what was. So he could sit here, try to picture how the man he knew now would deal with a perfectly cooked steak and a glass of fine wine. And he could imagine the man who'd been able to command much, much more at the flick of a finger.

The man who'd taken Julie MacBride to bed the first time.

I want to tell you how it was when Julie and I became lovers.

It hadn't been an angle Noah had expected Sam to take, not so soon, and not so intimately. But none of his surprise came through in his voice as he'd told Sam to go ahead.

Listening now, Noah let himself slide into Sam's place, into the warm southern California night. Into a past that wasn't his. The words on the recording became images, and the images more of a memory than a dream.

There was a full moon. It sailed the sky and shot beams of light, like silver swords, over the dark glint of the ocean. The sound of the surf as it rose, crested, crashed on shore was like the constant beat of an eager heart.

They'd taken a drive down the coast, stopped for a ridiculous meal of fried shrimp served in red plastic baskets at a smudgy little diner where they'd hoped to go unnoticed.

She'd worn a long flowered dress and a foolish straw hat to hide that waterfall of rich blond hair. She hadn't bothered with makeup and her youth, her beauty, her outrageous freshness hadn't been any sort of disguise.

She'd laughed, licked cocktail sauce from her fingers. And heads had turned.

They wanted to keep their relationship private, though so far it consisted of drives like this one, a few more-elegant meals, conversations and their work. Shooting had begun the month before, drastically cutting into any personal time they could steal.

Tonight, they'd stolen a few hours to walk along that foaming surf, their fingers linked, their steps meandering.

"I love doing this." Her voice was low and smooth, with just a hint of huskiness. She looked like an ingenue and sounded like a siren. It was part of the mystique that made her. "Just walking, smelling the night."

"So do I." Though he never had before her. Before Julie he'd craved the lights, the noise, the crowds and the attention centered on him. Now, being with her filled all those needy corners. "I love doing this even more."

He turned her, and she circled fluidly into his arms. Her lips curved as his met them, and they parted, inviting him in. She flowed into him, with tastes both sweet and sharp, scents both innocent and aware. The quiet sound of pleasure she made echoed in his blood like the crash of the surf.

"You do it so well, too," she murmured, and instead of easing away as she most often did, she pressed her cheek to his, let her body sway in tune to the sea. "Sam." His name sighed out of her. "I want to be sensible, I want to listen to the people who tell me to be sensible."

Desire for her was an ache in his belly, a burning in the blood. It took every ounce of control to keep his hands gentle. "Who tells you to be sensible?"

"People who love me." She leaned back, her deep amber eyes steady on his. "I thought I could be, then I thought, Well, if I'm not, I'll enjoy myself. I'm not a child, why shouldn't I be one of Sam Tanner's women if I want?"

"Julie—"

"No, wait." She stepped back, lifted a hand palm out to stop him. "I'm not a child, Sam, and I can deal with reality. I only want you to be honest with me. Is that where we're heading? To me becoming one of Sam Tanner's women?"

She'd accept that. He could see it in her eyes, hear it in her voice. The knowledge both thrilled and terrified him. He had only to say yes, take her hand, and she would go with him.

She stood, her back to the dark sea with its white edges, the moon-light spearing down to cast their shadows on the sand. And waited.

For the truth, he thought, and realized the truth was what he wanted for both of them.

"Lydia and I aren't seeing each other anymore. Haven't been for weeks now."

"I know." Julie smiled a little. "I read the gossip columns like anyone else. And I wouldn't be here with you tonight if you were still involved with someone else."

"It's over between us," he said carefully. "It was over the first minute I saw you. Because the first minute I saw you, I stopped seeing anyone else, stopped wanting anyone else. The first minute I saw you . . ." He stepped to her, slipped the straw hat away so that her hair tumbled down. "I started falling in love with you. I still am. I don't think I'll ever stop."

Her eyes filled so that the sheen of tears sparkled like diamonds against gold. "What's the point of being in love if you're going to be sensible? Take me home with you tonight."

She stepped back into his arms, and this time the kiss was dark and edged with urgency. Then she was laughing, a quick river of delight as she grabbed the hat from him and sent it sailing over the water.

Hands clasped again, they raced back to his car like children eager for a treat.

WITH ANOTHER WOMAN HE MIGHT HAVE RUSHED GREED-ily into the oblivion of movement and mating, gulping it down, taking what his body craved and seeking the brutal pleasure of release.

With another woman he might have played the role of seducer, keeping part of himself separated, like a director orchestrating each step.

In both of those methods were power and satisfaction.

But with Julie he could do neither. The power was as much hers as his. Nerves hummed along his skin as they walked up the stairs in his house.

He closed the door of the bedroom behind them. He knew pieces of Lydia were still there, though she'd been viciously methodical in removing her things—and a number of his own—when she'd moved out. But a woman never shared a man's bed without leaving something of herself behind to force him to remember.

He had a moment to wish he'd tossed out the bed, bought a new one, then Julie was smiling at him.

"Yesterday doesn't matter, Sam. Only tonight matters." She laid her hands on his cheeks. "We're all that matters, all that's real. Touch me." She whispered it as her mouth cruised over his. "I don't want to wait any longer."

It all slipped into place, the nerves fading away. When he swept her up, he understood this wasn't simply sex or need or gratification. It was romance. However many times he'd set the scene before, or had scenes set for him, he'd never believed in it.

He laid her on the bed, covering her mouth with his as this new feeling flowed through him. Love, finally, love. Her arms, soft, smooth, wrapped around him as the kiss went deep. For a moment, it seemed his world centered there. In that mating of lips.

He didn't tell himself to be gentle, to move slowly. He couldn't separate himself and direct the scene. He was lost in it, and her, the scent of her hair, the taste of her throat, the sound of her breath as it caught, released, caught again.

He slipped the thin straps of the dress from her shoulders, urged it down, down her body as he savored that lovely mouth. She shivered when he stroked her breast, gasped when he skimmed tongue and teeth over the nipple, then moaned when he drew her deep into his mouth.

She fit beneath him, slid against him, rose and fell with him. She said his name, only his name, and made his heart tremble.

He touched, and took, and gave more than he'd known he had to give to a woman. Her skin dewed, adding one more flavor, her muscles quivered, adding another layer of excitement.

He wanted to see all of her, to explore everything she had, everything she was. She was long and slender and lovely, so that even the ripple of ribs against her skin was a fascination.

When she opened for him, rose up to meet him, he slipped into her like a sigh and watched those eyes film with tears.

Slow, silky movement built to shudders. She cried out once, her nails biting into his hips, then again, like an echo as he poured himself into her.

NOAH BLINKED HIS VISION CLEAR AND HEARD ONLY SILENCE. The tape had run out, he realized. He stared at the machine, more than a little stunned that the images had come quite so clear. And more than a little embarrassed to find himself hard and unquestionably aroused.

With Olivia's face in his mind.

"Jesus, Brady." He picked up his wine with a hand not quite steady and took a long sip.

It was one of the side effects of crawling inside Sam Tanner, imagining what it was like to love and be loved by a woman like Julie MacBride. Remembering what it had been like to want the daughter that love had created.

But it was damned inconvenient when he didn't have any outlet for the sexual frustration now kicking gleefully in his gut.

He'd write it out, he decided. He'd finish his meal, turn on the tube for noise and write it out. Since the story had a core of possessive love and sexual obsession, he'd write in Sam's memory of the night he and Julie had become lovers.

Maybe it was idealized, he thought, and maybe there were times, moments, connections that produced the kinds of feelings Sam had spoken of.

For Noah, sex had always been a delightful part of life, a kind of sport that required some basic skills, a certain amount of protection and a healthy sense of team spirit.

But he was willing to believe that for some it could contain gilded emotions. He'd give Sam that night, and all the romantic swells that went with it. It was after all how the man remembered it—or wanted to. And the shimmering romance of it would only add impact to the murder itself.

He booted up his laptop, poured coffee from the room-service carafe that had kept it acceptably hot. But when he rose to turn on the television, he stopped by the phone, frowned at it.

What the hell, he thought, and going with impulse dug out the number for River's End. Within ten minutes, he'd made reservations for the beginning of the following week.

Sam Tanner had still not spoken of his daughter. Noah wanted to see if she would speak of him.

HE WORKED UNTIL TWO, WHEN HE SURFACED BRIEFLY TO stare with no comprehension whatsoever at the television where a giant lizard was kicking the stuffing out of New York.

He watched a uniformed cop, who obviously had more balls than brains, take a few plugs at the lizard with his handgun, then get eaten alive.

It took Noah a moment to process that he was watching an old movie and not a news bulletin. That's when he decided his brain was fried for the night.

There was one more chore on his agenda, and though he knew it was just a little nasty to have waited until the middle of the night to deal with it, he picked up the phone and called Mike in L.A.

It took five rings, and the slur of sleep and bafflement in his friend's voice gave Noah considerable satisfaction.

"Hey. Did I wake you up?"

"What? Noah? Where are you?"

"San Francisco. Remember?"

"Huh? No . . . sort of. Jesus, Noah, it's two in the morning."

"No kidding?" His brows drew together as he heard another voice, slightly muffled, definitely female. "You got a woman there, Mike?"

"Maybe. Why?"

"Congratulations. The blonde from the club?"

"Ah . . . *hmmmm.*"

"Okay, okay, probably not the time to go into it. I'm going to be gone at least another week. I didn't want to call my parents and wake them up, and I'm going to be pretty busy in the morning."

"Oh, but it's okay to call and wake me up?"

"Sure—besides, now that you're both awake, you might get another round going. Remember to thank me later."

"Kiss my ass."

"That's gratitude for you. Since you're so fond of calling my mother, give her a buzz tomorrow and let her know I'm on the road."

There were some rustling sounds, making Noah imagine Mike was finally getting around to sitting up in bed. "Listen, I just thought you needed a little . . ."

"Interference in my life. Stop pulling on your lip, Mike," he said mildly, knowing his friend's nervous habits well. "I'm not pissed off, particularly, but I figure you owe me. So give my mom a call and take care of my flowers while I'm gone."

"I can do that. Look, give me a number where I can—whoa."

The low smoke of female laughter had Noah raising an eyebrow. "Later. I don't really want to have phone sex with you and the blonde. You let my flowers die, I'll kick your ass."

The response was a sharp intake of breath, a great deal of rustling and whispering. Rolling his eyes, Noah hung up on a wild burst of laughter.

Terrific, he thought and rubbed his hands over his face. Now he had two sexual adventures in his head. He decided to take a cold shower and go to bed.

The Forest

Enter these enchanted woods, You who dare.
—GEORGE MEREDITH

SEVENTEEN

H E was surprised he remembered it so well, in such detail, with such clarity. As he drove, Noah caught himself bracing for the sensory rush as he came around a switchback, heartbeats before his field of vision changed from thick wood and sheer rock to stunning blue sky painted with the dazzling white peaks of mountains.

It was true that he'd driven this way once before, but he'd been only eighteen, it had been only one time. It shouldn't have been like coming home after a trip away, like waking up after a dream.

And it had been summer, he reminded himself, when the peaks were snowcapped, but the body of them green with the pines and firs that marched up their sides to give them the look of living, growing giants rather than the cold and still kings that reigned over the valleys.

He'd done his research, he'd studied photographs, the brochures, the travelogues, but somehow he knew they couldn't have prepared him for this sweep, for the contrasts of deep, silent forest and wildly regal peaks.

He continued the climb long after he passed the turnoff for River's End. He had time, hours if he chose, before he needed to wind his way down to the lowlands, the rain forest, the job.

Choices again. And his was to slip into a pull-off, get out of the car and stand. The air was cold and pure. His breath puffed out, and had little knives scoring his throat on the inhale. It seemed to him that the world was spread out before him, field and valley, hill and forest, the bright ribbon of river, the flash of lake.

Even as a car grinding into low gear passed behind him, he felt isolated. He couldn't decide if it was a feeling he enjoyed or one that troubled him, but he stood, letting the wind slap at his jacket and sneak under to chill his body, and studied the vast blue of the sky, with the white spears of mountains vivid against it like a design etched on glass.

He thought perhaps he'd stopped just here with his parents all those years ago, and remembered standing with his mother reading the guidebook.

The Olympic Range. And however vast and encompassing it seemed from this point, he knew that at lower elevations, in the forest where the grand trees ruled, it didn't exist. You would walk and walk in that dimness, or clatter up rocks on the tumbling hills and not see the stunning scope of them. Then you would take a turn, step out on a ridge, and there it would be. The vast sky-stealing stretch of it snatching your breath as if it had sneaked up on you instead of the other way around.

Noah took one last look, climbed back in his car and started down the switchback the way he'd come.

The trees took over. Became the world.

The detour took him a little more than an hour, but he still arrived at the lodge by three in the afternoon. He traveled up the same bumpy lane, catching glimpses of the stone and wood, the fairy-tale rooflines, the glint of glass that was the lodge.

He was about to tell himself it hadn't changed, when he spotted a structure nestled in the trees. It mirrored the style and materials of the lodge, but it was much smaller and not nearly as weathered.

The wooden sign over the double doorway read RIVER'S END NATU- RALIST CENTER. There was a walking path leading to it from the lane and another from the lodge. Wildflowers and ferns appeared to have been allowed to grow as they pleased around it, but his gardener's eye detected a human hand in the balance.

Olivia's hand, he thought, and felt a warm and unexpected spurt of pride.

It was undoubtedly man-made, but she had designed it to blend in so well it seemed to have grown there as naturally as the trees.

He parked his car, noted that the lot held a respectable number of vehicles. It was warmer here than it had been at the pull off. Warm enough, he noted, to keep the pansies and purple salvia happy in their long clay troughs near the entrance.

He swung on his backpack, took out his single suitcase and was just locking his car when a dog loped around the side of the lodge and grinned at him.

Noah couldn't think of another term for the expression. The dog's tongue lolled, the lips were peeled back and seemed to curve up, and the deep brown eyes danced with unmistakable delight.

"Hey there, fella."

Obviously seeing this as an invitation, the big yellow lab pranced across the lot, plopped down at Noah's feet and lifted a paw.

"You the welcoming committee, boy?" Obligingly, Noah shook hands, then cocked his head. "Or should I say girl. Your name wouldn't happen to be Shirley, would it?"

At the name, the dog let out one cheerful woof, then danced toward the entrance as if to tell Noah to come on, pal, get the lead out.

He was charmed enough to be vaguely disappointed when the dog didn't follow him inside.

He didn't see any dramatic changes in the lobby. Noah thought perhaps some of the furnishings had been replaced, and the paint was a soft, toasty yellow. But everything exuded such an aura of welcome and settled comfort that it might have been exactly so for a century.

The check-in was quick, efficient and friendly, and after having assured the clerk he could handle his baggage himself, he carried his bags, a package of information and his key up two squat sets of stairs in the main lobby and down a hallway to the right.

He'd requested a suite out of habit and because he preferred a separate area to set up his work. It was smaller than the rooms he remembered sharing with his parents, but certainly not cramped.

There was a nap-taking sofa, a small but sturdy desk, a table where guides and literature on the area were fanned. The art—running to watercolor prints of local flora—was better than decent, and the phone would support his modem.

He glanced at the view, pleased to have been given the side facing the back so it was untainted by cars. He dropped his suitcase on the chest at the foot of the sleigh bed of varnished golden wood and tossed the lid open. As his contribution to unpacking, he removed his shaving gear and dumped it on the narrow shelf over the white pedestal sink in the adjoining bath.

He considered the shower—he'd been in the car since six A.M.—and thought of the beer he might find in the lobby bar. After a mild debate he decided to take the first, then go hunt up the second.

He stripped, letting his clothes lay where they fell, then diddled with the controls of the shower until the water came out fast and hot. The minute he stepped under the spray, he groaned in pleasure.

Right decision, Brady, he thought as he let the water beat on his head. And after the beer, he'd wander around, scope out the place. He wanted to get a feel for the owners, to see if he could judge by how the staff and guests spoke of them which one of the MacBrides would be the best to approach.

He wanted to go over to the Center, find Olivia. Just look at her awhile.

He'd do that in the morning, he thought. After he got his bearings and a good night's sleep.

He toweled off, tugged on jeans. He gave some consideration to actually putting away the clothes in his bag. He opted instead to just dig out a shirt, when there was a hard rap on the door.

Noah quickly grabbed a shirt and carried it with him to the door.

He recognized her instantly. Later he would wonder why the recognition had been so immediate, and so intense. She'd certainly changed.

Her face was thinner, honed into sharp planes. Her mouth was firmer, still full and unpainted as it had been at nineteen, but it didn't strike him as innocent any longer.

And that gave him one hard tug of annoyance and regret.

He might have noted it wasn't smiling in welcome if he hadn't been dealing with the ridiculous and completely unexpected flash of pleasure.

Her hair had darkened to a color that reminded him of the caramels Mike's mother had always melted down at Halloween and swirled onto apples. And she'd lopped it off. Lopped off all that gorgeous shiny hair. And yet it suited her better this way. On another woman he supposed the short, straight cut with the fringe of bang would have been called pixyish. But there was nothing fairylike about the woman in the doorway with her tall and leanly athletic build.

She smelled like the woods and carried a stoneware bowl filled with fresh fruit.

He felt the foolish grin break out on his face and could think of nothing to say but: "Hi."

"Compliments of River's End Lodge." She thrust the bowl at him, straight into the gut and with enough force to earn a grunt from him.

"Ah, thanks."

She was in the room in one long stride that had him backing up automatically. When she slammed the door at her back, he lifted his eyebrows. "Do you come with the fruit? They hardly ever give you complimentary women in California."

"You have a hell of a nerve, sneaking in here this way."

Okay, he decided, all right, it wasn't going to be a friendly reunion. "You're right, absolutely. I don't know what I was thinking of, calling ahead for reservations, registering at the desk that way." He set the bowl down, gingerly rubbed his stomach. "Look, why don't we take a minute to—"

"I'll give you a minute." She rammed a finger into his chest. "I'll give you a minute, then you can get your butt back to Los Angeles. You have no right coming here this way."

"Of course I have a right. It's a goddamn hotel." He lifted a hand. "And don't poke at me again, okay?"

"I told you to stay away from me."

"And I damn well did." The flash in her eyes was a clear warning that had him narrowing his own. "Don't hit me again, Liv. I mean it. I'm pretty well fed up with female abuse. Now we can sit down and discuss this like reasonable adults, or we can just stand here and snarl at each other."

"I don't have anything to discuss with you. I'm *telling* you to go away and leave us alone."

"That's not going to happen." Deciding to play it another way, he sat, chose an apple from the bowl and stretched out his legs as he bit in. "I'm not going anywhere, Olivia. You might as well talk to me."

"I'm entitled to my privacy."

"Sure you are. That's the beauty of it. You don't tell me anything you don't want to tell me." He took another bite of the apple, then gestured with it. "We can start with something simple, like what you've been doing with yourself the last half dozen years."

Smug, smirky son of a bitch, she thought and spun away to pace. She hated that he looked the same, so much the same. The sun-streaked, wind-tossed hair; the full, firm mouth; the fascinating planes and angles of his face.

"If you were half the man your father is, you'd have some respect for my mother's memory."

That edgy little barb winged home and hooked itself bloodily in his heart. Noah studied his apple, turning it around in his hand until he was certain he could speak calmly. "You measured me by my father once before." He lifted his gaze, and it was hard as granite. "Don't do it again."

Olivia jammed her hands in her pockets, shot a withering glance over her shoulder. "You don't care what I think of you."

"You don't know what I care about."

"Money. They'll pay you big bucks for this book, won't they? Then you can bounce around on all the talk shows and spout off about yourself and the valuable insights you dug up on why my father butchered my mother."

"Don't you want to know why?" He spoke quietly and watched those wonderful eyes reflect fury, misery, then snap back to fury.

"I know why, and it doesn't change anything. Go away, Noah. Go back and write about someone else's tragedy."

"Liv." He called out to her as she strode toward the door. "I won't go away. Not this time."

She didn't stop, didn't look back, but slammed the door smartly enough to have the pictures rattling on the walls. Noah tossed his apple in the air. "Well, that was pleasant," he muttered, and decided he'd more than earned that beer.

SHE WENT DOWN THE BACK STAIRS, AVOIDING THE LOBBY and the people who would be milling around. She cut through the kitchen, only shaking her head when her name was called. She needed to get out, get out, get away until she could fight off the hideous pressure in her chest, the vicious roaring in her ears.

She had to force herself not to break out in a run, to try to outrace the panic that licked at her. She moved quickly into the forest, into the deep and the damp. Still, her breath wanted to come in pants, her knees wanted to shake. It wouldn't be permitted.

When she'd gone far enough, when the chances of anyone hiking down the path were slim, she sat down, there on the forest floor and rocked herself.

It was stupid. She'd been stupid, Olivia admitted as she pressed her forehead to her knees. She'd known he was coming. Jamie had told her he would, told her what he intended to do. Told her that she herself had decided to cooperate with him on the book.

That had generated the first genuine argument between them Olivia could remember.

Already, Noah Brady and his book were causing rifts in her family.

But she'd prepared herself to face him again. To deal with it. She wasn't the same naive, susceptible girl who'd fallen stupidly in love with him.

She hadn't expected that rush of feeling when he'd opened the door and smiled at her. So much the way he had six years before. She hadn't expected her heart to break again, not after she'd spent so much time and effort to heal it.

Temper was better than pain.

Still, she'd handled it—handled him—poorly.

She'd kept her eye out for his reservation. When it had come in, she'd promised herself she would go to his room after he'd checked in, so that she could talk to him, reason with him, in private. She would be calm, explain each one of her objections.

He was Frank Brady's son, after all. And Frank was one of the few people she trusted absolutely.

She arranged to take the fruit bowl up herself, had worked out exactly what she would say and how she would say it.

Welcome to River's End again, Noah. It's nice to see you. Can I come in for a minute?

Reasonable, calm, rational. But as she'd started toward his room the fear had crawled into her and she'd gripped her anger like a weapon to beat it back.

Then he'd opened the door, and smiled at her. Smiled, she thought now as she turned her head to rest her cheek on her updrawn knees, with absolute delight. As if there had never been betrayal, never been deceit.

And he'd looked so pleased and attractive—his hair dark and wet from the shower, his moss-green eyes lit with pleasure—that some ridiculous part of her had wanted to smile back.

So she'd attacked. What other choice had she had? she thought now. Instead of persuading him, or intimidating him, into backing away from the book, she was dead sure she'd convinced him to dig in his heels.

She wanted to be left alone. She wanted to protect her world and to be left alone inside it.

Why had Sam Tanner contacted Noah? No. Furious, she squeezed her eyes shut. She didn't want to think about that, about him. She didn't want to know. She'd put all that away, just as her grandmother had put her memories in the chest in the attic.

It had taken years to accomplish it. Years of secret visits to that attic, of nightmares, years of painful, guilty searches for any snippet of information about her parents.

And once she'd found all there was to find, she'd put it away, focused on the present and the future rather than the past. She found peace of mind, contentment in her work, a direction to her life.

All that was threatened now. Because Sam Tanner was getting out of prison, and Noah Brady was writing a book. Those were facts she couldn't ignore.

She glanced over as the lab raced down the path. The greeting took the form of a dancing leap and many sloppy kisses that had Olivia's tension breaking open so that a laugh could pour out.

"I can always count on you, can't I?" She nuzzled into Shirley's neck before she rose. "Let's go home, girl. Let's just go home and worry about all this later."

THE FOOD WAS GREAT. NOAH GAVE THE MACBRIDES HIGH marks on the lodge kitchen, particularly after indulging himself in two passes through the breakfast buffet. The service was right up there on a level with the food—warm, friendly, efficient without being obvious.

His bed had been comfortable, and if he'd been in the mood, he could have chosen from a very decent list of in-room movies.

He'd worked instead and now felt he deserved a morning to piddle.

Trouble was, he mused, looking out the window of the dining room at the steady, drumming rain, the weather wasn't quite as appealing as the rest of the fare.

Then again, the brochures had warned him to expect rainy springs. And he couldn't say it wasn't picturesque in its way. A far cry from his own sun-washed California coast, but there was something compelling about the shadowy grays and greens and the liquid wall of rain. It didn't make him long to strap on his foul-weather gear and take a hike, but it was pleasant to study from inside the cozy warmth of the lodge.

He'd already made use of the health club and had found it expanded and nicely modernized since his last visit. They'd added an indoor pool, and even as he considered a swim he tossed the idea aside. He couldn't imagine he'd be the only one with the idea and the prospect of families splashing around and hooting at one another just didn't fit his plans.

He could get a massage, or make use of the lodge library, which he'd wandered into the evening before and found well stocked and welcoming.

Or he could do what he'd come for and start poking around.

He could hunt up Olivia and argue with her again.

The bark of male laughter had him glancing over, then narrowing his eyes in speculation. The man was dressed in a plaid flannel shirt and work trousers. His hair was thick, a Cary Grant silver that caught the overhead lights as he worked the dining room, stopping by tables of those who, like Noah, were lingering over that last cup of coffee.

His brows were defiantly dark, and though Noah couldn't catch the color of his eyes, he imagined they would be that odd and beautiful golden brown. He had the whipcord build and appearance of impossible fitness of an elderly outdoorsman.

Rob MacBride, Noah thought, and decided that lingering over coffee and rain watching had been the perfect way to spend his morning.

He sat back and waited for his turn.

It didn't take long for Rob to complete the circuit and pause by Noah's table with a quick grin. "Pretty day, isn't it?"

"For ducks," Noah said, since it seemed expected. He was rewarded with that deep, barking laugh.

"Rain's what makes us what we are here. I hope you're enjoying your stay."

"Very much. It's a great place. You've made a few changes since I was here last, but you've kept the tone."

"So, you've stayed with us before."

"A long time ago." Noah held out his hand. "I'm Noah Brady, Mr. MacBride."

"Welcome back."

He watched for it, but saw no hint of recognition in Rob's eyes. "Thanks. I came here with my parents, about twelve years ago. Frank and Celia Brady."

"We're always pleased to have the next generation . . ." The recognition came now, and along with it quiet grief. "Frank Brady? Your father?"

"Yes."

Rob stared out the window at the rain. "That's a name I haven't thought of in a long time. A very long time."

"If you'll sit down, Mr. MacBride, I'll tell you why I'm here."

Rob shifted his gaze back, glanced at Noah's face. "I guess that's the thing to do, isn't it? Hailey?" he called out to the waitress just clearing another station. "Could you get us some coffee over here?"

He sat, laid his long, thin hands on the table. They showed the age, Noah noted; his face didn't. There was always some part of you, he mused, that was marked with time.

"Your father's well?"

"Yeah, he's good. Retired recently, drove my mother crazy for a while, then found something to keep himself busy and out of her hair."

Rob nodded, grateful Noah had slipped into small talk. He found it kind. "Man doesn't keep busy, he gets old fast. The lodge, the campground, the people who come and go here, that's what keeps me young. Got managers and such doing a lot of the day-to-day work now, but I still keep my hand in."

"It's a place to be proud of. I've felt at home since I walked in the door." Except for one small incident with your granddaughter, Noah thought, but decided it wouldn't be politic to mention it.

"I'll top that off, Mr. Brady," Hailey said, then poured a cup for Rob.

"So did you go into police work like your dad?" he questioned.

"No. I'm a writer."

"Really." Rob's face brightened. "Nothing like a good story. What sort of things do you write?"

"I write nonfiction. True crime." He waited a beat as he could already see the awareness moving over Rob's face. "I'm writing a book about what happened to your daughter."

Rob lifted his cup, sipped slowly. When he spoke it wasn't anger in his voice, but weariness. "Over twenty years now. Hasn't everything been said already?"

"I don't think so. I've had an interest in what happened since I was a kid. My father's connection, how it affected him made an impression on me."

He paused, weighed his words, then decided to be as honest as he was able. "I think, on some level, I'd always planned to write about it. I didn't know how I'd approach it, but I knew when the time came, I'd write it. The time came a few weeks ago when Sam Tanner contacted me."

"Tanner. Why won't he let her rest?"

"He wants to tell his story."

"And you think he'll tell you the truth?" Bitterness crackled in his voice like ice. "You think the man who murdered my daughter, who sliced her to ribbons, is capable of telling the truth?"

"I can't say, but I can tell you I'm capable of separating truth from lies. I don't intend for this book to be Tanner's. I don't intend for what I write to be simply his view noted down on paper. I'm going to talk to everyone who was touched or involved. I've already begun to. That's why I'm here, Mr. MacBride, to understand and incorporate your view."

"Julie was one of the brightest lights of my life, and he snuffed her out. He took her love, twisted it into a weapon and destroyed her with it. What other view could I possibly have?"

"You knew her in a way no one else could. You know them in a way no one else could. That's what matters."

Rob lifted his hands, rubbed them over his face. "Noah, do you have any idea how many times we were approached during the two years after Julie's death? To give interviews, to endorse books, movies, television features?"

"I can imagine, and I'm aware you refused them all."

"All," Rob agreed. "They offered us obscene amounts of money, promises, threats. The answer was always no. Why do you think I would say yes now, after all these years, to you?"

"Because I'm not going to offer you money, or make any threats, and I'll only give you one promise. I'll tell the truth, and by telling it, I'll do right by your daughter."

"Maybe you will," Rob said after a moment. "I believe you'll try to. But Julie's gone, Noah, and I have to think of the family I have left."

"Would it be better for them for this book to be written without their input?"

"I don't know. The wound's not raw anymore, but it still aches from time to time. There have been moments I wanted to have my say, but they passed." He let out a long sigh. "A part of me, I admit, doesn't want her to be forgotten. Doesn't want what happened to her to be forgotten."

"I haven't forgotten." Noah waited while Rob's gaze jerked back to his face. "Tell me what you want remembered."

EIGHTEEN

THE Naturalist Center was Olivia's baby. It had been her concept, her design and in a very real sense her Holy Grail.

She'd insisted on using the money she'd inherited from her mother, and at twenty-one, degree fresh and crisp in her hand, she'd reached into her trust fund and built her dream.

She'd supervised every aspect of the center, from the laying of stone to the arrangement of seats in the small theater where visitors could watch a short documentary on the area's flora and fauna. She'd chosen every slide and each voice-over in the lobby area personally, had interviewed and hired the staff, commissioned the to-scale model of the Quinault Valley and rain forest and often worked as guide on the hikes the center offered.

In the year since she'd opened the doors to the public, she'd never been more content.

She wasn't going to allow Noah Brady to spoil that carefully structured contentment.

With her mind only half on the job, she continued to take her small group of visitors on their indoor tour of the local mammals.

"The Roosevelt, or Olympic, elk is the biggest of the wapiti. Large herds of Roosevelt elk make their home along the Olympic Peninsula. In a very real way, we owe the preservation of this area to this native animal, as it was to protect their breeding grounds and summer range that President Theodore Roosevelt, during the final days of his administration, issued the proclamation that created Mount Olympus National Monument."

She glanced up as the main door opened and instantly felt her nerves fray.

Noah gave her a slight nod, a half grin, then began to wander around the main area, leaving a trail of wet behind him. As a matter of pride, Olivia continued her lecture, moving from elk to black-tailed deer, from deer to marten, but when she paused by the *Castor canadensis,* the beaver, and the memory of sitting on the riverbank with Noah flashed into her mind, she signaled to one of her staff to take over.

She wanted to turn around and go lock herself in her office. Paperwork was, always, a viable excuse. But she knew it would look cowardly. Worse, it would *feel* cowardly. So, instead, she walked over and stood beside him as he examined one of the enlarged slides with apparent fascination.

"So, that's a shrew."

"A wandering shrew, *Sorex vagrans,* quite common in this region. We also have the Trowbridge, the masked and the dusky shrew. There are Pacific water shrews, northern water shrews and shrew moles, though the masked shrew is rare."

"I guess I'm only acquainted with city shrews."

"That's very lame humor."

"Yeah, but you've gotta start somewhere. You did a great job here, Liv. I knew you would."

"Really? I didn't realize you'd paid attention to any of my ramblings back then."

"I paid attention to everything about you. Everything, Olivia."

She shut down, shuttered over. "I'm not going back there. Not now, not ever."

"Fine, let's stay here then." He wandered over and studied what he decided was a particularly ugly creature called a western big-eared bat. "Want to show me around?"

"You don't give a damn about natural science, so why waste each other's time?"

"Pardon me, but you're talking to someone who was raised on whale song and the plight of the pelican. I'm a card-carrying member of Greenpeace, the Nature Conservancy and the World Wildlife Federation. I get calendars every year."

Because she wanted to smile, she sighed. "The documentary runs every hour on the half hour in the theater. You can catch it in ten minutes right through those doors to your left."

"Where's the popcorn?"

Because she nearly did smile, she turned away. "I'm busy."

"No you're not." He caught her arm, held it in what he hoped she'd consider a light, nonthreatening grip. "You can make yourself busy, just as you can take a few minutes."

"I don't intend to discuss my family with you."

"Okay, let's talk about something else. How'd you come up with this? The design, I mean." He used his free hand to gesture. "It's no small deal, and looks a lot more entertaining than most of the nature places my mother dragged me into before I could fight back."

"I'm a naturalist. I live here."

"Come on, Liv, it takes more than that. Did you study design, too?"

"No, I didn't study design, I just saw it this way."

"Well, it works. Nothing to scare the little kids away in here. It doesn't whisper educational in that dry, crackling voice or bounce out with chipper graphics that give the parents migraines. Nice colors, good space. What's through here?"

He moved past the reception counter, where books and postcards of the area were neatly displayed for sale, and through a wide doorway.

"Hey, this is very cool." Centered in a room where more displays of plant and animal life were on view was the model of the valley. "Hawk's-eye view," he said, leaning over it. "And here we are. The lodge, the center." He tapped his finger on the protective dome. "There's the trail we took that day, isn't it, along the river? You even put in the beaver dam. Your grandparents have a house, though, don't they? I don't see it here."

"Because it's private."

He straightened, and his gaze seemed to drive straight into hers. "Are you under this glass dome, Liv, tucked away where no one can get to you?"

"I'm exactly where I want to be."

"My book isn't likely to change that, but what it might do is sweep out all the shadows that still hang over what happened that night. I've got a chance to bring the truth out, the whole of it. Sam Tanner's talking, for the first time since the trial, and a dying man often chooses to clear his conscience before it's over."

"Dying?"

"The tumor," Noah began, then watched with shocked alarm as her face went sheet white. "I'm sorry. I thought you knew."

All she felt was her throat, the burn of the words forcing their way out. "Are you telling me he's dying?"

"He has brain cancer; he only has months left. Come on, you need to sit down."

He took her arm, but she jerked herself free. "Don't touch me." She turned quickly and strode through the next doorway.

He would have let her go, told himself to let her go. But he could still see the shock glazing her eyes. Swearing under his breath, he went after her.

She had a long stride and the dead-ahead gait of a woman who would plow over obstacles on her way to the finish line. He told himself to remember that if he ever had to get in her way.

But he caught up just as she turned into an office past the theater area and nearly got flattened when she swung the door closed.

He managed to block it instead of walking face-first into it, then shut it behind him.

"This is an employees-only area." Which was a stupid lie, she thought, but the best she had. "Take a hike."

"Sit down." It appeared he was going to have to get in her way already, and so he took her arm once again, steered her around the desk and into the chair behind it. He had the impression of a small space, methodically organized, and crouching down, concentrated on her.

"I'm sorry." He took her hand without either of them really being aware of the gesture. "I wouldn't have dropped it on you that way. I thought Jamie would've told you."

"She didn't. And it doesn't matter."

"Of course it matters. Want some water or something?" He looked around hoping to spot a cooler, a jug, anything that would give him something to do.

"I don't need anything. I'm perfectly fine." She looked down, saw her hand in his. With baffled shock she noted her fingers had linked with his and curled tight. Mortally embarrassed, she shook free.

"Stand up, for God's sake. All I need is someone coming in here and seeing you kneeling at my feet."

"I wasn't kneeling." But he straightened up, then opted to sit on the corner of the desk.

It was more than her hair she'd changed. This Olivia was a hell of a lot tougher, a hell of a lot edgier than the shy college student he'd tumbled for.

"You did speak with Jamie, didn't you, about my wanting to talk with you?"

"Yes."

"Why didn't she tell you that Sam was dying?"

"We argued." Olivia leaned back in her chair. Her head didn't feel light any longer. She just felt tired. "We never argue, so that's one more thing I have to thank you and your book for. If she'd intended to tell me, I suppose it got lost in the fray."

"He wants to tell his story before he dies. If he doesn't, it dies with him. Is that really what you want?"

The need she'd worked so hard to bury tried to claw its way free. "It doesn't matter what I want, you'll do it anyway. You always planned to."

"Yeah, I did. And I'm telling you straight out this time, up-front. The way I should have before."

"I said I won't discuss that." And just that coolly, she snapped the door shut. "You want what you want. And as for him, he wants to purge him-self before it's too late, and look for what? Forgiveness? Redemption?"

"Understanding, maybe. I think he's trying to understand himself how it all happened. I want your part of it, Liv. All the others I'll talk to are pieces of the whole, but you're the key. Your grandfather claims you have a photographic memory. Is that true?"

"Yes," she said absently. "I see words. It's just . . . my grandfather?" She leaped to her feet. "You spoke to my grandfather."

"Just after breakfast."

"You stay away from him."

"He came up to my table, which from what I observed, he's in the habit of doing with guests. I told him who I was and why I was here. If you have a problem with his agreeing to talk to me, you'll have to take it up with him."

"He's over seventy. You have no business putting him through this."

"I should be in such good shape at seventy. I didn't strap him on the rack and crank the wheel, for Christ's sake." Damn it, would she forever make him feel guilty? "We had a conversation over coffee. Then he agreed to a taped interview in my room. And when we finished the session, he didn't shuffle out bent and broken. He looked relieved. Sam isn't the only one with something to purge, Liv."

It shook her enough to have her running a nervous hand through her hair. "He agreed to it? He spoke with you about it? What did he say?"

"Oh, no." Intrigued, Noah studied her. "I don't prime the pump that way. I want what you tell me to come from you, not to be a reflection of what other people think and feel."

"He never talks about it."

What was that, under the surprise, Noah wondered. Hurt? "He did today, and he agreed to at least one more interview before I leave."

"What's going on? I don't understand what's going on around here."

"Maybe it's just time. Why don't we try this? I'll talk to you, tell you about my wild and exciting life and all my fascinating opinions on the world in general. Once you see how charming and brilliant I am, you'll have an easier time talking to me."

"You're not nearly as charming as you think you are."

"Sure I am. Let's have dinner."

Oh, they'd gone that route before. "No."

"Okay, that was knee-jerk, I could tell. Let's try again. Let's have dinner."

This time she angled her head, took a steady five seconds. "No."

"All right, I'll just have to pay for you."

Her eyes went molten, a deep, rich gold that made him think of old paintings executed by masters. "You think I care about your money? That you can bribe me. You sleazy son of a——"

"Hold it, that's not what I meant. I meant I'd have to hire you—as in *ask for information on our day packages, including hikes guided by one of our professional naturalists.* The professional would be you. So which trail would you recommend for a nice, scenic hike tomorrow?"

"Forget it."

"Oh no, you advertise, you follow through. I'm a paying customer. Now do you want to recommend a trail, or should I just pick one at random?"

"You want to hike?" Oh, she'd give him a hike, Olivia thought. She'd give him one for the books. "That's fine, that's just what we're here for. Make the reservation out at the desk. Just give them my name and book it for seven tomorrow."

"That would be A.M.?"

"Is that a problem, city boy?"

"No, just clarifying." He eased off the desk and found himself a great deal closer to her than was comfortable for either of them. She smelled the same. For several dizzy minutes, it was all he could think about.

She smelled the same.

He felt the tug, the definite, unmistakable jerk in the gut of basic lust. And though he told himself not to do it, his gaze lowered to her mouth just long enough to make him remember.

"Well, *hmmm.*" He thought the reaction damn inconvenient all around and stepped aside. "I'll see you in the morning, then."

"Be sure to take one of our hiker's guides along with you, so you know how to dress for the trail."

"I know how the hell to dress," he muttered, and more annoyed with himself than he thought was fair, he strode out.

She made him feel guilty one minute, he thought, and angry the next. Protective, then aggressive. He damn well didn't want to be attracted to her again and add one more layer to cloud the issue.

He stopped by reception as instructed and booked the time. The clerk tapped out the information on her keyboard and offered him a cheery smile. "If I could just have your name?"

"Just use my initials," he heard himself saying. "S.O.B."

He had a feeling Olivia would get it.

OLIVIA KNEW HER GRANDMOTHER HAD BEEN CRYING. SHE came in the back door out of habit, the wet dog prancing at her heels. It only took one look to have her heart squeezing.

Val insisted on preparing the evening meal. Every day, like clockwork, she could be found in the kitchen at six o'clock, stirring or slicing, with good homey scents puffing out of pots and Vanna White turning letters on the under-the-counter TV. Often, Val could be heard calling out advice or muttering pithy comments such as *Don't buy a vowel, you moron.* Or shaking her head because the contestant at the wheel couldn't guess A Stitch in Time Saves Nine to save his immortal soul.

It was a comforting routine, and one that rarely varied. Olivia would come in, pour a glass of wine—it had been a soft drink or juice in her youth—and set the table while the two of them just talked.

But tonight, she came in chilled to the bone, her rain gear slick with wet from the aimless walk she and Shirley had indulged in, and there was no incessant clapping or bright colors on the little TV screen. Pots simmered, Val stirred, but she kept her back to the room. There was no smile of greeting tossed over her shoulder.

"You keep that wet dog in the mudroom, Livvy."

Because her voice was thick and a little rusty, Olivia recognized tears. "Go on, Shirley, go lie down now." Olivia shooed the dog back into the mudroom, where she curled up, a sulky look in her eyes, with her chew rope.

Olivia poured them both a glass of wine, and leaving the table unset, walked over to set her grandmother's on the counter by the stove. "I know you're upset. I'm sorry this is happening."

"It's nothing we need to talk about. We're having beef and barley stew tonight. I'm about ready to add the dumplings."

Olivia's first instinct was to nod and get out the deep bowls. To let the subject bury itself again. But she wondered if Noah wasn't right about at least one thing. Maybe it was just time.

"Grandma, it's happening whether we talk about it or not."

"Then there's no point in bringing it up." She reached for the bowl where the dough was already mixed and ready. And, reaching blindly, knocked the glass off the counter. It shattered on the floor, a shower of glass and bloodred wine.

"Oh, what was that doing there? Don't you know better than to set a glass on the edge of the counter? Just look at my floor."

"I'm sorry. I'll clean it up." Olivia turned quickly to get the broom out of the closet and shushed the dog, who'd leaped up as if to defend the womenfolk from invaders. "Relax, Shirley, it's broken glass not a gunshot."

But any amusement she felt vanished when she turned back and saw her grandmother standing, shoulders shaking, her face buried in a dish towel.

"Oh, I'm sorry, I'm sorry, I'm so sorry." She dropped the broom and rushed over to grab Val close.

"I won't deal with it again. I can't. I told Rob to tell that young man to go. Just to pack his bags and go, but he won't do it. He says it's not right, and it won't change anything anyway."

"I'll make him go." Olivia pressed her lips to Val's hair. "I'll send him away."

"No, it won't matter. I knew that, even when I was fighting with Rob. It won't matter. It can't be stopped. We weren't able to stop any of the talk or the books twenty years ago; we won't stop it now. But I can't open my heart to that kind of grief again."

She stepped back, wiping at her face. "I can't and I won't. So you're

to tell him not to come here asking me to talk. And I won't have it discussed in this house."

"He won't come here, Grandma. I'll make sure of it."

"I shouldn't have snapped at you about the glass. It's just a glass." Val
pressed her fingers to her left eye, then her temple. "I've got a headache,
that's all. Makes my temper short. You see to those dumplings for me,
Livvy. I'll just go take some aspirin and lie down for a few minutes."

"All right. Grandma—"

Val cut her off with a look. "Just put the dumplings on, Livvy. Your
grandfather gets cross if we eat much later than six-thirty."

Just like that, Olivia thought as Val walked out of the kitchen. It was
closed off, shut out. Not to be discussed. Another chest for the attic, she
decided, and turned to pick up the broom.

But this time around, the lock wasn't going to hold.

JUST AFTER NINE, ABOUT THE TIME NOAH WAS DEBATING
between a couple of hours' work or a movie break, Mike whistled his
way up the walk of the beach house.

He'd meant to get there earlier, to give Noah's plants and flowers a
good watering before full dark, but one thing had led to another. Namely
one of his co-workers had challenged him to a marathon game of Mortal
Kombat, which had led to dueling computers for two hours and eighteen
minutes.

But victory was its own reward, Mike thought. And to sweeten the
pot, he'd called his date and asked if she'd like to meet him at Noah's for
a walk on the beach, a dip in his friend's hot tub and whatever else struck
their fancy.

He didn't figure Noah would mind. And he'd pay off the usage by
getting up early and seeing to the gardens.

He flipped the porch light on, then moseyed into the kitchen to see
if good old Noah had any fancy wine suitable for hot tub seductions.

He studied labels, and trusting Noah's judgment on such details, chose
one with a French-sounding name. He set it on the counter, wondering

if it was supposed to breathe or not, then with a shrug, opened the refrigerator to see if Noah had any interesting food stocked.

He was still whistling, cheerfully debating between a package of brie and a plate of sad-looking fried chicken when he caught a flash of movement out of the corner of his eye.

He straightened fast, felt a brilliant burst of pain. He staggered back, reaching up thinking he'd bashed his head on the refrigerator.

His hand came away wet; he stared dumbly at the blood smearing his fingertips. "Oh shit," he managed, before the second blow buckled his knees and sent him down into the dark.

NINETEEN

I T was still raining when Noah's alarm buzzed at six. He slapped at it, opened his eyes to the gloom and considered doing what any sensible man did on a rainy morning. Sleeping through it.

But a few hours' cozy oblivion didn't seem worth the smirk and snippy comments Olivia would lay on him. Maybe it was pride, maybe he had something to prove to both of them, but either way, he rolled out of bed. He stumbled into the shower, which brought him up one level of consciousness, stumbled out again, then dressed for the day.

He decided anyone planning on tromping around in the trees in the rain had to be crazy. He figured out Olivia had known it was going to rain, had probably *arranged* for it to rain just to pay him back for being a jerk. He groused about it all the way down to the lobby, where he found several small groups of people suited up for the day and helping themselves to the complimentary coffee and doughnuts the inn provided for early hikers.

Most of them, Noah noted with complete bafflement, looked happy to be there.

At seven, riding on a caffeine-and-sugar high, he felt nearly human.

He drummed up enough energy to flirt with the desk clerk, then snagged one last doughnut for the road and headed out.

He spotted Olivia immediately. She stood in the gloom, rain pattering on her bush-style hat, fog twisting around her boots and ankles as she spoke to a quartet of guests about their planned route for the morning. The dog milled around, charming head scratches and handshakes out of the early risers.

She acknowledged Noah with a nod, then watched the group head off. "You set?"

Noah took another bite of his tractor wheel. "Yeah."

"Let's see." She stood back, skimmed her measuring glance up, then down, then up again. "How long have those boots been out of the box, ace?"

Less than an hour, Noah thought, as he'd bought them in San Francisco. "So I haven't been hiking in a few years. Unless we're planning on climbing the Matterhorn, I'm up for it. I'm in shape."

"Health-club shape." She pressed a finger against his flat belly. "Fancy health club, too. This won't be like your StairMaster. Where's your water bottle?"

Already irritated with her, he held out a hand, cupped it and let rain pool in his palm. Olivia only shook her head. "Hold on a minute." She turned on her heel and headed back into the lodge.

"Is it just me," Noah asked Shirley, "or does she browbeat everyone?" When the dog merely sat, shot the doughnut a hopeful look, Noah broke what was left in half, tossed it. Shirley caught it on the fly, gulped it whole, then belched cheerfully.

Noah was still grinning when Olivia jogged back out with a plastic water bottle and belt loop. "You always take your own water," Olivia began and to Noah's surprise began to nimbly hook the bottle to his belt.

"Thanks."

"I had them charge it to your room."

"No, I meant for the personal service, Mom."

She nearly smiled. He caught the start of one in her eyes, then she shrugged and snapped her fingers for the dog, who went instantly to heel. "Let's go."

She intended to start him off on the basic nature trail, the mile loop recommended for inexperienced hikers and parents with small children. To lull him into complacency, she thought with an inner smirk.

Fog smoked along the ground, slid through the trees, tangled in the fronds of ferns. Rain pattered through it, a monotonous drum and plunk. The gloom thickened as they entered the forest, pressing down as if it had weight and turning the fog into a ghost river.

"God what a place." He felt suddenly small, eerily defenseless. "Can't you just see a clawed hand coming up out of the fog, grabbing your ankle and dragging you down? You'd have time for one short scream, then the only sound would be . . . slurping."

"Oh, so you've heard about the Forest Feeder."

"Come on."

"We lose an average of fifteen hikers a year." She lifted a shoulder in dismissal. "We try to keep it quiet. Don't want to discourage tourists."

"That's good," Noah murmured, but gave the fog a cautious glance. "That's very good."

"That was easy," she corrected. "Very easy." She took out a flashlight, shined it straight up. It had the effect of slicing a beam through the gloom and casting the rest into crawling shadows.

"The overstory here is comprised of Sitka spruce, western hemlock, Douglas fir and western red cedar. Each is distinctive in the length of its needles, the shape of its cones and, of course, the pattern of its bark."

"Of course."

She ignored him. "The trees, and the profusion of epiphytes, screen out the sunlight and cause the distinctive green twilight."

"What's an epiphyte?"

"Like a parasite. Ferns, mosses, lichen. In this case they cause no real harmful effect to their hosts. You can see how they drape, form a kind of canopy in the overstory. And here, below, they carpet the ground, cover the trunks. Life and death are constantly at work here. Even without the Forest Feeder."

She switched off her light, pocketed it.

She continued the lecture as they walked. He listened with half an ear to her description of the trees. Her voice was attractive, just a shade husky. He had no doubt she kept her spiel in simple terms for the layman, but she didn't make him feel brainless.

It was enough, Noah realized, just to look. Enough just to be there with all those shapes and shadows and the oddly appealing scent of rot. To draw in air as thick as water. He'd thought he'd be bored or at the most resigned to using this route to draw her out. Instead, he was fascinated.

Despite the rain and fog there was a quiet green glow, an otherworldly pulse of it that highlighted thick tumbles of ferns and knotty hillocks coated with moss. Everything dripped and shimmered.

He heard a cracking sound from above and looked up in time to see a thick branch tumble down and crash to the forest floor. "You wouldn't want to be under one of them, would you?"

"Widow maker," she said with a dry smile.

He glanced at the branch again, decided it would have knocked him flat and out cold. "Good thing for me we're not married."

"Occasionally, the epiphytes absorb enough rain to weigh down the branch. Overburdened, it breaks. Down here, it'll become part of the cycle, providing a home for something else." She stopped abruptly, held up a hand. "Quiet," she told him in a soft whisper and motioned for him to angle behind the wide column of a spruce.

"What?"

She only shook her head, pressed two fingers to his lips as if to seal them. She held them there, while he wondered how she'd react if he started to nibble. Then he heard whatever had alerted her and felt the dog quivering between them.

Without a clue as to what to expect, he laid a hand on her shoulder in a protective move and scanned through the trees and vines toward the sound of something large in motion.

They stepped out of the gloom, wading knee high through the river of fog. Twelve, no fifteen, he corrected, fifteen enormous elk, their racks like crowns.

"Where are the girls?" he muttered against Olivia's fingers and earned a quick glare.

One let out a bellow, a deep bugling call that seemed to shake the trees. Then they slipped through the shadows and the green, their passing a rumble on the springy ground. Noah thought he caught the scent of them, something wild, then they were moving away, slowly sliding into the shadows.

"The females," Olivia said, "travel in herds with the younger males. More mature males, such as what we just saw, travel in smaller herds, until late summer when all bets are off and they become hostile with one another in order to cull out or keep their harem."

"Harem, huh?" He grinned. "Sounds like fun. So, were those Roosevelt elk?" Noah asked. "The kind you were talking about yesterday?"

If she was surprised he'd been paying attention, and had bothered to remember, she didn't show it. "Yes. We often see them on this trail this time of year."

"Then I'm glad we took it. They're huge, a long way from Bambi and family."

"You can see Bambi and family, too. During rutting season there're some high times in the forest."

"I'll just bet. Why didn't she bark? Or chase after them?" he asked, lowering a hand to Shirley's head.

"Training over instinct. You're a good girl, aren't you?" She crouched down to give Shirley a good, strong rub, then unwound the leash on her belt and hooked it to the dog's collar.

"What's that for?"

"We're moving off MacBride land. Dogs have to be leashed on government property. We don't like it much, do we?" she said to Shirley. "But that's the rule. Or . . ." She straightened and looked Noah in the eye. "We can circle back if you've had enough."

"I thought we were just getting started."

"It's your dime."

They continued on. He saw she had a compass on her belt, but she didn't consult it. She seemed to know exactly where she was, and where she was going. She didn't hurry, but gave him time to look, to ask questions.

Rain sprinkled through the canopy, plopped onto the ground like the drip of a thousand leaky faucets. But the fog began to lift, thinning, tearing into swirls, creeping back into itself.

The trail she chose began to climb and climb steeply. The light changed subtly until it was a luminous green pearled by the weak sunlight that fell through small breaks in the canopy, and in the breaks he caught glimpses of color from wildflowers, the variance of shades and textures of the green.

"It reminds me of snorkeling."

"What?"

"I've been snorkeling in Mexico," he told her. "You get good enough at it, you can go under for pretty decent periods and play around. The light's odd, not green like this really, but different, and the sun will cut through the surface, angle down. Everything's soft and full of shapes. Easy to get lost down there. Ever been snorkeling?"

"No."

"You'd like it."

"Why?"

"Well, you're stripped down to the most basic of gear and you're taking on a world that isn't yours. You never know what you'll see next. You like surprises?"

"Not particularly."

"Liar." He grinned at her. "Everybody likes surprises. Besides, you're a naturalist. The marine world might not be your forte, but you'd like it. My friend Mike and I spent two very memorable weeks in Cozumel a couple of years back."

"Snorkeling?"

"Oh yeah. So what do you do for play these days?"

"I take irritating city boys through the forest."

"I haven't irritated you for at least an hour. I clocked it. Wow! There it is."

"What?" Thrown off, she spun around.

"You smiled. You didn't catch yourself that time and actually smiled at me." He patted a hand to his heart. "Now I'm in love. Let's get married and raise more labradors."

She snorted out a laugh. "There, you irritated me again. Mark your time."

"No, I didn't." He fell into step with her and thought how easy it was to slide back into a rhythm with her as well. "You're starting to like me again, Liv. You're not going to be able to help yourself."

"I may be edging toward tolerate, but that's a long way from like. Now here, if you watch the trail, you'll notice oxalis, liverwort—"

"I can never get enough liverwort. You ever get down to L.A.?"

"No." She flicked a glance toward him, didn't quite meet his eyes. "No."

"I thought you might go visit your aunt now and then."

"They come here, at least twice a year."

"I got to tell you, it's tough to imagine Jamie tramping through the woods. That's one very impressive lady. Still, I guess that since this is where she grew up, she'd slide back in easily. What about her husband?"

"Uncle David? He loves her enough to come, to stay and to let my grandmother haul him off to fish on the lake. That's been the routine for years, even though everyone knows he hates fishing. If his luck's running bad, he actually catches some, then he has to clean them. Once we talked him into camping."

"Only once?"

"I think that's how Aunt Jamie got her pearl-and-diamond necklace. It was his bribe that she never make him sleep in the woods again. No cell phones, no laptops, no room service." She slid him a sidelong glance. "You'd relate, I imagine."

"Hey, I can give up my cell phone any time I want. It's not an addiction. And I've slept outside plenty."

"In a tent pitched in your backyard."

"And in Boy Scout camp."

The laugh bubbled out without her realizing it. "You were never a Boy Scout."

"I was, too. For one brief, shining period of six and a half months. It was the uniforms that turned me away. I mean, come on, those hats are really lame."

He was getting a little winded, but didn't want to break the flow now that he had her talking. "You do the Girl Scout thing?"

"No, I was never interested in joining groups."

"You just didn't want to wear that dumb beanie."

"It was a factor. How're the boots holding up?"

"Fine. You can't miss with L. L. Bean."

"You're starting to chug, ace. Want to stop?"

"I'm not chugging. That's Shirley. How come I'm supposed to use your name, but you don't use mine?"

"It keeps slipping my mind." She tapped a finger on the water bottle dangling from his belt. "Take a drink. Keep your muscles oiled. You'll note here that the vine maples are taller, more treelike than they are on the bottomland. You can see patches of soil through the mat. We've climbed about five hundred feet."

The world opened up again, with smoky peaks and green valleys, with a sky that was like burnished steel. The rain had stopped, but the ground beneath his feet was still moldering with it and the air tasted as wet as the water he swallowed.

"What's this place?"

"We switched over to Three Lakes Trail."

He could see how the river, the winding run of it, cut through forest and hill, the jagged islands of rock that pushed up through the stone-colored water like bunched fists. The wind flew into his face, roared through the tops of the trees at his back and was swallowed up by the forest.

"Nothing gentle about it, is there?"

"No. It's good to remember that. A lot of Sunday hikers don't, and they pay for it. Nature isn't kind. It's relentless."

"Funny, I would have said you prefer it to people."

"I do. Got your wind back?"

"I hadn't lost my wind." Exactly.

"If we cross the bridge here, then follow the trail another three and a half miles, we'll come to the lake area. Or we can turn back."

"I can do another three and a half miles."

"All right, then."

Big Creek Bridge spanned the water. He heard the rush of it as they crossed, felt the push and pull of the wind and adjusted his body to brace against it. Olivia hiked ahead as if they'd been strolling down Wilshire Boulevard.

He tried not to hate her for it.

In less than a mile, his feet were killing him and his quads were screaming. She hadn't bothered to mention the last leg was straight up. Noah gritted his teeth and kept pace.

He tried to keep his mind off his abused body by taking in the scenery, thinking about the massage he was going to book the minute he got back to the lodge, speculating on what Olivia had brought along for lunch.

He caught a flash out of the corner of his eye, glanced up in time to see something spring through the thinning trees. "What was that?"

"Flying squirrel. That's a rare sighting during the day. They're nocturnal."

"No shit? Like Rocky? Rocky and Bullwinkle," he explained when she frowned at him. "You know, the cartoon."

"I don't watch a lot of TV."

"You had to catch it when you were a kid." He craned his neck, trying to get another glimpse. "It's not just a cartoon; it's an institution. What else is up here, besides Rocky?"

"We provide a list of wildlife at the center." She gestured to a tree where the bark had been stripped and the trunk scored with deep grooves. "Bear. Those are bear scratchings."

"Yeah?" Rather than being alarmed as she expected, he stepped closer, examining the scar with apparent fascination. "Are they still hibernating now, or could we run into one?"

"Oh, they're up and about now. And hungry," she added, just for the hell of it.

"Well." He ran his fingers down one deep groove. "As long as one doesn't come along for a midday snack and mistake me for a tree, it'd be interesting."

He nearly forgot his aching muscles as they continued to climb. Chipmunks frolicked around the ground, up in the trees, chattering and scolding. A hawk sailed overhead with a regal spread of wings and a single wild cry that echoed forever. There was the glinting black passing of a raven and the first thin patch of snow.

"We can stop here." Olivia shrugged off her pack and sent Noah a considering look as she crouched down to open it. "I didn't think you'd make it, at least not without whining."

"The whining was a close call a few times, but it was worth it."

He looked out over the three lakes, each one the dull silver of an old mirror. Softly reflected in them, the mountains rippled on the surface, more shadow than image. The air was sharp with pine and cold and the soggy smell of the rain-soaked ground.

"As your prize for not whining, we have some of my grandmother's famous beef and barley stew."

"I could eat an ocean of it."

She pulled a small blanket out of her pack. "Spread that out and sit down. You won't get an ocean, but you'll get enough to warm your belly and take your mind off how much your feet hurt."

"I brought some of my complimentary fruit." He smiled as he snapped the blanket. "In case your plan was to starve me."

"No, I thought about just ditching you in the forest and seeing if you ever found your way out. But I like your parents, and they would've been upset."

He folded his legs and accepted the coffee she poured from a thermos into a cup. He wanted to slip off her hat so he could touch her hair. He loved the look of it, that sleek caramel cap with the sassy fringe. "You could learn to like me, too."

"I don't think so."

He ruffled Shirley's head when she came over to sniff at his coffee. "Your dog likes me."

"She's Grandpop's dog. And she likes drinking out of toilets. Her taste is not to be trusted."

"You're a hard woman, Liv. But you make great coffee. If we got married you could make it for me every morning and I'd treat you like a queen."

"How about you make the coffee and I treat you like a serf?"

"Does that include tying me up and demanding sexual favors? Because I should tell you I've recently taken a vow of celibacy."

She only laughed and got out a second thermos. "Your virtue's safe with me."

"Well, that's a load off my mind. Christ, that smells fabulous."

"My grandmother's a hell of a cook." She poured soup out of the wide-mouthed thermos into bowls.

"So, can I come to dinner?"

She kept her gaze focused on the thermos as she replaced the lid. "When I got home last night, she'd been crying. My grandfather had told her you were here, what you wanted and that he'd talked to you. I don't know what they said to each other, but I know they haven't said much to each other since. And that she'd been crying."

"I'm sorry for that."

"Are you?" She looked up now. He'd expected her eyes to be damp, but they were burning dry and hot. "You're sorry that you brought back an intolerable grief, caused a strain between two people who've loved each other for over fifty years and somehow shoved me straight into the middle of it?"

"Yes." His eyes never wavered from hers. "I am."

"But you'll still write the book."

"Yes." He picked up his bowl. "I will. It's already opened up, already gone too far to turn back. And here's a fact, Liv. If I back off this time, Tanner's still going to tell his story. He'll just tell it to someone else. That someone else might not be sorry, sorry enough to tread as carefully as possible, to make sure that whatever he writes is true. He wouldn't have the connection, however tenuous it is, to you and your family that makes it matter to him."

"Now you're a crusader?"

"No." He let her bitterness roll off him, though there were a few sharp pricks on his skin. "I'm just a writer. A good one. I don't have any illusions that what I write will change anything, but I hope it'll answer questions."

Had he been this sure of himself before? She didn't think so. They'd both grown up quite a bit in the last six years. "It's too late for the answers."

"We disagree. I don't think it's ever too late for answers. Liv, hear me out." He pulled off his hat, raked his fingers through his hair. "There are things I never got to explain to you before."

"I said—"

"Damn it, let me finish. I was ten when all this happened. My father was the biggest hero in my life; I guess he still is. Anyway, I knew about his job, and not just the ten-year-old's perception of him going after the bad guys. What he did mattered to me, made an impression on me. And I paid attention. When he came home after your mother's murder, there was grief on his face. I'd never seen it before, not from the job. Maybe there'd be anger, God knows sometimes he'd come home and look sick and tired, but I'd never seen him grieve. And I never forgot it."

To give herself something to do, she picked up her bowl, stirred without interest at the stew. She heard more than frustration in his voice. She heard passion. And purpose. "Isn't what you're doing now bringing back that grief?"

"You can't bring back what's never really gone away, and it hasn't, for any of you. I saw you on TV," he continued. "You were just a baby. They showed that clip dozens of times, when you ran out of the house, crying. Holding your hands over your ears. Screaming."

She remembered the moment perfectly, could relive it if she chose— had relived it when she didn't. "Are you offering me pity now?"

"So you can spit it back in my face." He shook his head, studying her as he spooned up stew. She wasn't a defenseless and terrified little girl now. She'd toughened, and if she didn't take steps otherwise, she'd soon be hardened. "I'm telling you I won't do that. I won't crowd and push. We'll take it at your pace."

"I don't know if I'll agree or not," she said after a moment. "But I won't even consider talking to you unless you promise to leave my grandmother out of it. Leave her completely alone. She can't handle it. And I won't have you try to handle her."

"All right." He sighed at her suspicious frown. "What? You want me to sign it in blood?"

"Maybe." She ate only because she knew she'd need fuel for the hike back. "Don't expect me to trust you."

"You did once. You will again before we're finished."

"You're annoyingly sure of yourself. There's a pair of harlequin ducks on the lake. You can just spot them, on the far side."

He glanced over. He'd already figured out that she shifted over into the nature mode when she wanted to change the subject.

"I'll be here through the week," he said. "My home number's on file at the lodge. If you haven't decided by the time I leave, you can get in touch later. I'll come back."

"I'll think about it." She gave Shirley a biscuit out of the tin. "Now be quiet. One of the best parts of being here is the quiet."

Satisfied with the progress, Noah dug into his stew. He was toying with asking if there was more when the scream had him flipping the bowl in the air and leaping to his feet.

"Stay here," he ordered. "Stay right here."

Olivia gaped at him for five seconds, then scrambled to her feet as he turned to run toward the sound. "Stop, wait!" The breath hitched in her chest as she debated tackling him or just throwing herself in his path. She managed to grab his sleeve, yank, then nearly plowed into him after all as Shirley barreled into her, hoping a tussle was coming.

"Someone's in trouble." The shriek stabbed the air again and had him pushing her back. "I want you to stay here until I—"

"It's a marmot." She fought back a laugh. "Probably an Olympic marmot."

"What the hell is that?"

She managed to compose her face. "Also known as rockchuck, whistle-pig or whistler, though the warning call it makes isn't a whistle as it's made with the vocal cords. It isn't a damsel in distress, but a . . . there."

With her hand still gripping his sleeve, she gestured. There were two of them with grizzled coats of gray-brown, their heavy bodies lumping along toward an outcrop of rocks. One of them stood up on its hind legs, sniffing the air, then eyeing dog and humans with a jaundiced eye.

"They're just out of hibernation, usually go into torpor in September and don't surface until May. Most likely their burrow is close by. The, ah, call is their early-warning system as they're slower than any of their predators."

"Terrific." He turned his head, eyed Olivia narrowly.

"Well, you were really brave. I felt completely protected from any terrifying marauding marmots."

"Smart-ass." He tapped his fist on her chin, then left it there. Her eyes were deep and gold with humor, her lips curved and soft. Color glowed in her cheeks, and the wind ruffled her hair.

He saw the change in her eyes, the darkening of awareness as he'd seen it years before. He thought he heard her draw in one breath, sharply, as his fingers uncurled and turned up to skim her jaw.

He didn't calculate the move. He just made it. The minute his mouth closed over hers, his mind clicked in and shouted *mistake!* But his other hand was already sliding through her hair, his teeth were already nibbling on that full lower lip to enhance the taste.

She jerked once, as if that touch of mouth to mouth had shocked her, then went very still. In that stillness he felt the faintest of quivers, and her lips warmed under his.

The combination had him nudging her closer, had him deepening the kiss though some part of him knew he should never have turned down this road again.

She'd meant to shove him away, to stop him the instant she'd seen the thought come into his eyes, the instant she'd felt the answering trip of her own pulse.

He paralyzed her. The rush of feelings that geysered up inside her body stunned her, left her open to more, with her hand gripping his sleeve and the blood swirling dizzily in her head.

The way it had been between them before. Exactly as it had been.

The wind rushed by them, through them, sighing through the trees, and still she couldn't move. Not toward him or away, not to hold on or reject.

That drenching sensation of helplessness terrified her.

"Olivia." He skimmed his hands over her face, fascinated by the angles of it, the texture.

Both of them had changed, and yet her flavor was the same, the shape of her mouth the same, the need swimming between them, exactly the same.

When he eased away, wanting to see it, needing to see it, he murmured again. Just "Olivia."

Now she pulled back, taking defense in temper. "This isn't going to happen again."

"Liv." His voice was quiet and serious. "It already is."

No, she told herself. Absolutely not. "Typical. That's just typical." She spun around and strode back to the blanket to begin tossing everything back in her pack.

Typical? Noah couldn't think of anything typical about having the top of his head sheared off. He still couldn't pull all his thoughts back in, but he managed to walk over, turn her around.

"Listen—"

"Hands off." She knocked them away. "Do you think I don't know what this is about? If you can't convince me with your so-called logic and charm, add some physical stimuli. Just like before."

"Oh no, you don't." With a wiry strength she'd underestimated, he held her still when she would have shoved away. His eyes flashed with a temper she realized was much more potent than his lazy good looks indicated. "You're not turning that around, not this way. You know damn well I didn't hike for four fucking hours just so I could cop a feel. If I'd wanted to move on you, I'd have done it in some nice, warm room before I had blisters."

"You did move on me," she corrected icily and only made him bare his teeth.

"I didn't plan it, it just happened. And you weren't fighting me off. You want to be pissed off about it, fine, but let's have it for the real reason."

They glared at each other while Shirley whimpered and bumped her body between theirs. "All right." Olivia opted to retreat behind dignity. "I'll be pissed off because you took advantage of a momentary weakness."

"There's not a weak bone in your body," he muttered and let her go. "How long are you going to make me pay for a mistake I made six years ago? How many ways do you want me to apologize for it?"

"I don't want an apology. I want to forget it."

"But you haven't. And neither have I. Do you want to know how many times I thought of you?"

"No." She said it quickly, the single word a rush. "No, I don't. If we want to find a way to deal with each other on this, Noah, then we concentrate on where we are now, not where we were then."

"Is that the MacBride way? If it's tough to deal with, bury it?" He regretted it instantly, not only because it was out of line, but because of the unguarded flare of shock and misery in her eyes. "Liv, I'm sorry."

He reached for her, swearing under his breath as she jerked away. "I'm sorry," he said again, and very precisely. "That was uncalled for. But you weren't the only one who was hurt. You sliced me in half that day. So maybe you're right. Maybe it's better to put it away and start now."

They packed up in silence, taking scrupulous care not to touch in any way. When they were back in the forest, she became the impersonal guide, pointing out any plants of interest, identifying wildlife and blocking any personal conversation.

Noah decided she might as well have snugged that glass dome over herself. She was inside it now, and untouchable.

That would make it simpler all around, he told himself. He didn't want to touch her again. Couldn't, for his own survival, risk it.

He spent the last two hours of the hike dreaming about burning his boots and washing the lingering taste of her out of his mouth with a good, stiff drink.

TWENTY

As the lodge came in sight, Noah's plan was simple. He was simple. He was going straight to the bar to buy a bottle, make that two bottles of beer. He was taking both up to his room where he would drink them during his hour-long hot shower.

If that didn't make him feel human again, well, he'd just order up some raw meat and gnaw at it.

The light was fading to a pearly gray with a few wild streaks of color in the western sky. But he wasn't in the mood to appreciate it.

For God's sake, he'd only kissed her. It wasn't as if he'd ripped her clothes off and dragged her to the ground for maniac sex. The fact that the image of doing just that held entirely too much appeal only made him grind his teeth as he pulled open the door to the lodge.

He turned to her, started to make some blisteringly polite comment on her ability as guide, when the desk clerk hurried over.

"Mr. Brady, you had a call from your mother. She said it was urgent."

Everything inside him froze, then started to churn sickly. "My mother?"

"Yes, she called about an hour after you left this morning, and again at three. She asked that you call her at home as soon as you came in."

He had a horrible and vivid image of cops coming to the door. Every family of those on the job knew what it meant when you opened the door and cops were standing there, their faces carefully blank.

His father was retired. It couldn't be. It couldn't.

"I—"

"You can call from in here." Olivia took his arm gently, spoke with absolute calm. The blank fear on his face set off screams of alarm in her head, but her hand was steady as she led him past the desk and into a back office.

"You can dial direct from here. I'll just—" She started to step back, intending to give him privacy, but his hand clamped over hers.

He said nothing at all, just held on while he dialed the number. His grip on her anchored him as a dozen terrors spun through his head. His palm went sweaty on the receiver as it rang once, twice, then his mother's voice, rushed and breathless, had a spike of ice slicing into his gut.

"Mom?"

"Oh, Noah, thank goodness."

"Dad?" He lived a thousand hells in the heartbeat it took her to answer.

"No, no, honey. It's not Frank. Your father's fine." Before his knees could buckle with relief, she was rushing on. "It's Mike, Noah."

"Mike?" His fingers tightened on Olivia's, turning both their knuckles white. "What's wrong? What happened?"

"Noah, I—God . . . He's in the hospital. He's in a coma. We don't know how bad. They're running tests, they're doing everything they . . ."

When she began to weep, Noah felt his guts slide into greasy knots. "What happened? A car accident?"

"No, no. Someone hurt him. Someone hit him and hit him. From behind, they say. He was in your house last night."

"At the beach house? He was at my place?" Denial and fear pounded through him. "It happened last night?"

"Yes. I didn't hear about it until this morning, early this morning. Your father's at the hospital now. I'm going back. They'll only let one of us sit with him at a time, for just a few minutes. He's in Intensive Care."

"I'll be there as soon as I can. I'll take the first flight out."

"One of us will be at the hospital. Maggie and Jim—" Her voice broke again when she spoke of Mike's parents. "They shouldn't be alone there."

"I'm on my way. I'll come straight there. Mom . . ." He could think of nothing. Nothing. "I'm on my way," he said again. He hung up the phone, then just stared at it. "My friend, he was attacked. He's in a coma. I have to go home."

He still had her hand, but his grip was loose now. She could feel his fingers tremble. "Go pack what you need. I'll call the airport, book you a flight."

"What?"

Her heart broke for him. Looking at his pale face and stunned eyes, there was room for no other feeling but pity. "It'll save time, Noah. Just go up and get what you need. I'll get you to the airport."

"Yeah . . . God." He snapped back, eyes clearing, face going hard and tight. "Just get me a seat, whatever gets me to L.A. quickest. Standby if nothing else. I'll be ready in five minutes."

He was as good as his word and was back at the office door before she'd completed the booking. He hadn't bothered to change, she noted, and carried only his backpack and laptop.

"You're set." She rose quickly from behind the desk. "It's a private airstrip about forty minutes from here, friends of my grandparents. They'll take off as soon as you get there."

She snagged a set of keys off a board as she headed out of the office. She jogged to a Jeep in the side lot, unlocked it and climbed in as he tossed his pack in the back.

"I appreciate it."

"It's all right. Don't worry about the rest of your things and your car. We'll deal with it." She drove fast, her hands competent on the wheel, her eyes straight ahead. "I'm sorry about your friend."

The initial shakes had passed, but he laid his throbbing head back against the seat. "I've known him forever. Second grade. He moved into the neighborhood. Pudgy kid, a complete dork. You were honor bound to beat the shit out of him. I was going to take my shot but just couldn't do it. He was so oblivious of his own dorkiness. Still is. He had this ridiculous crush on Marcia Brady."

"Is she your cousin?"

"Huh? Oh, Brady. No, Marcia, Marcia, Marcia. *The Brady Bunch*." He opened his eyes long enough to give her a look of astonishment, then sighed. "Right, no TV. Doesn't matter. He's the sweetest person I know. Dead loyal and completely harmless. Son of a bitch!" He pounded his fist on the dash, then pressed his hands to his face. "Son of a bitch. He's in a coma, a fucking coma. My mother was crying. She holds, she always holds. If she's breaking like that it has to be bad. Really bad."

She wanted to pull over, for just a minute, to take him to her, hold on to him until he found some comfort. It was an urge she'd never felt with anyone other than family. So she tightened her hands on the wheel and punched the gas.

"It's my fault." Noah dropped his hands on his lap, let them lie there limply.

"That's a ridiculous thing to say." She kept her voice brisk, practical. Logic, she thought, was more productive than a comforting hug. "You weren't even there."

"I didn't take it seriously enough. I didn't take *her* seriously enough. I sent him over there. Water the goddamn plants. Water the plants, Mike. And I knew she was half crazy."

"Who are you talking about?"

"I was seeing this woman for a while. It wasn't serious on my end, but I should have seen it. I just sort of drifted along with it—why the hell not? Good sex with a great body, a snappy-looking woman to hang out with. When it got complicated, I broke things off. Then it got nasty. There were some altercations, then the big one where she trashed my house while I was away."

"Trashed your house?"

"Big time. I had to scoop up most of what was left with a shovel."

"That's horrible. Really. Why didn't you have her arrested?"

"Couldn't prove it. Everybody knew she'd done it, just her style, but there wasn't much to be done about it. She tossed a few more threats in my face, made another scene. Then I go flying off, and tell Mike to water my flowers while I'm gone."

"If this very bizarre woman is the one who hurt your friend, then it's her fault. It's her responsibility. It's her guilt."

He said nothing to that. He was suffering, Olivia thought. She could feel the pain coming off him in shaky waves. And couldn't stand it. "When . . . after my mother's death I went through a period where I blamed myself. I'd run away and I'd hidden in the closet. I didn't do anything to help her."

"Jesus, Liv, you were four."

"Doesn't matter. That doesn't matter, Noah. When you love someone and something terrible happens to them, it doesn't matter how old you are. After that," she continued, "I went through another stage when I blamed her. What the hell was she thinking? She let him in the house. She let the monster in," she murmured and shuddered once. "She let him in, and he took her away from me. She left me. I blamed her for that."

She flinched when he lifted a hand to touch her cheek, then blew out a steadying breath. "Maybe you have to go through those stages before you can get to the truth of it. Sam Tanner was to blame. He was the only one to blame. Not me, not my mother."

"You're right. I owe you for this."

"The lodge would have done the same for anyone."

"No. I owe *you.*" He laid his head back again, closed his eyes and rode the rest of the way in silence.

NOAH WAS RUNNING ON NERVES ALONE BY THE TIME HE rushed off the elevator in ICU. During the flight he'd imagined Mike dead. Then jumped to giddy images of his friend popping up in bed and making a lame joke. When the cab had dropped him at the hospital, he was nearly ready to believe it had all been some weird dream.

Then he saw his mother sitting on a bench in the silent hallway, her arm around Maggie Elmo. Guilt and fear balled messily in his throat.

"Oh, Noah." Celia got quickly to her feet to throw her arms around him. He felt her stomach quiver against his. "I'm so glad you're here. There's no change," she added in a whisper.

"I need to see him. Can I . . ." He shook his head, then forced himself to ease away and face Maggie. "Mrs. Elmo."

"Noah." Tears began to trickle out of her already swollen eyes as she reached for him. He lowered to the bench, wrapped his arms tight around her. "He'll want you here. He'll want to see you when he wakes up. He's going to wake up. Any minute now."

He hung on to her faith as desperately as he held on to her. "We've been taking turns going in." Celia rubbed a hand over Noah's back. "Frank and Jim are in there now. But Maggie has to lie down for a while."

"No, I—"

"You said you'd lie down when Noah got here." All but crooning the words, Celia drew Maggie to her feet. "They've got a bed for you, remember? You just need to stretch out for a few minutes. We want to give Noah some time with Mike, don't we? I'll sit with you." She sent Noah a quiet look, then still murmuring, led Maggie down the hall.

Swamped with grief, Noah lowered his head to his hands. He hadn't moved when Frank came through the double doors to the left and saw him. Saying nothing, Frank sat, laid an arm over Noah's shoulders.

"I don't know what to do," Noah said when he could speak again.

"You're doing it. You're here."

"I want to hurt her. I'm going to find a way to make her pay for this."

"That's not what you need to focus on now."

"You know she did this." Noah straightened, stared at Frank with burning eyes. "You know she did."

"It's very possible. She'll be questioned as soon as they locate her, Noah." He gripped Noah's shoulder, cutting off the vicious stream of oaths. "She can't be charged without evidence."

"She'll dance. Goddamn it, Dad, you know she'll dance around this. I'm not letting her get away with it."

"I don't know that," Frank said firmly. "Neither do you. But I am telling you, as your father and as a cop, to stay away from her. If you follow through on what you're feeling right now, you'll only make matters worse. Let her box herself in, Noah, so we can put her away."

If Mike died, Noah thought, they wouldn't be able to put her away deep enough.

HE STAYED AT THE HOSPITAL UNTIL DAWN, THEN WENT TO his parents' house, collapsed facedown on his childhood bed and dropped into oblivion for four hours.

When he'd showered off twenty-four hours of sweat and fatigue, he went into the kitchen.

His mother was there, dressed in an ancient terry-cloth robe and breaking eggs into a bowl. Because love for her burst through him, he went to her, wrapped his arms around her and hugged her back against him.

"Who are you and what have you done with my mother?"

She managed a quiet laugh, lifting a hand up and around to pat his face. "I threw out the house rules this morning. Real eggs, real coffee all around. It's going to be another long day."

"Yeah." He looked over the top of her head, through the kitchen window into the yard beyond. "Remember when Mike and I tried to build that fort out back? We got all this scrap wood together and these rusted nails. Of course, he stepped on one and had to get a tetanus shot."

"Screamed bloody murder when he stepped on the nail. I thought he'd cut off an arm." She let out a laughing sigh that ended perilously close to a sob. "I love that boy. And I'm ashamed that after I heard what happened, my first thought was thank God it wasn't Noah. Oh, poor Maggie."

She eased away, picked up the bowl again and began briskly beating eggs. "We have to think positively. Think in healing white light. I've read a lot of books on it."

He had to smile a little. "I bet you have."

"We're going to bring him out of this." She got out a skillet, and the look she sent Noah was fierce and strong. "Believe it."

He wanted to, but every time he went into the tiny room in the hospital and saw Mike still and pale, his head swathed in bandages, his eyes sunk in shadowed bruises, his faith faltered.

As morning swam toward afternoon, he paced the corridor while rage built inside him. He couldn't let Caryn get away with what she'd done. He couldn't do anything but hope and pray and stand at his friend's bedside and talk nonsense just to block out the monotonous beep of machines.

She'd wanted a shot at him, he thought. By Christ, he'd give it to her. He turned toward the elevator, strode toward it, with hate blooming black in his heart.

"Noah?"

"What?" Fists already clenched, he glanced at the brunette. She wore a lab coat over shirt and trousers, with a stethoscope in her pocket. "Are you one of Mike Elmo's doctors?"

"No. I—"

"I know you," he interrupted. "Don't I?"

"We met at the club—you and Mike, my friend and I. I'm Dory."

"Right." He rubbed his tired eyes. The pretty brunette with the Southern drawl who stood up for him the night Caryn had come in. "You're a doctor?"

"Yes. Emergency medicine. I'm on my break and wanted to see how Mike was doing."

"They just keep saying no change."

"I'll check on that in a minute. You look like you could use some air. Let's take a walk."

"I was just heading out."

"Let's take a walk," she repeated. She'd seen murder in a man's eye before. It wasn't a look you forgot. "The last time I checked in, Mike's vitals were stable. His tests have been good." She punched the elevator button. "He's critical, but he's also young and healthy."

"He's been in a coma for a day and a half."

She nudged him into the elevator with her. "Sometimes a coma is just the body's way of focusing in on healing. And he did come around once in the ambulance on the way here. It was brief, but I think he recognized me, and that's a very positive sign."

"You? You were with him?"

She stepped out on the main lobby, took his arm to lead him to the doors. "We had a date. I was meeting him at your place. I was running late. We had a double suicide attempt come in. Lost one, saved the other. It was nearly ten by the time I got there."

Outside she turned her face up to the sun, rolled her shoulders. "God, it feels good out here. In any case, the door was open. Mike was on the kitchen floor, facedown. Glass all over the place. Wine bottle. It's probably what he was hit with. I went to work on him. I had my bag in the car. I called it in, did what I could on the scene. We had him in ER within thirty minutes."

"Is he going to die?"

She didn't answer right away, but sat down on the curb, waited for Noah to join her. "I don't know. Medically, he's got an even chance, maybe even a little better than even. There were no bone fragments in his brain, and that was a big one. Still, medicine has limits, and it's up to him now. I'm half crazy about him."

"No kidding?"

"Yeah. I know he started off that night with this thing for Steph. And actually, I had the same kind of focus on you." She tilted her face toward him and smiled. "You were a little too distracted to notice, so I went back and sulked a little."

"Yeah?"

She had to smile. "Just a little. Mike and Steph went through the moves and motions. They sort of ran out of steam, and I felt sorry for Mike because he was worried about you and didn't know what to do about it. We started talking and had this big click happen. We started going out. Then we started staying in."

"That was you the other night on the phone."

"Yeah."

"Mike Elmo and the sexy doctor." Absurdly pleased, Noah shook his head. "That's just terrific." He grabbed her face in his hand and kissed her noisily. "That's just great."

She laughed and gave him a friendly pat on the knee. "He thinks you walk on water. I didn't say that to make you sad," she hurried on when the light went out of Noah's eyes. "I said it because I think he's a pretty great guy, and he thinks you're a pretty great guy. So, I figure he's right. And I figure that when I ran into you upstairs you'd had about enough and were going to go find that lunatic Caryn and . . . I was going to say do something you'd regret, but I don't think you'd regret it. Something that wouldn't help, that wouldn't solve anything, and that in the end would put you in the kind of jam Mike wouldn't like."

"She wanted to hurt me. She didn't give a damn about Mike."

"Noah, she did hurt you. She hurt you where it matters the most. Let's go back up. I only have a few more minutes left, and I want to see him."

He nodded, got to his feet, then held down a hand for hers. "I guess it's lucky I ran into you."

"Why don't you buy me a beer after shift?" She grinned as they went back inside. "You can tell me all kinds of embarrassing Mike stories."

"What kind of friend would that make me?"

"He told me you got piss-faced the spring of your senior year in high school, and he dared you to run around the track bare-assed naked. And when you did, he took videos and showed them at your graduation party. He still has a copy, by the way." Her smile brightened as they moved onto the elevator. "You had very nice form at eighteen."

"Oh yeah. Well, that's nothing. I've got much better stories on Mike. What time do you get off shift?"

"Seven, please God."

"It's a date." His mood almost light, he stepped off the elevator. Then his heart crashed to his feet as he saw Maggie sobbing in his mother's arms.

"No." The roar inside his head was so loud he couldn't hear his own voice as he repeated the denial over and over, as he raced down the corridor, yanking free of Dory's restraining hand.

"Noah, wait!" Celia shifted quickly to block his path before he could shove through the doors into ICU. "Wait. Maggie, tell him. Tell Noah."

"He opened his eyes." She rocked back and forth on her heels, back and forth, then held out both hands to Noah. "He opened his eyes. He said 'Mom.' He looked at me, and he said 'Mom.'"

"Stay here," Dory ordered. "Stay out here. Let me check."

"The nurse came in, she called for the doctor." Celia wiped at her own tears while Noah held Maggie. "Frank and Jim are down in the cafeteria. Frank browbeat Jim into getting something to eat, then I was going to browbeat Maggie. He woke up, Noah." She laid her head on the side of his shoulder. "He woke up."

Dory came back through the doors. Noah took one look at the brilliant smile on her face and buried his face in Maggie's hair.

TWENTY-ONE

So, when were you going to tell me about Doctor Delicious?"

Mike grinned, with most of his old twinkle. "Is she a babe or what?"

"A prime babe, a brainy babe. So what's she doing hanging around with you?"

"She digs me. What can I say?" He still tended to tire easily, and the headaches came with tedious regularity. But they'd jumped him up to good condition after his stint in ICU and into a regular room.

His room was full of flowers, cards, balloons. He'd told Noah the nurses called it Party Central, a fact that pleased him enormously.

The day before Noah had brought in a brand-new laptop, loaded with every computer game it would hold. He'd called it occupational therapy, but knew it was part guilt, part unspeakable gratitude.

"I think I'm in, you know. With her," Mike said, scrupulously staring at his fingers.

Noah gaped. "You got a major bash on the head ten days ago. Ruined a damn fine bottle of wine, by the way. I think your brains are still scrambled."

"I don't think this has a lot to do with brains."

At a loss, Noah blew out a breath. "'You know' is a very big thing. You were only seeing her for a little while before you had your head broken. You've been stuck in a hospital bed ever since."

"I have a really fond feeling for this hospital bed." Mike gave the white sheets an affectionate pat. "After last night."

"Last night? *Here?* You had sex with her here?" It was fascinating.

"*Shh.* Tell the floor nurse, why don't you?" But Mike was still grinning. "She came in to see me after her shift, one thing led to another. The another was really amazing, by the way."

"Why the hell am I feeling sorry for you?" Noah wondered. "You're getting all the action."

He grabbed the can of Coke he'd brought in with him, chugged deeply. "I asked her to marry me."

And choked. "Huh? What? Jesus, Mike."

"She said yes." Mike's grin turned into his puppy dog smile and turned his eyes soft. "Can you beat that?"

"I think I'm having a stroke." Noah pressed his fingers to his twitching eye. "Call the nurse. No, better, call a doctor. Maybe I can get some action."

"We're going to get married next spring, because she wants the works. You know, the church, the flowers, the white dress."

"Wow." It was the best he could do. Noah figured he'd better sit down, then realized he already was. "Wow."

"They're letting me out of here tomorrow. I want to buy her a ring right away. I need you to go with me. I don't know squat about buying an engagement ring."

"What do I know about it?" Noah dragged his free hand through his hair and took a good, hard look. Mike's eyes were clear behind the thick lenses of his glasses. His smile was easy, almost lazily content. "You really mean it, don't you?"

"I want to be with her. And when I am I keep thinking, this is right. This feels exactly right." Vaguely embarrassed, he moved his shoulders. "I don't know how to explain it."

"I guess you just did. Nice going, Mike."

"So, you'll give me a hand with the ring, right?"

"Sure. We'll get her a doozy." With a sudden laugh, he surged to his feet. "Goddamn. Married. And to a doctor. Damn good thing. She'll be able to stitch you up every time you walk into something or trip over your feet. Does she know you're a complete klutz?"

"Yeah, she loves that about me."

"Go figure." To show his affection, he punched Mike on the shoulder. "I guess you won't be coming over and raiding my fridge every other night after . . ." He trailed off, remembering.

"It wasn't your fault. Look, we know each other well enough for me to see what's in your head." To keep Noah from backing off, Mike grabbed his hand. "You didn't know she was going to go postal."

"I knew enough."

"I knew as much as you did, and I didn't give a thought to going over there. For Christ's sake, Noah, Dory was coming." Shaken by just the thought of it, Mike rubbed his hands over his face, his fingers sliding under his glasses to press against his eyes. "Something could've happened to her, too. I'm the one who told her to meet me over there."

"That's not—"

"It's the same thing," Mike interrupted. "I was there at the club that night. I heard what she said, saw how she was." He turned to brood out his window at his view of palm trees. "I wish I could remember, but I keep coming up against the blank. Nothing, not a fucking thing after the marathon after work. I remember kicking Pete Bester's ass at Mortal Kombat. Next thing I'm clear on is waking up and seeing Mom. All I know about the between is what people tell me. Maybe I saw her. If I could say I saw her, they'd lock her up."

"They'd have to find her first. She skipped," Noah added when Mike looked back at him. "None of her friends know where she is, or they're not saying. She packed clothes, got a cash advance on her credit cards and split."

"Can't they go after her for that, like *The Fugitive*."

Even a half laugh felt good. "Richard Kimble was innocent."

"Yeah, but still."

"She wasn't charged. I guess if they come up with some evidence they might take a look for her. Otherwise . . ." He lifted his shoulders, let them fall. "Anyway, I don't think she'll be hassling either one of us, not for a while at least."

"That's something. So, now that you know I'm going to live, and that crazy bitch is off somewhere, I guess you better get back to work."

"Who says I haven't been working?"

"Your mother."

"Man, what is it with you and my mother?"

"I'd always planned to marry her, but I thought your father might shoot me. Dory knows she's my second choice, but she's so madly in love with me she doesn't care. But I digress," he said with a grin. "She said you've been letting the book coast, really only playing at it for the last week or so. I'd say it's time to get your lazy ass in gear."

"I'll get to it." Muttering, Noah wandered to the window.

"You don't have to worry about me anymore. I'm cool. Aside from the blank spot, I'm nearly back to normal."

"You were never normal. I've been thinking about talking to Jamie Melbourne again, getting her husband to talk to me. Hassling that asshole admin of Smith's."

"So do it."

"I'm waiting for my car." He knew it was stalling. "The lodge arranged to have someone drive it down for me. Should be here tomorrow or the next day."

"Then you can go home, make your calls and set up your interviews."

Noah glanced back over his shoulder. "You kicking me out?"

"What are friends for?"

WHAT WAS SHE DOING? WHAT IN GOD'S NAME WAS SHE DOING?

Olivia sat in the car, her fingers clamped on the steering wheel, and struggled to breathe. If she took slow, even breaths her heart would stop pounding. She could control it, control the frenzied jerk and throb of her pulse and beat back the panic attack.

She could do it, she could fight it off. She wouldn't let it take over.

But her hands wanted to tremble on the wheel, and the sheen of sweat had already pearled on her face as waves of heat then ice, heat then ice, surfed over her skin, through her belly, into her throat. She knew what she'd see if she looked in the rearview mirror. The wild, wide eyes, the glossy, translucent pallor.

The nausea rolled up, one long sick crest, from her feet to her stomach to her throat.

She gritted her teeth and fought it back, shoved it down even as the shudders shimmered over her in icy little bumps.

The scream wanted to rip out, it tore at her chest, clawing with sharpened demon claws. But all she released was a moan, a long keening sound drenched in despair, pressing her head back against the seat as she held on, held on.

Five seconds, then ten. Twenty. Until she willed herself, warred with her own mind, to snap clear.

Her breath came fast, as if she'd been running, but the sharpest edge of panic began to fade. Slowly, she ordered herself to relax, one muscle at a time. She opened her eyes, stared at her fingers, made them flex and release, flex and release.

Control. She had control. She was not a victim, would never, never be a victim. Not of circumstance or her own ill-buried fears.

With one last shuddering breath, she leaned back again. Better, that was better, she thought. It was just that it had come on so fast, had taken her completely by surprise. It had been more than two years since she'd had a full-blown panic attack.

Two years ago, she remembered, when she'd made plans to come to Los Angeles and visit her aunt and uncle. Then, she'd gotten as far as the airport when it had washed over her. The cold sweats, the shakes, the terrible need to get out, just get out and away from all the people.

She'd beaten it back, but she hadn't been able to face the plane, hadn't been able to face where it was going. The shame of that failure had drowned her in depression for weeks.

This time she'd gotten here, she reminded herself. She'd batted back the onslaught of the panic twice on the drive down and had been so certain she'd won completely.

She had won, she corrected. She was here, she was all right. She was back in control.

She'd been right to follow her impulse, to take the chore of returning Noah's car herself. Even though it had caused difficulties with her grandparents, she'd done the right thing. Concentrating on the drive had gotten her where she'd wanted to go. Where she hadn't been able to go for twenty years.

Or nearly gotten her there, she corrected, and, pushing the damp hair off her brow, she studied Noah's house.

It wasn't what she'd envisioned at all. It was pretty, almost feminine in the soft tones of the wood, the cheerful sweeps and spears of flowers.

His garden wasn't some haphazard bachelor attempt to brighten up his real estate, but a careful, clever arrangement by someone who not only knew flowers, but appreciated them.

She slipped out of the car, relieved that her legs were nearly steady. She intended to go straight to the door, knock, give him his keys and a polite smile. She'd ask him to call a cab, and get out and on her way to her aunt's as quickly as possible.

But she couldn't resist the flowers, the charm of verbena, the fresh chipper colors of Gerber daisies, the bright trumpets of the reliable petunias. He hadn't stuck with the ordinary, she noted, and had used the small space available on either side of the walk very well. Experimenting, she noted, crowding specimen to specimen so that it all tangled together in a natural burst rather than an obviously planned design.

It was clever and creative, and both the planting and maintaining must have involved a great deal of work. Still, he hadn't been quite as conscientious with the weeding as he might have been, and her gardener's heart had her crouching down to tug up the random invaders.

Within a minute she was humming and losing herself in a well-loved task.

• • •

NOAH WAS SO HAPPY TO SEE HIS CAR SITTING IN ITS USUAL spot that he overtipped the driver and bolted out of the cab.

"Oh baby, welcome home." He murmured it, stroked a loving hand over the rear fender and had nearly executed a snappy dance of joy when he spotted Olivia.

The surprise came first, or he assumed the quick jerk in his stomach was surprise. Then came the warmth. She looked so damn pretty, kneeling by his flowers, a faded gray cap shading her eyes.

He started toward her, then hooked his thumbs in his front pockets because his hands wanted to touch. "This is a surprise," he said, and watched her head snap up, watched her body freeze. Like a doe in the crosshairs, Noah mused. "I wasn't expecting to see you weeding my gummy snaps."

"They needed it." Furiously embarrassed, she got to her feet and brushed garden dirt off her hands. "If you're going to plant flowers, you should tend to them."

"I haven't had a lot of time just recently. What are you doing here, Liv?"

"Returning your car. You were told to expect it."

"I was also expecting some burly guy named Bob behind the wheel. Not that I'm complaining. Come on in."

"I just need you to call me a cab."

"Come on in," he repeated and moved past her to the door. "At least I can give you a drink to pay for the weeding service."

He unlocked the front door, glanced back to where she continued to stand. "Don't be a nitwit. You might as well. Damn it!"

Liv's eyes widened as he leaped inside the door. She could hear him cursing. Curiosity won and had her following him inside.

He jabbed a code into a security panel just inside the door. "Just had this installed. I keep forgetting it's here. If I set off the alarm again, my neighbors are going to lynch me. There." He blew out a breath when the signal light blinked on green. "Another small victory of man against machine. Have a seat."

"I can't stay."

"Uh-huh. I'll just get us a glass of wine while you think of the reason you can't sit down for fifteen minutes after driving all the way down the coast."

"My aunt and uncle are expecting me."

"This minute?" he asked from the kitchen.

"No, but—"

"Well, then. You want some chips with this? I think I have some."

"No. I'm fine." But since she was here, what harm would it do to have one civil glass of wine?

She thought his living room was sparsely furnished, no-frills male, but not unattractive. Then she remembered he'd told her his home had been trashed. It certainly explained why everything looked showroom fresh and unused.

"I was glad to hear your friend's going to be okay."

"It was touch-and-go the first couple of days." And the thought of it could still give him a raw sensation in the gut. "But yeah, he's going to be okay. In fact, he's going to be great. He got his skull fractured, fell in love and got engaged, not necessarily in that order—in just over a two-week period."

"Good for him, on two out of three anyway."

"We just bought her a ring this morning."

"We?"

"He needed guidance. Let's drink to Mike."

"Why not?" She touched the rim of her glass to his, then sipped. Then lifted her eyebrows. "Pouilly-Fuissé on a weekday evening. Very classy."

His grin flashed. "You know your wine."

"Must be the Italian from my grandmother's side."

"And can the MacBride half build a Guinness?"

"I imagine." It was just a little too comfortable, being here, being with him. It smacked of old patterns. "Well, if you'd call—"

"Let's go out on the deck." He took her hand, pulled her to the sliding door. He wasn't about to let her shake him off that quickly. "Too early for sunset," he continued, releasing her long enough to slide the door open. "You'll have to come back. They can be pretty spectacular."

"I've seen sunsets before."

"Not from this spot."

The breeze fluttered in off the ocean, whispered warm over her face. The water was bold and blue, chopping in against the shore, then rearing back for the next pass. The scent was of salt and heat, and the light undertone of sunscreen from the people sprinkled along the beach.

"Some backyard."

"I thought the same thing about yours when I saw your forest." He leaned against the rail, his back to the view, his eyes on her. "Wanna come play in my backyard, Liv?"

"No, thanks. You've got a nice hand with flowers." She flicked a finger over the soapwort, johnny-jump-ups and artesisa sharing space artistically in a stone tub.

"It shows my sensitive side."

"It shows you know what looks good and how to keep it that way."

"Actually, I learned out of compassion and annoyance. My mother was always planting something, then killing it. She'd go to the nursery, and the plants would scream and tremble. Once, I swear, I heard this coreopsis shrieking, 'No, no, not me! Take the Shasta daisies.' I couldn't stand it," he continued when she laughed. "I started having nightmares where all the plants she killed came back to life, brown, withered, broken, trailing dry dirt that crumbled from their roots as they formed an army of revenge."

"Zombie zinnias."

"Exactly." He beamed, delighted with her, fascinated by the way her face warmed when she was amused and relaxed. "Vampire violas, monster marigolds and gardenia ghouls. Let me tell you, it was pretty terrifying. In fact, I'm scaring myself just thinking about it."

"As a naturalist, I can certify you're safe. As long as you keep them alive."

"That's comforting." He trailed a finger down her arm, from elbow to wrist, in the absentminded gesture of a man used to touching. She stepped back, the deliberate gesture of a woman who wasn't.

"I really have to go. I called Uncle David from Santa Barbara, so they're expecting me by now."

"How long are you staying?"

"Just a few days."

"Have dinner with me before you go."

"I'm going to be busy."

"Have dinner with me before you go." As he repeated it, he touched her again, just an easy slide of fingertips along her jaw. "I like seeing you. You wanted to start with a fresh slate. Give me a chance, Olivia."

She could see it clearly, standing there with him while the sky exploded with sunset, music drifting out, something quiet with a throb to the bass. And while the sun turned red, while it melted into the sea, he would touch her as he had before. Cupping his hand on her face. He would kiss her as he had before. Slow and skilled and sexy.

And she'd forget why he was doing it. She'd forget to care why.

"You want a story." She shifted away from his hand. "I haven't decided if I'm giving it to you."

"I want a story." Temper simmered in his eyes, but his voice was cool. "That's one level. I said I liked seeing you, and I meant it. That's another level entirely. I've thought about you, Olivia."

He made a small move, a reangling of his body, and caged her between him and the rail. "I've thought about you for years. Maybe I wish I hadn't, and you've made it clear you'd rather I didn't think of you at all."

"It doesn't really matter what I'd rather." He was crowding her, and along with the irritation from that was a sly lick of excitement.

"We can agree on that." He set his wineglass on the rail. "Do you know what went through my mind when I got home and saw you out front? This. Just this."

It wasn't slow this time. She could taste the bite of temper as his mouth crushed down on hers, the snaps of frustration as his hand fisted on the back of her shirt. Just as she could feel the hot surge of need that pumped from his body to slam against hers.

It was as primal as the world she lived in, as elemental as the sea that crashed behind them. As inevitable as the quest to mate. Want. Had she always wanted him? And had the wanting always been so savage?

She had to take. She had to feed.

She understood the feral, and threw herself into the edgy demand of the kiss. Her hands gripped fistfuls of all that thick sun-streaked hair, her tongue slashed against his. The vicious heat that burst in her blood told her she was alive and could seize whatever she wanted. As long as she wanted.

Power plunged into him, feeding off her reckless response. The taste of her was a rage through his system, shearing away everything else. He wanted to gorge himself on her in fast, greedy gulps until the frantic, clawing hunger was sated.

But the more he took, the more he craved.

He pulled back far enough to see her face, the wild wash of color, the sharp edge in her eyes. "If you want me to believe you're pissed off about that, you're going to have to stop cooperating."

She thought anger was probably the only sensation she wasn't feeling. "Back off, Brady."

"Look—"

"Just . . ." She blew out a breath, lifted a hand to his chest. "Back off a minute."

"Okay." It was a surprise how much it cost him to step away, to break that contact of body to body. "That far enough?"

"Yeah, that's fine. I'm not going to pretend I didn't expect that or wasn't looking for it on one of those levels you were talking about. I have some basic kind of attraction to you. I didn't intend to act on it."

"Why?"

"Because it's not smart. But . . ." She picked up her glass again, or perhaps it was his, and sipped while she studied him. "If I decide to be stupid, then we'll have sex. I'm not against sex, and I think you'd be pretty good at it."

He opened his mouth, shut it again. Cleared his throat. "Excuse me while I restart my heart. Let me get this clear in my head. You're considering being stupid and having sex with me."

"That's right." Good, she decided and sipped again. Damn good. Finally she'd thrown his rhythm off. "Isn't that where you were heading?"

"In my own bumbling way, yeah, I suppose so."

"There was nothing bumbling about that kiss."

He rubbed a hand over the back of his neck. Had he actually thought he was getting to know her all over again? "Why do I feel like I should thank you?"

She laughed, shrugged a shoulder. "Look, Noah, why clutter up healthy animal instincts with emotions and excuses? I don't indulge in sex very often because, well, I'm busy and I'm picky. But when I do, I consider it a natural, sometimes entertaining act that shouldn't be tied up with a bunch of sticky pretenses. In other words, I approach it like a man."

"Yeah, well. *Hmmm.*"

"If you're not interested on that level, no hard feelings." She finished the wine, set it aside. "And I do recall you mentioning a vow of chastity, so maybe this conversation is moot."

"I wouldn't call it a vow, exactly. More like a . . . concept."

"Then we both have something to think about. Now I really have to go."

"I'll drive you."

"A cab's fine."

"No, I'll take you. A drive might clear my head. You're fascinating, Olivia. No wonder you've been stuck in my mind for years." He took her hand again, a habit she was almost getting used to. "Your stuff's still in the car, right?"

"Yes."

"Let's go, then. Keys?"

She dug them out of her pocket, handed them over as they walked through the house. "Aren't you going to set the alarm?"

"Shit. Right." Conversation, he thought, after he'd punched in the code and locked up. Fresh conversation because he didn't think his system could handle any more on the subject they'd just discussed. "So, did you have any trouble finding your way down here?"

"I had a map. I'm good at reading maps. And this is a great ride," she added as she settled in the passenger seat. "Handles like a dream."

"You open her up?"

She gave him a wisp of a smile. "Maybe." Then she laughed, enjoying the rush of wind as the car picked up speed. "It's a bullet. How many speeding tickets do you collect in the average year?"

He winced. "I'm a cop's son. I have great respect for the law."

"Okay, how many does your father have fixed for you during the average year?"

"Family doesn't keep track of small acts of love. You know he'd like to see you while you're here. My mother, too."

"I don't know what plans my aunt may have made, if there'll be time."

"I thought you didn't like pretenses."

She picked up the sunglasses she'd left on his dash, slipped them on. "All right. I don't know how I'll handle seeing him. I don't know how I'll handle being back here, even for a few days. I decided to come to find out."

She balled her fists in her lap, then deliberately relaxed them. "I don't remember Los Angeles. All I really remember is . . . Do you know where my mother's house is? Was?"

"Yeah." He was working on the current owners to let him take a tour.

"Go there. I want to go there."

"Liv, you can't get in."

"I don't need to. I just need to see it."

PANIC WAS A WHISPER INSIDE HER HEAD, AN ICY CARESS along her skin. But she made herself stand at the gate. The walls surrounding the estate were tall and thick and brilliantly white. Trees and distance screened the house, but she could catch glimpses of it, brilliantly white as well, with the soft red tile of the roof.

"There are gardens, I'm not sure I knew how many. Elaborate, wonderful gardens. One was tucked away under big, shady trees and had a little pool with goldfish and water lilies. It had a bridge over it. A white bridge, that my mother said was for the fairies."

She crossed her arms over her chest, hugging her biceps and hunching over as if to fight off sudden cold. "There was another with just roses. Dozens and dozens of rosebushes. He bought a white one when I was born and planted it himself. I remember him telling me that. He'd planted it himself because it was special, and when he had to go out of town, or whenever he came back, he'd leave a white rose on my pillow. I wonder if they kept the gardens the way they were."

Noah said nothing, simply rubbed a hand over her back and listened.

"The house was so big. It seemed like a palace to me. Soaring ceilings and huge windows. Room after room after room, every one of them special somehow. I slept in a canopy bed." She shuddered once, violently. "I can't stand to have anything overhead while I sleep now. I hadn't realized why. Someone would tell me a story every night. My mother or him, or if they were going out, Rosa. But Rosa didn't tell the really good stories. Sometimes they'd have parties, and I could lie in bed and hear the music and people laughing. My mother loved having people around. They'd come all the time. Aunt Jamie, Uncle David. Her agent. Uncle Lou. He'd always bring me a peppermint stick. One of those thick, old-fashioned ones. I can't imagine where he got them.

"Lucas Manning came over a lot. It must've been around the time my—he left." She couldn't say "my father." Simply couldn't bring herself to form the words. "I just remember Lucas being there, in the house, out by the pool. He made my mother laugh. He was nice to me in an absent sort of way. Kids know that it's just show. I wanted to like him, because he made Mama laugh, but I just kept wishing Lucas would stop coming over, because if he did maybe my . . . maybe he'd come home."

She rested her head against the bars of the gate. "Then, of course, he came home. He came home and he killed her. And I can't do this. I can't do this. I can't."

"It's all right." Noah gathered her to him, holding her tight even though she stood stiffly with her fisted hands pressed to his chest to separate them. "You don't have to. You don't need to be here now, Olivia."

She made herself open her eyes again, stare over his shoulder at those flashes of white. "I've been running away from and running toward this all my life. It's time I decided on a direction and stuck with it."

Part of him wanted to scoop her up, cuddle her as he carried her back to the car and took her away. But someone had taken her away for most of her life. "When you run away it comes after you, Liv. And it always catches up."

Afraid he was right, feeling the monster nipping at her heels, she turned and walked back to the car.

TWENTY-TWO

S HE had her color back by the time Noah swung up the drive toward the Melbourne mansion. It seemed to him she'd all but willed it back, just as she'd willed away that lost and grieving look from her eyes.

"Wow." Her smile seemed natural, effortless as the house came into view. "We have pictures of it, even videos, but they don't come up to the in-your-face."

"One of those nice fixer-uppers priced for the young marrieds."

She laughed, then swiveled in her seat as the dogs raced over the yard. "There they are! Oh, I wish I could've brought Shirley."

"Why didn't you?"

"I thought you might object to dog hair and slobber all over your pretty-boy car. And my grandfather would be lost without her." She pushed out as soon as he'd stopped and all but dived into the dogs.

The vulnerable woman with haunted eyes who'd stood outside the gate of her childhood home might not have existed. It certainly wasn't the face she showed to her uncle as David Melbourne came out of the house.

She let out a whoop of delight and bounded toward him, half leaping into his arms for a fierce hug.

He'd aged well, Noah thought, comparing the man who held Olivia with the photos that dated back to the murder. He'd kept the weight off, and had either discovered the fountain of youth or had an excellent cosmetic surgeon.

The lines on his face were dashing rather than aging, as were the streaks of silver in his hair. He was dressed casually in buff-colored trousers and a Henley shirt the color of kiwis.

"Welcome, traveler." He laughed, cupped her face. "Let's look at you. Pretty as ever."

"Missed you."

"Goes double." He kissed her, then hugging a protective arm around her shoulders, turned to Noah. The cooling of voice and eyes was subtle but unmistakable. "It was nice of you to deliver my girl."

"My pleasure."

"Uncle David, this is Noah Brady."

"Yes, I know."

"I just need to get my things out of the trunk."

"I'll get them." Noah unlocked the trunk, took out the single suitcase.

"That's it?" David wanted to know.

"I'm only going to be here a couple of days."

"How about giving Jamie some tips on packing light while you're here?"

"You pack as much as she does. Clotheshorse."

He winced, took the case from Noah. "Jamie got caught on the phone. She should be off by now. Why don't you run in, Livvy? Rosa's paced a rut in the foyer waiting for you to get here."

"Aren't you coming?"

"Be right there."

"All right. Thanks for the lift, Brady."

"No problem, MacBride," he said in the same tone. "I'll be in touch."

She said nothing to that, only jogged up the stairs and inside.

"I hope you'll forgive me for not asking you in," David began. "This reunion's a family affair."

"Understood. You can say what you have to say to me out here."

David inclined his head. "You're perceptive, Noah. I imagine that's why you're good at your work." He set Olivia's suitcase down, glanced toward the house. "You seem to have established some kind of rapport with Livvy."

"We're beginning to understand each other." Again, he thought. Or maybe it was at last. "Is that a problem for you?"

"I have no idea." In what might have been a gesture of peace, David spread his hands. "I don't know you."

"Mr. Melbourne, I was under the impression you were supportive of the book I'm writing."

"I was." David sighed out a breath. "I thought enough time had passed, enough healing had been done. And I believed that a writer of your caliber could do justice to the tragedy."

"I appreciate that. What changed your mind?"

"I didn't realize how much this would upset Val." Concern clouded his eyes, and he slipped his hands into his pockets. "My mother-in-law. I feel partially responsible as I did support it, and that support certainly influenced Jamie into giving you her cooperation and then encouraged Livvy to do so. I lost my own mother when I was very young. Val's one of the most important people in my life. I don't want her hurt."

Protection, Noah mused. The family was a puzzle made up of pieces of protection and defense. "I've already given Liv my word that I won't contact her grandmother or ask her to talk to me. I'll keep her out of it as far as I'm able to."

"The book itself pulls her into it." He held up a hand before Noah could speak. "I can't expect you to turn your back on your work because the ripple effect of that work will hurt people I love. But I want you to be aware of it. And I want you to consider that a man who murders would hardly flinch at lying. Sam Tanner isn't to be trusted, and my biggest regret is that he'll have time to die outside of prison rather than in it."

"If you're worried he'll lie to me, if your feelings are that strong, you'd be smart to put them on record."

David laughed, shook his head. "Noah, personally, I'd love to sit down with you and tell you exactly what I feel, what I remember. I'm going to do my best to ease my mother-in-law's feelings over it, then, if I can, I'll talk to you. You'll have to excuse me now." He picked up the suitcase. "It's the first time Livvy's come to visit. I don't want to miss any time with her."

OLIVIA LOVED THE HOUSE AND EVERYTHING THEY'D DONE with it. She loved it for them—it was so obviously perfect for them with its elegance and pastels and soaring ceilings. But she preferred the rambling style and rooms soaked in colors of her grandparents' home.

She was glad she'd finally made herself come.

By the time she crawled into bed, she was worn to the bone by the drive, the emotion, the elaborate dinner her aunt had arranged and the nonstop conversation as they'd caught up with one another.

Still, her last thought before sleep sucked her under was of Noah standing on the deck of his pretty house, with his back to the sea.

OLIVIA CAME TO THE CONCLUSION VERY QUICKLY THAT WHILE southern California suited Jamie down to her pedicure, it wasn't the town for Liv MacBride. She was sure of it halfway between the shopping expedition her aunt insisted on and the lunch at some trendy restaurant with a name she immediately forgot.

The lunch portions were stingy, the wait staff glossy enough to glow in the dark and the prices so remarkably outrageous she could do nothing but gasp.

"I had my stylist pencil in appointments later this afternoon," Jamie began as she toyed with her field-green-and-wild-pepper salad. "Marco is a genius and an event in himself. We can squeeze in a manicure, maybe a paraffin treatment."

"Aunt Jamie." Olivia sampled what had been billed as the nouveau-club and was in reality two pieces of bark bread cut into tiny triangles and filled with mysterious vegetables. She wondered if anyone ate real food in L.A. "You're trying to make a girl out of me."

"No, I'm not." Jamie pouted. "I'm just trying to give you a . . . well, just one girl day. You should have let me buy you that little black dress."

"That little black dress was four thousand dollars and wouldn't hold up through one hike."

"Every self-respecting female needs at least one killer black dress. I say we go back for it, and the lizard sandals, the Pradas. You put those together on that fabulous body of yours, men will start diving out of windows to fall at your feet."

Olivia shook her head, laughed. "I don't want to be responsible for that. And I don't need the dress, or the shoes, or the warehouse full of other things you tried to talk me into."

"How can we be related?"

"Genetics are a tricky business."

"I'm so glad you're here. I'm so glad you're not angry with me anymore." Tears flooded her eyes, and she reached over and gripped Olivia's hand.

"I wasn't angry with you. Not you, not really. I'm sorry we argued." She turned her hand over, gripped Jamie's tight. "I was angry at Noah, which was just as useless. All those years ago, when you came up to visit and we went out into the forest that evening . . . you were honest with me. You let me be honest with you. Ever since, whenever I needed to talk about Mama, you listened. Whenever I had questions, you answered them."

"Until you stopped asking," Jamie murmured.

"I thought I should put it away. I thought I could. Someone who's smarter than I gave him credit for told me that whenever you run away from something it chases after you and it always catches up. I think I'm ready to change directions."

"It won't be easy."

"God, no. But I'll be honest with you again. I want to hear what he says about that night. I want to hear Sam Tanner's story."

"So do I. We loved her," Jamie said squeezing Olivia's hand. "How could we not want to hear it for ourselves?"

"Grandma—"

"Has dealt with this in her own way, always. It doesn't make your way wrong or your needs wrong."

"No, it doesn't. I guess I'm going to get in touch with Noah before I go back."

"He's a nice man." Jamie's smile changed texture, crept toward feline. "And a very attractive one."

"I noticed. I've just about decided to sleep with him."

The little sound that popped out of Jamie's mouth was something between a grunt and a squeak. "Well. Well then. Ah . . . Listen, why don't we blow this joint, go get a pizza and you can elaborate on that very interesting statement."

"Great." With relief, Olivia pushed her plate aside. "I'm starved."

FRANK WAS SITTING IN HIS KITCHEN, ENJOYING THE SINGLE predinner light beer his wife allowed him. On a notepad, he drew circles, squiggles, exes as he toyed with a new play for the basketball team he coached.

He'd have enjoyed some potato chips or Fritos with his beer, but Celia had come across his secret stash a few days before. He still couldn't figure out what the hell she'd been doing looking on the top shelf of the den closet, but he couldn't ask as he'd denied knowing the sour cream and onion chips were there.

He claimed Noah had probably left them. That was his story, Frank thought as he made do with a handful of salt-free pretzels. And he was sticking to it.

When the doorbell rang, he left his beer and his doodling on the table, thinking it might be one of his players. He didn't think it set the right tone for Coach to come to the door with a cold one in his hand.

It was a young woman, with the tall, rangy build he could have used on the court. A little too old to fit into his twelve-to-sixteen-year-old league, he thought; then images overlapped in his mind and had him grabbing for her hands.

"Liv. Livvy! My God, you're all grown up."

"I didn't think you'd recognize me." And the fact that he had, with such obvious delight, warmed her. "I'd have known you anywhere. You look just the same."

"Never lie to a cop, even a retired one. Come in, come in." He pulled her inside. "I wish Celia were here. She had a late-afternoon meeting. Sit down." He fussed around the living room, picking up the newspaper, scooping a magazine off a chair. "Let me get you something to drink."

"I'm all right. I'm fine." There was a pressure in her chest, heavy, tight. "I told myself to call first. Then I didn't. I just came."

He saw the battle for composure on her face. "I'm glad you did. I knew you were grown-up, but every time I pictured you, even when I'd read your letters, I'd see a little girl."

"I always see a hero." She let herself go into his arms, let herself be held. And the jitters in her stomach quieted and eased. "I knew I'd feel better. I knew it would be all right, if I could see you."

"What's wrong, Livvy?"

"A lot of things. I'm figuring them out but—"

"Is this about Noah's book?"

"Part of it. About that, about him. He's your son." She said it with a sigh and stepped back to stand on her own. "And as much as I didn't want to, as much as I told myself I wouldn't, I trust him to do it right. It's going to be painful for me to talk to him, but I can do it. I will do it, in my own time. In my own way."

"You can trust him. I don't understand his work, but I understand Noah."

Puzzled, she shook her head. "You don't understand his work? How can you not understand his work? It's brilliant."

It was Frank's turn for confusion. He sat on the arm of the sofa, staring at her. "I have to say, I'm surprised to hear you say that. How could you feel that, as a survivor of a murder victim?"

"And the daughter of a murderer," she finished. "That's exactly why. I read his first book as soon as it came out. How could I resist it with his name on the cover?" And she'd hidden it in her room like a sin. "I didn't expect to like it." Hadn't wanted to, she thought. Had wanted to read it and condemn him. "I still don't know if I can say I liked it, but I understood what he was doing. He takes the most wicked of crimes, the most horrid, the most unforgivable. And he keeps them that way."

She waved a hand in annoyance at her own fumbling attempt to explain. "When you hear about a murder on the news, or read about it in the paper, you say, oh, how awful, then you move on. He humanizes it, makes it real—so vividly real that you can't say, 'Oh, how awful,' then slide down the pillows and go to sleep. Everyone who was involved—he strips them down to their most desperate and agonized emotions."

That, she realized, was what she feared about him the most. That he would strip her to the soul.

"He makes them matter," she continued. "So that what was done matters."

She smiled a little, but her eyes were horribly sad. "So that what his father did, every day, year in and year out, matters. You're his standard for everything that's right and strong."

Just, she thought, as her father was her standard for everything evil and weak.

"Livvy." Words clogged in Frank's throat. "You make me ashamed that I never looked close enough."

"You just see Noah. I'm nervous about talking to him." She pressed her hand to her stomach. "I don't want him to know that. I want us to try to do this on equal ground. Well, not quite equal," she corrected, and her smile steadied. "I'm going back home tomorrow, so he'll have to deal with me on my turf. I wondered, one of the things I wanted to ask, was if you and Mrs. Brady would like to come up sometime this summer, have a couple of free weeks at the lodge on the MacBrides. We've made a number of improvements, and I'd love you to see my Center and . . . Oh God. I'm sorry. God."

She pressed both hands to her mouth, stunned that the words had tripped out, stumbling over one another in her rush to conceal the truth.

"Livvy—"

"No, I'm all right. Just give me a minute." She walked to the front window, stared out through the pretty sheer curtains. "I know he gets out in a few weeks. I thought, somehow I thought, if you were there, just for the first couple of days after . . . it would be all right. I haven't let myself really think about it, but the time's coming. Just a few weeks."

She turned back, started to speak, to apologize again. But something in his face, the grim line of his mouth, the shadow in his eyes stopped her. "What is it?"

"It's about him getting out, Liv. I was contacted this morning. I have some connections, and whenever there's something new about Tanner, I get a call. Due to his health, the hardship, overcrowded system, time served, his record in prison . . ." Frank lifted a hand, let it fall.

"They're letting him out sooner, aren't they? When?"

Her eyes were huge, locked on his. He thought of the child who'd stared at him from her hiding place. This time, he could do nothing to soften the blow.

"Two weeks ago," he told her.

THE PHONE SHATTERED NOAH'S CONCENTRATION INTO A thousand irretrievable shards. He swore at it, viciously, ignoring the second ring as he stared at the last line he'd written and tried to find the rhythm again.

On the third ring he snatched up the portable he'd brought in by mistake, squeezed it with both hands as if to strangle the caller, then flipped it on.

"What the hell do you want?"

"Just to say good-bye. 'Bye."

"Wait. Liv. Wait, don't hang up, damn it. You don't return my calls for two days, and then you catch me at a bad moment."

"I've been busy, which you obviously are, too. So—"

"Okay, okay. I'm sorry. That was rude. I'm a jerk. I've got the sackcloth right here. You got my messages?" All ten thousand of them, he thought.

"Yes, I haven't had time to return them until now. And I only have a minute as it is. They're already boarding."

"Boarding? What? You're at the airport? You're leaving already?"

"Yes, my plans changed." Her father was out of prison. Was he already in L.A.? Is this where he would come first? She rubbed a hand over her mouth and schooled her voice to sound casual. "I have to get back, and I thought I'd let you know. If you still want to talk to me, regarding your book, you can reach me at the lodge, the Center most likely."

"Go back in the morning. One night can't make any difference. Olivia, I want to see you."

"You know where to find me. We'll work out some sort of schedule that's convenient for the interviews."

"I want . . ." You, he realized. How the hell had it gotten so mixed up a second time? "The book isn't everything that's going on here, between us. Change your flight." He hit keys rapidly to save data and close. "I'll come pick you up."

"I don't want to be here," she said flatly. "I'm going home." To where it was safe. To where she could breathe. "If you want interviews with me, you'll have to come to the lodge. It's final boarding. I'm leaving."

"It's not just the damn interviews," he began, but she'd already broken the connection.

Noah swung the phone over his shoulder, then halfway back to the desk before he managed to resist the urge to just beat it to bits of plastic.

The woman was making him nuts. She ran hot, cold, jumped up, down and sideways. How the hell was he supposed to keep up with her?

Now she was gone, leaping out of his reach before he had a real chance to grab hold. Now he was supposed to go chasing after her? Was that the game?

Disgusted, he kicked back in the chair, stared at the ceiling. No, she didn't work that way. It wasn't games with Olivia so much as it was a match. There was a big difference between the two.

There were details he needed to deal with, more data he needed to work through. And then, he thought, tossing the phone on the cluttered desk, then they'd just see about that match.

He was more than willing to go one-on-one.

OLIVIA DIDN'T RELAX UNTIL THE PLANE WAS IN THE AIR AND she could nudge her seat back, close her eyes. Below, Los Angeles was falling away, out of reach and soon out of sight. There was nothing there for her now, no need to go back. The house that had once been her own personal castle was locked behind iron gates and belonged to someone else.

And the murder that had been done there, long since scrubbed away.

If and when Noah contacted her, she'd deal with it, and him. She'd proven to herself that she could get through that swarm of memories. Retelling them would only be words, words that couldn't hurt her now.

The monster was loose.

It seemed to whisper in her ear, a warning edged with a kind of jumping glee.

It didn't matter. She wouldn't let it matter. Whether or not they'd unlocked his cell, given him a suit of clothes and the money he'd earned over his years in a cage, he'd been dead to her for a long, long time.

She hoped she'd been dead to him as well. That he didn't think of her. Or if he did, she prayed that every thought caused him pain.

She turned her head away from the window and willed herself to sleep.

SLEEP DIDN'T COME EASILY TO SOME. IT WAS FULL OF FEAR and sound and bloody images.

The monster was loose. And it cavorted in dreams, shambled on thick legs into the heart and poured out in bitter tears.

The monster was loose, and knew there would be no end, no finish without more death.

Livvy. The name was a silent sob, trembling in a desperate mind. The love for her was as real as it had been from the moment she'd been born. And the fear of her was as real as it had been on the night blood had been spilled.

She would be sacrificed only if there was no choice.

And the loss of her would be, forever, an open wound in the heart.

TWENTY-THREE

O UT? What do you mean he's out?"

"He got out two weeks ago. His lawyer filed a hardship plea, and they bumped up his release date." Frank settled down on a deck chair where his son had taken advantage of an overcast day and a quiet beach to work outside.

"Son of a bitch." Noah pushed to his feet, paced from one end of the deck to the other. "Son of a bitch. He must have known the last time I went to see him. He didn't tell me. I finally got a conference call scheduled with Smith this afternoon, and his assistant didn't mention it either. Well, where the hell did he go?"

"I don't have that information. Actually, I thought you might. I wouldn't mind keeping tabs on Tanner." Frank thought of the shock and fear in Olivia's eyes. "For old times' sake."

"He hasn't bothered to give me his fucking forwarding address. The book's dead without him." He stared down at his piles of papers, anchored with bottles, a conch shell, whatever came most handily. "Without him and Liv, it stops. The rest fans out from them. Early release?" He looked back at Frank. "Not parole, so he doesn't have to check in."

"He served his time. The state of California considers him rehabilitated."

"Do you?"

"Which part of you is asking the question? My son or the writer?"

Noah's face closed up immediately, went blank. "Never mind."

"I didn't mean I wouldn't answer, Noah. I was just curious."

"You're the one who compartmentalizes what I am and what I do. For me, they're in the same drawer."

"You're right. I've been giving that some thought recently." Frank sighed, laid his hands on his knees. "I thought you'd be a cop. I guess I had that idea in my head for a long time. I had this image of you coming on the job while I was still on it."

"I know I disappointed you. But it's not what I am."

The instinctive denial was on his tongue. Frank paused and gave his son the truth instead. "I had no right to be disappointed. And I know it's not what you are, Noah, but some things die hard. You were always interested in what I did when you were a kid. You used to write up reports." He laughed a little. "You'd ask me all these questions about a case and write it all up. I didn't see that for what it was. When you went into journalism, I thought, well, he'll snap out of that. But you didn't and I was disappointed. That's my failure, not yours."

"I never wanted to close cases, Dad. I wanted to study them."

"I didn't want to hear that. Pride has two edges, Noah. When you started writing books, started digging into things that were over and done, I took it as a reflection on what I had done, as if you were saying that it wasn't enough to do the job, gather the evidence, make the arrest, get the conviction."

"That's not it. That was never it."

"No, but I let my pride get in the way of seeing what you were doing, why you were doing it and what it meant to you. I want you to know I'm sorry for that. More sorry that I never gave you the respect you deserved for doing work you were meant to do, and doing it well."

"Well." Emotion slid through him, carrying out the tension in his shoulders he hadn't been aware of. "It's a day for surprises."

"I've always been proud of who you are, Noah. You've never been anything but a joy to me, as a son and as a man." Frank had to pause a moment before his tongue tangled.

"I wouldn't be what I am if you hadn't been there."

"Noah." Love was a swollen river in his throat. "I hope one day you have a grown child say that to you. It's the only way to know how much it means." He had to clear his throat before he embarrassed both of them. "I'm going to give more consideration to what you do. Fair enough?"

"Yeah, that's fair enough."

"I'll start by telling you I'll do that interview sort of thing, when you have the time for it."

"I've got time now. How about you?"

"Now? Well, I . . ." He hadn't been prepared for it and found himself limping for an excuse.

"Just let me get a fresh tape."

Noah knew when he had a fish on the line and made it fast. He came back out with a tape and two cans of Coke. "It's not as hard as you think," he said while he labeled the tape and snapped it into the recorder. "You just talk to me, tell me about the case. Just the way you used to. You told me some about this one. I made notes on it even back then. Tanner made the nine-one-one call himself. I've got a transcript of it."

Wanting accuracy rather than memory, Noah dug out the right file. "He called it in at twelve forty-eight. *She's dead. My God, Julie. She's dead. The blood, it's everywhere. I can't stop the blood. Somebody help me.*" Noah set the paper aside. "There's more, but that's the core of it. The nine-one-one operator asked him questions, kept getting the same response, but managed to get the address out of him."

"The uniforms went in first," Frank said. "Standard procedure. They responded to the nine-eleven. The gate was open; so was the front door. They entered the premises and found the body and Tanner in the front parlor area. They secured the scene, reported a homicide and requested detectives. Tracy Harmon and I took the call."

• • •

FOR NOAH, IT WAS AS IF HE'D WALKED INTO THE HOUSE THAT
night with his father. He felt the warm rustle of air that stirred the palm
fronds and danced through gardens silvered in moonlight. The house
stood, white as a wish with windows blazing gold with lights.

Police cruisers were guard-dogging the front, one with its blue and
red lights still spinning to shoot alarming color over the marble steps,
the faces of cops, the crime scene van.

More light poured out of the open doorway.

A rookie, his uniform still academy fresh, vomited pitifully in the
oleanders.

Inside, the grand chandelier dripped its waterfall of light on virgin
white floors and highlighted the dark stain of the blood trail.

It smeared in all directions, across the foyer, down the wide hall, up
the polished-oak stairway that swept regally to the left.

The smell of it was still ripe, the look of it still wet.

He was used to death, the violence of it. The waste of it. But his first
glimpse of what had been done to Julie MacBride broke his heart. He
remembered the sensations exactly, the sudden, almost audible snapping,
the resulting churn of pity and horror in his gut. And the fast, overpow-
ering flood of fury that burst into his head before he shut them away,
locked them away, and did his job.

At first glance it appeared to have been a vicious struggle. The broken
glass, the overturned furniture, the great spewing patterns of blood.

But there were patterns within patterns. The dead always left them.
Her nails were unbroken and clean, the defensive wounds on her hands
and arms shallow.

He'd come at her from behind. Later Frank would have this verified
by the ME's findings, but as he crouched beside the body, he played the
scene in his head.

The first blow had gone deep into her back, just below the shoulder
blades. She'd probably screamed, stumbled, tried to turn. There would have
been shock along with the pain. Had she seen his face? Seen what was in it?

He'd come at her again. Had she lifted an arm to block the blow? *Please, don't! God, don't!*

She'd tried to get away, knocking over the lamp, shattering glass, slicing her bare feet on it even as he sliced at her. She'd fallen, crawled, weeping. He'd driven the blades into her again and again, plunging with them, slashing with them even after she was still. Even after she was dead.

Two uniforms watched Sam in the adjoining room. As with his first glimpse of Julie, this image would implant itself on Frank's mind. He was pale and handsome. He smoked in quick jerks, his arm pistoning up and down, up and down as he brought the cigarette to his lips, drew in smoke, blew it out, drew it in again.

His eyes were off—glassy and wheeling in his head. Shock and drugs.

His wife's blood was all over him.

"Somebody killed her. Somebody killed Julie." He said it again and again.

"Tell me what happened, Mr. Tanner."

"She's dead. Julie's dead. I couldn't stop it."

"Couldn't stop what?"

"The blood." Sam stared down at his hands, then began to weep.

Sometime during that initial, disjointed interview, Frank remembered there was a child. And went to look for her.

IN HIS OFFICE, NOAH TYPED UP HIS NOTES FROM THE INTERview with his father. It helped to write it down, to see the words.

When his phone rang, he jolted, and realized that he had been lost, working for hours. The first streaks of sunset were now staining the sky through his window.

Noah pressed his fingers to his aching eyes and answered.

"It's Sam Tanner."

Instinctively, Noah snatched up a pencil. "Where are you?"

"I'm watching the sun go down. I'm outside, and I'm watching the sun go down over the water."

"You didn't tell me they were letting you out early, Sam."

"No."

"Are you in San Francisco?"

"I was in San Francisco long enough. It's cold and it's damp. I wanted to come home."

Noah's pulse picked up. "You're in L.A.?"

"I got a room off of Sunset. It's not what it used to be, Brady."

"Give me the address."

"I'm not there now. Actually I'm down the road from you. Watching the sun set," he said almost dreamily. "Outside a place that serves tacos and beer and salsa that makes your eyes sting."

"Tell me where you are. I'll meet you."

SAM WORE KHAKIS AND A SHORT-SLEEVED CHAMBRAY SHIRT, both so painfully new they'd yet to shake out the folding pleats. He sat at one of the little iron tables on the patio of the Mexican place and stared out over the water. Though business wasn't brisk, there was a sprinkling of people at other tables, kids with fresh faces who scooped up nachos and sipped at the beers they were barely old enough to order.

In contrast, Sam looked old, pale and inexplicably more naive.

Noah ordered more tacos, another beer for each of them.

"What does it feel like?"

With a kind of wonder, Sam watched an in-line skater skim by. "I spent a few days in San Francisco, to get my bearings. Then I took a bus down. Part of me kept expecting someone to stop me, take me back, say it had all been a mistake. Another part was waiting to be recognized, to hear someone call out, 'Look, there's Sam Tanner,' and run over for my autograph. There're two lives crossed over in the middle, and my mind keeps jumping back and forth between them."

"Do you want to be recognized?"

"I was a star. An important actor. You need the attention, not just to feed the ego, but to stroke the child. If you weren't a child, how good an actor could you be? After a while, inside, I had to put that away. When I knew the appeals weren't going to work, the cage wasn't going to open, I had to put it away to survive. Then I got out and it all came flooding back. And as badly as I wanted someone to look at me, to *see* me and remember, it scared the shit out of me that someone would. Stage fright." Sam gave a small, sick smile. "There's something I haven't had to deal with in a long time."

Noah said nothing while the waitress clunked their food and drinks down. Once she'd walked away, he leaned forward. "Coming to L.A. was a risk, because someone's bound to recognize you sooner or later."

"Where else would I go? It's changed. I got lost twice walking around. New faces everywhere, on the street, on the billboards. People driving around in big chunky Jeeps. And you can't smoke any fucking where."

Noah had to laugh at the absolute bafflement in the statement. "I imagine the food's some better than San Quentin's."

"I forgot places like this existed." Sam picked up a taco, studied it. "I'd forgotten that before I went inside. If it wasn't the best, I wasn't interested. If I wasn't going to be seen, admired, envied, what was the point?"

He bit in, crunching the shell, ignoring the little bits of tomato and lettuce and sauce that plopped onto his plate. For a few moments he ate in concentrated silence, a kind of grim focus Noah imagined came from prison meals.

"I was an asshole."

Noah lifted a brow. "Can I quote you?"

"That's what this is about, isn't it? I had everything—success, adula-tion, power, wealth. I had the most beautiful woman in the world, who loved me. I thought I deserved it, all of it, so I didn't value what I had. I didn't value any of it or see it as any more than my due. So I lost it. All of it."

Keeping his eyes on Sam's face, Noah sipped his beer. "Did you kill your wife?"

He didn't answer at first, only watched the last sliver of sun sink red into the sea. "Yes." His gaze shifted, locked on Noah's. "Did you expect me to deny it? What's the point? I served twenty years for what I did. Some will say it's not enough. Maybe they're right."

"Why did you kill her?"

"Because I couldn't be what she asked me to be. Now ask me if I picked up the scissors that night and stabbed them into her back, her body, sliced them across her throat."

"All right. Did you?"

"I don't know." His eyes shifted to the water again, went dreamy again. "I just don't know. I remember it two ways, and both seem absolutely real. I stopped thinking it mattered, then they told me I was going to die. I need to know, and you're going to figure out which of the two ways is real."

"Which one are you going to tell me?"

"Neither, not yet. I need the money. I opened an account at this bank." He brought out a scrap of paper. "That's my account number. They do this electronic transfer. That'd be the best way."

"All right." Noah pocketed the paper. "It'll be there tomorrow."

"Then we'll talk tomorrow."

NOAH CALLED OLIVIA THE NEXT MORNING, CAUGHT HER AT her desk at the Center. He was still damp from the shower after his run on the beach, just starting to pump up his system with coffee. The sound of her voice, brisk, businesslike, husky around the edges made him smile.

"Hello back, Ms. MacBride. Miss me?"

"Not particularly."

"I don't believe it. You recognized my voice too easily." He heard her sigh, certain she'd wanted it audible and full of exasperation.

"Why wouldn't I? You talk more than any three people I know put together."

"And you don't talk enough, but I've got your voice in my head. I had a dream about you last night, all soft, watery colors and slow motion. We made love on the bank of the river, and the grass was cool and damp and wild with flowers. I woke up with the taste of you in my mouth."

There was a moment of silence, a quiet catch of breath. "That's very interesting."

"Is someone in your office?"

"Momentarily. Thanks, Curtis, I'll take care of that." There was another pause. "That riverbank is a public area."

He laughed so hard he had to slide onto a stool. "I'm becoming seriously crazy about you, Liv. Did you like the flowers?"

"They're very nice and completely unnecessary."

"Sure they were. They make you think of me. I want you to keep me right in the front of your mind, Liv, so we can pick things up when I get there."

"When do you plan to make the trip?"

"One or two weeks—sooner, if I can manage it."

"The lodge is booked well in advance this time of year."

"I'll think of something. Liv, I need to tell you I've seen Tanner, spoken with him. He's here in Los Angeles."

"I see."

"I thought you'd feel better knowing where he is."

"Yes, I suppose I do. I have to go—"

"Liv, you can tell me how you feel. Aside from the book, just as someone who cares about you. You can talk to me."

"I don't know how I feel. I only know I can't let where he is or what he's doing change my life. I'm not going to let anything or anyone do that."

"You may find out some changes don't have to hurt. I'll let you know when I plan to come in. Keep thinking about me, Olivia."

She hung up, let out a long breath. "Keep dreaming," she murmured and skimmed a finger over the petals of a sunny daisy.

She hadn't been able to resist keeping them in her office where she could see them when she was stuck at her desk and itching to get outside.

She'd recognized what he'd done as well, and found it incredibly sweet and very clever. The flowers he ordered were all from the varieties he had in his own garden. The garden she hadn't been able to resist. He had to know that looking at them would make her think of him.

She'd have thought of him anyway.

And she'd lied when she'd told him she didn't miss him. It surprised her how much she did and worried her just a little to realize she wished they were different people in a different situation. Then they could be lovers, maybe even friends, without the shadows clinging to the corner of their relationship.

She'd never been friends with a lover, she thought. Had never really had a lover, as that term added dimension and intimacy to simple sex.

But she thought Noah would insist on being both. If she wanted him, she would have to give more than she'd been willing, or able, to give to anyone before.

One more thing to think about, she decided, and rubbing the tension from her neck, swiveled back to her keyboard and began to input her ideas for the fall programs with an eye to the elementary school field trips she hoped to implement.

She answered the knock on her door with a grunt.

"Was that a come in or go to hell?" Rob wanted to know as he gently shook the package he carried.

"It's come in to you, and go to hell for anyone else. I'm just working out some fall programs." She angled her head as she swiveled her chair around. "What's in the box?"

"Don't know. It came to the lodge, looks like an overnight from Los Angeles, to you."

"Me?"

"I'd guess it's from the same young man who sent you the flowers." He set the package on the desk. "And I say he has fine taste in women."

"Which you say with complete objectivity."

"Of course." Rob sat on the corner of the desk, reached for her hands. "How's my girl?"

"I'm fine." She gave his hand a reassuring squeeze. "Don't worry about me, Grandpop."

"I'm allowed to worry. It's part of the job description." And she'd been so tense, so pale when she'd come back from California. "It doesn't matter that he's out, Livvy. I've made my peace with that. I hope you will."

"I'm working on it." She rose, moved away to tidy files that didn't need tidying. "Noah just called. He wanted to let me know he'd seen him, spoken to him."

"It's best you know."

"Yes, it is. I appreciate that he understands that, respects that. That he doesn't treat me as if I were so fragile I'd break, that I needed to be protected from . . ." She trailed off, felt a wave of heat wash into her face. "I didn't mean—"

"It's all right. I don't know if we did the right thing, Livvy, bringing you here, closing everything else out. We meant it for the best."

"Bringing me here was exactly the right thing." She dropped the files and stepped over to hug him tight. "No one could have given me more love or a better home than you and Grandma. We won't let thoughts of him come in here and make us question it." Her eyes stormed with emotion when she drew back. "We won't."

"I still want what's best for you. I'm just not as sure as I once was what it is. This young man . . ." He nodded toward the flowers. "He's bringing you an awful lot to face at one time. But he's got a straight look in his eye, makes me want to trust him with you."

"Grandpop." She bent, kissed his cheek. "I'm old enough, and smart enough, to decide that for myself."

"You're still my baby. Aren't you going to open the package?"

"No, it'll only encourage him." She grinned. "He's trying to charm me."

"Is he?"

"I suppose he is, a little. He's planning on coming back soon. I'll decide just how charmed I am when I see him again. Now, go to work, and let me do the same."

"He comes back around, I'm keeping an eye on him." Rob winked as he got up and headed for the door. Then he stopped, one hand on the knob, and glanced back. "Did we keep you too close, Livvy? Hold you too tight?" He shook his head before she could answer. "Yes or no, you grew your own way. Your mother'd be proud of you."

When the door closed behind him, she sat down, struggled with the tears that were a hot mix of grief and joy. She hoped he was right, that her mother would be proud, and not see her daughter as a woman who was too aloof, too hard, too afraid to open herself to anyone but the family who'd always been there.

Would Julie, bright, beautiful Julie, ask her daughter, Where are your friends? Where are the boys you pined for, the men you loved? Where are the people you've touched or made part of your life?

What would the answer be? Olivia wondered. There's no one. No one.

It made her so suddenly, so unbearably sad the tears threatened again. Blinking them away, she stared at the package on her desk.

Noah, she thought. He was trying to reach her. Wasn't it time she let him?

She dug out the Leatherman knife from her pocket, used the slim blade to break the sealing tape. Then she paused, let herself feel the anticipation, the pleasure. Let herself think of him as she lifted the lid.

Hurrying now, she probed through the protective blizzard of Styrofoam chips, spilling them out onto the desk as she worked the contents out. Glass or china, she thought, some sort of figurine. She wondered if he'd actually tracked down a statue of a marmot, was already laughing at the idea when she freed the figure.

The laugh died in her throat, tumbled with the avalanche of icy panic that roared through her chest. Her own rapid breathing became a crashing scream in her head. She dropped the figurine as if it were a live snake, poised to strike.

And stared, trembling and swaying, at the benevolent and beautiful face of the Blue Fairy poised atop the music box.

TWENTY-FOUR

I never wanted to be alone." Sam held the coffee Noah had given him and squinted against the sun. "Being alone was like a punishment to me. A failure. Julie was good at it, often preferred it. She didn't need the spotlight the way I did."

"Did or do?" Noah asked, and watched Sam smile.

"I've learned there are advantages to solitude. Julie always knew that. When we separated, when I bought the place in Malibu, the prospect of living there alone was nearly as terrifying as living without her. I don't remember much about the Malibu house. I guess it was similar to this."

He glanced back at the house, the creamy wood, clear streams of glass, the splashes of flowers in stone tubs. Then out to the ocean. "The view wouldn't have been much different. You like it here, being alone?"

"My kind of work requires big chunks of solitude."

Sam only nodded and fell silent.

Noah had debated the wisdom of conducting the interviews at his own place. In the end, it had seemed most practical. They'd have the privacy he required and, by setting up on the deck, give Sam his wish to be outside. He hadn't been able to come up with a good argument against it, as Sam already had his address.

He waited while Sam lit another cigarette. "Tell me about the night of August twenty-eighth."

"I didn't want to be alone," Sam said again. "I wasn't working, had just fired my agent. I was pissed off at Julie. Who the hell did she think she was, kicking me out of the house when she was the one fucking around? I called Lydia. I wanted company, I wanted sympathy. She hated Julie, so I knew she'd say what I wanted to hear. I figured we'd get high and have sex—like old times. That'd teach Julie a lesson."

His hand bunched into a fist on his knee, and he began to tap it there, rhythmically. "She wasn't home. Her maid said she was out for the evening. So I was pissed off about that, too. Couldn't depend on anyone, no one was there when you needed them. Worked myself up pretty good. There were others I could have called, but I thought fuck them. I did a line to prime myself up, then got in the car and headed into L.A."

He paused, rubbing lightly at his temple as if he had a headache brewing, then went back to tapping his fist on his knee. "I don't know how many clubs I hit. It came out in the trial, different people seeing me at different places that night. Saying I was belligerent, looking for trouble. How did they know what I was looking for when I didn't?"

"Witnesses stated you were looking for Lucas Manning, got into a shoving match with security at one of the clubs, knocked over a tray of drinks at another."

"Must have." Sam moved his shoulder casually, but his hand continued its hard, steady rhythm. "It's a blur. Bright lights, bright colors, faces, bodies. I did another line in the car. Maybe two before I drove to our house. I'd been drinking, too. I had all this energy and anger and all I could think of was Julie. We'd settle this, goddamn it. Once and for all."

He sat back, closed his eyes. His hand stilled, then began to claw at his knee. "I remember the way the trees stood out against the sky, like a painting. And the headlights of other cars were like suns, burning against my eyes. I could hear the sound of my heartbeat in my head. Then it goes two ways."

He opened his eyes, blue and intense, and stared into Noah's. "The gate's locked. I know he's in there with her. The son of a bitch. When she comes on the intercom I tell her to open the gate, I need to talk to her. I'm careful, really careful, to keep my tone calm. I know she won't let me in if she knows I've been using. She won't let me in if she knows I'm primed. She tells me it's late, but I persist, I persuade. She gives in. I drive back to the house. The moonlight's so bright it hurts my eyes. And she's standing in the door, the light behind her. She's wearing the white silk nightgown I'd bought her for our last anniversary. Her hair's down around her shoulders, her feet are bare. She's so beautiful. And cold, her face is cold, like something carved out of marble. She tells me to make it quick, she's tired, and walks into the parlor.

"There's a glass of wine on the table, and the magazines. The scissors. They're silver and long-bladed sitting on the glass top. She picks up her wine. She knows I'm high now, so she's angry. 'Why are you doing this to yourself?' she asks me. 'Why are you doing this to me, to Livvy?'"

Sam lifted a hand to his lips, rubbed them, back and forth, back and forth. "I tell her it's her fault, hers because she let Manning put his hands on her, because she put her career ahead of our marriage. It's an old argument, old ground, but this time it takes a different turn. She says she's through with me, there's no chance for us, and she wants me out of her life. I make her sick, I disgust her."

Still the actor, he punched the words, used pauses and passion. "She doesn't raise her voice, but I can see the words coming out of her mouth. I see them as dark red smoke, and they choke me. She tells me she's never been happier since she kicked me out and has no intention of weighing herself down with a has-been with a drug problem. Manning isn't just a better actor, he's a better lover. And I was right all along, she's tired of denying it. He gives her everything I can't."

Noah watched Sam's eyes go glassy and narrowed his own.

"She turned away from me as if I was nothing," Sam muttered, then lifted his voice to a half shout. "As if everything we'd had together was nothing. The red smoke from her words is covering my face, it's burning in my throat. The scissors with the long silver blades are in my hands. I want to stab them through her, deep inside her. She screams, the glass flies out of her hand, shatters. Blood pours out of her back. Like I'd pulled a cork out of a bottle of perfect red wine. She stumbles, there's a crash. I can't see through the smoke, just keep hacking with the scissors. The blood's hot on my hands, on my face. We're on the floor, she's crawling, the scissors are like part of my hand. I can't stop them. I can't stop."

His eyelids shuttered closed now, and the hands on his knees were bone-white fists. "I see Livvy in the doorway, staring at me with her mother's eyes."

His hand shook as he picked up his coffee. He sipped, long and deep like a man gulping for liquid after wandering the desert. "That's one way I remember it. Can I have something cold now? Some water?"

"All right." Noah switched off the recorder, rose, went inside to the kitchen. Then he laid his palms on the counter. Icy sweat shivered over his skin. The images of the murder were bad enough. He'd read the transcripts, studied the reports. He'd known what to expect. But it had been the perfect artistry of Sam's narrative that knotted his stomach. That, and the thought of Olivia crawling out of her child's bed and into a nightmare.

How many times had she relived it? he wondered.

He poured two glasses of mineral water over ice, braced himself to go back out and continue.

"You're wondering if you can still be objective," Sam said when Noah stepped out again. "You're wondering how you can stand to sit here with me and breathe the same air."

"No." Noah passed him the water, sat. "That's part of my job. I'm wondering how you live with yourself. What you see when you look in the mirror every morning."

"They kept me on suicide watch for two years. They were right. But after a while, you learn to go from one day to the next. I loved Julie, and that love was the best part of my life. It still wasn't enough to make me a man."

"And twenty years in prison did?"

"Twenty years in prison made me sorry I'd destroyed everything I'd been given. Cancer made me decide to take what was left."

"What's left, Sam?"

"The truth, and facing it." He took another sip of water. "I remember that night another way, too. It starts off the same, toking up, cruising, letting the drug feed the rage. But this time the gates are open when I get there. Boy, that pisses me off. What the hell is she thinking? We're going to have a little talk about that. If Manning's inside . . . I know damn well he's in there. I can see him pumping himself into my wife. I think about killing him, with my bare hands, while she watches. The door of the house is wide open. Light's spilling out. This really gets me. I walk in, looking for a fight. I start to go upstairs, sure I'll catch them in bed, but I hear the music from the parlor. They must be fucking in there, with the music on, the door open and my daughter upstairs. Then I . . ."

He stopped, took a long drink, then set the glass aside. "There's blood everywhere. I didn't even recognize it for what it was at first. It's too much to be real. There's broken glass, smashed. The lamp we'd bought on our honeymoon is shattered on the floor. My head's buzzed from coke and vodka, but I'm thinking Jesus, Jesus, there's been a break-in. And I see her. Oh God, I see her on the floor."

His voice broke, wavered, quavered, just as perfectly delivered as the stream of violence in his first version. "I'm kneeling beside her, saying her name, trying to pick her up. Blood, there's blood all over her. I know she's dead, but I tell her to wake up, she has to wake up. I pulled the scissors out of her back. If I took them out, they couldn't hurt her. And there was Livvy, staring at me."

He took a cigarette from the pack on the table and struck a match, and the flame shivered as if in a brisk wind. "The police didn't buy that one." He blew out smoke. "Neither did the jury. After a while, I stopped buying it, too."

"I'm not here to buy anything, Sam."

"No." He nodded but it was a sly look, a con's look. "But you'll wonder, won't you?"

• • •

"ACCORDING TO MANNING, HE AND JULIE NEVER HAD AN affair. Not for lack of trying on his part, he was up-front about that." Noah stood with his father outside the youth center while a group of kids fought through a pickup game on the newly blacktopped basketball court. "He was in love with her—or infatuated, spent a lot of time with her— but she considered him a friend."

"That's the way he played it during the investigation."

"Did you believe him?"

Frank sighed, shook his head as he watched one of his boys bobble a pass. "He was convincing. The housekeeper's testimony backed him up. She swore no man had ever spent the night in that house but the man her mistress had been married to. She was fiercely loyal to Julie and could have been covering. But we never shook her on it. The only evidence to the contrary was Sam Tanner's belief and the usual gossip. As far as the case went, it didn't matter one way or the other. Tanner believed in the affair, so to him it was real and part of the motive."

"Don't you find it odd that Manning and Lydia Loring ended up as lovers even for only a few months?"

"That's why they call it Holly-Weird, pal."

"Just hypothetically, if you hadn't had Tanner cold, where else would you have looked?"

"We had him cold, and we still looked. We interviewed Manning, Lydia, the housekeeper, the agent, the family. Particularly the Melbournes, as they both worked for Julie. Actually, we took a long look at Jamie Melbourne. She inherited a considerable sum upon her sister's death. We went through Julie's fan mail, culled out the loonies and took a look at them in case an obsessed fan had managed to get in through the security. The fact is, Tanner was there. His prints were all over the murder weapon. He had motive, means and opportunity. And his own daughter saw him."

Frank shifted. "I had some trouble with the case during the first few days. It didn't hold as solid as I wanted it to."

"What do you mean, it didn't hold?"

"Just that the way Tanner behaved, the way he mixed up two different nights—two different altercations with Julie in his head—or pretended to . . . It didn't sit at first. Then he lawyered and went hard. I realized he'd been playing me. Don't let him play you, Noah."

"I'm not." But he jammed his hands into his pockets, paced away, paced back. "Just hear me out. A few days ago he told me two versions of that night. The first jibes with your findings, almost a perfect match. He's into the part when he's describing it. He could've been replaying a murder scene in a brutal movie. Then he tells me the other way, the way he got there and found her. His hands shake, and he goes pale. His voice races up and down like a roller coaster."

"Which did you believe?"

"Both."

Frank nodded. "And he told you last the way that makes him innocent. Let that impression dig the deepest."

Noah hissed out a breath. "Yeah, I thought of that."

"Maybe he still wishes it was the second way. One thing I believed, Noah, is that after, he wished she hadn't opened the door that night. And you can't ever forget that one vital point," Frank added. "He's an actor and knows how to sell himself."

"I'm not forgetting," Noah murmured. But he was wondering.

HE DECIDED TO SWING BY AND SEE HIS MOTHER. HE PLANNED on heading to Washington the following day. This time he'd fly up, then rent a car. He didn't want to waste time on the road.

Celia was sitting on their little side deck, going through the mail and sipping a tall glass of herbal sun tea. She lifted her cheek for Noah to kiss, then wagged a form letter at him. "Have you seen this? They're threatening to cut the funding for the preservation of the northern elephant seal."

"Must've missed that one."

"It's disgraceful. Congress votes itself a raise, spends millions of taxpayer dollars on studies to study studies of studies, but they'll sit back and let another of the species on our planet become extinct."

"Go get 'em, Mom."

She huffed, put the letter aside and opened another. "Your father's at the youth center."

"I know, I was just there. I thought I'd come by and see you before I headed to Washington tomorrow."

"I'm glad you did. Why don't you stay for dinner? I've got a new recipe for artichoke bottoms I want to try out."

"Gee, that sounds . . . tempting, but I have to pack."

"Liar," she said with a laugh. "How long will you be gone?"

"Depends."

"Is the book giving you trouble?"

"Some, nothing major."

"What then?"

"I've got a little hang-up going." He picked up her tea, sipped. Winced. She refused to add even a grain of sugar. "A personal-level hang-up. On Olivia MacBride."

"Really?" Celia drew out the word, giving it several syllables, and grinned like a contented cat. "Isn't that nice?"

"I don't know how nice it is or why you'd be so pleased about it. You haven't seen her since she was a kid."

"I've read her letters to your father. She appears to me a smart, sensible young woman, which is a far cry from your usual choice, particularly that creature Caryn. She still hasn't turned up, by the way."

"Fine. Let her stay in whatever hole she dug for herself."

"I suppose I have to agree. And to backtrack, I like hearing you say you're interested in someone. You never tell me you're interested in a woman. Just that you're seeing one."

"I've been interested in Liv for years."

"Really? How? She was, what, twelve, when you last saw her."

"Eighteen. I went up to see her six years ago, when she was in college."

Surprised, Celia stopped opening mail. "You went to see her? You never mentioned it."

"No, mostly because I wasn't too happy with the way it worked out." He blew out a breath. "Okay, condensed version. I wanted to write the book, even then. I went to see her to talk her into cooperating. Then I saw her, and . . . Man, it just blasted through me. I couldn't think, with all the stuff going on inside me just looking at her, I didn't think."

"Noah." Celia closed a hand over his. "I had no idea you'd ever felt that way, with anyone."

"I've felt that way with her, and I ruined it. When she found out why I was there, it hurt her. She wouldn't listen to apologies or explanations. She just closed the door."

"Has she opened it again?"

"I think she's pulled back a couple of the locks."

"You weren't honest with her before, and it ended badly. That should tell you something."

"It does. But first I have to wear her down." Because he felt better having just said it all out loud, he smiled. "She's a hell of a lot tougher than she was at eighteen."

"You'll think more of her if she makes you work." She patted his hand, then went back to the mail. "I know you, Noah. When you want something, you go after it. Maybe not all at once, but you keep at it until you have it."

"Well, it feels like I've been going after Olivia MacBride most of my life. Meanwhile . . . Mom? What is it?" She'd gone deadly pale, had him leaping up fearing a heart attack.

"Noah. Oh God." She gripped the hand he'd pressed to her face. "Look. Look."

He pulled the paper out of her hand, ignoring it while he struggled to keep them both calm. "Take it easy. Just sit still. Catch your breath. I'll call the doctor."

"No, for God's sake, look!" She took his wrist, yanked the paper he held back down.

He saw it then. The photocopy was fuzzy, poorly reproduced, but he recognized the work of the police photographer documenting the body of Julie MacBride at the scene of the murder.

He had a copy of the picture in his own files, and though he'd looked at it countless times, the stark black and white was freshly appalling.

No, not a photocopy, he realized. Computer-scanned, just as the bold letters beneath the picture were computer-generated.

IT CAN HAPPEN AGAIN.
IT CAN HAPPEN TO YOU.

Rage, cold and controlled, coated him as he looked into his mother's horrified, baffled eyes. "He flicked the wrong switch this time," Noah murmured.

He waited until his father came racing home. But no amount of arguing or pleading could make him wait until the police arrived.

The son of a bitch had played him all right and had nearly sucked him in. Now he'd threatened his family. Revenge, Noah supposed as he slammed out of his car and strode down Sunset. Revenge against the cop who'd helped lock him away. Go after the family. Lure the son in, dangle the story, take the money, then terrorize the wife.

Noah pushed through the front entrance of the apartment unit, flicked a glance at the elevator and chose the stairs. The mighty had fallen here, he thought. The paint was peeling, the treads grimy, and he caught the sweet whiff of pot still clinging to the air.

But he hadn't fallen far enough.

The bastard liked women as his victims. Noah pounded a fist on the door of the second-floor apartment. Women and little girls. They'd just see how well he handled it when he had a man to deal with.

He pounded again and seriously considered kicking the door in. The cold edge of his rage had flashed to a burn.

"If you're looking for the old man, he split."

Noah glanced around, saw the woman—hell, the hooker, he corrected.

"Split where?"

"Hey, I don't keep tabs on the neighbors, honey. You a cop?"

"No, I've got business with him, that's all."

"Look a little like a cop," she decided after an expert up-and-down survey. "Parole officer?"

"What makes you think he needs one?"

"Shit, you think I can't spot a con? He did some long time. What he do, kill somebody?"

"I just want to talk to him."

"Well, he ain't here." She kept moving, giving Noah an unattractive whiff of cheap perfume and stale sex. "Packed up his little bag and moved out yesterday."

LONG AFTER THE CENTER HAD CLOSED FOR THE DAY, OLIVIA worked in her office. The paperwork had a nasty habit of building up on her during late spring and summer. She much preferred taking groups on the trail, giving lectures or heading a tour of the backcountry for a few days.

She caught herself staring at the phone, again, and muttered curses under her breath. It was humiliating, absolutely mortifying, to realize that part of the reason she was working late again was the hope that Noah would call.

Which he hadn't done in two days, she reminded herself. Not that he was under any obligation to call her, of course. Not that she couldn't, if she wanted to, call him. Which she wouldn't do because, damn it, it would look as if she was hoping he'd call.

She was acting like a high school girl with a crush. At least she thought she was. She'd never been a high school girl with a crush. Apparently she'd had more sense at sixteen than she had now.

Now she daydreamed over the flowers he'd sent. She remembered the exact tone of his voice when he'd said her name. After he'd kissed her. The texture of his hands against her face. The little lurch of shock and pleasure in her own stomach.

The way he talked and talked, she thought now, poking and prodding at her until she gave up and laughed. He'd been the first man she'd ever been attracted to who could make her laugh.

He was certainly the only man she'd ever thought about after he was out of sight.

No, maybe she should say the second man, as the younger version of Noah had attracted her, charmed her, confused her. They were both just different enough now for this . . . whatever it was between them, to be somehow new. And very compelling.

Which, she supposed, said as much about her as it did about him.

She hadn't wanted anything but surface involvements, and she hadn't wanted many of those.

Why in the world was she sitting here analyzing her feelings when she didn't want to have any feelings in the first place? She had enough to worry about without adding Noah Brady to the mix.

She glanced toward her little storage closet. She'd buried the music box under the packing, stuffed it in the closet. Why had he sent it? Was it a peace offering or a threat? She didn't want the first and refused to be intimidated by the second.

But she hadn't been able to throw it away.

When the phone rang, she jumped foolishly, then rolled her eyes in annoyance. It had to be Noah, she thought. Who else would call so late? She caught herself before she could snatch eagerly at the receiver, deliberately let it ring three full times while she took careful breaths.

When she picked it up, her voice was cool and brisk. "River's End Naturalist Center."

She heard the music, just the faint drift of it, and imagined Noah setting a scene for a romantic phone call. She started to laugh, to open her mouth to make some pithy comment, then found herself unable to speak at all.

She recognized it now, Tchaikovsky's *Sleeping Beauty*.

The soaring, liquid, heartbreaking notes of it that took her back to a warm summer night and the metallic scent of blood.

Her hand tightened on the receiver while the panic-trip of her heart filled her head. "What do you want?" Her free hand pressed and rubbed between her breasts as if to shove back the rising pressure. "I know who you are. I know what you are."

The monster was free.

"I'm not afraid of you."

It was a lie. Terror, hot, greasy flows of it swam into her belly and slicked over her skin. She wanted to crawl under her desk, roll up into a ball. Hide. Just hide.

"Stay away from me." Fear broke through, spiking her voice. "Just stay away!"

She slammed the receiver down and, with panic bubbling madly in her throat, ran.

The doorknob slipped out of her hand, making her whimper with frustration until she could cement her grip. The Center was dark, silent. She nearly cowered back, but the phone rang again. Her own screams shocked her, sent her skidding wildly across the floor. Her breath tore out of her lungs, sobbed through the silence. She had to get out. To run. To be safe.

And as she reached for the door, the knob turned sharply. The door opened wide, and in its center was the shadow of a man.

Her vision went gray and hazy. Dimly she heard someone call her name. Hands closed over her arms. She felt herself sway, then slide through them into the black.

"Hey, hey, hey. Come on. Come back."

Her head reeled. She felt little pats on her face, the brush of lips over hers. It took her a moment to realize she was on the floor, being rocked like a baby in Noah's lap.

"Stop slapping me, you moron." She lay still, weak from embarrassment and the dregs of panic.

"Oh yeah, that's better. Good." He covered her mouth with his, poured an ocean of relief into the kiss. "That's the first time I ever had a woman faint at my feet. Can't say I like it one damn bit."

"I didn't faint."

"You did a mighty fine imitation, then." She'd only been out for seconds, he realized, though it had seemed to take a lifetime for her to melt in his grip. "I'm sorry I scared you, coming in that way. I saw your office light."

"Let me up."

"Let's just sit here a minute. I don't think my legs are ready to try standing yet." He rested his cheek on hers. "So, how've you been other-wise?"

She wanted to laugh, and to weep. "Oh, just fine thanks. You?"

He shifted her so he could grin into her face. Then just the look of her, clear amber eyes, pale skin, had something moving inside him. "I really missed you." His hand roamed through her hair now, stroking. "It's so weird. Do you know how much time we've actually spent together?"

"No."

"Not enough," he murmured, and lowered his mouth to hers again. This time her lips were soft and welcomed him. Her arms lifted and enfolded him. He felt himself sink, then settle so that even the wonder of it seemed as natural as breathing.

She had no defenses now. He drew her in, soft, slow, sure until there was nothing but that stirring mating of lips.

"Liv." He traced kisses along her jaw, up to her temple. "Let me close the door."

"Hmm?"

Her sleepy answer had sparks of heat simmering inside the warmth. "The door." His hand brushed over her breast, his fingers spreading as she arched toward him. "I don't want to make love with you in an open doorway."

She made another humming sound, scraping her teeth over his bottom lip as she slapped at the door in an attempt to close it herself.

Then the phone rang, and she was clawing to get free.

"It's just the phone. Christ." To defend himself, he clamped his arms over hers.

"It's him. Let me go! It's him."

He didn't ask whom she meant. She only used that tone when she spoke of her father. "How do you know?"

Her eyes wheeled white with panic. "He called before—just before."

"What did he say to you?"

"Nothing." Overwhelmed, she curled up, clamped her hands over her ears. "Nothing, nothing."

"It's okay, it's all right. Stay right here." He nudged her aside and, with blood in his eye, strode into the office. Even as he reached for the receiver, the ringing stopped.

"It was him." She'd managed to get up, managed to walk to the door. But she was shaking. "He didn't say anything. He just played the music. The music my mother had on the stereo the night he killed her. He wants me to know he hasn't forgotten."

TWENTY-FIVE

H<small>E'D</small> managed to book a room, but had been warned it was only available for one night. For the remainder of the month, the lodge was fully booked. There were a couple of campsites still available, but he couldn't work up any enthusiasm in that area.

Still, he was going to have to snag one, and buy himself some camping equipment if he meant to stay.

And he meant to stay.

His original plan had been to rent a snazzy suite in some hotel within reasonable driving distance where he could work in comfort and seduce Olivia in style. After what he'd learned the night before, he wasn't willing to stay that far away.

He intended to keep an eye on her. The only way to accomplish that was to stay put and to be more stubborn than she was.

There'd been a test of that the night before as well. She'd told him about the phone call, the music box, and her fear had been alive in the room with them. But the moment she'd gotten it out, she'd toughened up again, stepped back from him.

He thought part of it had been an incredibly misplaced sense of embarrassment at showing a weakness. But on another level, he decided this was the way she'd shored up any holes in her defenses for years. She set it aside, closed it off and refused to talk about it.

She'd fired up when he'd said he was taking her home. She knew the way, he'd get lost on the way back, she didn't need a bodyguard. And wouldn't be *taken* anywhere by anyone.

Noah stepped out on his tiny first-floor patio and scanned the deep green of the summer forest.

He'd never actually dragged a woman to his car before, he thought now. Never seriously wrestled with one in a personal match that didn't have the end goal of sex on the minds of both participants. And he'd never come quite so close to losing to a girl.

He rubbed his bruised ribs absently.

He wondered if he should be ashamed of having enjoyed it quite so much, then decided against it. He'd gotten her home safely, had managed to block her last punch long enough to punctuate his victory with a very satisfying kiss.

Until she'd bitten him.

God, he was crazy about her.

And concerned enough to make him determined to deal with Sam Tanner. To keep Olivia safe and to give her some peace of mind.

He went back inside and called his father. "How's Mom?"

"She's fine. I drove her in to work today and browbeat a promise out of her that she wouldn't go anywhere alone. I'll be driving her to and from until . . . until."

"No word on Tanner?"

"No. He withdrew two thousand in cash from his bank account. He rented his room by the week and had paid up. We're—the police are interested in questioning him about the picture, but there's not a lot they can do. I tugged some strings and had a couple of my buddies check the airports and train stations for reservations in his name. Nothing."

"He needs to be found. Hire a detective. The best you know. I can afford it."

"Noah—"

"This is my party, I foot the bill. I'll arrange for you to leave messages for me here at the lodge. I'm going to be doing the tent thing for a while and I might not have my cell phone on me, so I won't always be reachable. I'll be checking in as often as I can."

"Noah, if he's decided it's payback, you're a target. He's dying, he's got nothing to lose."

"I grew up with a cop. I know how to handle myself. Take care of Mom."

Frank waited a beat. "I know how to take care of what's mine. Watch yourself, Noah."

"Same goes." He hung up, then paced the little room while he tried to juggle an idea out of his mind. When it came, it was so simple, so perfect, he grinned. "I know how to take care of what's mine, too," he murmured. And hoping she'd cooled off, he went to find Olivia.

SHE HADN'T COOLED OFF. IN FACT, SHE WAS NURSING HER temper as a devoted mother would a fretful baby. She'd take spit-in-his-eye temper over the sick, shaky panic she felt every time her office phone rang.

So she nurtured it, she used it, she all but wallowed in it.

When Noah walked into her office, she got to her feet, slowly, her eyes cold, steady. Like a gunfighter, she shot fast and from the hip.

"Get your sorry ass out of my office. And off MacBride property. If you're not checked out and gone inside of ten minutes, I'm calling the cops and having you charged with assault."

"You'll never make it stick," he said with a cheer he knew would infuriate her. "I'm the one with the bruises. Don't swear," he added quickly and shut the door at his back. "There're young, impressionable children out there. Now, I've got a deal for you."

"A deal for me?" She bared her teeth in a snarl, then jerked back when the phone rang.

Before she could move, Noah snatched it off the hook himself. "River's

End Naturalist Center. Ms. MacBride's office. This is Raoul, her personal assistant. I'm sorry, she's in a meeting. Would you like—"

"Idiot." She hissed at him and wrestled the phone out of his hand. "This is Olivia MacBride."

Noah shrugged, then wandered around the room as she dealt with business. When she ended the conversation, then said nothing, he checked the soil of a nicely blooming African violet. "I've been thinking about taking a few days to get away from technology," he decided. "To test myself. Man against nature, you know." He looked back.

She was still standing, but she had her hands linked together now. The fire had gone out of her eyes, leaving them carefully blank.

"I'd think less of you if you weren't afraid, because then I'd think you were stupid." He said it quietly, with just the slightest edge of annoyance. How could he see so much, she wondered, without even seeming to look?

"I'm not a damsel in distress. I can take care of myself."

"Good, because I'm hoping you'll be looking after me the next few days. I want to do some hiking and camping in the backcountry."

Her laugh came fast and was none too flattering. "The hell you do."

"Three days. You and me." He held up a finger before she could laugh again. "We get away for a while. You do what you do best. And so do I. You'd agreed to interviews, so we'll talk. This place is something you love, and I want you to show it to me. I want to see what you see when you look at it."

"For the book."

"No, for me. I want to be alone with you."

She could feel her resolve, and her temper, melting. "I've rethought that situation, and I'm not interested."

"Yes, you are." Unoffended, he took her hand, skimming his thumb over her knuckles. "You're just mad at me because I outmuscled you last night. Actually, it wasn't—" He broke off as he glanced down at her hand and saw the faint trail of bruises just above her wrist. "I guess I'm not the only one with bruises." He lifted her wrist, kissed it. "Sorry."

"Cut it out." She slapped his hand away. "All right, I'm mad because you saw me at my worst, my weakest, and I let you see it. I'm mad because you wouldn't leave me alone, and I'm mad because I like being with you even when you irritate me."

"You can count on staying mad for a while, then. I'm not going anywhere until we figure everything out. Let's go play in the forest, Livvy."

"I have work."

"I'm a paying client. And as part of the deal, you can give me a list of what I need and I'll buy what's available at the lodge. Between the guide fee and the equipment, you're going to take in a couple of grand easy. Delegate, Liv. You know you can."

"You also need backcountry permits."

"What'll they think of next?"

"Twenty-four hours, you'll be crying for your laptop."

"Bet?"

"Hundred bucks."

"Deal." He gave her hand a squeeze.

HE HADN'T EXPECTED HER TO SEND OVER A LIST THAT included wardrobe, detailing down to how many pairs of socks and underwear she recommended he take for the trip. It was like being twelve again and getting a to-do list from his mother.

He bought the gear, including a new backpack, as she'd pointed out on her list that his was too small and had a number of holes in it. And though they were going to weigh him down, he bought two bottles of wine and nested them inside spare socks.

Camping was one thing. Going primitive was another.

By the time he was done, he figured he'd be carrying thirty-five pounds on his back. And imagined after five miles or so it would weigh like a hundred.

With some regret he locked his cell phone and laptop in the trunk of the rental car. "I'll be back, boys," he murmured.

"Looks like I'm going to win that hundred bucks before we leave."

"That wasn't whining. It was a fond farewell."

He turned and studied her. She wore jeans, roomy and faded, a River's End T-shirt and a light jacket tied around her waist. Sturdy boots, he noted, with a number of impressive nicks and scars on the leather. She carried her pack as though it were weightless.

The smirk suited her. "You sure you're up for this?"

"I'm raring."

She adjusted the cap that shaded her eyes, then jerked her thumb. "Let's get started."

He found the forest more appealing if no less primitive without the rain they'd hiked through the last time. Little slivers of sunlight fought their way through gaps in the overstory, shimmering unexpectedly on the now-lush green leaves of the maples and the fragile blades of ferns.

The air cooled. Ripened.

He remembered and recognized much of the life around him now. The varied patterns of bark on the giant trees, the shape of leaves of the shrub layer. The vast, nubby carpets of moss didn't seem quite so foreign, nor did the knobs and scallops of lichen.

He gave her silence as his muscles warmed to the pace and tuned his ears to the rustles and calls that brought music to the forest.

She waited for him to speak, to ask questions or fall into one of those casual monologues he was so skilled at. But he said nothing, and the vague tension she'd strapped on with her pack slid away.

They crossed a narrow stream that bubbled placidly, skirted a leafy bed of ferns, then began to climb the long, switchbacking trail that would take them into backcountry.

Vine maple grew thick, an elastic tangle of inconvenience along the trail. Olivia avoided it when she could, worked through it when she couldn't and once grabbed at it quickly before it would swing back and thwack Noah in the face.

"Thanks."

"I thought you'd lost your voice."

"You wanted quiet." He reached over to rub his hand over the back of her neck. "Had enough?"

"I just tune you out when you talk too much."

Noah chuckled then went on.

"I really like being with you, Liv." He took her hand, sliding his fingers through hers. "I always did."

"You'll throw off your pace."

"What's the hurry?" He brought her hand to his lips in an absent gesture. "I thought you'd bring Shirley."

"She sticks with Grandpop most days, and dogs aren't allowed in the backcountry. Here, look." She stopped abruptly and crouched, tapping a finger beside faint imprints on the trail.

"Are those——"

"Bear tracks," she said. "Pretty fresh, too."

"How do you know that? They always say that in the movies. The tracks are fresh," he said in a grunting voice. "He passed through here no more than an hour ago wearing a black hat, eating a banana and whistling 'Sweet Rosie from Pike.'"

He made her laugh. "All the bears I know whistle show tunes."

"You made a joke, Liv." He ducked his head and gave her a loud kiss. "Congratulations."

She scowled at him and rose. "No kissing on the trail."

"I didn't read that in my camper's guide." He got to his feet and started after her. "How about eating? Is there eating on the trail?"

She'd anticipated his stomach. Digging into her pocket, she pulled out a bag of trail mix, passed it to him.

"Yum-yum, bark and twigs, my favorite." But he opened the bag and offered her a share.

He would have taken her hand again, but the trail narrowed and she bumped him back. Still, he thought she'd smiled more in the last ten minutes than she usually did in a full day. Some time alone together in the world she loved best was working for both of them.

"You have a great butt, Liv."

This time she didn't bother to hold on to the vine maple and smiled again when she heard the slap and his muffled curse. Olivia took a swig from her canteen as they climbed. The light sweat she'd worked up felt good; it felt healthy. Her muscles were limber, her mind clear. And, she admitted, she was enjoying the company.

She'd chosen this trail, one that skirted up the canyon, because other hikers rarely chose to negotiate it. Long switchbacks leading to steep terrain discouraged many. But she considered it one of the most beautiful and appreciated the solitude.

They moved through the lush forest, thick with green, climbing up and down ridges, along a bluff that afforded views of the river that ran silver and smooth. Wildlife was plentiful here where the majestic elk wandered and raccoon waddled to wash.

"I have dreams about this." Noah spoke half to himself as he stopped, just to look.

"About hiking?"

"No, about being here." He tried to catch hold of them, the fragments and slippery pieces of subconscious. "Green and thick, with the sound of water running by. And . . . I'm looking for you." His gaze snapped to hers, held with that sudden intensity that always rocked her. "Olivia. I've been looking for you for a long time."

When he stepped forward, she felt her heart flutter wildly. "We have a long way to go."

"I don't think so." Gently, he laid his hands on her shoulders, slid them down to cuff her wrists. "Come here a minute."

"I don't—"

"Want kissing on the trail," he finished. "Too bad." He dipped his head, brushed his lips over hers once. Then again. "You're shaking."

"I am not." Her bones had gone too soft to tremble.

"Maybe it's me. Either way, it looks like this time I finally found you."

She was afraid he was right.

She drew away and, too unsteady to speak, continued up the trail.

The first wet crossing was over a wide stream where the water ran clear and fast. A log bridge spanned it, and dotting the banks were clumps of wild foxglove with deep pink bells and a scatter of columbine with its bicolored trumpets. The scenery took a dramatic turn, from the deep, dank green of the river basin to the stunning old-growth forest where light speared down in shafts and pools.

And the ancient trees grew straight as soldiers, tall as giants, their tops whispering sealike in the wind that couldn't reach the forest floor.

Through their branches he could see the dark wings of an eagle picked out against the vivid blue of the summer sky.

Here among the ferns and mosses were bits and splashes of white, the frilly tips of fringecups, the bloodred veins of wood sorrel against its snowy petals, the tiny cups of tiarella.

Fairy flowers, Noah thought, hiding in the shade or dancing near the fitful stream.

Saying nothing, he dragged off his pack.

"I take that to mean you want a break."

"I just want to be here for a while. It's a great spot."

"Then you don't want a sandwich."

His brows went up. "Who says?"

Even as she reached up to release her pack, he was behind her, lifting it off. She figured it was fifty percent courtesy, fifty percent greed for the food she had packed inside. Since she could appreciate both, she unzipped the compartment that held sandwiches and vegetable sticks.

He was right about the spot. It was a great one in which to sit and relax, to let the body rest and recharge. Water in the thin stream chugged over rocks and sparkled in the narrow beams of sunlight filtering through the canopy. The scent of pine sharpened the air. Ferns fanned over the bank, lushly green. A duet of wood thrush darted by with barely a sound, and deeper in the woods came the cackling call of a raven.

"How often do you get out here?" Noah asked her when only crumbs remained.

"I take groups out four or five times a year."

"I didn't mean a working deal. How often do you get out here like this, to sit and do nothing for a while?"

"Not in a while." She breathed deep, leaning back on her elbows and closing her eyes. "Not in too long a while."

She looked relaxed, he noted. As if at last her thoughts were quiet. He had only to shift to lay his hand over hers, to lay his lips over hers.

Gently, so sweetly her heart sighed even as she opened her eyes to study him. "You're starting to worry me a little, Noah. Tell me, what are you after?"

"I think I've been pretty up-front about that. And I wonder why it surprises both of us that through all this, maybe right from the beginning of all this, I've had feelings for you. I want some time to figure out what those feelings are. Most of all, Liv, right now, I want you."

"How healthy is it, Noah, that this connection you believe in has its roots in murder? Don't you ever ask yourself that?"

"No. But I guess you do."

"I didn't before six years ago. But yes, I do now. It's an intricate part of my life and who I am. An intimate part of it. Monster and victim, they're both inside of me." She drew her knees up, wrapped her arms around them. It disturbed her to realize she'd never spoken like that to anyone before, not even family. "You need to think about that before any of this goes . . . anywhere."

"Liv." He waited until she turned her head toward him, then his hands caught her face firmly, his mouth crushed down hard and hot and heady on hers. "You need to think about that," he told her. "Because this is already going everywhere, and for me at least, it's going there pretty damn fast."

More disturbed than she wanted to admit, she got to her feet. "Sex is easy, it's just a basic human function."

He kept his eyes on hers as he rose, the deep green diving in and absorbing her. "I'm going to enjoy, really enjoy proving you wrong." Then in an abrupt change of mood she couldn't keep up with, he hauled up his pack, and shot her a blatantly arrogant grin. "When I'm inside you, Olivia, the one thing I promise you won't feel is easy."

She decided it was wiser not to discuss it. He couldn't understand her, the limitations of her emotions, the boundaries she'd had to erect for self-preservation. And he, she admitted as they headed up the trail again,

was the first man who had made her feel even a twinge of regret for the
necessity.

She liked being with him. That alone was worrying. He made her
forget he'd once broken her heart, made her forget she didn't want to
risk it again. Other men she'd dealt with had bored or irritated her within
weeks. Olivia had never considered that a problem, but more a benefit.
If she didn't care enough to get involved, there was no danger of losing
her way, losing her head or her heart.

And ending up a victim.

The sunlight grew stronger as they climbed, the light richer. White
beams of it shot down in streams and bands and teased the first real spots
of color out of the ground.

There were the deep scarlet bells of wild penstemon, the crisp yellow
of paintbrush. New vistas flashed as they hiked along a ridge with the long,
long vees of valleys below, the sharp rise of forested hills rising around
them.

At the next wet crossing, the river was fast and rocky with a thunder-
ing waterfall tumbling down the face of the cliff.

"There. Over there." Olivia gestured, then dug for her binoculars.
"He's fishing."

"Who?" Noah narrowed his eyes and followed the direction of her
hand. He saw a dark shape hunched on an island of rock in the churning
river. "Is that—Christ! It's a bear." He snatched the binoculars Olivia
offered and stared through them.

The bear slammed into his field of vision, nearly made him jolt. He
leaned forward on the rustic bridge and studied the bear as the bear studied the water. In a lightning move, one huge black paw swept into the
stream, spewing up drops. And came out again locked around a wriggling
fish that flashed silver in the sun.

"Got one! Man, did you see that? Snagged it out of the water, first try."

She hadn't seen. She'd been watching Noah—the surprise and excitement on his face, the utter fascination in it.

Noah shook his head as the bear devoured his snack. "Great fishing skills, lousy table manners." He lowered the binoculars, started to hand them back and caught Olivia staring at him.

"Something wrong?"

"No." Maybe everything, she thought, is either very wrong or very right. "Nothing. We'd better go if we want to make camp before we lose the light."

"Got a specific place in mind?"

"Yes. You'll like it. We'll follow the river now. About another hour."

"Another hour." He shifted his pack on his shoulders. "Are we heading to Canada?"

"You wanted backcountry," she reminded him. "You get backcountry."

She was right about one thing, Noah decided when they reached the site. He liked it. They were tucked among the giant trees with the river spilling over tumbled rocks. The light was gilded, the wind a whisk of air that smelled of pine and water.

"I'm going upstream to catch dinner." As she spoke she took a retractable rod out of her pack.

"Very cool."

"If I get lucky, we eat like bears tonight. If I don't, we have some dehydrated food packs."

"Get lucky, Liv."

"Can you set up the tent while I'm fishing?"

"Sure, you go hunt up food, I'll make the nest. I have no problem with role reversal whatsoever."

"Ha. If you want to wander, just stay in sight of the river, check your compass. If you get lost——"

"I won't. I'm not a moron."

"If you get lost," she repeated. "Sit down and wait for me to find you." He looked so insulted, she patted his cheek. "You've done just fine so far, city boy."

He watched her go and promised himself he would do a whole lot better.

TWENTY-SIX

THE tent didn't come with instructions, which Noah thought was a definite flaw in the system. By his calculation, setting up camp took him about triple the amount of time and energy it would have taken Olivia. But he decided he'd keep that little bit of information to himself.

She'd been gone more than an hour by the time he was reasonably sure the tent would stay in an upright position. Assuming she wasn't having the same luck the bear had had with fishing, he explored their other menu choices. Dry packs of fruit, dehydrated soup and powdered eggs assured him that while they might not eat like kings, they wouldn't starve.

With nothing left on his chore list and no desire to explore after a full day of hiking, he settled down to write in longhand.

It was Olivia he concentrated on, what she had done with her life, the goals she'd focused on, what, in his mind, she'd accomplished and the ways he calculated she'd limited herself. The roots of her childhood had caused her to grow in certain directions, even while stunting her in others.

Would she have been more open, more sociably inclined if her mother had lived? Would she have been less driven to stand on her own if she'd grown up the pampered, indulged child of a Hollywood star?

How many men would have walked in and out of her life? Did she ever wonder? Would all that energy and intelligence have been channeled into the entertainment field, or would she still have gone back to her mother's roots and chosen the isolation?

Considering it, considering her, he let his notebook rest on his knee and just looked. The stream gurgled by. The trees towered, their topmost branches spearing through sky and dancing to the wind. The stillness was broken by the music of the water, the call of birds that nested and fed in the forest around him. He saw a lone elk, its rack crown-regal, slip out of the trees and pause to drink downstream.

He wished he had the skill to draw, but contented himself with etching the memory on his mind as the elk strode without hurry into the deepening shadows of the great firs.

She would have come back, Noah decided. Perhaps her life wouldn't have been centered here, but she would have been pulled back to this, time and again. As her mother had been.

Sense memory, he thought, or the roots that dig themselves into the heart before we're old enough to know it. She would have needed this place, the smells and the sounds of it. She needed it now, not only for her work and her peace of mind. It was here she could find her mother.

The cry of an eagle had him looking up, watching the flight. She spread her wings here, too, Noah decided. But did she realize that for every time she soared, she offset it by running back to the closet and closing herself into the dark?

He wrote down his thoughts, his impressions, listened to the life ebb and swell around him. When his mind drifted, he stretched out on the bank and slipped into dreams.

SHE HAD THREE FINE TROUT. SHE'D CAUGHT THE FIRST TWO within an hour, but knowing his appetite, she'd taken the time to wait for the third to take the hook. She'd found a nice bramble of huckleberries. Her hat was full of them, and their sweet taste sat nicely on her tongue as she wandered back to camp.

The time alone had quieted her mind, and soothed away the edge of nerves being too close and too long in Noah's company seemed to produce. Her problem, she reminded herself. She just wasn't used to being with a man on the level Noah Brady insisted on. She was no more ready for him now than she'd been at eighteen.

Sexually it should have been simple enough. But he kept tangling intimacy and friendship so casually she found herself responding in kind before she'd thought it through.

Thinking it through was vital.

She liked him well enough, she thought now. He was a likable man. So much so she tended to forget how close he could get, how much he could see. Until his eyes went dark and quiet and simply stripped her down to her deepest secrets.

She didn't want a man who could see inside her that way. She preferred the type that skimmed the surface, accepted it and moved on.

If admitting that caused an ache around her heart, she'd live with it. Better an ache than pain.

Better alone than consumed.

She thought they'd deal with each other well enough now. This was her turf, after all, and she had the home advantage. She'd made the decision to talk to him about her childhood, what she remembered, what she'd experienced. It wouldn't be without difficulty, but she'd made the choice.

A choice, she understood, she couldn't have made when he'd come to her at college. She'd been too soft yet, too unsteady. He might have talked her into it, because she'd been so in love with him, but it would have been a disaster for her.

In some part of her heart she'd always wanted to say it all, to get it out and remember her mother in some tangible way. Now she was ready for it. This was her opportunity, and she was grateful she could speak of it to someone she respected.

To someone, she realized, who understood well enough to make it all matter.

She saw him sleeping by the stream and smiled. She'd pushed him hard, she thought, and he'd held together. A glance around camp showed her he'd done well enough there, too. She secured her line and placed the fish into the running water to keep them fresh, then settled down beside him to watch the water.

He sensed her, and she became part of the dream where he walked through the forest in the soft green light. He shifted toward her, reached out to touch. Reached out to take.

She pulled away, an automatic denial. But the half-formed protest she'd begun to make slipped back down her throat as his eyes opened, green and intense. Her breath caught at what she saw in them, in the way they stayed locked on hers as he sat up and took her face in his hands. Held it as if he had the right. As if he'd always had the right.

"Look, I don't—"

He only shook his head to stop the words, and his eyes never left hers as he drew her closer, as his mouth covered hers. And the taste was ripe and hot and ready.

She trembled, maybe in protest, maybe in fear. He wouldn't accept either. This time she would take what he had to give her, what he'd just come to realize he'd held inside for years to give her, only.

His hands moved from her face, through her hair, over her shoulders as the kiss roughened, and he pushed her back on the ground and covered her.

Panic scrambled inside her to race with desire that had sprung up fast and feral. She pushed at his shoulders as if to hold him off even as she arched up to grind need against need.

"I can't give you what you want. I don't have it in me."

How could she not see what he saw? Not feel what he felt? He took his mouth on a journey of her face while she quivered under him. "Then take what you want." His lips brushed hers, teasing, testing. "Let me touch you." He skimmed his hand up her ribs, felt the ripple of reaction as his fingers closed lightly over her breast. "Let me have you. Here, in the sunlight."

He lowered his mouth to within a whisper of hers, then shifted it to her jaw and heard her moan. The taste of her there, just there along that soft, vulnerable spot where her pulse beat thick and fast, flooded into him.

He said her name, only her name, and she was lost.

Her fingers dug into his shoulders, then dragged through his hair to fist hard, to bring his mouth back to hers so she could pull him under with her.

A savage rush of delight, a raw edge of desire. She felt them both as his mouth warred with hers, knew the reckless greed as he yanked her shirt up, tore it away and filled his hands with her.

Strong and possessive, flesh molding flesh with the rocky ground under her back and the primitive beat of blood in her veins. For the first time when a man's body pressed down on hers, she yielded. To him, to herself. As something inside her went silky, her mind went blissfully blank, then filled with him.

He felt the change, not just in the giving of her body, the deepening of her breath. Surrender came sweet and unexpected.

She was still the woman he'd fallen headlong in love with.

His hands slowed, gentled, soothing trembles, inciting more. With a kind of lazy deliberation that sent her head reeling, he began a long, savoring journey.

Pleasure shimmered over her skin, warmed it, sensitized it. She rose fluidly when he lifted her, cradled her. With a murmur of approval, she stripped his shirt away and reveled in the slick slide of flesh against flesh, of the surprising bunch of muscles under her hands, the comforting beat of his heart against hers.

"More." In that dreamy altered state, she heard her own breathless demand and arched back to offer. "Take more."

She was willow slim and water soft. The lovely line of her throat drew his lips over and down. The curve of her breast a fascination, the taste of it fresh and his. Her breath hitched and released as he closed his mouth over her.

Need leaped in his belly.

There was more. More to taste, more to take. As her skin and muscles quivered, his mouth grew more urgent. Every demand was answered, a moan, a movement, a murmur.

He unhooked her jeans and when he skimmed his tongue under denim, her shocked jerk of response had dark and dangerous images swirling in his mind. He dragged them over her hips, and even as she reared up, took what he wanted.

It was a hot, smothering swell of sensation, air too thick to breathe, blood roaring to a scream in her ears. With mouth and teeth and tongue he drove her toward a peak she wasn't prepared to face. She choked out his name, fighting against a panicked excitement that threatened to swallow her whole.

Then her hands were gripped in his, held fast. Heat pumped through her, dewing her skin, scorching through her system until pain and pleasure fused into one vicious fist. The pressure of it had her strangling for air, straining for freedom even as her hips arched.

Then everything inside her broke apart, shattered into pieces that left her limp and defenseless.

Her cry of release shuddered through him. Her hands went lax in his. Everything he wanted whittled down to her, this place, this moment. So he watched her face as he drove her up again. Again.

Her eyes flew open, wide with shock, blind with pleasure. Her lips trembled as her breath tore through them. Sunlight scattered over her skin as she poured into his hand.

Blood screaming, muscles quivering, he held himself over her. "Olivia." Her name was raw in his throat and full of need. "Look at me when I take you." His eyes were as green and deep as the shadows behind them. "Look at me when we take each other. Because it matters."

He drove himself deep, buried himself inside her. Even as his vision dimmed at the edges he held on. The woman, the moment, and his certainty of each. Clinging to that clarity for another instant, he lowered his brow to hers. "It's you," he managed. "It's always been you."

Then his mouth took hers in a kiss as fierce as the sudden plunging of his body.

SHE COULDN'T MOVE. NOT ONLY BECAUSE HE PINNED HER to the ground with the good, solid weight of a satisfied man, but because her own body was weak and her system still rocking from the sensory onslaught.

And because her mind, no matter how she fought to clear it, remained dazzled and dim.

She told herself it was just sex. It was important to believe it. But it had been beyond anything she'd ever experienced, and beneath the drugged pleasure was a growing unease.

She'd always considered sex a handy release valve, a necessary human function that was often an enjoyable exercise. Orgasms ranged from a surprising burst of pleasure to a slight ping of sensation, and she'd always considered herself responsible either way.

With Noah she didn't feel she'd had a chance to be responsible. He'd simply swept her up and along. She'd lost control, not only of her body but also of her will. And because of it she'd given him a part of herself she hadn't known existed. A part she hadn't wanted to exist.

She needed to get it back and lock it away again.

But when she started to shift, to push him aside, he simply tucked her up, rolled over and trapped her in a sprawl over him.

She wanted to lay her head over his heart, close her eyes and stay just as they were forever.

It scared her to death.

"It'll be dark soon. I have to get the cook camp set up, a fire started."

He stroked a hand over her hair, enjoying the way it flowed to a stop at the nape of her neck. "There's time."

She pushed off, he pulled her back. It infuriated her that she was continually underestimating his strength—and his stubbornness. "Look, pal, unless you want to go cold and hungry, we need wood."

"I'll get it in a minute." To make sure she stayed where he wanted her to, he reversed positions again, studied her face.

"You want to pull away, Liv. I won't let you. Not again." He tried to disguise his hurt. "You want to pretend that this was just a nice, hot bout of sex in the woods, no connection to what we started before, years ago." He fisted a hand in her hair. "But you can't. Can you?"

"Let me up, Noah."

"And you're telling yourself it won't happen that way again," Noah said angrily. "That you won't feel what you felt with me again. But you're wrong."

"Don't tell me what I think, what I feel."

"I'm telling you what I see. It's right there, in your eyes. You have a hard time lying with them. So look at me." He lifted her hips and slipped inside her again. "Look at me and tell me what you think now. What you feel."

"I don't—" He thrust hard and deep, hammering the orgasm through her. "Oh, God." She sobbed it out, arms and legs wrapping around him.

Driven as much by triumph as frustration he took her in a wild fury until he emptied.

When she was still shuddering, he rolled aside and, saying nothing, rose, dressed, then went to gather firewood.

She wondered why she'd ever believed she could handle him or herself around him. No one else had ever managed to befuddle her quite so much or so often.

He'd convinced her to be with him alone when she knew it was best if she conducted business with him in more traditional surroundings. He made her laugh when she didn't want to find him amusing. He made her think about things, about pain she'd so carefully tucked away.

Now he'd lured her into sex on the bank of a stream in daylight, along a route that, while not well traveled, was public land. If it had gone according to her own plans, they would have had their evening meal, perhaps some conversation, then some civilized, uncomplicated sex in the dark privacy of the tent.

Once that was out of the way, it would have been back to business.

Instead, everything was tangled up again. He was angry with her for something she couldn't, and wouldn't, change. And yes, something she hadn't quite forgiven him for. She was left feeling unsteady, inadequate and uneasy.

To compensate, she ignored him and went about the business of setting up the cook camp several safe feet from the sleeping area. She hung the food high, then gathered her tools and got down to the business of cleaning the fish for their dinner.

He was just like every other man, she told herself. Insulted because a woman isn't tongue-tied with delight at his sexual prowess. Miffed because she wasn't moony-eyed in infatuation, which he'd use up then discard anyway the minute it started to cramp his style.

It was a hell of a lot smarter to think like a man yourself, she decided, and avoid the pitfalls.

Let him sulk, she thought as she carefully buried the fish waste. When she heard him approach, she sniffed in derision and had no clue just how sulky her own face was when she lifted it to look up at him.

"What do you want?"

He decided, wisely, that she'd kick him in the ass if she had any idea just how easily he could read her. So he just held out the wine he'd poured. "I brought some along. It's been cooling in the stream. Figured you'd be up for a glass about now."

"I need to cook this fish." She ignored the wine and strode back toward the fire.

"Tell you what." Tongue tucked in his cheek, he strolled after her. "Since you caught it and cleaned it—neither of which I have any experience in—I'll cook it."

"This isn't your pretty kitchen. I don't want my catch going to waste."

"Ah, a direct challenge." He pushed the wine at her and snatched the skillet. "Sit down, drink your wine and watch the master."

She shrugged her shoulders and plucked a berry out of her hat. "You screw it up, I'm not catching more."

"Trust me." His eyes met hers, held. "I won't disappoint you, Liv."

"You don't risk disappointment if you handle things yourself."

"True enough, but you miss some interesting adventures. I had to learn to cook," he continued, and changed the tone to light as he dribbled oil in the skillet. "Out of self-defense. My mother believes tofu is all four of the major food groups. You have no idea what it's like to be a growing boy and be faced with a meal of tofu surprise after a hard day of school."

Despite herself, her interest was caught. He'd unearthed the bag of herbed flour she'd packed and was expertly coating the fish. Without thinking, she sipped the wine and found the light Italian white perfect.

She barely managed to muffle a sigh. "I don't understand you."

"Good, that's progress. You've spent most of our time together this round being sure you did and getting it dead wrong." Satisfied, he slipped the fish into the hot oil to sizzle.

"An hour ago you were furious with me."

"You got that right."

"And now you're pouring wine, frying fish and sitting there as if nothing happened."

"Not as if nothing happened." For him everything had happened. He just had to wait for her to catch up. "But I figure you're pissed off enough for both of us, so why waste the energy?"

"I don't like to be handled."

His gaze flashed back to her. "Neither do I."

"We both know you wanted to come up here so I'd talk to you about your book without distractions or interruptions. But you haven't said anything about it."

"I wanted to give you a day, to give us both a day. I wanted you." He ran a finger down her arm. "I still want you. I'd like it better if you were more comfortable with that."

"I'd like it better if you'd keep it simple."

"Well." He poked at the fish. "One of us isn't going to get what he or she wants. Better get the plates, partner. These boys are nearly ready."

"Noah."

"Hmm?" He glanced up, a tender look on his face, and her heart wanted to melt. So she shook her head. "Nothing," she said and reached for the plates.

LATER, WHEN THE MEAL WAS FINISHED AND THE FOREST dark and full of sound, it was she who turned to him. She who needed arms around her to chase away the dreams that haunted her and the fear that stalked with them.

And he was there, to hold her in the night, to move with her in a sweet and easy rhythm.

So when she slept, she slept curled against him, her hand fisted over his heart, her head in the curve of his shoulder. Noah lay awake, watching the play of moonlight over the tent, listening to the call of a coyote, the hoot of an owl and the short scream of its prey.

He wondered how it was possible that he'd never stopped loving her and what either of them, both of them, were going to do about it.

The Monster

Deep into that darkness peering, long I stood there wondering, fearing, Doubting, dreaming dreams no mortal ever dared to dream before.

—EDGAR ALLAN POE

TWENTY-SEVEN

GROGGY, achy, Noah woke to birdsong. He sat up, tugged his jeans on and thought vaguely of breakfast. Through the sharp scent of pine and earth, he caught the wonderfully civilized aroma of coffee. And could have wept with gratitude for Olivia's consistent efficiency.

She'd built the morning campfire and had the coffeepot heating nicely. He burned his fingers on the handle, hissed a mild curse, then snatched up the cloth she'd left folded nearby to protect his hand.

One long sip had his eyes clearing and his system revving up. God bless a woman who appreciated strong black coffee, he thought, then stepped closer to the river to look for her.

Mists climbed up from the water to twine with sunbeams into silver and gold ribbons. A herd of deer drank lazily at the point where the stream curved like a bent finger and vanished into the trees.

And he saw her, hair wet and gleaming as she floated through the gilt-edged mists upstream, watching him with eyes as tawny as a cat's and just as wary.

She looked as though she belonged there, in the wild, in that unearthly, shimmering light.

The water rippled as she moved her arms, her shoulders rising over the surface. The mists seemed to open for her, then close again.

"I didn't expect you up so soon." Her voice was quiet, but her eyes seemed full of storms.

"I'm an early riser. How's the water?"

"Wet."

And freezing, he imagined. Still, he drank down the last of his coffee, then set the cup aside to pull off his jeans. He saw her eyes waver, then steady. What worries you, Olivia? he wondered. That it won't be the way it was between us last night? Or the possibility it will be?

The water was dazzlingly cold on his bare skin, and he saw her lips twitch when he winced. For no other reason than that, he bit back a yelp as he let himself slide in. He imagined his body going blue from the neck down.

"You're right," he said when he was reasonably sure his teeth wouldn't chatter. "It's wet, all right."

It surprised her that he kept two arm spans' distance between them. She'd expected him to move toward her, move in. He never seemed to do exactly what she expected. That, she could have told him, was what worried her most.

He was never precisely what she anticipated.

And her feelings for him were anything but what she'd planned.

When he closed the distance between them, she was almost relieved. This followed logic. Morning sex, basic human need. Then they would get along with the business of the day on equal footing.

But he only curled his fingertips around hers and watched her face. "You make great coffee, Liv."

"If you can't dance on it, it isn't coffee."

"Where are we going today?"

She frowned at him. "I assumed you'd want to get started on the interview."

"We'll get to it. Which trail do you like from here?"

It was his party, she reminded herself, and shrugged. "There's a nice route up into the mountains from here. Wonderful views, some good alpine meadows."

"Sounds like a plan. Do you want me to touch you?"

Her gaze jerked back to his. "What?"

"Do you want me to touch you, or would you rather I didn't?"

"We've had sex," she said carefully. "I liked it well enough."

He let out a short laugh. "No need to pump up my ego," he said and brushed a wet strand of hair from her cheek. "Besides, that's not what I asked you. I asked if you wanted me to touch you now." With his eyes locked on hers, he skimmed his finger down her throat, over her shoulder. "To make love with you *now*."

"You're already touching me."

Her skin shivered as he traced his finger down the center of her body, slicked it into her. "Yes or no," he murmured when her breath snagged.

The liquid weight settled low in her stomach, urging her hips to move, setting a pace for her own pleasure. Heat ran up her body in one long, shuddering roll. Giving in to it, to him, she gripped his hair, dragged him to her. "Yes," she said against his mouth.

She opened to him, clamping her legs around his waist, prepared for that fast, hard race to climax. Craving it. But he used his hands on her, drove her up and over, up and over until she was gasping out his name.

He wondered that the water didn't simply churn red and burst into flame from his need for her. He wondered how he could have lived all his life not having her wrapped around him just like this. Long limbs, slim and strong, soft, slippery skin that sparkled with wet in the sun. He drew her head back so that the kiss could go deep and deep, spin out endlessly while the sun broke through the mist with a burst of light, turned the water to a clear moving mirror around them.

He found purchase on the rough riverbed, braced, then slid into her in one long, slow stroke. "Hold on to me, Liv." His breathing was ragged, and he buried his face in the curve of her throat, nipped there to hear her moan. "Come around me," he murmured, and felt her muscles clamp him like a hot vise as the climax shot through her.

Through the drumbeat of her heart, in her head, she heard him murmur to her, but could no longer separate promises from demand. His voice was only one more velvet layer, one more source of fogged pleasure. But when she felt his body tighten, she curled herself around him, holding fast so they could tumble off the last edge together.

He didn't let her go. She waited for him to release her, to drift back, aim a quick, triumphant grin and climb out of the water for a second shot of coffee.

But he held her fast, held her close, his lips rubbing lightly from her temple to her jaw in a sweet and soothing motion that left her more shaken than sex.

She had to get away, she thought, ease back before she let herself slip into intimacy. "The water's cold."

"Cold, hell. It's freezing." He nibbled his way to her ear, enjoying the way her heart continued to riot against his. "You know, the minute your mind clears, your body tenses up. Why do you do that?"

"I don't know what you mean. We have to get out. We need to get started if—"

He turned his head, crushed his mouth against hers. "We've already started, Liv. We started a long time ago." He cupped her chin in his hand, then released her to turn to the bank. "We have to figure out where we want to finish."

She fixed powdered eggs, and they polished off the pot of coffee. He agreed with her plan to keep camp where they were and consider the hike she outlined a day trip that could be managed round trip in an easy five hours.

Carrying light packs, they started the climb on a rough track that led to rougher ridges. The valley fell away to their right, the forest marched toward the sky to the left. With the river winding below, they moved up into cool, crisp air where eagles soared and no sign of man could be seen.

He thought she maneuvered the dizzying switchbacks as other women would a ballroom floor, with a kind of casual feminine grace that spoke of supreme confidence.

She was patient when he stopped to take pictures, and he stopped often.

She answered his questions—and he had more than she'd expected—in clear and simple terms. And she stood by, silently amused, when he drew to a halt and stared as the trail curved and the sky was swept by mountains.

"If you planted a house here, you'd never get anything done. How could you stop looking?"

Why couldn't he be shallow and simple as she'd wanted him to be? "It's public land."

He only shook his head, taking her hand to link fingers. "Just think of it for a minute. We're the only two people in the world, and we've landed here. We could spend our whole life right here, with our brains dazzled."

Blue, white, green and silver. The world was made up of those strong colors and just the blurred smudges of more. Peaks and valleys and the rush of water. The feel of his hand warm in hers, as if it was meant to be.

And nothing else, no one else existed. No fear, no pain, no memories, no tomorrows.

Because she discovered she could yearn for that, she drew away. "You wouldn't be so happy with it in the dead of winter when you'd freeze your ass off and couldn't get a pizza delivery."

He looked at her, quiet, patient and made her ashamed. "What would you miss most if you could never go back?"

"My family."

"No, not people. What thing would you miss most?"

"The green," she said instantly and without thought. "The green light, and the green smell of the forest. It's different up here," she continued as they began to walk again. "Open, cool, with the forest well past peak."

"Not as many places to hide."

"I'm not hiding. This is iceland-moss," she told him, gesturing to a curly clump of yellow-green. "It's the best-known lichen in human consumption. In Sweden it's sold as an herbal medicine." She caught his look and lifted her eyebrows. "What?"

"I just like that snippy tone you get when you're annoyed and start a nature lecture."

"If you don't want to know what you're looking at, fine."

"No, I do. Besides, when you start talking about lichens and fungi, I get this urge to make wild animal love with you."

"Then I'll have to switch to wildflowers."

"It won't help. I'll still want to jump you." A flash of pink caught his eye. "Hey, are those bleeding hearts? Growing wild."

"That's right." Her annoyance didn't have a chance against his honest enthusiasm as he scrambled over some rocks to get a closer look. "Very much like your garden variety in appearance. Don't touch," she warned. "We maintain low impact here."

"I don't have the right shade or soil to grow these at home. Tried them at Mom's, but that was the next thing to murder. I've always liked the look of them."

"We have some nice specimens in the garden at my grandparents'. We'll go this way." She climbed over the rocks and chose a new heading. "I think I know a spot you'll like."

The track moved inside the edge of the forest, a steep incline with tumbles of rocks to one side where flowers forced their way through cracks and rooted ruthlessly in thin soil.

He heard the sound of drumming and grinned like a boy when they passed a cliff face sheared with a roaring fall of water. A dozen times he had to resist the urge to stop and pluck up handfuls of the hardy wildflowers.

His muscles began to burn, his feet to beg for rest. He was about to give in to both when she clattered over a hunched fist of rocks and turned to give him a hand up.

"That five hours was round trip, right, bwana?" Puffing a little, he gripped her hand and hauled himself up. "Because otherwise I'm just going to—Oh, Jesus."

He forgot his aches and pains and fatigue and filled himself on the view.

It was an ocean of flowers, rivers of color flowing through green and washing up toward a slope of forested peak that shot into the blue like the turret of a castle. At the highest points, curving pools of snow shimmered through the rock and trees and made the flowers only more of a miracle to him.

Butterflies danced, white, yellow, blue, flirting with the blooms, or settled delicately onto them with a quiet swish of wings.

"Amazing. Incredible. This is where we put the house."

This time she laughed.

"What are those, lupines?"

"You have a good eye. Broadleaf lupines—the common western blue butterfly prefers them. Those are mountain daisies mixed with them. Those there, the white with the yellow center, are avalanche lilies."

"And yarrow." He studied the fernlike leaves and flat white blossoms.

"You know your flowers. You don't need me up here."

"Yes." He took her hand again. "I do. It was worth every step." He turned and caught her unprepared with a soft and stirring kiss. "Thanks."

"At River's End you get what you pay for." She started to turn away, but he had her arms, eased her back around. "Don't." She closed her eyes before his mouth could capture hers again.

"Why?"

"I—" She opened her eyes again and could do nothing about the emotions that swirled into them. "Just don't."

"All right." Instead he lifted her hand to his lips, pressed them lightly to the knuckle of each finger and watched confusion join the clouds in her eyes.

"What are you looking for, Noah?"

He kept his eyes on hers, opened her fisted hand to press his lips to the center of her palm. "I've already found it. You just have to catch up."

He was afraid there was only one way for that to begin. "Let's sit down, Liv. This is a good spot. It's a good time." He shrugged off his pack, sat on a rock and opened it to find his tape recorder.

Seeing it in his hand, she felt her breath go thick and hot in her lungs. "I don't know how to do this."

"I do. I want to tell you something first." He set the recorder beside him, then hunted out his notepad. "I considered giving up the idea of this book. Setting it aside, as I did when I hurt you before." He opened the notebook, then looked at her. "It wouldn't have done any good, this time around. It would've been in the back of my mind. Always. Just as it would be in the back of yours. I can't quite figure out, Liv, if that's standing between us or if it's why we're here together. Why we've come back together after all this time. Why we're lovers now. But I do know that if we don't finish it, we'll keep running in place. I need to go forward. So do you."

· "I said I'd do it. I keep my word."

"And hate me for it? Blame me for being the one who brought it to the surface? Just the way you hated me that day in the hotel?"

"You lied to me."

"I know I did. I've never been sorrier for anything in my life."

She'd expected him to deny it, to make excuses, rationalize. And she should have known better. He was a man with honor, one who'd been raised with it and with compassion. It was why what he did mattered, she thought now. Why he mattered.

"I don't hate you, Noah, and I won't hate you for being honest about doing what you feel you need to do. But what I do feel is my own business."

"Not anymore it isn't." He said it lightly, but she heard the undercoating of steel in the tone. "But we can talk about that—about us—later."

"There is no us."

"Think again." This time the steel was in his eyes. "But for now, why don't you sit down?"

"I don't need to sit." But she dragged off her pack, uncapped her water bottle.

"Fine. Tell me about your mother."

"I was four when she died. You'd learn more about her from other sources."

"When you remember her, what do you think of first?"

"Her scent. The scent she kept in one of her bottles on her vanity. I thought they were magic. There was one in cobalt with a silver band winding around it. It was something unique to her, warm, lightly sweet with a faint hint of jasmine. Her skin always carried that scent, and when she'd hug me or pick me up, it was strongest just . . ." Olivia touched her fingers to her own throat just under the jaw. "I liked to sniff her there, and she'd laugh.

"She was so beautiful." Her voice thickened as she turned away to stare out over the sea of flowers. "You can't know, really. I've seen her movies now, all of them. Countless times. But she was so much more beautiful than they could capture. She moved like a dancer, as if gravity were simply something she tolerated. I know she was a brilliant actress. But she was a wonderful mother. Patient and fun and . . . careful. Careful to be there, to pay attention, to let me know that whatever else there was, I was the center of the world. Do you understand that?"

"Yes. I was lucky in that area, too."

She gave in and sat beside him. "I suppose I was spoiled. I had time and attention and a houseful of toys and indulgences."

"To me the only spoiled children are the ones who have no appreciation or respect for those things. I'd say you were just loved."

"She loved me very much. I never had any cause to doubt that, even when she scolded me about something. And I adored her. I wanted to be exactly like her. I used to look at myself in the mirror and imagine how I would grow up to be just like Mama."

"You look very much like her."

"I don't." She pushed off the rock in one sharp movement. "I'm not beautiful. I don't want to be. And I'll never be judged on my looks as she was, too often was. That's what killed her. In this fairy tale, the beast killed beauty."

"Because she was beautiful?"

"Yes. Because she was desirable. Because men wanted her and he couldn't stand that. He couldn't tolerate the very thing that had drawn him to her in the first place. Her face, her body, her manner. If it appealed to him, it appealed to other men, and there would be no other men. The one way he could keep her only to himself was to destroy her. No matter how much she loved him, it wasn't enough."

"Did she love him?"

"She cried for him. She didn't think I knew, but I did. I heard her one night with Aunt Jamie after I was supposed to be in bed. Earlier that summer when it stayed light until late. They were in Mama's room, and I could see from where I stood beside the door, in the mirror, the reflection of them as they sat on the bed. My mother crying and Aunt Jamie with her arms around her."

And just like that, she took both of them back.

>"What will I do? Jamie, what will I do without him?"
>
>"You'll be fine, Julie. You'll get through this."
>
>"It hurts." Julie turned her face into Jamie's shoulder, felt the sturdiness, longed for it. "I don't want to lose him, to lose everything we have together. But I just don't know how to keep it."
>
>"You know you can't keep going on the way you have been these last few months, Julie." Jamie eased back to brush the deep gold hair from her sister's face. "He's hurt you, not just your heart, but you. I can't sit by when I see bruises on you that he put there."
>
>"He doesn't mean it." Julie rubbed her hands over her face, drying the tears as she rose. "It's the drugs. They change him. I don't understand why he started them again. I don't know what he finds in them that I haven't given him."
>
>"Listen to yourself." A whip of anger in her voice, Jamie pushed to her feet. "Are you taking the blame for this? For him finding his kicks and his ego in cocaine and pills and alcohol?"
>
>"No, no, but if I could just understand what's missing, what he's looking for that isn't there . . . Oh God." She squeezed her eyes tight and raked back her hair. "We were so happy. Jamie, you know we were happy. We were everything to each other, and when Livvy came it was like . . . like a circle completed. Why didn't I notice when he started to crack that circle? How wide was the gap before I saw what was happening? I want to go back. I want my husband back, Jamie." She turned around, one hand pressed to her belly. "I want another child."
>
>"Oh God. Oh, Julie." She was across the room, wrapped around her sister in two strides. "Don't you see what a mistake that would be now? Just now?"
>
>"Maybe it is, but maybe it's the answer. I told him tonight. I had Rosa fix us this wonderful dinner. Candles and music and champagne. And I told him I wanted us to have another child. He was so happy at first. So much like Sam.

We laughed and held each other and started thinking up names, just as we did for Livvy. Then all at once, all of a sudden, he got moody and distant and he said . . ." The tears began to stream again. "He said how did he know it would be his? How did he know I wasn't already carrying Lucas's bastard?"

"That son of a bitch. How dare he say such a thing to you."

"I hit him. I didn't think, I just struck out and shouted at him to get out, get the hell out. And he did. He stared right through me, and he left. I don't know what to do."

She sat on the bed again, covered her face with her hands and wept. "I don't know what to do."

Noah said nothing as Olivia stood as she was, one hand still covering her stomach as her mother's had. She'd taken him back, taken him there into the intimacy of that bedroom, into the female misery and despair. The words, the voices, the movements flowing out of her.

Now, without looking at him, she dropped her hand. "I went back to my room, and I told myself Mama was rehearsing. She did that a lot. So I told myself Mama was being a movie, that she wasn't talking about my father. I went to sleep. And later that night I woke up and he was in my room. He'd turned on my music box and I was so happy. I asked him to tell me a story."

Her eyes cleared when she focused on Noah again. "He was high. I didn't know it then. I only knew he was angry when he shouted and he broke my music box. I only knew he wasn't the way Daddy was when my mother came rushing in and he hurt her. I hid in the closet. I hid while she cried and fought with him and locked him out of the room. Then she came and sat with me and told me everything would be all right. She called the police on my little phone, and she filed for divorce.

"It took him less than four months to come back and kill her."

Noah turned off his recorder, slid off the rock and walked to her.

In automatic defense she stepped back. "No. I don't want to be held. I don't want to be comforted."

"Tough luck, then." He wrapped his arms around her, holding firm when she struggled. "Lean a little," he murmured. "It won't hurt."

"I don't need you." She said it fiercely.

"Lean anyway."

She held herself stiff another moment, then went limp. Her head rested on his shoulders, and her arms came up to wrap loosely around his waist.

She leaned a little, but she kept her eyes open. And she didn't weep.

TWENTY-EIGHT

NOAH asked questions on the hike back to camp, dozens of them. But he didn't mention her parents. He asked about her work, her routines, the Center and the lodge. She recognized what he was doing and couldn't decide if she resented or appreciated his deliberate attempt to put her at ease again.

Couldn't quite fathom why it worked so well.

Every time she put up a barrier, he wiggled around it and made her comfortable again. It was a skill she had to admire. And when they stopped again, to look again, she found herself sitting shoulder to shoulder with him as if she'd known him all her life.

She supposed, in some odd way, she had.

"Okay, so we build the house right up there." He gestured behind him to a rocky incline.

"I told you, this is public land."

"Work with me here, Liv. We put it up there, with big windows looking out this way so we catch the sunset at night."

"That'd be tough, since that's south."

"Oh. You sure?"

She gave him a bland look with humor ghosting around her mouth. "West," she said and pointed.

"Fine. So the living room faces that way. We need a big stone fireplace in there. I think we should keep it open, really high ceilings with like a balcony deal. No closed spaces. Four bedrooms."

"Four?"

"Sure. You want the kids to have their own rooms, don't you? Five bedrooms," he corrected, enjoying the way her eyes widened. "One for a guest room. Then I need office space, good-sized room, lots of shelves and windows. That should face east. Where do you want your office?"

"I have an office."

"You need a home office, too. You're a professional woman. I think it should be next to mine, but we'll have to have rules about respecting each other's space. We'll put them on the third floor." His fingers linked with hers. "That'll be our territory. Kids' play area should be on the main level, with windows looking into the forest so they never feel closed in. What do you think about an indoor pool?"

"I wouldn't consider a home without one."

He grinned, then caught her off balance by leaning in, capturing her mouth in a long, hard kiss. "Good. The house should be stone and wood, don't you think?"

His hand was in her hair, just toying with the ends. "This is hardly the spot for vinyl siding."

"We'll plant the garden together." His teeth scraped lightly over her bottom lip. "Kiss me back, Olivia. Slide in. Just once."

She already was, couldn't do otherwise. The picture he painted was so soft, so dreamy she glided inside it. And found him. Found him surprisingly solid and real. And there. The sound she made was equal parts despair and delight as her arms locked tight around him.

How could it be he who snapped it all into place? Who made it all fit? All the misty wishes of childhood, all the half-formed fantasies of a young girl, all the darker needs of a woman swirled together inside her and re-formed into just one question.

He was the answer.

Rocked by the tumble of her own heart, she jerked back. She couldn't let it happen, not with him. Not with anyone. "We have to get started."

There was fear in her eyes. He wasn't quite sure how he felt about being the one to cause it. "Why are you so sure I'll hurt you again?"

"I'm not sure of anything when it comes to you, and I don't like it. We need to go. There's more than an hour left to hike before we hit camp."

"Time's not the problem here. So why don't we——" He broke off as a movement behind her caught his eye. He shifted his gaze, focused and felt the blood drain out of his head. "Jesus Christ. Don't move."

She smelled it now——the wild and dangerous scent. Her heart slammed once against her ribs, and before she could get to her feet, Noah was springing up to put himself between her and the cougar.

It was a full-grown male, perched on the rocks just above with his eyes glinting in the sunlight. Now he shifted, let out a low, guttural growl and flashed teeth.

"Keep your eyes on his," Olivia instructed as she rose. "Don't run."

Noah already had his hand on the hilt of his knife. He had no intention of running. "Go." He bared his own teeth and shifted when Olivia tried to step out from behind him. "Start moving back down the trail."

"That's exactly right." She kept her voice calm. "No sudden moves, no fleeing motions. We just ease back, give him room. He's got the advantage. Higher ground. And he's showing aggressive behavior. Don't take your eyes off him, don't turn your back."

"I said, 'Go.'" It took every ounce of willpower not to turn around and shove her down the trail. One thin stream of sweat trickled down his back.

"He must have a kill near here. He's just trying to protect it." She bent, keeping her eyes on the cat's, and scooped up two rocks. "Back away, we just back away."

The cat hissed again, and his ears went back flat. "Yell!" Olivia ordered, continuing the backward motion even as she winged the first rock. It struck the cougar sharply on the side.

She continued to shout, heaved the second rock. The cat spat furiously, swiped at the air. And as Noah drew the knife from his belt, the cat slunk away.

Noah continued to move slowly, kept Olivia behind him, scanning rock and brush. "Are you all right?"

"Stupid! Just plain stupid!" She tore her cap off, kicked at a rock. "Sitting there necking as if we were in the backseat of a Buick. I wasn't paying attention. What the hell is wrong with me?"

Furious with herself, she pulled the cap back on, wiped her sweaty palms on her thighs. "I know better than that. Sightings of cougar are rare, but they happen. So do attacks, especially if you're just an idiot." She pressed her hands to her eyes, rubbed hard. "I wasn't looking for signs, I wasn't even looking. And then sitting there that way, without keeping alert. I'd fire any one of my guides for that kind of careless behavior."

"Okay, you're fired." He'd yet to sheathe his knife and remained braced. "Let's just keep moving."

"He's not bothered with us now." She blew out a breath. "He was protecting a kill, doing what he's meant to do. We're the intruders here."

"Fine. I guess we'll build the house somewhere else."

She opened her mouth, shut it, then shocked herself by laughing. "You're a moron, Noah. I almost got you killed or certainly maimed. What the hell were you going to do with that, city boy?" She swiped a hand over her face and tried to choke back a giggle as she eyed his knife.

He turned the knife in his hand, considering the blade. "Protect the womenfolk."

She snorted out another laugh, shook her head. "I'm sorry. I'm sorry. It's not funny. This must be a reaction to gross stupidity. I've seen cougar a few times, but never that close up, and I've always been on higher ground."

She blew out another breath, relieved that her stomach was settling down from its active jumping. And that's when she noticed his hands were rock steady.

He hadn't so much as flinched, she realized. Wasn't that amazing? "You handled yourself."

"Gee, thanks, Coach." He slid the knife away.

"No." Calm again, she laid a hand on his arm. "You really handled yourself. I wouldn't have expected it. I keep underestimating you, Noah. I keep trying to fit you into a slot, and you won't go."

"Maybe you just haven't found the right slot yet."

"Maybe, but I don't think you fit into anything unless you want to."

"And what about you? Where do you want to fit, Liv?"

"I'm where I want to be."

"Not the place, Liv. We're not talking about forest or ocean here."

"I'm where I want to be," she repeated. Or where, she admitted, she'd thought she wanted to be.

"I have work that matters and a life that suits me."

"And how much room is there, in your slot?"

She looked at him, then away again. "I don't know. I haven't had to make any."

"Get ready to," was all he said.

Neither of them was sure if it was a command or a suggestion.

HE OFFERED TO TRY HIS HAND AT FISHING, BUT SHE POINTED out he didn't have a license and shot that down. Accepting that, he insisted on making soup instead, and entertained her with stories of childhood adventures with Mike.

"He decides in-line skating is the way to get chicks."

Noah sampled the soup, decided it could have been worse. "Coordination isn't Mike's strong point, but at sixteen a guy's brain is really just one big throbbing gland, so he blows most of his savings on the blades. I figure, what the hell, maybe he's on to something and get myself a pair, too. We head to Venice to try out his theory."

He paused, poured them both more wine. The light was still strong, the air wonderfully cool. "The place is lousy with girls. Tall ones, short ones, wearing tiny little shorts. You gotta cruise first, scope things out. I home in on this little blonde in one of the girl packs."

Olivia choked. "Girl packs?"

"Come on, your species always travels in packs. Law of the land. I'm working out how to cull her out of the herd while we strap on the blades. Then Mike gets up on his feet for about three seconds before his feet go out from under him. He pinwheels his arms, knocks this guy skating by in the face, they both go down like redwoods. Mike smacks his head on the bench and knocks himself out cold. By the time he comes to, I've lost the blonde, and end up taking Mike to the ER, where he had a standing appointment."

"A little accident-prone?"

"He could hurt himself in his sleep."

"You love him."

"I guess I do." And because there'd been something wistful in his statement, he studied her face. "Who'd you hang with when you were a kid?"

"No one. There were a few when—before I moved up here, but after . . . Sometimes I'd play with kids at the lodge or campground, but they came and went. I don't have any lasting attachments like your Mike. He's doing all right now?"

"Yeah. He bounces."

"Did they ever find the person who broke into your house and hurt him?"

"No. Maybe it's better that way. I'm not sure what I'd do if I got my hands on her. She could've killed him. Anything I could do to her wouldn't be enough."

There was a dark side here, a latent violence she could see in his eyes. She'd had glimpses of it once or twice before. Oddly enough it didn't make her uneasy, as hints of violence always did. It made her feel . . . safe, she supposed. And she wondered why.

"Anything you could do wouldn't change what already happened."

"No." He relaxed again. "But I'd like to know why. Knowing why matters. Don't you need to know why, Olivia?"

She took his empty bowl, and hers, then rose. "I'll wash these." She started toward the stream, hesitated. "Yes. Yes, I need to know why."

While she washed the bowls, Noah took out his tape recorder, snapped in a fresh tape. He had his notepad and pencil ready when she came back.

He saw the stress. It showed in the way her color faded to a delicate ivory. "Sit down." He said it gently. "And tell me about your father."

"I don't remember that much about him. I haven't seen him for twenty years."

Noah said nothing. He could have pointed out that she remembered her mother very clearly.

"He was very handsome," Olivia said at length. "They looked beautiful together. I remember how they'd dress up for parties, and how I thought everyone's parents were beautiful and had beautiful clothes and went out to parties, had their pictures in magazines and on TV. It just seemed so natural, so normal. They seemed so natural together.

"They loved each other. I know that." She spoke slowly now, a line of concentration between her elegant, dark brows. "They loved me. I can't be wrong about that. In their movie together, they just . . . shimmered with what they felt for each other. It radiates from them. I remember how it did that, how they did that whenever they were in the same room. Until it started to change."

"How did it change?"

"Anger, mistrust, jealousy. I wouldn't have had words for it then. But that shimmer was smudged, somehow. They fought. Late at night at first. I'd hear not the words so much but the voices, the tone of them. And it made me feel sick."

She lifted her glass, steadied herself. "Sometimes I could hear him pacing the hall outside, saying lines or reciting poetry. Later I read some article on him where he said he often recited poetry to help him calm down before an important scene. He suffered from stage fright.

"Funny, isn't it? He always seemed so confident. I think he must have used the same sort of method to calm himself down when they were fighting. Pacing the hall, reciting poetry. 'For man, to man so oft unjust, is always so to women; one sole bond awaits them, treachery is all their trust.'" She sighed once. "That's Byron."

"Yes, I know."

She smiled again, but her eyes were so horribly sad. "You read poetry, Brady?"

"I was a journalism major. I read everything." He feathered his fingers along her cheek. "'Give sorrow words; the grief that does not speak whispers the o'er-fraught heart and bids it break.'"

It touched her. "With or without words, my heart's survived. It's my mother's heart that was broken, and she who didn't survive what he wanted from her, or needed. And I haven't spoken of it to anyone except Aunt Jamie, and then only rarely. I don't know what to say now. He'd pick me up."

Her voice cracked, but she tried to control herself. "In one fast swoop so that my stomach would stay on my feet for a minute. It's a delicious feeling when you're a child. 'Livvy, my love,' he'd call me, and dance with me around the living room. The room where he killed her. And when he'd hold me, I'd feel so safe. When he'd come in to tell me a story—he told such wonderful stories—I'd feel so happy. I was his princess, he'd say. And whenever he had to go away to a shoot, I'd miss him so much my heart would hurt."

She pressed a hand to her mouth, as if to hold in the words and the pain. Then made herself drop it. "That night when he came into my room and broke the music box, and shouted at me, it was as if someone had stolen my father, taken him away. It was never, never the same after that night. That whole summer I waited for him to come back, for everything to be the way it was. But he never did. Never. The monster came."

Her breath caught, two quick inward gasps. And her hand shook, spilling wine. Instinctively, Noah snagged the glass before it slipped out of her fingers. Even as he said her name she pressed both fists to her rampaging heart.

"I can't." She barely managed to get the words out. Her eyes were huge with pain and shock and staring blindly into his. "I can't."

"It's all right. Okay." He dropped his pad, the glass, everything and wrapped his arms around her. Her hands were trapped between them, but he could feel her heart race, he could feel the sharp, whiplash shudders that racked her. "Don't do this to yourself. Don't. Let go. If you don't let go, you'll break to pieces."

"I can still see it. I can still see it. Him kneeling beside her, the blood and broken glass. The scissors in his hand. He said my name, he said my name in my father's voice. I'd heard her scream, I'd heard it. Her scream, breaking glass. That's what woke me up. But I went into her room and played with her bottles. I was playing in her room when he was killing her. Then I ran away and never saw her again. They never let me see her again."

There was nothing he could say; there was no comfort in words. He held her, stroking her hair while the sun left the sky and sent the light to gloaming.

"I never saw either of them again. We never talked of them in our house. My grandmother locked them in a chest in the attic to save her heart. And I spoke of her secretly to Aunt Jamie and felt like a thief for stealing the pieces of my mother she could give me. I hated him for that, for making me have to steal my mother back in secret whispers. I wanted him to die in prison, alone and forgotten. But he's still alive. And I still remember."

He pressed his lips to her hair, rocking her as she wept. The hot tears dampening his shirt relieved him. However much they cost her to shed, she'd be better for them. He swung her legs over, drawing her into his lap to cradle her there like a child until she went lax and silent.

Her head ached like a fresh wound, and her eyes burned. The fatigue was suddenly so great she would have stumbled into sleep if she hadn't held herself back. But the raw churning in her stomach had ceased, and the agonizing pressure in her chest was gone.

Tired and embarrassed, she pulled back from him. "I need some water."

"I'll get it." He shifted her aside to get up and fetch a bottle. When he came back, he crouched in front of her, then brushed a tear from her cheek with his thumb. "You look worn out."

"I never cry. It's useless." She uncapped the bottle, drank deep to ease her dry throat. "The last time I cried was because of you."

"I'm sorry."

"I was so hurt and angry when I found out why you'd really come.

After I made you leave, I cried for the first time since I was a child. You had no idea what I'd let myself feel about you in those two days."

"Yes, I did," he murmured. "It scared me. Nearly as much as what I felt for you scared me."

When she started to get up, he simply planted his hands on her thighs, locked his gaze to hers and held her in place. "What? You don't want to hear about it?"

"It was a long time ago."

"Not so long, but maybe just long enough. It's a good thing you booted me out, Liv. We were both too young for what I wanted from you then. Both parts of what I wanted."

"You're getting your book now," she said evenly. "And we're acting on the attraction. So I guess we're both finally grown-up."

He moved fast, stunning her when he dragged her to her feet, nearly lifted her off them. His eyes had gone sharp, like the keen edge of a blade. "You think all I want from you is the book and sex? Goddamn it, is that what you think or is that what you choose to think? That way, you don't have to give too much back or take any real risks."

"You think baring my soul to you about my parents isn't a risk?" She shoved him back, hard. "You think knowing anyone with the price and the interest will buy my memories and feelings isn't a risk?"

"Then why are you doing it?"

"Because it's time." She pushed her hair back from her damp cheeks. "You were right about that. Does that satisfy you? You were right. I need to say it, to get it out, and maybe somewhere in your damn book I'll see why it had to happen. Then I can bury them both."

"Okay." He nodded. "That covers that part. What about the rest? What about you and me?"

"What about it?" she shot back. "We had a few sparks some years ago and decided to act on them now."

"And that's it for you? A few sparks?"

She stepped back as he moved in. "Don't crowd me."

"I haven't even started crowding you. That's your problem, Liv, never letting anyone get quite close enough to share your space. I want your body, fine if you're in the mood, but everything else is off-limits. That doesn't work for me. Not with you."

"That's your problem."

"Damn right." He grabbed her arm, spinning her back when she turned. "And it's yours, too. I have feelings for you."

He released her abruptly to pace away, to stand all but vibrating with frustration on the bank of the stream. The light was gone now, so the low fire flickered gold and the first shimmer of the rising moon shifted through the trees.

"Do you think this is a snap for me?" he said wearily. "Because I've had other women in my life, it's a breeze for me to deal with the only one who's ever mattered?"

He turned back. She stood where he'd left her, but had lifted her arms to cross them defensively around her. Those delicate fingers of moonlight shivered over her, pale silver.

"Olivia, the first time I saw you, you were a baby. Something about you reached right out, so much more than that sad image on the television screen, and grabbed me. It's never let go. I didn't see you again until you were twelve, gangly and brave and all haunted eyes. There was a connection. There was nothing sexual about it."

He started back toward her, watched her shift slightly, as if to brace. "I never forgot you. You were in and out of my head. Then you were eighteen. You opened the door of your apartment, and there you were, tall and slender and lovely. A little distracted, a little impatient. Then your eyes cleared. God, I've had your eyes in my head as long as I can remember. And you smiled at me and cut me off at the knees. I've never been the same." He stopped a foot away from her and saw she was trembling.

"I've *never* been the same."

Her skin was shivering, her heart beating too fast. "You're fantasizing, Noah. You're letting your imagination run wild."

"I did plenty of fantasizing about you." He was calm now, certain because he could see her nerves. "But it didn't come close. I did some compensating, too. But there was never a woman who pulled at me the way you do. Straight from the gut. I know I hurt you. I didn't understand you or myself well enough then. Even when I came here and saw you again, I didn't understand it. I just knew seeing you thrilled me. I've never gotten over you. Do you know what it was like to realize I'd never gotten over you?"

Panic wanted to rise, taunted her to run. Pride had her standing her ground. "You're mixing things up, Noah."

"No, I'm not." He reached up, touched her face, then framed it in his hands. "Look at me, Liv. Look. There's one thing I'm absolutely clear on. I'm so completely in love with you."

A messy mix of joy and terror clogged her throat. "I don't want you to be."

"I know." He touched his lips gently to hers. "It scares you."

"I don't want this." She gripped his wrists. "I won't give you what you're looking for."

"You are what I'm looking for, and I've already found you. Next step is to figure out what you want, and what you're looking for."

"I told you I already have everything I want in my life."

"If that were true, I wouldn't scare you. I'm going to build a life with you, Olivia. I've been waiting to start and didn't even know it. It's only fair I give you time to catch up."

"I'm not interested in marriage."

"I haven't asked you yet," he pointed out and his lips parted as they covered hers again. "But I'll get to that. Meanwhile, just tell me one thing." He cruised into the kiss so that they could both float on it. "Is what you're feeling for me just a few sparks?"

It was warmth she felt, a steady stream of it, and a longing so deep, so aching, it beat like a heart. "I don't know what I feel."

"Good answer. Let me love you." He walked her backward toward the tent, muddling her brain with hands and lips. "And we'll see if the answer changes."

He was patient and thorough and showed her what it was to be touched by a man who loved her. Each time she tried to hold back, he would simply find a new way to slide through her defenses. To fill a heart reluctant to be filled. To steal a heart determined not to be taken.

When he moved inside her, slow and smooth and deep, he saw the answer he wanted in her eyes. "I love you, Olivia."

He closed his mouth over hers, drew in her ragged breath and wondered how long he would wait to hear her say it.

TWENTY-NINE

THE man was so carelessly cheerful, Olivia thought, it was all but impossible not to respond in kind. It didn't matter that the morning had dawned with a thin, drizzling rain that would undoubtedly have them soaked within an hour of the hike back.

He woke up happy, listened to the drumming and said it was a sign from God that they should stay in the tent and make crazy love.

Since he rolled on top of her and initiated a sexy little wrestling match, she couldn't come up with a logical argument against the plan. And for the first time in her life laughed during sex.

Then just when she'd convinced herself that good sex shouldn't be a barometer of her emotions, he nuzzled her neck, told her to stay put and that he'd see to the coffee.

She snuggled into the warm cocoon of the tent and wallowed in the afterglow of lovemaking. She hadn't let herself be pampered since childhood. She had taught herself to believe that if she didn't take care of herself, see to details personally and move consistently forward in the direction she'd mapped out, she would be handing control of her life over to someone else.

As her mother had done. And yes, she thought closing her eyes, perhaps even as her father had done. Love was a weakness, or a weapon, and she'd convinced herself that she'd never permit herself to feel it for anyone beyond family.

Didn't she have both potentials inside her? The one to surrender to it completely, and the one to use it violently? How could she risk turning that last key in that last lock and open herself to what she already knew she had inside her for Noah?

Then he nudged his way back into the tent, two steaming cups in his hand. His sun-streaked hair was damp with rain, his feet bare and the jeans he'd tugged on unbuttoned. The wave of love swamped her, closed over heart and head.

"I think I saw a shrew." He passed her the coffee and settled down with his own. "Don't know if it was a wandering or a dusky, but I'm pretty sure it was a shrew."

"The wandering's found more often in the lowlands," she heard herself say. "At this altitude it was probably a dusky."

"Whichever, it looked mostly like a mouse and was rooting around, for breakfast, I guess."

"They eat constantly, rarely go over three hours without a meal. Very like some city boys I know."

"I haven't even mentioned breakfast." He fortified himself with coffee. "I thought about it, but I haven't mentioned it. The weather's going to get better." She merely lifted an eyebrow and glanced up toward the roof of the tent and the steady tapping of rain. "An hour, tops. And it'll clear," he insisted. "If I'm right, you cook breakfast in the sunshine. If I'm wrong, I do it in the rain."

"Deal."

"So, how about a date when we get back?"

"Excuse me?"

"A date, you know. Dinner, a movie, making out in my rental car."

"I thought you'd be heading back to L.A. soon."

"I can work anywhere. You're here."

It was so simple for him, she realized. "I keep trying to take a step back from you. You keep moving forward."

He smoothed her tousled hair with his fingers. "Is that a problem for you?"

"Yes, but not as much as I thought it would be. Not as much as it should be." She took a breath, braced herself. "I care about you. It's not easy for me. I'm no good at this."

He leaned forward, pressed his lips to her forehead and said, "Practice."

WHILE NOAH AND OLIVIA WERE INSIDE THE TENT IN THE rain-splattered forest, Sam Tanner looked out the window of the rented cabin and into the gloom.

He'd never understood what had drawn Julie to this place, with its rains and chill, its thick forests and solitude. She'd been made for the light, he thought. Spotlights, the elegant shimmer of chandeliers, the hot white flash of exotic beaches.

But she'd always been pulled back here by some invisible tie. He realized now that he'd done his best to break that tie. He'd made excuses not to go with her, or he'd juggled their demands to prevent her from going alone. They'd only made the trip twice after Olivia was born.

He'd ignored Julie's need for home because he hadn't wanted anyone or anything to be more important to her than he was.

Before they could slide away from him, he picked up the mini-recorder he'd bought and put those thoughts on tape. He intended to speak with Noah again, but wasn't sure how much more time he had. The headaches were raging down on him like a freight train and with terrifying regularity now.

He suspected the doctors had overestimated his time, and the tapes were his backup.

Whatever happened, whenever it happened, he was going to be sure the book found its way.

He had everything he needed. He'd stocked the kitchen with food from the resort's grocery store. There were times he didn't have the energy for the dining room. He had plenty of tapes and batteries to continue his story until he was able to reach Noah again.

Where the hell is he? Sam thought with a flush of anger. Time was running out, and he needed that connection. He needed not to be alone.

The headache began to build in the center of his skull. He shook pills out of bottles—some prescription, some he'd risked buying on the street. He had to beat the pain. He couldn't think, couldn't function if he let the pain take over.

And he had so much to do yet. So much to do.

Olivia, he thought grimly. There was a debt to pay.

He set the bottles back on the table, beside the long gleaming knife and the Smith & Wesson .38.

NOAH MIGHT HAVE FELT SMUG ABOUT BEING RIGHT ABOUT the rain, but he felt even better when they reached the lowland forest. He could start dreaming of a hot shower now, a quiet room and several hours alone with his computer and a phone.

"You've lost two bets to me now," he reminded her. "It stopped raining, and I never whined for my laptop."

"Yes, you did. You just did it in your head."

"That doesn't count. Pay up. No, forget I said that. I'll take it in trade. We'll call it even if you find me a room where I can work for a few hours."

"I can probably come up with something."

"And a place I can shower and change?" He smiled when she slanted him a look. "I'm on line for a room at the lodge if you get any cancellations, but meanwhile I'm relegated to a campsite and public showers. I'm very shy."

Delighted with her giggle, he grabbed her hand. "Except around you. You can shower with me. We take conservation very seriously in my family."

She scowled, but only for form's sake. "We can swing by the house," she said after checking her watch. "My grandmother should be out with one of the children's groups for a while yet, then she generally goes marketing. You've got an hour, Brady, to get yourself cleaned up and out. I don't want her upset."

"That's not a problem." He told himself he wouldn't let it be. "But she's going to have to meet me eventually, Liv. At the wedding, anyway."

"Ha ha." She tugged her hand free.

"We can make another bet. I say I can charm her inside of an hour."

"No deal."

"You're just afraid because you know she'll come over to my side and tell you what a blind fool you are for not throwing yourself at my feet."

"You really need to get a grip."

"Oh, I've got one." And I've got you, he thought. We're both just figuring that out.

He saw the flickers of color first, through the trees and the green wash of light. Dabs and dapples of red and blue and yellow, then the glint that was stronger sunlight shooting off glass.

When he stepped into the clearing, he stopped, pulling Olivia to a halt beside him.

When he'd driven her home, it had been dark, deep and dark, and he'd only seen the shape of shadow against night, and the flickers of light in a window.

Now, he thought the house looked like a fairy tale with its varied rooflines and sturdy old wood and stone, flowers flowing at its base and sprinkling into sweeps of pretty colors and shapes.

There were two rockers on the porch, pots filled with more brilliant flowers and generous windows on all sides that would have opened the inside world up to the forest.

"It's perfect."

She watched his face as he said it, as surprised to see he meant just that as by the rush of pleasure it gave her.

"It's been the MacBrides' home for generations," she told him.

"No wonder."

"No wonder what?"

"No wonder it's your place. It's exactly right for you. This, not the house in Beverly Hills. That would never have been you."

"I'll never know that."

He turned from the house to look into her eyes. "Yes, you do."

With someone else she might have shrugged it off. With anyone else, she wouldn't have spoken of it. "Yes, I do know that. How do you?"

"You've been inside me for twenty years."

"That doesn't make sense."

"It doesn't have to. What I know is that when I try to project twenty years from now, you're still there."

Her heart did one long, slow roll. She had to look away to steady it. "God, you get to me." She shook her head when his hands came to her shoulders, when he shifted her back to him. "No, not now."

"Always," he said quietly, and settled his lips softly, dreamily on hers.

Without a sound, without a struggle, her arms came up and around him, her body leaned in. Not surrender, not this time. This time acceptance.

Emotions stormed through him, fast and hot and needy. And his mouth grew rough on hers. "Tell me," he demanded. He was wild to hear the words, to hear from her lips what he could taste on them.

She wanted to, wanted to fling herself off the edge and trust him to fall with her. The fear and the joy of it roared in her head. She teetered there, pulled in both directions, and only jerked away when she heard the sound of an engine laboring up the lane.

"Someone's coming."

He kept his hands on her shoulders, his eyes on hers. "You're in love with me. Just say it."

"I—it's the truck. It's my grandmother." She pressed a hand to her mouth. "God, what have I done?"

The truck was already rounding the turn. Too late to ask him to go, Olivia realized. Too late even if the glint in his eye told her he wouldn't have quietly slipped into the trees.

She turned away, braced herself as the truck pulled up. "I'll handle this."

"No." He took her hand in a firm grip. "We'll handle it."

Val sat where she was as they walked to the truck. Her fingers were tight on the wheel. She saw the distress and apology on Olivia's face and looked away from it.

"Grandma." Olivia stopped at the driver's side, rested her free hand on the base of the open window.

"So, you're back."

"Yes, just now. I thought you'd be with the children's group."

"Janine took it." Rage had her by the throat, whipping the words out before she could stop them. "Did you think to sneak in and out before I got home?"

Stunned, Olivia blinked, stood numbly as Noah shifted in front of her, much as he had to shield her from the cougar. "I asked Olivia if I could shower and change, since the lodge is booked. I'm Noah Brady, Mrs. Mac-Bride."

"I know who you are. This is Livvy's home," she said shortly. "If she's told you that you can use it to clean up, that's her right. But I have nothing to say to you. Move aside," she ordered. "I have groceries to put away."

She dragged at the wheel and, without another glance at either of them, drove around the back of the house.

"I broke my word to her," Olivia murmured.

"No, you didn't."

She let out a shuddering breath that caught in her throat as he started after the truck. "What are you doing? Where are you going?"

"To help your grandmother carry in the groceries."

"Oh, for Christ's sake." She caught up, dragged at his arm. "Just go! Can't you see how I hurt her?"

"Yeah, I can see it. And I can damn well see how she's hurt you." The steel was back in his voice as he took her wrist, pulled her hand away. "I'm not backing off. You're both going to have to deal with that."

He strode to the back of the house and, before Val could protest, plucked a bag out of her hand. Reaching into the bed of the truck, he hauled out another. "I'll take these in."

He carted them onto the back porch and let himself in through the kitchen door.

"I'm sorry." Olivia rushed to Val. "Grandma, I'm so sorry. I wouldn't have—I'll make him go."

"You've already made your choices." Back stiff, Val reached in for another bag.

"I wasn't thinking clearly. I'm sorry." She could taste hysteria bubbling in her own throat. "I'm so sorry. I'll make him go."

"No, you won't." Struggling to hold his temper, Noah came back out. He walked to the truck, took the last two bags. "Any more than I'll make you do anything. If you want to take it out on someone, Mrs. MacBride, take it out on me."

"Noah, would you just *go*?"

"And leave you here feeling guilty and unhappy?" He gave her a long, quiet look that had Val's eyes narrowing. "You know better. I'm sorry we disagree about the book," he continued, turning back to Val. "I'm sorry that my being here upsets you. But the fact is, I'm going to write the book, and I'm going to be a part of Olivia's life. I hope we can come to terms about both, because she loves you. She loves you enough, and is grateful enough for everything you've done for her and been to her, that if it comes down to a choice between your peace of mind and her own happiness, she'll choose you."

"That's not fair," Olivia began, and Val cut her off with a lifted hand.

The wound inside her might have broken open again, might have been raw and viciously painful. But her eyes were still clear, they were still sharp. She wanted to dislike his face, to find it cold and hard and ruthless. She wanted to see self-interest, perhaps coated with a thin sheen of polish.

Instead she saw the glint of anger that hadn't faded since it had flashed into his eyes when she'd snapped at Olivia. And she saw the strength she'd once seen in his father's face.

"That book will not be discussed in this house."

Noah nodded. "Understood."

"There're perishables in those bags," Val said as she turned away. "I have to get them put away."

"Just give them to me," Olivia began, then hissed in frustration when he simply walked past her and into the house behind her grandmother.

Left with no choice, Olivia dragged off her pack, dumped it on the porch and hurried in after them.

Already unloading bags, Val glanced toward the door as Olivia came in. She saw nerves, ripe and jittery, in her granddaughter's eyes. It made her feel ashamed.

"You might as well take that pack off," she said to Noah. "I imagine you're sick of carrying it by now."

"If I admitted that, Liv would smirk at me. She wants me to think she thinks I'm a shallow urbanite who can't tell east from west."

"You can't," Olivia murmured and had Noah grinning at her.

"I was just testing you."

"And are you?" Val asked. If she'd been blind, she would have seen the bond in the look that passed between them. "A shallow urbanite."

"No, ma'am, I'm not. The fact is I've fallen in love, not just with Liv—though that came as a jolt to both of us—but with Washington. At least your part of it. I've already picked some spots where we could build our house, but Liv says we'd run into trouble because it's a national park."

"He's just babbling," Olivia managed when she had untangled her tongue. "There isn't—"

"Spending a few days at the lodge or camping isn't like living here," Val interrupted.

"I don't guess it is." Noah leaned back comfortably against the counter. "But I'm a pretty flexible guy about some things. And this is where she's happy. This is home for her. As soon as I saw this place, I thought she'd like to get married right here in the yard, between the flowers and the forest. That would suit her, wouldn't it?"

"Oh, stop it!" Olivia burst out. "There isn't—"

"I wasn't talking to you," Noah said mildly, then offered Val an easy smile. "She's crazy about me, but she's having a little trouble, you know, settling into it."

Val nearly smiled. It broke her heart, then filled it again to see the amused exasperation on her little girl's face. "You're a clever young man, aren't you?"

"I like to think so."

She sighed a little as she neatly folded the last brown bag. "You might as well go get the rest of your things. You can stay in the guest room."

"Thanks. I'll just leave the pack here." He turned, caught Olivia by the chin while she was still trying to catch up and kissed her, warmly, deeply. "I won't be long."

"I—" The screen door slapped smartly behind him, and Olivia threw up her hands. "You didn't have to do that. He'll be fine at the campground. You'll just be uncomfortable if he stays here."

Val walked over to tuck the bags away in the broom closet. "Are you in love with him?"

"I—it's just . . ." She trailed off helplessly as Val turned back to look at her.

"Are you in love with him, Livvy?"

She could only nod as tears swam into her eyes.

"And if I said I don't want him around here, I don't want you to have anything to do with him? That you owe me the loyalty to respect my feelings on this?"

"But—"

"I'll never have peace if you let that man into your life."

She went white, white and rigid with the lance of pain. This was the woman who had given her everything, who had opened her arms, her heart, her home. She had to grip the edge of the counter to steady herself. "I'll go . . . I'll go tell him he has to leave."

"Oh. Oh, Livvy." Val dropped into a chair, covering her face as she burst into tears.

"Don't! Don't cry. I'll send him away. He won't come back." Already on her knees, Olivia wrapped her arms around Val's waist. "I won't see him again."

"He was right." Eyes drenched, Val framed Olivia's pale face. "I wanted to throw it back in his face, but he was right. You'd turn away from him, from your own heart if you thought it was what I needed. I wanted him to be the selfish one, but I'm the one who's been selfish."

"No. Never."

"I've hoarded you, Livvy." With an unsteady hand, Val brushed at Olivia's hair. "As much for your sake as mine in the beginning, but . . . As time passed, just for me. I lost my Julie, and I promised myself nothing would ever happen to you."

"You took care of me."

"Yes, I took care of you." Tears streaming still, Val pressed a kiss to Olivia's forehead. "I loved you, and, Livvy, I needed you. I needed you so desperately. So I never let you go, not really."

"Don't cry, Gran." It ripped her to shreds to see the tears.

"I have to face it. We both do. I never let either of us face it, Livvy. Every time your grandfather would try to talk to me about it, to make me see, I closed off. Even just a few days ago, I wouldn't listen to him. I knew he was right, but I wouldn't listen. Now it's taken an outsider to make me face it."

"Everything I have, everything I am, I owe to you."

"It's not a debt." Anger with herself made Val's voice sharp. "I'm ashamed to know I let you think it was or should be. I'm ashamed that I pulled back from you when you chose to cooperate with this book. I could see it was something you needed, but I pulled back, deliberately, and made you suffer for it. I put a wedge between us, and I was too proud, too afraid to pull it out again."

"I have to know why it happened."

"And I've never let you. I've never let any of us." Val drew Olivia closer, rested her cheek on the soft cap of hair. "I still don't know if I can face it all. But I do know I want you to be happy. Not just safe. Being safe isn't enough to live on."

Steadier, Val eased back, rubbed the tears away. "It's best if your young man stays here."

"I don't want him to upset you."

Val took what she hoped was the next step and managed a smile. "I'd rather he stay here where I can keep an eye on him and see if he's good enough for you. If I decide he's not, I'll see that your grandfather whips him into shape."

Olivia turned her cheek into Val's hand. "He claims he can charm you in less than an hour."

"Well, we'll just see about that." Rising, Val plucked out a tissue, blew her nose. "It takes more than a pretty face to charm me. I'll make up my own mind in my own time." Her head felt a little hollow from the emotional ride. "I suppose I'd better go up and see that the guest room's in order."

"I'll do it. I'll just take my pack up." She hefted it. "I should run over to the Center, check on things. It won't take me long."

"Take your time. It'll give me a chance to interrogate your young man. You never brought one home with you before for me to make squirm."

"He's slippery."

"I'm quick."

"Gran, I love you so much."

"Yes, I know you do. Go on. I need to make myself presentable. We'll talk more, Livvy," she murmured after Olivia started up the stairs. "It's long past time we talked."

Her step was light as she crossed the upstairs hall to her room. She was in love, and it didn't hurt a bit. The gaps that had widened between her and her grandmother over the past months were closing.

The future was a wide, wonderful space overflowing with possibilities. Wanting to hurry, she flung open the door of her room. And the joy that had just begun to fill her soul fell away.

There, on the pillow of her bed, bathed in a quiet stream of sunlight, lay a single white rose.

THIRTY

S HE couldn't breathe. Her head rang, wild, frantic bells that vibrated down from her skull, pealed down her spine, beat along her numbed legs until she simply collapsed forward on her hands and knees and began to suck for air like a woman drowning.

There was a terrible urge to crawl away.

Into the closet, into the dark.

She fought it and the ice-pick jabs of panic in her chest. She pressed her hand to her shirt, then stared down at it, surprised it wasn't covered with blood.

The monster was here.

In the house. He'd been in the house. With the thought of that chuckling hideously in her ear, she lunged to her feet, stumbled over the pack she'd dropped. Momentum carried her forward so that she fell on the bed, her fingers inches away from the stem of that perfect white rose.

She snatched her hand away as if the flower were a snake, filled with venom and ready to strike.

She reared back, her eyes wide and round, the scream tearing at her throat for release.

In the house, she thought again. He'd come into the house. And her grandmother was down in the kitchen, alone. Her hand might have shook, but she reached for the knife at her belt, unsheathed it so that blade hissed against leather. And she moved quietly toward the door.

She wasn't a helpless child now, and she would protect what she loved.

He wouldn't still be inside. She tried to reason with herself, to follow logic, but she could still taste the fear.

She slipped out into the hall, keeping her back against the wall. Her ears were cocked for any sound, and the hilt of the knife was hot in her hand.

She moved quietly from room to room, carefully as she would when tracking a deer. She searched each one for a sign, for a scent, a change in the air. Her knees trembled as she crossed to the attic door.

Would he hide there where the memories were locked away? Would he know somehow that everything precious of her mother was neatly stored up those narrow stairs?

She imagined herself going up, climbing those steps, hearing the faint creak of her weight against the old wood. Then seeing him, standing there with the chest lid flung open, and her mother's scent struggling to life in the musty air.

The bloody scissors in his hand, and the deranged eyes of the monster looking out from her father's face.

She all but willed it to be so as her fingers trembled against the knob. She would raise her knife and drive it into him, as he'd once driven the blades into her mother. And she would end it.

But her hand lay limply on the knob, and her brow pressed against the wood of the door. For the first time in two decades, she wanted desperately to weep and couldn't.

At the sound of a car rounding the lane, she slid the bolt home under the knob and ran on jellied legs to a window.

The first fresh spurt of fear when she didn't recognize the car shimmered into relief when she saw Noah climb out. Her hands curled on the sill as she scanned the trees, the lengthening shadows.

Was he out there? Was he watching?

She spun around, desperate to run downstairs now, to let the terror spill out so someone else could take it away.

And thought of her grandmother.

No, no, she couldn't frighten her that way. She would handle it herself. Cautious, she slid the knife back in its sheath, but left the safety unsnapped.

She leaned against the wall again, taking slow, even breaths. When she heard Noah's step on the stairs, she moved back into the hall.

"She's starting to warm up to me. Asked if I liked grilled pork chops."

"Let me give you a hand with that." How steady her voice was, she thought. How cool. She reached out to take his laptop case and left him with his bag and gear. "The guest room's in here. It has its own bath."

"Thanks." He followed her inside, glancing around as he dropped his bags on the bed. "This is a hell of a lot more appealing than a pup tent on a campsite. And guess who's here?"

"Here?"

His eyes narrowed on her face at the thready ring to her voice. "What's the matter, Liv?"

She shook her head, lowered to the edge of the bed. She needed a minute, just another minute. "Who's here?"

"My parents." He took a good look at her now and, sitting beside her, took her hand. It was clammy and cold.

"Frank? Frank's here?" Her hand turned over in his, gripped like a vise.

"At the lodge," Noah said slowly. "They'd booked a room a while back. I want you to tell me what's wrong."

"I will. Frank's here." She let her head drop weakly on Noah's shoulder. "I asked him to come. When I was in L.A. I went to his house and asked him if he could. And he did."

"You matter to him. You always did."

"I know. It's like a circle, and it keeps going. All of us around and around. We can't stop, just can't stop going around until it's all finished. He's been in the house, Noah."

"Who?"

She straightened up, and though her cheeks were still pale, her eyes were level. "My father. He's been in the house."

"How do you know?"

"There's a rose on my bed. A white rose. He wants me to know he's come back."

The only change was a hardness that came into his eyes and a coldness that glinted into the green. "Stay here."

"I've looked." She tightened her grip on his hand. "I've already looked through the house. Except for the attic. I couldn't go into the attic because . . ."

"Damn right you couldn't go into the attic." The idea of it made his stomach churn. "You stay in here or go downstairs with your grandmother."

"No, you don't understand. I couldn't go up because I wanted him to be there. I wanted it because I wanted to go up and kill him. Kill my father. God help me, I could see it, the way I'd ram the knife into him. The way his blood would run over my hands. I wanted it. I wanted it. What does that make me?"

"Human." He snapped it out, the word as effective as a slap. She jerked back, shuddered once.

"No. It would have made me what he is."

"Did you go up, Olivia?"

"No. I locked the door from the outside."

"Lock this one from the inside, and wait for me."

"Don't go."

"He's not here." He got to his feet. "But you'll feel better if we make sure. Lock the door," he ordered. "And wait."

Despising herself, she did just that. Hid, as she had hidden before. When he came back, she opened the door and looked at him with empty eyes.

"There's no one there. I didn't see any indication there had been. We need to tell your grandparents."

"It'll frighten my grandmother."

"She has to know. See if you can track down your grandfather. Call the lodge. I'll call my parents." He skimmed his knuckles over her cheek. "You'll feel better if you have your cop."

"Yes. Noah." She laid a hand on his arm. "When I saw you get out of the car just now, I knew I could lean on you. I wanted to."

"Liv. If I told you I'd take care of you, it'd just piss you off, wouldn't it?"

She gave a watery laugh and sat back on the bed again. "Yeah, not now because I'm shaky, but later."

"Well, since you're shaky, I'll risk it. I'm going to take care of you." He took her face in his hands and kissed her. "Believe it. Now call your grandfather."

HE'D TAKEN SUCH A RISK. SUCH A FOOLISH AND SATISFYING risk. How easily he could have been caught.

And then what?

He wasn't ready to face that yet. Not quite yet. As he sat in his room, he lifted a glass of bourbon to his lips with a hand that still shook slightly.

But not with fear. With excitement. With life.

For twenty years, he'd had no choice but to follow the rules. To do what was expected. To play the game. He couldn't have known, could never have anticipated what it was like to be free of that.

It was terrifying. It was liberating.

She would know what the rose meant. She wouldn't have forgotten the symbolism of it.

Daddy's home.

He drank again, felt such power after so many years of powerlessness.

He'd nearly been caught. What incredible timing. He'd barely left the house by the back door—wasn't it wonderful that such people trusted the fates and left their doors unlocked—when he'd seen them step out of the trees.

Livvy, little Livvy and the son of the cop. That was irony enough for any script. The cycle, the circle, the whims of fortune that would have the daughter of the woman he loved connect with the son of the cop who'd investigated her murder.

Julie, his beautiful Julie.

He'd thought it would be enough just to frighten Livvy, enough to make her think of that bloody night so many years ago, to remember what she'd seen and run from.

How could he have known, after all these years, that he would look at her as she turned to another man and see Julie? Julie pressing that long, slim body against someone else?

How could he have known he'd remember, in a kind of nightmare frenzy, what it was to destroy what you loved? And need so desperately to do it all again?

And when it was done . . . He picked up the knife and turned it under the lamplight . . . It would be over. The circle finally closed.

There would be nothing left of the woman who'd turned him away.

"YOU'LL NEED TO TAKE BASIC PRECAUTIONS." FRANK SAT IN the MacBride living room, his blood humming. Back on the job, he thought. To finish one that had never felt closed.

"For how long?" Olivia asked. It was her grandmother who concerned her most. But the crisis appeared to have steadied Val. She sat, shoulders straight, eyes alert, mouth hard.

"As long as it takes. You're going to want to avoid going out alone, staying in groups as much as possible. And start locking the doors."

Olivia had had time to settle, time to think. So she nodded. "There really isn't anything we can do, is there?"

He remembered the little girl hiding in the closet, and the way she'd reached out to him. She was a woman now, and this time he couldn't just pick her up and take her to safety. "I'm going to be as honest with you as I can, Livvy. So far, he hasn't done anything we can push him on."

"Stalking," Noah snapped out. "Trespassing. Breaking and entering."

"First you have to prove it." Frank held up a hand. "If we manage to do that, the police might be able to hassle him, but not much more. A phone call with no specific threat, a gift and a flower put into an unlocked house. He could argue that he just wanted to make contact with the daughter he hasn't seen in twenty years. There's no law against it."

"He's a murderer." Rob stopped his restless pacing and laid a hand on Olivia's shoulder.

"Who's served his time. And the fact is . . ." Frank scanned the faces in the room. "The contact may be all he wants."

"Then why didn't he speak to me, over the phone?"

Frank focused on Olivia. She was a little pale, but holding up well. Underneath the composure, he imagined her nerves were screaming. "I can't get into his head. I never could. Maybe that's why I could never put this one aside."

You're what's left of Julie, Frank thought. All he has left of her. And you're what helped put him away. And she knew it. He could see the knowledge of it burning in her eyes.

"What we can do is ask the local police to do some checking," he continued. "Do what they can to find out if Tanner's in the area."

Olivia nodded again, kept her hands still in her lap. "And if he is?"

"They'll talk to him." And so will I, Frank thought. "If he contacts you, let me know about it right away. If there's more, we may be able to push on the stalking." He hesitated, then got to his feet. "Remember one thing, Livvy. He's on your ground. Out of his element. And he's alone. You're not."

It bolstered her, as it was meant to. She rose as well. "I'm glad you're here." She smiled at Celia. "Both of you."

"We all are." Val stepped forward. "I hope you'll stay for dinner."

"You have so much on your mind," Celia began.

"We'd like you to stay." Val laid a hand on Celia's arm, and there was a plea in her eye, woman to woman.

"Then why don't I give you a hand? I haven't had a chance to tell you how much I like your home." As they started out, with Celia's arm draped over Val's shoulders, Olivia wondered who was leading whom.

"I haven't even offered you a drink." Rob struggled to slip into the role of host. "What can I get you?"

Coffee, Frank started to say. He always drank coffee when he was working. But Olivia moved to Rob, slid her arm through his. "We have a really lovely Fumé Blanc. Noah's fond of good wine. Why don't you make yourselves comfortable while we open a bottle?"

"That would be nice. Wouldn't mind stretching my legs a bit first. Noah, why don't we take a walk?"

He wanted to object, to keep Olivia in sight. But it had been more order than request, and he knew there was a reason for it. "Sure. We'll take a look at Mr. MacBride's garden so you can mourn your own failure." As much for himself as to make a point, he turned to Olivia, brushed a kiss over her mouth. "Be right back."

Frank waited until they were outside. Even as they stepped off the porch, his eyes were scanning. "I take it there's more between you and Livvy than the book."

"I'm in love with her. I'm going to marry her."

The sudden hitch in his step had Frank coming up short, blowing out a breath. "Next time, son, remember my age and tell me to sit down first."

Noah was braced for a fight, craved one. "You have a problem with that?"

"No, anything but." Calmly, Frank studied his son's face. "But it sounds like you do."

"I brought this on her."

"No. No, you didn't." Deliberately he moved away from the house, wanting to be certain their voices didn't carry through open windows. "If Tanner wanted to get to her, he'd have found a way. You didn't lead him here, Noah."

"The fucking book."

"Maybe he looked at it as a tool, maybe he just wanted the spotlight again." Frank shook his head. "Or maybe he started out wanting to tell his story, just as he told you. I've never been able to get a handle on him. I'll tell you this, if you don't keep your head clear, you never will either. And you won't help her."

"My head's clear." And his rage was cold. "Clear enough to know if I find him before the cops do, I'll do more than talk. He's terrorizing her, and he brought Mom into it. He's used me for part of it."

He strode around the edge of the garden, where the last soft light lay like silk over the celebration of flowers. "Goddamn it. I sat with him. I looked him in the eye. I listened to him. I'm supposed to know what's inside people, when they're stringing me along. And I'd started to believe he'd been innocent."

"So had I at one point. Why did you?"

Noah jammed his hands into his pockets, stared into the trees. "He loved her. However fucked-up he was, he loved her. He still does. You can see it when he talks about her. She was it for him. I know what that feels like now. When you have that inside you, how can you get past it to kill?"

He shook his head before Frank could speak. "And that's stupid because it happens all the time. Drugs, alcohol, obsession, jealousy. But a part of me bought into it, wanted to buy into it."

"You love her. He's her father. There's something else, Noah. They found Caryn."

"What?" For a minute the name meant nothing. "Doesn't matter now."

"It might. She turned up in New York. Hooked up with a photographer she met at a party. A rich photographer."

"Good for her. Hope she stays there. A whole continent between us ought to be enough." Then he thought of Mike. "Did they pull her in?"

"She was questioned. Denied it. Word is she got pretty violent in denying it."

"Typical."

"She also has an alibi for the night Mike was hurt. The party. A couple of dozen people saw her at this deal up in the hills."

"So she slipped out for a while."

"It doesn't look like it. The alibi's holding. We have the time of the attack narrowed to thirty minutes between when Mike got to the house and Dory found him. During that half-hour period, Caryn was snuggled up to the photographer in front of twenty witnesses."

"That doesn't . . ." He trailed off, felt his insides lurch. "Tanner? God." He dragged his hands free, pressed his fingers to his eyes. "He knew where I lived. He was out by then, and he knew where to find me. The son of a bitch, what was the point?"

"Did you let him see any of your work?"

"No, of course not."

"Could be as simple as that. He wanted to see where you were heading with it. Top billing was important to him, probably still is. And you'd have names, addresses in your files. Notes, tapes."

"Revenge? Does it come down to that? Getting back at the people who testified against him?"

"I don't know. But he's dying, Noah. What does he have to lose?"

HE HAD NOTHING TO LOSE. SO HE SAT, SIPPING HIS DRINK and watching night fall. The pain was nicely tucked under the cushion of drugs, and the drugs were dancing with alcohol.

Just like old times.

It made him want to laugh. It made him want to weep.

Time was running out, he thought. Wasn't it funny, wasn't it wonderfully funny how it had crawled for twenty years, only to sprint like a runner at the starting block now that he was free?

Free to do what? To die of cancer?

Sam studied the gun, lifted it, stroked it. No, he didn't think he'd let the cancer kill him. All he needed was the guts.

Experimentally he turned the gun, looked keenly into the barrel, then slipped it like a kiss between his lips.

It would be fast. And if there was pain, it would be over before it really began. His finger flirted with the trigger.

He could do it. It was just another kind of survival, wasn't it? He'd learned all about survival in prison.

But not yet. First there was Livvy.

Most of all, there was Livvy.

THROUGH THE MEAL, NO ONE SPOKE OF IT. CONVERSATION ran smoothly, gliding over underlying tensions. After the first ten minutes, Noah gazed at his mother with admiration. She drew Olivia out, chattering on about the Center, asking her opinion about everything from the plight of the northern pocket gopher—where did she get this stuff—to the mating habits of osprey.

He decided either Olivia was as skilled an actress as her mother had been, or she was enjoying herself.

Val lifted a bowl of herbed potatoes and passed them to Frank. "Have some more."

"I'm going to have to make serious use of your health club tomorrow." But he accepted the bowl and helped himself to another serving. "This is a fantastic meal, Val."

"Frank tolerates my cooking," Celia put in.

"Cooking?" Frank winked at Noah and handed off the bowl. "When did you start cooking?"

"Listen to that," she said as she gave him a playful punch. "All the years I've slaved over a hot stove for my men."

"All the tofu that gave their lives," Noah murmured, and earned a punch of his own. "But you sure are pretty, Mom. Isn't she pretty?" He grabbed her hand and kissed it.

"You think that gets around me?"

He scooped up potatoes. "Yeah."

And that's what did it for Val. How could she hold back against a boy who so clearly loved his mother? She lifted a basket, offered it. "Have another roll, Noah."

"Thanks." This time when he smiled at her, she smiled back.

They lingered over coffee. Under different circumstances, Noah mused, the MacBrides and the Bradys would have slipped into an easy friendship, without complications, with no shadows.

But the shadows were flickering back. He could see them in the way Olivia would glance at the windows, quick glimpses at the dark. The way his father studied the house, a cop's assessment of security.

And he saw the strain on Val MacBride's face when his parents got ready to leave.

"I'll be at your naturalist talk at the Center tomorrow." Celia slipped on a light jacket on. "And I'm hoping there's still room for one more on your guided hike."

"We'll make room."

Celia ignored Olivia's extended hand and caught her up in a hard hug.

"I'll see you in the morning, then. Val, Rob, thanks for a wonderful meal." And when she embraced Val, she murmured in her ear. "Stay strong. We're right here."

She gave Val's back a bolstering pat, then took Noah's arm. "Walk your mother to the car." It would, they both knew, give Frank a chance to reassure the MacBrides.

Celia breathed deep of the night and wondered how Frank would feel about buying a little holiday cabin in the area. They were used to having their chick close by, after all.

It was a good place for roots, she thought, drawing in the scent of growing things. A good place for her son.

She turned to him, took his face in her hands. "You're smart and you're clever and you've always been a joy to me. If you let that girl get away, I'll kick your butt."

He lifted an eyebrow. "Do you know everything?"

"About you, I do. Have you asked her to marry you?"

"Sort of. She's work. Yeah, just as you said she would be," he added when Celia rolled her eyes. "But she's not going to get away from me. And I'm not going to let anything happen to her."

"I always wondered who you'd fall in love with and bring into our lives. And I always promised myself that whoever it was, no matter how irritated I might be by her, I'd be a quiet, noninterfering mother-in-law. And you can wipe that smirk off your face right now, young man."

"Sorry. I thought I heard you say something about you being quiet."

"I'll ignore that, and tell you how much I appreciate you choosing a woman I can admire, respect and love."

"I didn't choose her. I think I ran out of choices the minute I saw her."

"Oh." Celia stepped back, sniffling. "That's going to make me cry. I want grandbabies, Noah."

"Is that from the quiet, noninterfering part of you?"

"Shut up." Then she hugged him, held on fierce and tight. "Be careful. Please, be very careful."

"I will. With her. With all of it." He stared over his mother's shoulder, into the shadows. "He's not going to harm us."

THIRTY-ONE

H E waited until the house was quiet to go to her. He knocked softly but didn't wait for her answer. And saw the moment she turned from the window that she hadn't expected him.

"Did you really think I'd leave you alone tonight?"

"I don't think it's appropriate that we sleep together in my grandparents' house."

He had to give himself a minute. "Are you saying that to make me mad or because you actually believe the only reason I'm here is to sleep with you?"

She shrugged, then turned away again. The wind had risen to sing through the treetops. That, and the sound of the night birds, was a music that always soothed her.

But not tonight.

She'd tried a hot bath, the herbal tea her grandmother enjoyed before bedtime. They'd added yet another layer of fatigue to her body and did nothing to soothe her mind.

"I don't have any objections to sex," she said coolly, willing him to leave before she pulled him in any deeper. "But I'm tired, and my grand-parents are sleeping at the end of the hallway."

"Fine, go to bed." He walked to her shelves, scanned the titles of books and plucked one at random. "I'll just sit here and read awhile."

She closed her eyes while her back was to him, then composing her features carefully, faced him. "Maybe we should straighten this out before it goes any further. The few days in the backcountry was fun. More fun than I'd expected. I like you, more than I anticipated. Because I do, I don't want to hurt you."

"Yes, you do." He set the book aside, sat down. "The question is why."

"I don't want to hurt you, Noah." Some of the emotion pumping inside her leaked into her voice. "We had an interesting time together, we had great sex. Now I've got a lot more on my mind. And the simple fact is I don't want what you seem to believe you want from us. I'm not built for it."

"You're in love with me, Olivia."

"You're deluding yourself." She shoved open the French doors and stepped out onto the narrow terrace.

"The hell I am."

She hadn't expected him to move that quickly, certainly not that quietly, but he was beside her, spinning her around, and the temper in his eyes was ripe and hot. "Do I have to make you say it?" He yanked her against him. "Is that the only way? You can't even give me the words freely?"

"What if I am in love with you? What if I am?" She fought her way free, stood back with the wind whipping at her thin robe. "It won't work. I won't let it." Her voice rose. With an effort, she controlled it before she gave in to the urge to shout. "Maybe if I didn't care, I'd let it happen."

"That makes sense, that explains everything. If you didn't love me, we could be together."

"Because it wouldn't matter. I'm afraid, and you'd see to it I wasn't alone. I'd let you do what you seem so hell-bent on doing and take care of me, at least until this is over."

A little calmer, he reached out to touch the ends of her hair. "I knew it was a mistake to say that. Taking care of you isn't taking you over, Liv."

"You've got this nurturing streak. You can't help yourself."

The idea so completely baffled him, he could only stare. "No, I don't."

"Oh, for God's sake." She stormed past him, back into the room. "You want to look after everyone you care about. Listen to yourself sometime when you talk about Mike. You're always coming to his rescue. You don't even realize it. It's second nature. It's the same with your parents."

"I don't rescue my parents."

"You tend to them, Noah. It's lovely, really lovely. Just tonight, I'm listening to your mother talk about how you come by their house and try to save her flowers. Or how you go hang out with your father at the youth center, take him pizza."

"He might starve otherwise. It's not tending." It was a word that made him want to squirm. "It's just family."

"No, it's just you." And she could have drowned in love with him for no other reason. He was beautiful—inside and out.

"You focus," she continued. "You listen, and you make things matter. All the things I wanted to believe about you, all the ways I tried to tell myself you were shallow or careless were just ways to stop myself from feeling. Because I can't."

"Won't," he corrected. "I sound like a pretty good catch." He started toward her. "Why are you trying to shake me off the hook?"

"I don't come from the kind of people you come from. My mother was a victim, my father a murderer. That's what I have inside me."

"So everyone who comes from a difficult or violent background isn't capable of love?"

"This isn't a debate. I'm telling you the way it is. I'm telling you I don't want to be involved with you."

"How are you going to stop it?"

"I already have." Her voice went flat and cool now as she turned toward the door. "We're done. I've given you all I can give you on the book. There's no need for you to stay past morning."

He walked toward the door she opened. Her heart was bleeding as she shifted aside. Later she would tell herself she should have seen it coming, should have recognized the cool, reckless light in his eye.

He gripped her wrist to move it away from the knob. Closed the door. Turned the lock. "If we play it your way and I go along with the idea that you can turn your feelings on and off as easily as I turned that lock, then all we really had between us was business—which is concluded—and sex. Would that be an accurate statement?"

He had her backed against the door, trapped there. When the first shock passed, she realized he frightened her. And along with the fear rode a terrible excitement. "Close enough. It's better that way, for both of us."

"Sure, let's keep it simple. If it's just about sex—" He yanked the tie of her robe away. "Then let's take it."

She jerked her chin up, forced herself to meet his eyes. "Fine."

But his mouth was already crushed to hers, tasting of fury and violence. His fingers plunged into her, ripping her over a brutal peak before her mind could keep pace with her body. She cried out, shock, denial, delight, and the sound was muffled against his ruthless mouth.

He tore her robe aside even as he drove her deeper, faster, into the pumping heat.

"It doesn't matter. It's just sex." Hurt and anger speared through him, and he let the keener edge of desire rule.

His hands were rough when he dragged her to the bed, his body hard and demanding when he pressed down on hers. He gave her no time, no choice. But he gave her pleasure.

Her nails dug into his shoulders, but not in protest. Beneath his, her body shuddered and writhed, and the sounds in her throat were the low animal moans of mating.

This was not the playful tumble he'd shown her or the gentle thoroughness of seduction. Heat instead of warmth, greed unbalanced by generosity.

She tore at his clothes, and raked her nails down his sweat-slicked back. With oaths instead of promises, he jerked up her hips and slammed himself into her. She was hot and wet and fisted around him urgently as her body bowed up, a quaking bridge.

Her skin glinted with damp in the lamplight, her eyes stared, dark with shock, into his. She couldn't survive it. It was one terrified thought that raced through her spinning brain. No one could survive this brutal heat, these battering fists of sensation.

She fought to swallow air and breathed out his name.

The orgasm sliced through her, twin edges of pleasure and pain. It opened her, left her helpless and exposed.

He hung on, like a man clinging to a ledge by his fingertips as the blood beat like thunder in his head, his heart, his loins. "Say it." He panted it out, gripping her hips so that she had no choice but to take more of him. "Give me the words. Damn it, Liv, tell me now."

His face filled her vision. There was nothing else. "I love you. Oh God." Her hand slid away from him to lie limply on the bed. "Noah."

He let go of the ledge, and when the last desperate thrust emptied him, he collapsed on her.

He could feel her trembling, and the staccato beat of her heart against his. Who won? he wondered and rolled away from her.

"I'm trying to be sorry for treating you that way," he said. "But I'm not."

"There wouldn't be any point in it." She was cold, she realized, growing cold because he was moving away.

"I won't leave in the morning. I won't leave until this is resolved. You'll have to find a way to deal with that."

"Noah." She sat up, then began to shiver. "The lack's in me. It's not you."

"That makes it just fine, then." He rolled off the bed, scooped up his jeans. "I told my mother you were work. That's not the half of it. You're a battle, Liv. You're a fucking combat zone, and I never know if you're going to wave the white flag, attack, or just turn tail and retreat. And maybe you're right." He jammed his legs into the pants and dragged them up. "Maybe it's just not worth it."

It was the first time in six years he'd hurt her, really hurt her. She stared, speechless as the shock wave of it shook through her. The words were lethal enough, but he'd said them with such steely finality, with such a wintry indifference that she wrapped her arms tight to ward off the vicious chill.

"You're cold." He reached down for her robe, tossed it onto the tangled sheets. "Go to bed."

"You think you can speak to me like that, then walk away?"

"Yeah, I do." He found what was left of his shirt and stuffed it in his pocket.

"You son of a bitch." He only lifted a brow when she scrambled off the bed, punched her arms through the sleeves of her robe. "I'm a combat zone? Well, who the hell asked you to sign up for the fight?"

"I guess we can say I was drafted. Lock those outside doors," he instructed and turned to leave.

"Don't you dare walk out. You started this. You can't possibly understand. You have no idea what it's like for me. You pop into my life whenever you damn well please, and I'm just supposed to go along?"

"You kick me out of your life whenever you damn well please," he retorted. "And I'm just supposed to go along."

"You want to talk about love and marriage, building houses, having children, and I don't know what's going to happen tomorrow."

"Is that all? Well, just let me consult my crystal ball."

Ordinarily, the killing look she shot him would have made him want to grin. Now he simply studied her with mild interest as she swore at him and spun away to pace. "Always a slick answer, always a joke. I just want to slap you."

"Go ahead. I don't hit girls."

He knew that would do it. She stopped on a dime, swung around all balled fists, quivering muscles and fiery eyes. Her breath heaved as she fought for control, and her cheeks flushed with furious color.

Under the wall of temper he'd built leaked a stream of sheer admiration for her willpower. She wanted to wale into him but wouldn't give him the satisfaction. God, what a woman.

"I prefer being civilized," she told him.

"No, you don't. But you're probably smart enough to know if you take a swipe at me we'll just end up in bed again. You lose control there, when I'm touching you, when I'm inside you. You forget to pick up all the emotional baggage you've carted around all your life, and it's just you and me."

"Maybe you're right. Maybe you're exactly right. But I can't spend my life in bed with you, and the baggage is right there waiting when I get up."

"So throw some of it out, Liv, and travel light."

"You're so smug, aren't you?" She detested the bitter taste of the words. "With your nice, cozy suburban childhood? Mom and Dad puttering around the house on weekends and you and all your pals ready to ride your bikes to the park after school."

Progress, he thought, and settled into the fight. Finally, she was cutting through the shield. "I'd say it wasn't quite like Beaver Cleaver, but you wouldn't know who the hell I was talking about since you didn't watch TV."

"That's right, I didn't. Because my grandmother was afraid they'd run a story on my mother, or I'd turn it on and see one of her movies or one of the movies made about her. I didn't go to school because someone might have recognized me, and there'd be talk. Or there'd be an accident. Or God knows. I didn't have my parents lazing around the house on a Sunday afternoon because one was dead and the other in prison."

"So how can you have a normal life now? That's a pitiful excuse for being afraid to trust your own feelings."

"And what if it is?" Shame tried to wash through her temper, but she damned it up. "Who are you to judge me? Who have you lost? You can't know what it's like to lose one of the most vital people in your life to violence. To see it. To be part of it."

"For Christ's sake, my father was a cop. Every time he strapped on his weapon and left the house, I knew he might not come back. Some nights when he was late, I'd sit by the window in the dark and wait for his car." He'd never told anyone that, not even his mother. "I lost him a thousand different ways over a thousand different nights in my head. Don't tell me I don't understand. My heart breaks for you, for what you lost, but goddamn it, don't tell me I don't understand."

Because it ripped at him, he swung around toward the door. "The hell with this."

"Wait." She would have rushed to the door to stop him, but her knees were shaking. "Please. I didn't think. I didn't think of it." Her eyes were damp and bleak. "I'm sorry. Don't go. Please, don't go. I need air."

She made it through the terrace doors, reached out for the banister and held on to it. When she heard him step out behind her, she closed her eyes. Relief, shame, love ran through her in a twisting river.

"I'm a mess, Noah. I've always set goals and marched right toward them. It was the only way I could get through everything. I could put what happened out of my head for long periods of time and just focus on what I was going to do, what I would accomplish. I didn't make friends. I didn't put any effort into it. People were just a distraction. No, don't." She said it quietly and shifted aside when he brushed a hand over her hair. "I don't think I can tell you if you're touching me."

"You're shivering. Come inside and we'll talk."

"I'm better outside. I'm always better outside." She drew a deep breath. "I took my first lover two weeks after you came to see me at college. I let myself think I was a little in love with him, but I wasn't. I was in love with you. I fell in love with you when you sat down beside me on the riverbank, near the beaver dam, and you listened to me. It wasn't a crush."

She gathered the courage to turn then, to face him. "I was only twelve, but I fell in love with you. When I saw you again, it was as if everything inside me had just been waiting. Just waiting, Noah. After you left, I closed all that off again. You were right, what you said about my turning my feelings on and off. I could. I did. I went to bed with someone else just to prove it. It was cold, calculated."

"I'd hurt you."

"Yes. And I made sure I remembered that. I made sure I could pull that out so you couldn't do it again. Even after all this time, I didn't want to believe you could understand what I felt. About what happened to my mother, to me, to my family. But I think a part of me always knew you were the only one who really could. The book isn't just for you."

"No, it isn't."

"I don't know if—I'm not sure—" She broke off again, shook her head in frustration. "I wanted to make you go. I wanted to make you mad enough to go because no one's ever mattered to me the way you do. It terrifies me."

"I won't hurt you again, Liv."

"Noah, it's not that." Her eyes glowed against the dark. "It's the other way around this time. What's inside of me, what could be in there and could leap out one day and—"

"Stop it." The order cut her off like a slap. "You're not your father any more than I'm mine."

"But you know yours, Noah." Still, for the first time she reached out to touch him, laid a hand on his cheek. "Everything I feel for you . . . it fills me up inside. All the places I didn't know were empty, they're just full of you."

"Christ, Liv." His voice went rough and thick. "Can't you see it's the same for me?"

"Yes. Yes, I can. I've been happier with you than I thought I could be. More with you than I thought I wanted to be. But even with that, I'm afraid of the things that you want. The things you have a right to expect. I don't know if I can give them to you or how long it'll take me. But I do know I love you."

She remembered the words he'd used to tell her and gave them back to him. "I'm so completely in love with you. Can that be enough for now?"

He reached up to take the hand that rested on his cheek, to press his lips to the center of her palm like a promise. "That's exactly enough for now."

Later, he dreamed of running through the forest, with the chill damp soaking through the fear sweat on his skin and his heart galloping in wild hoofbeats in his chest. Because he couldn't find her, and the sound of her scream was like a sword slicing through his gut.

He woke with a jerk to the pale silver of oncoming dawn with the last fierce call of an owl dying in the air. And Olivia curled warm against him.

THE RAIN WAS HOLDING OFF. BUT IT WOULD COME BEFORE nightfall. Olivia could just smell the testing edge of it in the air as she guided her group into the trees. She'd done a head count of fifteen and had been foolishly grateful to see Celia among them.

The fact that she was there had been enough to help Olivia convince Noah to take some time in his quiet room to work.

She explained the cycle of survival, succession, tolerance of the rain forest. The give and take, the nurturing of life by the dead.

It was the trees that always caught the attention first, the sheer height of them. Out of habit, Olivia took the time to let her audience crane their necks, murmur in awe, snap their pictures while she talked of the significance and purpose of the overstory. It always took a while before people began to notice the smaller things.

Her talks were never carved in stone. She was good at gauging the pace and rhythm of her group and gearing a talk to suit it. She moved along to point out the deep grooves that identified the bark of the Douglas fir, the faint purple cast of the cones of the western hemlock.

Every tree had a purpose, even if it was to die and become a breeding ground for saplings, for fungi, for lichen. If it was to fall, striking others down, it would leave a tear in the overstory so that busy annuals could thrive in the swath of sunlight.

It always amused her when they moved deeper and the light became dimmer, greener, that her groups would become hushed. As if they'd just stepped into a church.

As she lectured, she followed the familiar pattern, scanning faces to see who was listening, who was simply there because their parents or spouse had nagged them into it. She liked to play to those especially, to find something to intrigue them so that when they stepped out into the light again, they took something of her world with them.

A man caught her eye. He was tall, broad at the shoulders, with a fresh sunburn on his face that indicated someone unused to or unwise in the sun. He wore a hat and a long-sleeved shirt with jeans so obviously new they could have stood on their own. Despite the soft light, he kept his sunglasses in place. She couldn't see his eyes through the black lenses but sensed they were on her face. That he was listening.

She smiled at him, an automatic response to his attentiveness. And her gaze had already moved on when his body jerked in reaction.

She had an avid amateur photographer in the group who was crouched by a nurse log, lens to fungi. She used his interest as a segue, identifying the oyster mushroom he was trying to capture on film.

She shifted over, pointed out a ring of lovely pure white caps. "These are called Destroying Angels and while rare here are deadly."

"They're so beautiful," someone commented.

"Yes. Beauty is often deadly."

Her gaze was drawn back to the man in the sunglasses. He'd moved closer, and while most of the others were hunting up other groups of mushroom and chattering, he stood still and silent. As if waiting.

"Any of you who go on unguided hikes or camp in the area, please exercise caution. However appealing nature may be, however lovely, it has its own defenses. Don't think that if you see an animal has nibbled on a mushroom or a berry patch, that makes it safe. It's wiser, and your experience in the forest will be more enjoyable, if you simply look."

There was a peculiar tightness in her chest, a sensation that made her want to rub the heel of her hand between her breasts to loosen it. She recognized it—an early warning of a panic attack.

Stupid, she told herself, taking steady breaths as she took the group on a winding trail around nurse logs and ferns. She was perfectly safe. There was nothing here but the forest she knew and a handful of tourists.

The man had moved closer yet, close enough so that she could see a light sheen of sweat on his face. She felt cold and vaguely queasy.

"The cool dampness—" Why was he sweating? she wondered. "The cool dampness," she began again, "in the Olympic rain forest provides the perfect environment for the exuberant growth you see around you. It supports the greatest weight of living matter, per acre, in the world. All the ferns, mosses and lichens you see live here epiphytically. Meaning they make their life on another plant, whether in the overstory of the forest, on the trunks of living trees or in the corpse of a dead one."

The image of her mother's body flashed into her mind. "While many of the plants we see here grow elsewhere, it's only in this area that many of the species reach true perfection. Here on the west side of the Olympic Mountains, in the valleys of Ho, Quinault and Queets, there is the ideal blend of saturation, mild temperatures and topography in perfect proportions to support this prime-temperate rain forest."

The routine of lecture steadied her. The smattering of comments and questions engaged her mind.

The call of an eagle had everyone looking up. Though this thick canopy barred the sky, Olivia used the moment to shift into an explanation of some of the birds and mammals found in the forest.

The man in the sunglasses bumped against her, gripped her arm. She jolted and had nearly shoved him away when she saw he'd tripped in a tangle of vine maple.

"I'm sorry." His voice was barely a whisper, but his hand stayed on her arm. "I didn't mean to hurt you."

"You didn't. The vine maple's been tripping up hikers for centuries. Are you all right? You look a little shaky."

"I'm . . . You're so . . ." His fingers trembled on her arm. "You're very good at your job. I'm glad I came today."

"Thank you. We want you to enjoy yourself. Do I know you?"

"No." His hand slid down her arm, brushed lightly over the back of hers, then dropped away. "No, you don't know me."

"You look like someone. I can't quite place it. Have you—"

"Miss! Oh, Miss MacBride, can you tell us what these are?"

"Yes, of course. Excuse me a minute." She skirted over to a trio of women who huddled around a large sheet of dark red lichen. "It's commonly called dog lichen. You can see—if you use your imagination—the illusion of dog's teeth in the rows."

The pressure was back, like a vise around her ribs. She caught herself rubbing her hand where the man's fingers had brushed.

She knew him, she told herself. There was something . . . She turned around to look at him again. He was gone.

Heart pumping, she counted heads. Fifteen. She'd signed on for fifteen, and she had fifteen. But he'd been there, first at the edges of the group, then close in.

She walked over to Celia. "You're wonderful," Celia told her and gave her a brilliant smile. "I want to live right here, with dog lichen and Destroying Angels and licorice ferns. I can't believe how much you know."

"Sometimes I forget I'm supposed to entertain as well as educate and get too technical."

Celia skimmed her gaze over the group. "Looks to me like everyone is well entertained."

"I hope so. Did you happen to notice a tall man, short gray hair, sunglasses. Sunburned, good build. Mid-sixties, I guess."

"Actually, I haven't paid much attention to the people. I got caught up. Lose someone?"

"No, I . . . No," she said more firmly. "He must have been out on his own and just joined in for a bit. It's nothing." But she rubbed the back of her hand again. "Nothing."

WHEN SHE GOT BACK TO THE CENTER, OLIVIA WAS PLEASED to see several members of her group had been interested enough to head to the book area. A good guided hike could generate nice sales of books.

"Why don't I buy you lunch?" Celia asked.

"Thanks, but I really have work." She caught the look, sighed a little. "You don't have to worry. I'm going to be chained to my desk for quite a while. Then I have an interior lecture scheduled and another guided hike, then another lecture. The only place I'll be alone until six o'clock is in my office."

"What time's the first lecture?"

"Three o'clock."

"I'll be here."

"At this rate, I'll have to offer you a job."

Celia laughed, then gave Olivia's shoulder a little squeeze. "It's annoying, isn't it, having people hovering."

"Yes." The minute she said it, she winced. "I'm sorry. That was rude. I didn't mean—"

"I'd hate it, too," Celia interrupted, then surprised Olivia by kissing her cheek. "We'll get along very well, Liv. I promise. I'll see you at three."

Oddly amused, Olivia walked through the Center to the concession area and picked up a Coke and a box of raisins to fortify her through the paperwork on her desk.

She detoured, winding through each area on the way to her office. When she realized she was looking for the man with the sunburned face, she ordered herself to stop being an idiot.

She pulled off her cap, stuck it in her back pocket, then carried her snack to her office. As she stepped inside, she checked her watch to gauge her time.

Two paces from her desk, she froze. And stared at the single white rose lying across the blotter. The can of Coke slipped out of her hand and landed with a thud at her feet.

His face had changed. Twenty years—twenty years in prison had changed it. Somehow she'd known, but she hadn't been prepared. Breathing shallowly she rubbed the hand he'd touched.

"Daddy. Oh God."

HE'D BEEN SO CLOSE. HE'D TOUCHED HER. HE'D PUT HIS hand on her, and she hadn't known who he was. She'd looked into his face and hadn't known him.

All those years ago, with the security glass between them, Jamie had told him Olivia would never know him.

His daughter, and she'd given him the absent smile of one stranger to another.

He sat on a bench in deep shade, washed down pills with bottled water. Wiped the clammy sweat from his face with a handkerchief.

She *would* know him, he promised himself. Before another day passed, she would look at him and know him. Then it would be finished.

THIRTY-TWO

I T irritated Noah that he couldn't connect with Lucas Manning. Unavailable. Out of town. Incommunicado. He wanted a follow-up interview, and he wanted it soon.

Then there was Tanner himself.

Oh, they'd talk again all right, Noah thought as he pushed himself away from his laptop and paced to the window. He had a great deal to say to Sam Tanner. Maybe the son of a bitch thought the book would be a tool, perhaps even a weapon. But it was going to be neither.

When it was done, it would be the truth. And when it was done, if he had any skill, it would be a closing for Olivia.

The closing of that hideous part of her life and the opening of their life together.

She would be finished with her guided hike by now, he decided. And he could use a break from the book. So what was stopping him from going over to the Center? She might be a little annoyed, accuse him of checking up on her.

Well, that was something she'd have to get used to. He intended to spend the next sixty years, give or take, making sure she was safe and happy.

He shut down his machine and walked downstairs through the empty house. The MacBrides were at the lodge, and he imagined his mother had nudged them into having a meal with her. Bless her heart.

He checked the doors before he left, making sure they were secured. And, as a cop's son, just shook his head at the locks. Anyone who wanted in, he thought, would get in.

He'd learned that the hard way.

Following instinct, he detoured toward the garden, and casting one guilty look over his shoulder, plucked a handful of flowers to take to Olivia.

They'd make her smile, he thought, even as she pretended to be peeved that he'd stolen them from her grandfather.

He straightened quickly at the sound of a car and remembered he hadn't thought to hook his knife onto his belt. The wavering sun glinted off chrome and glass, then cleared so that he recognized Jamie Melbourne at the wheel.

By the time he'd walked to the car, she'd shoved the door open and jumped out. "Are they all right? Is everyone all right?"

"Everyone's fine."

"Oh God." She leaned weakly against the fender, dragged a hand through her hair. She wasn't quite as polished as usual, he noted. Her makeup was sketchy, her eyes shadowed and her simple slacks and blouse travel-crushed.

"I—all the way up here, I imagined all sorts of things." She dropped her hand, closed her eyes a moment. "My mother called me last night, told me. She said he'd been here. Inside the house."

"It looks that way. Why don't you sit down?"

"No, no, I've been sitting. On the plane, in the car. I couldn't get here any sooner. She didn't want me to come, but I had to. I had to be here."

"No one's seen him, at least not that I've heard. Liv's at the Center, and your parents are at the lodge with mine."

"Good. Okay." She heaved out a long breath. "I'm not a hysterical person. I think once you've faced the worst and survived it, you cope with anything. But I came very, very close to losing it last night. David was in Chicago, and I couldn't reach him for what seemed like hours. It probably wasn't more than twenty minutes until my brain clicked back and I thought of his cell phone."

Because she looked as if she needed it, Noah gave her a smile. "I love technology."

"I sure had good thoughts about it last night. Nothing's ever sounded so good as his voice. He's on his way. Canceled the rest of his meetings. We all need to be together until . . ." Her eyes went dark. "Until what, Noah?"

"Until it's over," was all he said.

"Well, I'd better get my bag inside—and have a good, stiff drink."

"I'll get it for you."

"No, it's just a carry-on. God knows what I threw in it this morning. I probably have a cocktail dress and hiking boots in there. And, to be honest, I could use a few minutes on my own to pull it together."

"I just locked up." He pulled the key Rob had unearthed for him out of his pocket.

"I bet they haven't done that more than half a dozen times since I was born." She took the key, studied it. "How's my mother holding up?"

"She's tougher than you think. Maybe than she thought."

"I hope you're right," Jamie murmured as she opened the trunk and pulled out a tote. "Well, I've got about six thousand calls to make to finish shifting my schedule around." She slung the tote strap over her shoulder, then glanced at the flowers in Noah's hand. "Going to see your girl."

"That was the plan."

"I like your plan. I think you're good for her." She studied his face. "You're a sturdy one under it all, aren't you, Noah Brady?"

"She'll never have to worry if I'll be there, never have to wonder if I love her."

"That's nice." The fatigue seemed to lift from her eyes. "I know just how important that is. It's funny, Julie wanted that—no, more than that— and I found it. I'm glad her daughter has, too."

He waited until she was in the house, until she'd locked the door behind her. With his senses alert, he walked into the trees to follow the trail to the Center.

• • •

FROM THE SHADOWS HE WATCHED, TURNING THE WEAPON in his hand. And weeping.

OLIVIA WAS DEAD CALM, AND SHE WAS DAMN WELL GOING to stay that way. For ten minutes after seeing the rose, she'd sat on the floor, shaking. But she hadn't run. She'd fought back the panic, pulled herself to her feet.

She'd ordered herself to be calm and to act. As quietly as possible, she asked every member of the staff she could find if they'd noticed any-one going into her office. Each time the answer was no, and each time she followed it up by giving a description of her father, as she'd seen him that morning.

When she had all the answers she could gather, she walked outside and started toward the lodge.

"Hey!"

Her body wanted to jerk, and she forced it still. Then absorbed the flow of relief when she saw Noah coming across the parking lot toward her.

Normal, she promised herself. She would be normal.

"My grandfather's going to scalp you for picking his prize lilies."

"No, he won't, because he'll know I was swept away by romance."

"You're an idiot. Thank you."

She gave him the smile he'd expected, but there was strain at the edges. "You need a break. Why don't you get someone to fill in for you the rest of the day?"

"I need to do my job. It's important to me. I was just about to go over and find Frank." She glanced around. People were coming and going. In and out of the lodge, the Center, the forest. "Let's sit down a minute."

She led him around the side and to a bench in the deep shade where her father had sat a short time before.

"There's another white rose. It was on my desk in my office."

"Go inside the lodge." Noah's voice was cool. "I'll look around."

"No, wait. I questioned the staff. No one noticed anyone going into my office. But a couple of them did notice someone this morning when I was setting up the group out here. A tall man, short gray hair, sunburned. He wore dark glasses and a fielder's cap, stiff new jeans and a blue long-sleeved shirt." She pressed her lips together. "I noticed him, too, during the hike. He slipped into the group. I kept getting this feeling, this uneasiness, but I couldn't pin it down. He spoke to me. He touched my hand. I didn't recognize him. He's changed, he looks old—years older than he should and . . . hard. But part of me knew. And when I saw the rose, his face was right there. My father."

"What did he say to you, Liv?"

"It wasn't anything important, just that I was good at my job, that he was glad he'd come. Funny, isn't it, twenty years down the road and he compliments me on my work. I'm all right," she said when Noah put his arm around her. "I'm okay. I always wondered what it would be like if I saw him again. It was nothing like I imagined. Noah, he didn't look like a monster. He looked ill, and tired. How could he have done what he did, how could he be doing this now, and just look tired?"

"I doubt he knows the answer to that himself. Maybe he's just caught up, Liv, in the then and the now. And he just can't stop."

He caught a movement, a bit of color, shifted his gaze. And watched Sam Tanner step out of the forest. Noah got to his feet, gripped a hand on Olivia's arm to pull her up beside him.

"Go into the lodge, find my father. Then stay there."

She saw him, too, just at the moment when he spotted them, when he stopped short on the far edge of the parking lot. They stared at each other in the windy silence, as they had once stared at each other across a bloody floor.

Then he turned and walked quickly toward the trees.

"Go find my father," Noah repeated and in a quick movement, unsnapped her knife sheath from her belt. "Tell him what happened here. Then stay." He turned, took her hard by the shoulders. "Do you hear me, Liv? You stay inside. With my mother. Call your aunt at the house. Tell her to stay put, with the doors locked."

"What? Aunt Jamie?"

"She got here just as I was leaving. Do it now."

She shook herself to break out of the fog, then watched in dull horror as Noah strapped her knife to his own belt. "No, you're not going after him."

He simply gave her one steel-edged look, then turned her in the direction of the lodge. "Go inside now."

"You won't find him." She shouted it, snatching at Noah's arm as he strode away. "You don't know what he's capable of if you do."

"He doesn't know what I'm capable of either. Goddamn it." He whirled on her, fury hardening his face. "Love isn't enough. You have to trust me. Go get your cop, and let's deal with this."

With no choice, Olivia watched him sprint to the trees and vanish.

NOAH HAD TO RELY ON HIS SENSES, HIS HEARING, STRAINING to catch the rustling of brush. To the left? The right? Straight ahead. As he moved deeper, the false green twilight fell so that he strained his eyes, waiting to see a movement, the subtle sway of a low branch, the vibration of a thickly tangled vine.

He was younger, faster, but the forest itself could cloak prey as well as hunter.

He moved deeper, keeping his breathing slow and even so the soft sound of it wouldn't distract him. As he walked, his boots treading silently on the cushion of moss, he could hear the low rumble of thunder.

A storm was brewing.

"There's no point in running, Tanner," he called out as he closed his hand over the hilt of Olivia's knife. It never occurred to him to wonder if he could use it. "It's already over. You'll never get to her. You'll never touch her."

His own voice echoed back to him, cold and still, and was followed by the strident call of a bird and the rush of wind through high branches.

Instinct had him winding in the direction of the house, into the thick beauty of the ripe summer forest, past the gleaming white river of deadly mushrooms, around the delicate sea of fanning ferns.

Rain began to hiss through the canopy and slither in thin trickles to the greedy green ground.

"She's your own daughter. What good will it do you? What point is there in hurting her now?"

"None." Sam stepped out from the bulk of a fir. The gun in his trembling hand gleamed dull silver. "There was never a point. Never a reason. I thought you knew."

OLIVIA HIT THE DOORS OF THE LOBBY AND BURST INSIDE. She looked frantically right and left. Guests were milling around or parked on the sofas and chairs. The hum of conversation roared in her ears.

She didn't know where to find Frank. The dining room, the library, his own suite, one of the terraces. The lodge was a honeycomb of rooms and carefully arranged spaces where guests could loiter at their leisure.

Noah was already in the forest. She couldn't take the time.

She spun on her heel, raced to the front desk. "Mark."

She grabbed the young desk clerk, dragged him toward the door leading to the back rooms. "My grandparents, have you seen them?"

"An hour or so ago. They came through with some people. What's the matter? What's the problem?"

"Listen to me." Panic was trying to claw through control. "Listen carefully, it's important. I need you to find Frank Brady. He's a guest here. I need you to find him as quickly as you can. You tell him . . . Are you listening to me?"

"Yeah." His Adam's apple bobbed. "Sure. Frank Brady."

"You find him, and you find him fast. You tell him that Sam Tanner went into the forest. The east side, Lowland Trail. Have you got that."

"East side, Lowland Trail."

"Tell him Noah went after him. Tell him that. Get one of the staff to call my house. My aunt's there. She's to stay inside. It's vital that she stay inside and wait to hear from me. No one's to go into the forest. Make an announcement. No one's to go in there until I clear it. Do whatever you can to keep guests in or around the lodge. Whatever it takes."

"Inside? But why——"

"Just do it," she snapped. "Do it now." And shoving him aside, she sprinted into the rear office.

She needed something, anything. Some kind of weapon. A defense. Frantic, she swept her hands over the desk, yanked open drawers.

She saw the scissors, the long silver blades, and snatched at them. Was it justice? she wondered as they trembled in her hand. Or was it just fate?

She slid the blades under her belt, secured the eyes of the handles and bolted.

The rain began to fall as she raced out of the clearing and into the trees.

NOAH'S MIND WAS CLEAR AS GLASS, DETACHED FROM THE physical jeopardy of the gun and focused on the man. A part of him knew he could die here, in the verdant darkness, but he moved past it and faced whatever hand fate had begun to deal him twenty years before.

"No point, Sam? All of it, all those years you spent away come down to you and me standing in the rain?"

"You're just a bonus. I didn't expect to talk to you again. I've got some tapes for you. For the book."

"Still looking to be the star? I won't make you one. Do you think I'll let you walk out of here, give her one more moment's pain? You'll never touch her."

"I did." Sam lifted his free hand, rubbed his thumb and fingertips together. "I was so close. I could smell her. Just soap. She grew up so pretty. She has a stronger face than Julie's. Not as beautiful, but stronger. She looked at me. She looked right at me and didn't know me. Why would she?" he murmured. "Why would she know me? I've been as dead to her as her mother for twenty years."

"Is that why you arranged all this? To come alive for her? Start me on the book so I'd dig up old memories. Put you back in her head, so when you got out you could start on her."

"I wanted her to remember me. Goddamn it, I'm her father, I wanted her to remember me." He lifted his hand again, drilled his fingertips into his temple where pain began to hammer. "I've got a right. A right to at least that."

"You lost your rights to her." Noah edged closer. "You're not part of her anymore."

"Maybe not, but she's part of me. I've waited nearly a third of my life just to tell her that."

"And to terrify her because she knows what you are, she saw what you were. She was a baby, innocent, and taking that innocence wasn't enough? You sent the music box to remind her that you weren't done. And the phone calls, the white roses."

"Roses." A dreamy smile came to his lips. "I used to put a white rose on her pillow. My little princess." He pressed his hand to the side of his head again, dragging it back, knocking his cap aside. "They don't make drugs like they used to. The kind I remember, you'd never feel the pain."

He blinked, his eyes narrowing abruptly. "Music box?" He gestured with the gun, an absent gesture that had Noah halting. "What music box?"

"The Blue Fairy. The one you broke the night you knocked your wife around in Olivia's room."

"I don't remember. I was coked to my eyeballs." Then his eyes cleared. "The Blue Fairy. I knocked it off her dresser. I remember. She cried, and I told her I'd buy her another one. I never did."

"You sent her one a few days ago."

"No. I'd forgotten. I should have made that up to her. I shouldn't have made her cry. She was such a good little girl. She loved me."

Despite the cold wall of rage, pity began to eke through. "You're sick and you're tired. Put the gun down and I'll take you back."

"For what? More doctors, more drugs? I'm already dead, Brady. I've been dead for years. I just wanted to see her again. Just once. And just once, I wanted her to see me. She's all I have left."

"Put the gun down."

With a puzzled expression, Sam glanced down at the gun in his hand. Then he began to laugh. "You think this is for you? It's for me. I didn't have the guts to use it. I've been gutless all my fucking life. And you know what, Brady? You know what I figured out when I stuck the barrel in my mouth? When I had my finger on the trigger and couldn't pull it?"

His voice became confident and clear. "I didn't kill Julie. I wouldn't have had the guts."

"Let's go talk about it." As Noah stepped forward, reaching out with one hand for the gun, there was a crash in the brush, a blur of movement.

He felt pain rip along his shoulder as he turned, heard a scream that wasn't his own. He saw David Melbourne's contorted face as the force of the attack sent him ramming against Sam, tumbling them both to the ground.

Noah rolled aside, agony spearing through his wounded shoulder as he thrust his hands up, caught the wrist of David's knife hand. Noah's lips peeled back in a snarl of effort as his bloody hands began to slip.

The blade stabbed into the rain-slimed moss, a breath from his face. Rearing up, Noah bucked him aside, then rolled for the gun that lay on the ground.

As he snatched it up, David fled into the trees.

"I never thought of him." With the side of his face scratched and oozing blood, Sam crawled over. His eyes were glassy from the pain rolling inside his head. "I should have known, because I never thought of him. A dozen other men, I thought of them. She would never have looked at them, that was my delusion, but I thought of them. Never him."

As he spoke, he fumbled to tie his handkerchief around the gash in Noah's shoulder. "He should've just waited for me to die instead of trying to kill me."

Wincing against the pain, Noah gripped Sam's shirtfront. "Not you. It's Olivia he wants now."

"No." Fear coated over the agony in his eyes. "No, not Livvy. We have to find him. Stop him."

There wasn't time to debate. "He's heading deeper in, but he may circle around, head toward the house." Noah hesitated only a moment. "Take this." He unsnapped Olivia's sheath. "They're looking for you by now. If my father comes across you with a gun—"

"Frank's here?"

"That's right. Melbourne won't get far. You head toward the house. I'll do what I can to pick up his trail."

"Don't let him hurt Livvy."

Noah checked the gun and raced into the green.

OLIVIA WANTED TO RUSH HEADLONG INTO THE TREES, RUN blindly through the shadows, shout for Noah. It took every ounce of control to move slowly, to look for signs.

Her turf, she reminded herself.

But there'd been dozens of people in that edge of the forest, leaving crisscrossing prints. The ground was percolating with rain now, and she would lose even these prints if she didn't choose soon. He'd come in at a sprint, she remembered, and judged the length between strides.

Noah had long legs.

So did her father.

She headed due south and into the gloom.

The rain was alive, murmuring as it forced its way through the tangle of vines and drapery overhead. The air was thick with it and the pervasive scent of rot. Small creatures scurried away, sly rustles in the dripping brush. And as the wind cooled the treetops, a thin fog skinned over the ground and smoked over her boots.

She moved more quickly now, trying to outpace the fear. Every shadow was a terror, every shape a threat. Ferns, slick with rain, slithered around her legs as she hurried deeper into the forest and farther away from safety.

She lost the trail, backtracked, could have wept with frustration. The quiet chuckle of panic began to dance in her chest. She focused on the forest floor, searching for a sign. And caught her breath with relief, with something almost like triumph, when she picked up the tracks again.

Nerves skipped and skidded over her skin as she followed the trail of the man she loved. And of the man who'd shattered her life.

When she heard the scream, fear plunged into her heart like a killing blade.

She forgot logic, she forgot caution and she ran as though her life depended on it.

Her feet slipped, sliding wild over the moldering ground. Fallen logs seemed to throw themselves into her path, forcing her to leap and stumble. Fungi, slimy with rain, burst wetly under her boots. She went down hard, tearing moss with the heels of her hands, sending shock waves stinging into her knees.

She lunged to her feet, breathless, pushed herself off the rough bark of a hemlock and pushed blindly through vines that snaked out to snatch at her arms and legs. She beat and ripped at them, fought her way clear.

Rain soaked her hair, dripped into her eyes. She blinked it away and saw the blood.

It was soaking into the ground, going pale with wet. Shaking, she dropped to her knees, touched her fingertips to the stain, and brought them back, red and wet.

"Not again. No, not again." She rocked herself, mourning in the sizzle of rain, cringing into a ball as the fear hammered at her, screamed into her mind, burst through her body like a storm of ice.

"Noah!" She shouted it once, listened to the grieving echo of it. Shoving to her feet, she ran her smeared fingers over her face, then screamed it.

With her only thought to find him, she began to run.

HE'D LOST HIS DIRECTION, BUT HE THOUGHT HE STILL HAD the scent of his quarry. The gun was familiar in his hand now, as if it had always been there. He never doubted he could use it. It was part of him now. Everything that was primitive about the world he was in was inside him now.

Life and death and the cold-blooded will to survive.

Twenty years, the man had hidden what he was, what he'd done. He'd let another grow old in a cage, had played the devoted husband to his victim's sister, the indulgent uncle to her daughter.

Murder, bloody murder had been locked inside him, while he prospered, while he posed. And when the key had started to turn in the door to Sam Tanner's cage, it had set murder free again.

The break-ins, the attack on Mike. An attempt to stop the book, Noah thought as he moved with deliberate strides through the teeming woods. To beat back the guilt, the fear of exposure that must have tried to claw out of him hundreds of times over twenty long years.

And once again, he'd turned the focus on Sam, once again structured his acts to point the accusations at an innocent man.

But this time it was Olivia he'd hunted. Fear that she'd seen him that night, would remember some small detail that had been tucked in a corner of her mind all this time. A detail that might jibe with the story Sam wanted to tell.

Yes, it was logical, the cold-blooded logic that would fit a man who could murder his wife's sister, then live cozily with her family for another generation.

Then the balance had shifted on him, with the possibility of a book, another in-depth look at the case, the interviews with Olivia urging her to talk about the night her family had conveniently buried along with Julie.

But she couldn't talk, couldn't think, couldn't remember if she was too afraid. Or if she was dead.

Then he heard her scream his name.

THIRTY-THREE

T HE monster was back. The smell of him was blood. The sound of
him was terror.

She had no choice but to run, and this time to run toward him.

The lush wonder of forest that had once been her haven, that had
always been her sanctuary, spun into a nightmare. The towering majesty
of the trees was no longer a grand testament to nature's vigor, but a living cage that could trap her, conceal him. The luminous carpet of moss
was a bubbling bog that sucked at her boots. She ripped through ferns,
rending their sodden fans to slimy tatters, skidded over a rotted log and
destroyed the burgeoning life it nursed.

Green shadows slipped in front of her, beside her, behind her, seemed
to whisper her name.

Livvy, my love. Let me tell you a story.

Breath sobbed out of her lungs, set to grieving by fear and loss. The
blood that still stained her fingertips had gone ice-cold.

Rain fell, a steady drumming against the windswept canopy, a sly
trickle over lichen-draped bark. It soaked into the greedy ground until
the whole world was wet and ripe and somehow hungry.

She forgot if she was hunter or hunted, only knew in some deep primal instinct that movement was survival.

She would find him, or he would find her. And somehow it would be finished. She would not end as a coward. And if there was any light in the world, she would find the man she loved. Alive.

She curled the blood she knew was his into the palm of her hand and held it like hope.

Fog snaked around her boots, broke apart at her long, reckless strides. Her heartbeat battered her ribs, her temples, her fingertips in a feral, pulsing rhythm.

She heard the crack overhead, the thunder snap of it, and leaped aside as a branch, weighed down by water and wind and time, crashed to the forest floor.

A little death meant fresh life.

She closed her hand over the only weapon she had and knew she would kill to live.

And through the deep green light haunted by darker shadows, she saw the monster as she remembered him in her nightmares.

Covered with blood, and watching her.

Fury that was as much hate as fear spurted through her in a bitter kind of power. "Where's Noah? What have you done to him?"

He was on his knees, his hand pressed to his side where blood spilled out of him. The pain was so huge it reached to the bone, to the bowels.

"Livvy." He whispered it, both prayer and plea. "Run."

"I've been running from you all my life." She stepped closer, driven forward by a need that had slept inside her since childhood. "Where's Noah?" she repeated. "I swear I'll kill you if you've taken someone else I love."

"Not me. Not then, not now." His vision wavered. She seemed to sway in front of him, tall and slim with her mother's eyes. "He's still close. For God's sake, run."

They heard it at the same moment, the thrashing through the brush. She spun around, her heart leaping with hope. At her feet, Sam's heart tripped with terror.

"Stay away from her." Sheer will pushed him to stand. He tried to shove Olivia behind him, but only collapsed against her.

"You should have died in prison." David's face was wet with rain and blood. The knife in his hand ran with both. "None of this would have happened if you'd just died."

"Uncle David." The shock of seeing him, his eyes wild, his clothes splattered, had her stepping forward. With a strength born of desperation, Sam jerked her back, held her hard against him.

"He killed her. Listen to me. He killed her. He wanted her and couldn't have her. Don't go near him."

"Step away from him, Livvy. Come here to me."

"I want you to run," Sam said urgently. "Run the way you did that night and find a place to hide. Find Noah."

"You know better than to listen to him." David's smile made her blood go cold. "You saw what he did to her that night. He was never good enough for her. Never right. I've always been there for you, haven't I, Livvy?"

"She never wanted you." Sam's voice was slurred and slow as he fought to stay conscious. "She never loved anyone but me."

"Shut up!" The parody of a smile became a snarl. His face flushed dark and ugly. "It should have been me. She would have come to me if you hadn't gotten in the way."

"Oh God. Oh, my God." Olivia stared at David and braced to take her father's weight. "You. It was you."

"She should have listened to me! I *loved* her. I always loved her. She was so beautiful, so perfect. I would have treated her like an angel. What did he do for her? He dragged her down, made her miserable, only thought of himself."

"You're right. I treated her badly." Sam slumped against Olivia, murmured, "Run." But she only shook her head and held on to him. "I didn't deserve her."

"I would have given her everything." Tears slipped out of David's eyes now, and his knife hand dropped to his side. "She would never have been unhappy with me. I settled for second best and gave Jamie everything I would have given Julie. Why should I have settled when she was finally going to divorce you? When she finally saw you for what you were. She was meant to come to me then. It was meant."

"You went to the house that night." Sam's side was numb. He levered himself straight, caught his breath and prayed for the strength to step away from his daughter.

"Do you know how much courage it took for me to go to her, to give her everything that was in my heart? She let me in and smiled at me. She was doing her clippings and having a glass of wine. The music was on, her favorite Tchaikovsky. She said it was nice to have company."

"She trusted you."

"I poured my soul out to her. I told her I loved her, always had. That I wanted her. That I was leaving Jamie and we could be together. She looked at me as if I were insane. Pushed me away when I tried to hold her. She told me to leave and we'd forget I'd ever spoken of it. Forget." He spat the word out.

"She loved my father," Olivia murmured. "She loved my father."

"She was *wrong!* I only tried to convince her she was wrong, I only wanted to make her see. If she hadn't struggled against me, I wouldn't have ripped her robe. Then she turned on me, shouted at me to get out of her house. She said she would tell Jamie everything. She said I was scum. Scum! That she would never see me again, never speak to me. I—I couldn't hear what she was saying, it was so vile. She turned her back on me, turned away as if I were nothing. And the scissors were in my hand. Then they were in her. I think she screamed," he said softly. "I'm not sure. I don't know. I only remember the blood."

His eyes focused again, fixed on Olivia. "It was an accident, really. One moment, one terrible mistake. But I couldn't take it back, could I? I couldn't change it."

She had to be calm, Olivia ordered herself. Her father was bleeding badly. She had no doubt that she could outdistance and lose her uncle in the forest. But how could she leave her father? How could she run away and hide again?

She would stand, protect. And pray for help to come. "You held me while I cried for her."

"I cried, too!" It enraged David that she didn't understand. Just like her mother. Just like Julie. "If she'd only listened, it would never have happened. Why should I have paid for that? He's the one who hurt her; he's the one who deserved to pay. I had to protect myself, my life. I had to get out. There was so much blood, I was nearly sick."

"How did you get out of the house and back home?" Olivia asked and strained her ears for a sound—heard only the thrashing of rain. "Aunt Jamie would have seen the blood."

"I stripped off my clothes, bundled them up. I went outside, to the pool, and washed the blood off. I washed it all away. There were always spare clothes in the changing house, no one would ever notice. I could get rid of my own later, a Dumpster in the city. I went back in the house because I thought it might be a dream. But it wasn't. I thought I heard you upstairs. I thought I heard you, but I couldn't be sure."

"I woke up. I heard Mama scream."

"Yes, I found out later. I had to get home in case Jamie woke up and realized I'd slipped out. It wasn't until they brought you to us that I wondered if you'd seen me. I wondered if you'd heard. Twenty years, I've wondered. I've waited."

"No, I didn't see you. I never knew."

"It would have stayed that way. Everyone put it aside, everyone closed the door, until the book. How could I be sure? How could I know for sure that you hadn't heard my voice, that you hadn't looked out the window, seen my car? It ruined my life, don't you see? I'd done everything to make it work, everything to make up for that one single night."

"You let my father go to prison."

"I was in prison, too." Tears leaked out of his eyes. "I was paying, too. I knew you'd be just like her. I knew when it came down to a choice, you'd choose him. I always loved you, Livvy. You should have been ours. Mine and Julie's. But that's over now. I have to protect myself. I have to end it."

He lunged toward her, leading with the knife.

•   •   •

IT WAS LIKE HIS DREAM, THE DARK, THE TREES, THE MUR-
mur of rain and wind. He could run until his heart burst out of his chest
and he couldn't find her. Every rustle had him turning in a new direction,
every call of a night bird was the sound of her voice.

The bone-numbing terror that he would be too late, that he would
never wake up from this nightmare and find her curled against him, drove
him harder.

She was somewhere in the vast, twisting maze of the forest. Somewhere just beyond his reach.

He stopped, leaning against the bulk of a hemlock to clear the tumble
of his mind. The air was so thick, every breath he took was like gulping
in water. His shoulder was on fire, the white handkerchief tied over the
wound long since gone red.

He stood very still for a moment and listened. Was that the murmur
of voices, or just the rain? Sound seemed to shoot at a dozen different
angles, then swallow itself. The only compass he had now was his gut.
Trusting it, he turned west.

This time, when she screamed, he was close.

SAM SHOVED HER CLEAR AND, WITH THE LITTLE STRENGTH
he had left, drove his body into David's. When the knife sliced through
him again, he felt nothing but despair. As he staggered and fell, Olivia
leaped to her feet and tried to catch him.

It happened quickly, her father slipping out of her hands, the sound of
running feet slapping against the saturated ground. And the quick prick of
a knife at her throat.

"Let her go." Noah braced his feet, held the gun in the classic police
grip. Fear was a hot river in his blood.

"I'll kill her. You know I will. Drop the gun, or I'll slice her throat
and be done with it."

"And lose your shield? I don't think so." Oh God, Liv, oh God, don't move. He gazed quickly at her face, saw the blank shock in her eyes, the thin trickle of red sliding down the slim column of her throat. "Step away from her, step back."

"Put the gun down!" He jerked Olivia's head up with the flat of the blade. "She's dead, do you hear me. She's dead if you don't do it now!"

"He'll kill me anyway."

"Shut up! Shut the hell up!" He nicked her again, and she saw Noah's hands jerk, then start to lower.

"Don't do it. Don't hurt her."

"Put it down!"

She heard the roar of their voices in her head, saw the decision in Noah's eyes. "He'll kill me no matter what you do. Then he'll kill you. Don't let him take someone else I love. Don't let him win."

Her hand closed over the cold metal eyes of the scissors, drew them out in one quick, smooth motion, then plunged them viciously into his thigh.

He screamed, high and bright, his knife hand jerking up, then dropping. She shoved her body away from his, yanking the scissors clear. Then held them out as he leaped toward her.

She heard the bullet ring out, one sharp snap. Saw the bright blossom of blood bloom high on his chest and the puzzled shock in his eyes as he fell toward her.

She didn't step back. And she would never ask herself if she'd had time to do so. The killing point of the scissors slid silently into his belly.

The weight of him bore her to the ground. Before she could roll clear, Noah pulled her up and against him. His arms that had been so steady began to quiver.

"You're all right. You're okay." He said it again, then once again as his hands ran shakily over her. "He cut you." His fingers brushed gently at her throat. "Oh God, Liv."

She was crushed against him again, burrowed into him. Her head went light, seemed to circle somewhere just beyond her shoulders. "I thought he might have killed you. I saw the blood and I thought . . . No!" She jerked back, her hands vising on Noah's face. "Daddy."

She pulled away and stumbled to the ground beside her father. "Oh no, no, no. Don't. Please. I'm so sorry. I'm sorry, Daddy." She had nothing but her hands to press against his wound to try to stem the bleeding.

"Don't cry, Livvy." He reached up to touch her face. "This is the best way for me. My time's running out, anyway. I needed to see you again. It was the last thing I had to do. You've got your mother's eyes." He smiled a little. "You always did. I let her down in so many ways."

"Don't, please don't." She pressed her face to his neck. "Noah, help me."

"If I'd been what I should have been, what she believed I could be, she'd still be alive."

"Don't talk now. We have to stop the bleeding. They'll find us soon." Her hands fumbled with the scraps of cloth Noah gave her. "They're looking, and we'll get you to the hospital."

"You're a smart girl, you know better." His eyes were clouding over, but they shifted to Noah. "She's a smart one, isn't she, Brady?"

"That's right." He pressed another scrap of his shirt to the wound in Sam's side. "So listen to her."

"I'd rather die a hero." His short laugh ended in a racking cough. "There's enough of the old me in here to rather enjoy that. Is that son of a bitch dead?"

"As Moses," Noah told him.

"Thank Christ for that." The pain was floating away. "Livvy." He gripped her hand. "When I was looking for you that night, when you saw me, I wasn't going to hurt you."

"I know that. I know. Don't leave me now that I've just gotten you back."

"I'm sorry, Livvy. I wanted you to look at me once, just once, and know who I was. In the end I kept you safe. Maybe that makes up for all the years I didn't." His vision wavered and dimmed. "Write the book, Brady. Tell the truth."

"Count on it."

"Take care of my little girl. Kiss me good-bye, Livvy love."

With tears flooding her throat, she pressed her lips to his cheek. And felt his hand go lax in hers. Her grief was one long, low moan.

Noah sat with her while she cradled her father's body and wept in the rain.

• • •

SHE SLEPT BECAUSE NOAH POURED A SEDATIVE DOWN HER throat. When she woke, logy with drugs and grief and shock, it was midday.

She heard the birdsong, felt the sun on her face. And, opening her eyes, saw him sitting beside her.

"You didn't sleep."

He was already holding her hand. He couldn't seem to let go. "I did for a bit."

"Everything that happened, it's all in my head, but it feels as if it's wrapped in cotton."

"Just leave it that way for now."

He looked so wonderful, she thought. So hers, with his exhausted eyes and stubble of beard. "You saved my life."

"Just part of the service." He leaned down to kiss her. "Don't make me do it again."

"That's a deal. How's your shoulder?"

"Well, I could say it's nothing, but why lie? It hurts like a bitch."

She sat up, tugged up the sleeve of his T-shirt and pressed her lips to the bandage.

"Thanks. Why don't you try to get some more sleep?"

"No, I really need to get out." She looked into his eyes. "I need to walk. Walk in the forest with me, Noah."

When she was dressed, she held out a hand for his. "My family?"

"They're still asleep. Your grandparents were up with Jamie until almost dawn."

She nodded, started out quietly. "Your parents?"

"In the spare room."

"They'll need us, all of them. I need this first."

They went down the back stairs and left through the kitchen door.

"Your father," she began. "When they found us, I don't think he knew whether he was proud of you or horrified." She let out a breath, drew another in. "I think he was both."

"He taught me how to handle guns, to respect them. I know he hoped I'd never have to use one."

"I don't know how to feel, Noah. All these years I thought my father was a murderer, the worst kind of murderer. I lost him when I was four, and now I have him back. I have him back in a way that changes everything. And I can never tell him."

"He knew."

"It helps to have that, to hold on to that." She tightened her hand on his as they moved into the trees. "I didn't run. I didn't leave him. This time I didn't run and hide. I can live with all the rest because this time, I didn't run."

"Liv, you gave him exactly what he wanted at the end of his life. You looked at him, and you knew him. He told me that was the last thing he needed."

She nodded, absorbing that into the grief. "All my life, I loved my uncle. I shifted him into my father figure, admired him, trusted him. He wasn't what I thought he was, any more than my father was what I thought he was. Oh God. God, Noah, how is Aunt Jamie going to cope with this? How is she going to live with it?"

"She has you, your family. She'll get through it."

"I hope she'll stay here, for a while at least. Stay here and heal."

"I think she needs to hear you say just that."

She nodded again and leaned against him a little. "You're good at knowing what people need to hear." She let out a sigh. "I was afraid I wouldn't be able to come in here again and feel what I've always felt. But I can. It's so beautiful. So alive. No monsters here."

"Not ever again."

"I love this place." It had sheltered her, given her life. Now, she had a choice. To stay with the old, or to start the new.

She let go of Noah's hand, turned in a circle. "But there's this other spot, along the coast. Heavily wooded, excellent old forest with a view of the Pacific raging up against the cliffs." She stopped, met his eyes soberly. "That's where we should build the house."

He stared at her while a rage of emotions gushed into him, then settled in quiet joy. "How many bedrooms?"

"Five, as previously discussed."

"Okay. Stone or wood?"

"Both." Her lips twitched, her eyes glowed now, as he nodded and stepped toward her.

"When?"

"As soon as you ask me to marry you, which you've neglected to do so far."

"I knew I'd forgotten something." She laughed when he hauled her into his arms. "I've waited a long time for you." He brushed his lips over hers, then lingered, deepened the kiss. "Don't make me wait anymore. Marry me."

"Yes." She framed his face with her hands. "Between the forest and the flowers. And soon." She smiled at him, drawing him close to touch her lips to his cheek. "I love you, Noah. I want to start a life with you. Now. We've both waited long enough."